TR$\underset{X}{}$IALS

TR℞IALS:

the risk/benefit ratio

a novel by M.E. Smith

Beaver's Pond Press, Inc.

Edina, Minnesota

ISBN 10: 1-59298-200-X
ISBN 13: 978-1-59298-200-4

Library of Congress Control Number: 2007933707
Printed in the United States of America
12 11 10 09 08   6 5 4 3 2 1

Cover and interior design by Clay Schotzko

Beaver's Pond Press, Inc.

Beaver's Pond Press, Inc.
7104 Ohms Lane
Edina, MN 55439-2129
(952) 829-8818
www.BeaversPondPress.com
Beaver's Pond Press is an imprint of Beaver's Pond Group.

To order, visit www.BookHouseFulfillment.com
or call 1-800-901-3480. Reseller discounts available.

for
Maureen & Evelyn
with love

risk/benefit ratio—

the probability of harm or injury as compared to a valued or desired outcome

Prologue—Saturday, September 21

He stared at her casket. *It's so small,* he thought. For the most part, Grant Adams was unable to think clearly, but this had penetrated the fog and registered. *That poor little girl.* While he felt a heavy sadness, he couldn't deny being grateful that it wasn't his own daughter lying there. *At least not yet,* he reminded himself.

Melanie Warner came up to Grant, her eyes glassy and swollen from tears. "Ashley was so glad she met you, Katie. You were a very good friend to her and I know she looked up to you a great deal."

Grant looked at his daughter standing next to him, and tried to see her as others did. Katie was tall for her age and thin, but not skinny. She had her mother's wavy, brown hair and his green eyes. The combination was striking. Even at thirteen, people often told her what a beautiful girl she was. *She is the one positive product of our marriage,* he thought bitterly. Katie was also mature for her age, and so it didn't surprise him when she grabbed Mrs. Warner's hand and offered words that he did not.

"I'm happy that I got to meet Ashley, too. But I think she helped me more than I helped her. We talked a lot, Mrs. Warner—about being sick and about regular stuff, too. She told me that even though it was hard to be sick all the time, she still felt lucky. She had good friends, a nice home, and really great parents. She loved you both so much."

"And yet there was nothing we could do to take away her pain or ..." Melanie's voice trailed off; the overwhelming feelings of helplessness and failure were just too much. She gave Katie's hand a quick squeeze and excused herself, nodding her head in Grant's direction. A brief moment of eye contact with him spoke volumes. *Cherish every moment.* He placed his arm around the shoulder of his little girl and tried to forget that the illness that took Ashley away from the Warners was one of the things the two girls had in common.

1

PHASE I

Monday, September 23

It was difficult to determine which was louder, the rain against the windowpane or the pounding inside Grant's head.

"Excuse us for a moment, Grant. We'll call the lab and see what's keeping Will." James MacPhearson slid his chair away from the table and his brother Steven followed suit. The brothers walked toward the door of the exquisitely appointed conference room. "Jessica, call down to the lab and tell Will he's late for the meeting with Mr. Adams." Jessica murmured something too low for Grant to hear. But he saw her hand over what looked like a document and both men spent a few minutes reading it before signing at the bottom.

Grant took the opportunity to size up the brothers while the interview was delayed. Both were well dressed and shared the same thinning salt-and-pepper hair. From appearance only, Grant would have guessed James was older. Wearing glasses, he was taller than his brother and had an easy confidence. Steven, with a thickened waistline and ruddy complexion, appeared somewhat awkward.

In preparation for the interview, Grant had done his research. MacPhearson Pharmaceuticals was just coming into its own. It was a small drug company owned by two brothers and their partner, William Adison. All three had been in the research labs at the University of Minnesota and had decided to start their own company. That was thirteen years ago. Grant looked at the surroundings. Professional, classy, expensive. *Not bad for thirteen years, boys.*

"He'll be in soon," James explained as he and Steven returned to the table. "But since we're already running late, let's get started. Our partner is known for getting wrapped up in a project and forgetting everything else, like meetings and ..."

"Eating." Steven smiled, but there was a sentiment of irritation rather than humor in his voice.

"Well, that's good for a company like MacPhearson, where research and development is critical." Grant hoped he hadn't come across as being too eager to please, but the truth was, he wanted this job. No, *needed* this job. Not only would it be a good career move for him in general, but MacPhearson Pharmaceuticals was a company heavily into research. It wasn't just a coincidence that one of their current research projects was the development of a treatment for bronchiosclerosis, the illness his daughter had. If he could land a position here, he might be able to get Katie involved in a clinical trial. Grant was willing to do anything to help her.

MacPhearson Pharmaceuticals had developed the only existing drug to treat bronchiosclerosis, or hardening of the bronchioles, which caused constriction of the breathing tubes in the lungs. It was a fatal disease and MacPhearson's breakthrough treatment was being tested in clinical trials. Grant had tried to get Katie involved in a study testing the MacPhearson drug some months before, but her symptoms were so mild that she did not qualify. And with so many new cases arising in the past year alone, the lengthy waiting list for potential candidates was discouraging. Although Katie's illness was in the earliest stages, Grant had done enough research on the disease to know that her condition could deteriorate rapidly. Time was critical. With the MacPhearson drug showing promising results in clinical trials, Grant knew he needed to get her into a study soon. Since doctors have substantial input as to which subjects participate in trials, Grant needed an "in" with a doctor conducting a study. If he were an employee of the sponsoring company, he might be able to pull some strings.

"In short," James explained, "your responsibilities as a Senior Clinical Research Associate would be similar to those of your current position in the research department at Webber Scientific. The primary difference is that you would be more of an in-house guy, meaning you would travel less, though we would expect you to go out to the clinics conducting studies to monitor with the less-experienced Clinical Research Associates. You'll show them the ropes of monitoring and see that they adhere to the study protocol, good clinical practices, and FDA guidelines to ensure subject safety. If a site gets behind or disorganized, you would go out to co-monitor with another CRA—or study monitor, as we sometimes call them here—and make sure everything at the site is in compliance with FDA regulations.

"You'd be the study manager for two new drugs: one is in Phase II and the other is in Phase III. Of course, we can't disclose to you any specifics about these drugs, at least not until you've accepted an offer and signed the proper confidentiality contracts, but I can say we are excited about both compounds. Each is proving effective in clinical trials.

"After receiving your résumé," James went on, "we checked your references. I have to ask; why, Grant, would you want to come to a little company like ours when you are moving up the ladder at Webber? It's a larger pharma company and it seems like it would be very stable."

"I know it seems cliché, but I'm ready for something new. I got into clinical research because I am a scientist at heart. As you've seen," Grant gestured toward his résumé on the table in front of them, "I started out of college working in a virology lab. But then I got interested in clinical research, took some courses, and made the jump to Webber. I'm much happier working with people than being in the lab. I am an outstanding CRA. I have a strong work ethic, excellent attention to detail, and my qualifications—"

"—are stellar," Steven interrupted, holding the résumé. "We can see your experience and credentials are more than adequate. But why *here*?"

Grant decided to lay it all out on the line. No sense in getting the job, and then have them find out later. "My thirteen-year-old daughter has recently been diagnosed with bronchiosclerosis. It's only in the initial stages, more of a nuisance to her right now. But I know what's coming, and so does she. She just watched a friend of hers die from it. I also know that MacPhearson is developing a treatment drug that has been successful in the lab and in earlier clinical trials. You're starting Phase III trials now. I want to work for you because I want to be with a company that is trying to fight this illness. And I won't deny that I would be very interested in Katie being considered for a future trial." There, he'd been honest. Now he could only hope it didn't cost him.

～

Later that afternoon, James MacPhearson rubbed his eyes. He looked out of his office's third-story window at the St. Croix River and the Wisconsin shore in the distance. After a cool summer, the leaves had already begun to turn. The shades of orange, gold, and crimson calmed him. It had been a long day. At Will's request, he'd come to the office earlier than usual. The request in itself wasn't anything extraordinary, but the fact that he had asked James to meet him there alone was. Why hadn't Will asked Steven? The three were in business together—partners—each with one-third share. One-third of the successes, one-third of the failures.

In truth, there hadn't been any real failures thus far. Oh, there had been some research projects that didn't pan out, but that was the name of the game in this business. You sacrifice time and money on hundreds of drugs, hoping one will make it. There was the initial research phase, which included testing on animals, then there were clinical trials involving human subjects, and, if proven safe and effective, the compound would be submitted to the FDA. On average, it took fifteen years and eight hundred million dollars to get a drug to market. MacPhearson Pharmaceuticals had two. It still amazed James that in just thirteen years they had two major medications that had not only been approved by the FDA, but were doing well on the market. They had become three wealthy men, and MacPhearson was catapulted from a lab in a warehouse to a state-of-the-art facility, housing both the corporate offices as well as several laboratories.

They had all agreed to build a smaller facility, but with only the best design and equipment. Expansion could come later. And so they found sixteen acres about twenty miles outside of St. Paul, a mile or so west of the Minnesota-Wisconsin border. Most of the lab workers lived in the eastern Twin Cities metro area, but a few made the commute across the St. Croix River Bridge from Wisconsin. Finally, MacPhearson Pharmaceuticals was on the map, literally and figuratively. There had been write-ups in medical journals and even an article in *Newsweek*.

There was the article Will had published earlier that summer about the research process in a small pharmaceutical company. With the costs of health care and medication rising, politicians and the general public often viewed pharmaceutical companies in a negative light. Will's article explained the resources necessary to fund medical research. In their early days, they relied on federal funding and grants to make ends meet. There had been many lean years. But the sales of their first drug to hit the market provided them with the resources to expand and continue more projects. In his article, he discussed the research and development of the drug used to treat bronchiosclerosis. It occurred to James that Grant Adams had probably read Will's article and decided to pursue an opportunity with their company. *Grant Adams is an intelligent man*, James reasoned.

MacPhearson Pharmaceuticals was still under private ownership, but lately they had been discussing the possibility of going public. It was a big step, though. And, in addition to several other potential compounds, it looked like successful drug number three was on the way. If they played their cards right, James thought, and timed going public with the marketing phase of the new drug, they might become three *very* wealthy men.

It had been a busy day. When James arrived at the lab that morning, Will had said he wanted to meet later. He was working on something and said he was getting close. James had heard that, of course, many times before. Since moving to the new facility, he and Steven had assumed more of the business-related responsibilities, since Will's first love was the lab. And so it was not surprising that Will missed the meeting with James as well as the interview with Grant Adams.

James had already made up his mind to hire Adams. The interview was just a formality, but Steven had insisted. "This is a critical time for the company," he had stressed to James and Will. "We don't want just anyone working for us."

James knew his brother was right about the interview. Being careful had paid off so far. They now had more than twenty Clinical Research Associates on staff, supervised by three managers. One of the managers in the clinical research department had recently decided to step down for family reasons. So they needed to hire a replacement for her, and preferably one with experience. After six years of working in the laboratory, seven years in clinical research monitoring at Webber, and an impressive record at both places, Adams was definitely qualified. And then Adams had mentioned his daughter.

"So is this how it works? I do all the work and you stare out the window all day?" Steven laughed as he threw himself down on one of the brown leather chairs across from James's desk. Not as comfortable as he hoped. *It's all about appearances with James*, he thought.

"Someone's got to be the brains of the operation, and if it were you, we'd still be research assistants at the U."

"So what'd you think of Adams?" Steven asked, ignoring James's comment. "I think he's our guy—seems smart, knows the ropes, is looking for a change. And what about his daughter? I was surprised he mentioned it today. If I were him I'd have waited."

"I think he wanted us to know up front. And I agree, he's a perfect fit. His daughter's situation only makes it better. He'll have an interest in MacPhearson doing well. He'll be loyal because we're working on a drug to help her."

"We scratch his back …"

"Exactly," James replied.

Tuesday, September 24

Grant knew as soon as the phone rang that the job was his. He had been confident yesterday when he left MacPhearson; he came home and started packing. Not full-fledged packing, but packing. He looked around his apartment. *Not much to leave behind*, he thought. After the divorce he decided to get an apartment until he could find something bigger, maybe a townhouse or condo. Elizabeth got the house. It was fair, since her parents were the ones who had given them the down payment. That was almost fourteen years ago. *Where did the time go?* The divorce became final just after Katie's eleventh birthday. Unfortunately, after a little more than two years, the apartment looked pretty much the same as when he moved in. The only room that could be considered decorated was the small bedroom where Katie stayed every other weekend, more often during the summer. He and Elizabeth had joint custody, but didn't want to have Katie going back and forth on a nightly or even weekly basis. Grant's sister was a teacher and had told him how hard it is for a kid that age to be bounced back and forth so much. His position with Webber required him to travel every week, so Katie stayed with Elizabeth in their house. *No*, he corrected himself, *her house*. It's incredible how fast a divorce divides two people and their belongings, families, and friends. But it takes much longer for it to actually sink in. In conversation, Grant sometimes even still referred to Elizabeth as his wife. Maybe deep down he still wanted her to be.

After accepting the offer, he decided to spend the day packing up the rest of his apartment. He had arranged to take a few personal days this week, so he wasn't due back at Webber until Thursday. Pete, his supervisor for the last two years, was going to be surprised. They had become friendly after the divorce, but not close enough for Grant to confide in him about leaving. Grant had not told Pete about Katie's illness. Her symptoms were mild enough; an outsider wouldn't think she had anything more than a cold or a tough spell with asthma. As he sorted things into piles to be saved, tossed, or looked at again later, he thought about what he would say to Pete.

I want to be there for Katie before she grows up and moves away to college. I'm tired of traveling and being on the road three or more days a week. MacPhearson is smaller and most of my sites will be regional. That means I can set up a real home, and maybe Elizabeth will let me have Katie on a more permanent basis. She's about to get married again, and I'm sure she and David would welcome some time alone. I've had a good run here, but this is something I have to do, both professionally and personally.

He knew Pete couldn't argue with that.

~

Once he called to offer the position to Adams, Steven went down to the lab to see Will. He was glad Grant accepted the offer right then, instead of playing the game and asking for a few days to think it over. *I like a man who can make up his mind*, thought Steven. He opened the door of the lab. Most of the research assistants were at lunch, so it was quiet. But he knew James and Will were around somewhere—both of their cars were still in the lot. They must be in the lab office. As he got closer, he heard them talking in hushed voices; he slowed his pace. What could be so important? And if it were important, why wasn't he there? All he could gather was that Will was apparently excited about something and James was trying to calm him down. Steven inched closer to the open door.

"I don't want Steven to know yet, James. He won't be happy that I've continued work on a project that we agreed to scrap six months ago," whispered Will.

"But that doesn't matter now, does it? You went ahead, and now it looks like you might have stumbled onto something. Will, your research is what has made MacPhearson so successful. Steven knows that. Let me talk to him first. You know how he gets when he feels like he's been blown off. My brother is a brilliant businessman and a good scientist, but he's never had the persistence to do the dirty work."

Steven clenched his jaw. James was right, of course. He hated being stuck in the lab. But he didn't appreciate his brother treating Will like the quarterback. After all, it was *MacPhearson* Pharmaceuticals.

"Fine, fine. I'll be up later today and we can all sit down and figure out how exactly we're going to handle this. This is big, James, really big! Talk to Steven today. Once he cools off he'll realize that this could change everything!"

"I'll let you know how it goes." James's voice was just enough to cover the sound of his brother's retreating footsteps.

It was nearly three-thirty before James went into Steven's office, but it was empty. He decided to sit down and wait. He picked up a photo of the two of them in San Francisco, toasting their new company with wine from Napa Valley. *So young*, he thought, *so idealistic.* They had planned to save the world with science, cure diseases like cancer and AIDS. The University of Minnesota had to rely on funding, and year after year funding was cut. Going out on their own was risky, but exciting. They were young and could recover if things didn't work out. Getting Will to come on board was James's idea. He was a genius—had a doctorate in biochemistry. Neither James nor Steven had his talent, his vision. The MacPhearsons only had master's degrees, James's in chemistry and Steven's in biology. But Steven also had a MBA, which gave him the advantage on the business side. *And look where we are now, little brother.*

All James had to do was convince his brother they could handle their partner's latest discovery.

Steven approached his office knowing James was already inside. He was still angry about the private meeting, but curiosity had taken over now and he just wanted to know what the hell was going on.

"I wanted to come in downstairs," Steven began, "but you guys never taught me the secret handshake."

"You heard?"

"Only some. James, what the hell is Will doing working on research that we *all* agreed to end last spring?"

"Steven, set aside the ego and listen to me. He thinks he's found it."

"Is he sure?" asked Steven.

"No," James answered, "but it sounds like he's getting close. He has to run more tests, but he may have the compound within the month."

"Well, then I guess we have a month to figure out exactly what we're going to do."

Friday, September 27

He was late—again. Barbara Adison sat impatiently in the driver's seat of her black Mercedes. She had only wanted to pick up Will on their way to the country club, not to have to park and go inside. *Damn it!* She pounded the steering wheel with the palm of her hand. They were going to drive together to the company cocktail party. She scanned the parking lot. No, there was no sign of the little black Honda. At least she knew Will hadn't left with *her*.

His affair had begun a few years ago. It had stung at first, but she and Will had been through a lot. In an ironic sort of way, it almost improved their relationship. He was discreet and she was able to maintain the lifestyle to which she'd grown accustomed. She glanced in the rearview mirror, checking her shoulder-length, dark brown hair, deep-set blue-gray eyes, and flawless make-up. She was a very attractive woman, and knew it. But she was also smart, and more of a realist than a romantic. Barbara ran her hand over the dashboard; *she drives a piece of crap, while I drive this. And,* she laughed to herself as she laid on the horn, *at least I don't have to sleep with him.*

～

Grant had just returned from a monitoring trip in Portland, Oregon, and of course, his connecting flight out of Denver had been delayed. He barely had had enough time to drive home, shower, and change before leaving for the MacPhearson party. He gave himself the once-over in the full-length mirror that hung on the back of his bedroom door. His light brown hair was still as thick as ever, and he had almost lost the extra pounds he gained after Katie was born. Being on the road and living out of hotels made it almost impossible for him to stick to his yearly resolution to get healthy. This year he accepted defeat in late February.

That was another reason to make the move to a smaller company. At Webber, he did quite a bit of traveling. His sites, a total of eleven in all, were scattered all over the country, which meant he was out of town at least three nights out of the week. But with his new position at MacPhearson, he would only have to travel a few times each quarter. Some sites would be local—right here in the Twin Cities—and a few were within driving distance in Wisconsin. Only three would require air travel.

Without Elizabeth to consult, he spent several minutes looking through his closet before choosing a charcoal gray suit, moss green shirt, and a tie that Katie had given him last Father's Day. The shirt was a favorite of Elizabeth's. She said it brought out the green in his eyes. All in all, he was pleased. Not too stuffy, not too casual, and since it was time to go anyway, it would have to do.

"Good enough," he mumbled to himself. Although he wouldn't officially start his job for another few weeks, tonight would be an opportunity to meet many of his new colleagues at MacPhearson. Grant was particularly looking forward to finally meeting the elusive Dr. William Adison.

∼

Jessica was the first to arrive at the St. Croix Country Club. Steven wanted everything to be perfect, so he had sent her ahead to make sure his instructions were followed—exactly. The staff at the club was very professional and she was assured that all of Mr. MacPhearson's requests were met. Typical, she thought as she looked over the menu. Shrimp cocktail, smoked salmon, filet mignon, and champagne. If I ever get married, I'll have Steven plan the wedding. His taste was impeccable and, as usual, tonight he wanted only the best. "If I ever get married," she repeated under her breath. She'd always pictured herself settled down by now, maybe even with a few kids. But then she'd met Will and her plans had changed.

In the ladies' room, Jessica studied herself in the mirror. Her long, blonde hair, held back with a band for work, was definitely due for a trim, and she was starting to lose the tan she had gotten over the summer. Will always said how pretty she was. He never said beautiful, always pretty or cute. And, she admitted, she did look young for her age. Even though she was twenty-seven, she still got carded whenever she went out with her friends. Twenty-seven and involved with a forty-six-year-old man. It still seemed unreal to her that she was seeing someone almost her father's age, let alone someone who was married. They met when she started as an administrative assistant at MacPhearson. It just sort of happened. She never believed other people when they said that, but in her case it was true. Jessica had never intended on breaking up a marriage—she wasn't raised that way—but nevertheless, here she was. She had told only her best friend, Amy, about the relationship with her boss. It would break her mother's heart. Jessica's father and older brothers were very protective of her. If they ever found out about Will, they'd probably kill him. "Oh Will," she said to her reflection, "we should have been more careful." They'd gotten comfortable, and comfort led to carelessness. Soon, everyone would know. She wouldn't be able to hide the truth for much longer.

She had tried to meet with him in the lab that morning—she needed to talk with him desperately—but he blew her off, said he was in the middle of some tests and needed to continue his work. Later, after lunch, he called up to her desk and had the audacity to ask that she not attend tonight. Barbara will be there, he had explained, and I don't want to create a scene. But Jessica had already decided that she'd show up at the party. She would try to catch him alone so they could talk, so they could decide what to do together. And if that didn't work, a scene is exactly what she would create.

~

Stepping into the club promptly at six, James was the first of the owners to arrive. He nodded to the employees sitting at the bar, and took in the room. Across from him, facing west, were several ten-foot-high windows providing a sweeping view of Minnesota and the river that separated it from Wisconsin. The sun was just beginning to slip in the evening sky, and a stream of gold light bathed the room. He saw several boats on the water and was envious of the families trying to catch every moment of autumn before the cold reality of winter arrived.

The St. Croix Club was originally a small golf course and clubhouse. But as the Twin Cities grew in size, so did the club. The grounds were expanded, and a new clubhouse was built to accommodate a wealthier clientele. Weddings, receptions, and business gatherings were often held there on the weekends, and it was the site of choice for many MacPhearson work parties and meetings. Earlier in the week, Steven requested this room, which held about thirty round tables dressed in ivory silk, each seating eight. The sunlight played off the wine glasses and the room sparkled. As the sole planner for the gathering, Steven had truly outdone himself.

James glanced at his watch. Tonight was important. Where was Steven? And Will? For all James knew, Will was still back at the lab. He had become completely obsessed with the project. And Steven was still bitter about the whole thing. It would have to be handled very carefully, regardless of the outcome. James turned to once again look out at the river, realizing he still had no idea *how* to handle it.

~

The party was officially underway by six-thirty. By then, all three partners were in attendance, talking together quietly near the bar. Their wives, a very exclusive club, chatted together at a table in the corner. Paula MacPhearson was dressed in a well-cut, ivory suit that complimented her chin-length, reddish-brown hair and large, brown eyes. The ensemble made her seem taller than her petite five-foot, four-inch frame. Her sister-in-law was laughing at something one of them had said. Audrey MacPhearson had been a friend of Paula's since college. They had been roommates their junior and senior years, and it was Paula who had introduced her to Steven. Although close in friendship and now related by marriage, the two women were opposites in appearance. Audrey currently wore her hair blonde, often swept up in a twist. She had keen, bluish-green eyes that were accentuated by her light blue pants suit and a stunning figure, the result of visits with both a personal trainer and a talented plastic surgeon. Barbara, Will's wife, seemed tense. She kept tugging at her black cocktail dress and fiddling with the cranberry-colored silk wrap around her shoulders.

Barbara had seen Jessica at another table as soon as she walked in the room. Will had promised her Jessica wouldn't be there. *Damn you*, she shot a contemptuous look over at her husband, but he faced the other direction. *I will not be played for a fool*, she thought. But she knew it was important to keep up appearances, especially tonight. Will swore to her that no one at MacPhearson knew, not even James or Steven. And so she returned her attention to Paula, who was gushing over plans for her youngest daughter's winter wedding. Audrey was genuinely interested in hearing about her niece, but Barbara had to force herself to concentrate. She failed yet again when she saw Jessica leave the room, followed by Will.

"You're what?" he asked in a loud whisper, pulling her into the nearby coatroom. Will couldn't believe what he heard.

"Pregnant." Jessica was angered by his reaction. "I'm not any happier than you. Do you really think I want to have a baby with a man who's married to someone else? Who doesn't love me enough to leave his wife?" Not that she expected him to be pleased about the baby, but she had thought that at least he would be supportive. "Trust me, Will, this is not what I had planned."

He did trust her. But a baby? His baby?

Oh God, his mind was racing. *What have I done?*

"So where do we go from here?" He could see this was as shocking for her as it was for him. She was not the kind of girl who would trap a man by getting pregnant with his child. She was too decent for that. He looked at her as though for the first time. *She's so young. Her whole life is ahead of her. And Barbara. How am I going to tell Barbara?* "What are we going to do?"

"I have absolutely no idea," Jessica murmured quietly. She leaned toward him and he held her.

He had no way of knowing that he wasn't going to have to tell Barbara anything. Standing just outside the doorway, she had heard every word.

~

Shortly after the dessert plates had been cleared, James stood and addressed the group.

"I'd like to thank you for coming this evening. I hope you are all enjoying yourselves. While I won't dominate Steven's party with office talk, I do have some very exciting news to share with you. Our preliminary third-quarter results are excellent, and we show no signs of slowing down. In fact, I'd like to finally end the speculation and office gossip that has been circulating for the last few months by officially announcing that MacPhearson Pharmaceuticals will be going public during the first or second quarter of the coming year. We're finally in the big leagues—which will benefit us all. On Monday morning, please take time to read a detailed e-mail, prepared by Robert Dawson, which describes the transition from our being a private to a public company and the advantages of this move."

James looked out across the crowd and continued, "*You* all make our company great. A team is only as strong as its weakest player, and let me say that we have no weak players. On that note, I'd like you to join me in welcoming our newest colleague, acquired from Webber—a formidable opponent—Grant Adams." James raised his glass. The rest of the room toasted in return.

Grant stood up from his seat, bowing awkwardly in the general direction of the crowd. Not used to being the center of attention, he felt his face flush. James's announcement had taken him by surprise, and he hoped it was over. To his relief, he heard Steven's voice, loud and slurred, from near the bar.

"Welcome to the MacPhearson family, Grant, and thank you, big brother. Now, with all of that out of the way, we have some serious celebrating to do. You are all under direct orders … to drink every last drop of liquor from the bar—it's already been paid for!"

~

Hours later, Grant lay awake in bed, his head swimming from both the party and the wine. He had met so many people, but only a few came to mind clearly.

Of course, the person he had most wanted to meet that evening was Dr. William Adison. Grant had seen his picture in an article published a few months earlier in a scientific journal. Either the photograph was much older than the article, or Will had aged dramatically since the photo was taken. He was tall and willowy, with brown eyes that were ringed with dark, puffy circles. Though clearly exhausted, he was energetic when he greeted Grant early in the evening.

"Welcome, welcome, Grant. I know a few boys at Webber. They had good things to say about you."

"Well, thank you. Dr. Adison, it's really an honor to finally meet you. Your research is impressive, to say the least. I'm so glad to be here, relieved to know that now I'm on your team, instead of playing against it." Grant wanted Will to know how much he respected him as a scientist.

"Stop inflating his ego, Grant," Steven said, as he joined their conversation. "As it is, he can barely get that big head through the lab door. We're considering expanding his office, just to accommodate it." Steven was smiling, but Grant got the distinct impression Steven was envious of his partner.

The second person to stick in Grant's mind was Oliver Klein, another PhD who worked in the lab, just under Will. The two were about the same height, but Dr. Klein had a good hundred pounds over Will. He looked to Grant like a retired football player, with cropped, brown hair, close-set blue eyes, and a huge neck. He was clearly in excellent shape for his age, which Grant assumed to be about fifty. He also had a military look to him, so it hadn't surprised Grant to learn Dr. Klein had played football and earned his doctorate in microbiology while serving in the army. Both he and the other research scientists, about ten who seemed to range in age from early twenties to late thirties, spent most of the evening at a few tables near the bar. Klein was unmarried. *At least I think so*, Grant mused, *judging by the way he was carrying on with those young female assistants.*

And then there was Jessica Monroe, Steven MacPhearson's administrative assistant. She seemed out of sorts during her conversation with Grant, as if her mind were a million miles away, and she hardly spoke to Dr. Klein when they all sat together at a table after dinner. Grant couldn't help but notice she kept looking over at Will, Steven, and James. Grant had seen her briefly at his interview last week. She was a beautiful girl, although Grant found it hard to believe she was old enough to be out of college. She had laughed when he said that, and for a moment her smile was genuine. When he asked her if he could refill her glass, she requested ginger ale. *Too bad*, Grant thought to himself hours later as he started to fall asleep, *if anyone needs a glass of wine to settle her nerves, it's Jessica Monroe.*

Monday, September 30

Grant walked around the first floor of the townhouse. This would be perfect, he thought. He had followed up on a recommendation from Audrey MacPhearson. She had overheard him saying at the party that he was looking for a townhouse. A friend of hers had recently bought a beautiful, brand-new unit in Hudson, she told him, just across the river from the office. According to her friend there were other models available.

This two-bedroom unit had three levels. The first level contained a tuck-under garage, a laundry room, and a small room with a separate entrance that he would use as his office. The second story had a modern, open floor plan with high ceilings and lots of natural light. Grant found himself thinking like a realtor, making mental notes of the generous kitchen, informal dining room, and family room. There was also a small bathroom at the end of the hall. The house would be a great place for Katie and her friends to hang out. The upstairs had two good-sized bedrooms and a full bath. Because the townhouse was brand new, it was clean and bright, and very neutral. He could probably rope his mother into helping him decorate. She could have free reign and the house could be almost finished by the time he moved in. That gave him just a few weeks to convince his ex-wife that Katie should come and live with him.

Things were falling into place, just as he had hoped. New job, new house, new life. It was time to make a fresh start. Now the only thing missing from this perfect image was his daughter. He wanted to come home to her every evening. He could see the two of them working at the kitchen table on her homework, sharing dinner at the dining room table, and watching movies in the family room. Elizabeth would agree; she had to. But, then again, what if she didn't? Maybe it was because things were going *so* well, or maybe because he had been burned by her before, but either way Grant Adams couldn't shake the feeling that something was about to go terribly wrong.

Friday, October 4

Katie Adams sat across the table from her father. She was spending the weekend with him, and the two had just finished touring his new townhouse. She was impressed; it was much more of a real home than the apartment had been. He told her all about his new job with MacPhearson, but did not tell her about the medications his new company was currently testing. They talked the entire way from the townhouse to the Northwoods Bar and Grill, a favorite restaurant near his apartment they had found about a year ago. Katie wanted to ask her father something, but decided to wait until they were eating before springing it on him. She wanted him to be in a good mood, and knew he would be more relaxed after he ate something and had a beer.

"So how's school? What's it like to be back on the bottom again?" he asked, referring to the fact that she had just begun the seventh grade, the lowest grade, at Pine Grove Middle School.

"It's fine. Most of my friends are at Willow Lane Middle, so that sucks, I mean stinks," she corrected herself, seeing her father's disapproving look. "Most of my teachers are pretty nice, except Mrs. Johnson, my phy. ed. teacher. She always gets on me because she thinks I'm dogging it."

"Doesn't she know that you're … sick?" Grant's concern turned from her language to the fact that someone was not treating his daughter fairly.

"I don't want anyone except the school nurse to know about that yet, not until they *have* to anyway. But Mom said she'd call Mrs. Johnson if I want her to."

"How is Beth?" he asked, hoping to sound casual. "And David?" he added, forcing a polite smile.

"Fine and fine. Mom is freaking out about all the wedding plans. They are planning on flying us out to Hawaii, getting married there, and then staying for a week. The trip sounds cool, and David even promised to take me snorkeling. But I'm not excited about being with them on their honeymoon. It kind of creeps me out when I think about being right next door to their room—*on their honeymoon*," she added dramatically. Grant said nothing in response, but completely understood Katie's feelings. It made him feel sick to think of Beth with another man.

When the waitress brought their drinks—lemonade for Katie and beer for Grant—she took their order. Without even looking over the menu, they decided on the fish, with baked potatoes and salads. Beth had never liked any kind of fish or seafood. But since the divorce, it had become a new tradition for Grant and Katie to go out for fish on Fridays.

"So, what do you think of my new place?" He had been so excited during their tour and it made Katie happy that her dad was happy. He deserved it.

"I think it's great, Dad. It's perfect for you. There's lots of room, and I was thinking . . ." It was clear to Grant that Katie had something on her mind. She was an open book to him.

"Spill it, little girl," he prompted. She started to play innocent, but immediately dropped it, knowing full well she'd never beat him at this game.

"Okay. I was thinking that since you have this great new townhouse and this new job where you won't have to travel so much that maybe I could come and live with you." She didn't even give him a chance to counter. "Mom is so into the wedding, and she's even busier since she started law school this fall. And once David moves in … I think it's a good time for me to be out of the house," she added, finishing her argument.

"Well, if your mom ever needs tips on how to effectively argue a case, she should go to you. Katie, we'll have to talk this over with her. I'm glad you told me how you feel, though. You know we just want you to be happy."

"I know, Dad," she said, her eyes starting to become glassy.

"The truth of the matter is that I was planning on discussing our arrangement with your mom anyway. The reason we had you live with her was to give you some stability after we divorced. You were able to keep your home, your school, and your friends. I was also traveling a lot in those days, and we didn't want you bounced back and forth. But—"

"But my school has changed, and like I said, all my friends go to a different school anyway, and now you're going to be home more, and—"

"Katie, I'll talk to her about it on Sunday. I agree that it seems like a good plan, especially with all Beth has on her plate right now. But moving in with me is not going to be a fast or easy decision for her, so let's take it slow, okay?" The last thing he wanted to do was make it seem to Beth as if the decision had already been made—without her. He would state his case, let Katie share her feelings on the subject, and hopefully the three of them would have a mature discussion. He hoped she would listen to reason. *But then again,* he thought sarcastically, *she is going to be a lawyer.*

~

Five miles away, in the laboratory of MacPhearson Pharmaceuticals, Oliver Klein and Tara Wolfe were waiting for the results of their experiment. Will Adison was also in the laboratory, anxiously awaiting the results of his own tests that he had been conducting all week. Dr. Klein glanced at the door of the lab office. He found it both annoying and surprising that Adison had practically yelled at Tara when she offered to help him. Adison, usually distracted but mild mannered, was obviously stressed or excited about something. Every night this week he had been in the lab until at least eight o'clock. He had always been a dedicated scientist, but he never stayed that late so many days in a row. *Maybe he had a fight with the wife,* thought Oliver. *Or the girlfriend,* he added wryly. He found it amusing that Will Adison could be such a brilliant scientist and yet so moronic about his supposedly secret affair with Jessica Monroe. Practically the whole lab knew what was going on, although no one dared let on about it.

Will stuck his head out of the office. "Tara, in a few minutes I'm going to be printing some test results. Should be about seven or eight pages in spreadsheet format. I'll be in here. Please call me when they begin printing," Will told the young research assistant.

"Sure Dr. Adison. If you like, I can just wait until it finishes printing and then bring the document to you," she offered. She was just finishing her inventory report and wasn't planning to start another test this late in the day.

"No, no, no. I'll get it myself," Will replied hastily, then added, "but thank you."

"No problem. I'll call when it starts printing," Tara assured him. She shot a puzzled glance at Oliver, as if to say, *what the hell was that all about?*

Will's earlier reaction, and his response to Tara now, piqued Oliver's curiosity. What was Adison working on? Why was he being so secretive?

"Hey, Tara, why don't you go home? I can take care of the rest of this stuff myself. It's Friday, enjoy the weekend," he told her.

"Are you sure?" Tara asked, as she walked over to her locker to grab her jacket. Oliver nodded and said he'd see her first thing on Monday to look over the results.

As she closed the door of the lab behind her, Oliver was already making his way over to Dr. Adison's lab computer.

Will Adison looked over the data again. He wasn't happy that Oliver, not Tara, had called to tell him his document was printing. Will certainly didn't want *him* getting a look at his work—this work. While he thought Dr. Klein was an adequate scientist, it was no secret that the two didn't see eye to eye. In Will's opinion, Oliver had no vision. He was an excellent lab manager, but would never be the type to generate a new theory or explore new territory. Whatever creativity he had, if any, must have been killed by years of military service. Adison, on the other hand, knew he was the exact opposite. He was all vision, and had been accused by more than one colleague of being impractical. When he came up with a new idea, he wanted to see it through. Even if the early work wasn't promising, he knew it might lead to something. Over his desk was a quotation from Edison: *I did not make one thousand errors. The light bulb was just an invention with one thousand and one steps.*

He felt that way now. They had already done so much research on this drug. In fact, a closely related compound was currently showing excellent results in clinical studies. This only deepened Will's belief that if they kept tinkering with old ideas, new ideas—valuable ideas—would come shining through. But not everyone agreed with him, and his trial and error method was costly. It had been the source of many arguments among the three owners.

Steven was more in line with Oliver's way of running a lab. You either "fish or cut bait." Steven felt that if a compound wasn't showing itself to be effective, you moved on to another project. As a businessman, this was logical. But as a scientist, Will believed more persistence was necessary. As partners, they simply agreed to disagree, each realizing that a successful pharmaceutical company needed a balance of leaders who had creative vision and leaders who were fiscally responsible. James, as always, was the tie between the two, and often served as mediator.

Will's office was dimly lit compared to the bright white glare of the lab. His eyes were having trouble focusing. He read over the data as he sank into his old, comfortable chair. It was finally quiet; even Oliver had gone home. Will took off his glasses, tossing them down on his desk, and closed his eyes for a moment. After all these months—no make that *years*—of work, the results were, even to him, unbelievable.

Sunday, October 6

As he pulled the car into Elizabeth's driveway, Grant felt a familiar ache forming in the pit of his stomach. Today was worse, though, because he dreaded talking with her about Katie's living arrangements. Katie must have felt the same way, because she barely spoke the entire ride over.

David must have been watching from the living room window; he opened the door for them just as they climbed the last step. He was a few inches shorter than Grant, which placed him at about five feet ten. He was an avid runner, and had the lean look of one. His brown eyes were penetrating, an asset in the courtroom. Grant would hate to be on the witness stand facing this guy.

"Hello, Grant. How are you? Hi, Katie. Did you have a good weekend?" He was polite, although not warm.

"Fine, and you? How are those wedding plans coming along?" Grant's response revealed a much cooler tone.

"We're almost done. Did Katie tell you about snorkeling?

"She did. I was going to warn you about the sharks, but with you being an attorney, they aren't likely to attack one of their own," Grant snipped.

"Another lawyer joke. Won't you ever run out?" Beth's voice drifted in from the kitchen. She came in a moment later as Grant and Katie moved into the living room, followed by David. *Attractive as always*, thought Grant, though he was glad to note she had gained a few pounds. Well, maybe that was just wishful thinking. She wore jeans and a flannel shirt. It stung Grant when he realized that it might be David's. She used to wear his shirts.

"Hi love," she kissed the top of Katie's head. "I'll be heading out to the library to study for an exam, but I'll be home for dinner, around four-thirty or so, okay? Be good!" She grabbed an overloaded book bag and headed for the door. "Grant, can I please speak with you outside?"

He kissed Katie's cheek and blatantly ignored David on his way out.

"I actually want to talk to you too, Beth," he started. It was important for him to speak first, but she beat him to it.

"Katie called me on Saturday night from your place and said she wants to live with you. While I don't want her to move away from me, I agree that it might be a good thing for her right now. She needs someone who can give her every second, and unfortunately, that can't be me right now. We can reverse the custody arrangement so that your place is her primary residence and she can spend some weekends …" at that moment her voice broke. He was absolutely shocked by what she was saying. Grant looked at her, and he felt for her right then. He knew she loved her child, their child, and it must have killed her to let her go like that. Time was precious, especially with Katie being sick.

"Thank you. I can't even begin to tell you how much this means to me," Grant replied. "You know she loves you. It's just that, with everything that's been going on, she's ready for a change. How's she been feeling, Beth?" he asked, needing more than his daughter's brief and uninformative updates on her condition.

"She seems fine, Grant. Honestly, if I didn't know better, I'd say the doctors are wrong. She seems tired sometimes, but what kid that age doesn't? I know we already got a second and third opinion, but I think we should bring her to another doctor. Really, Grant, she just doesn't seem that sick," Beth answered, swallowing hard.

"I would love to believe that, Beth," he assured her, nodding. "After her appointment with Dr. Billings next week, if you want, we'll take her to see someone new. Nothing would make me happier than to hear that there's been some terrible mistake," he said, struggling to get the words out.

"Has she talked to you about Ashley's funeral yet?" Beth asked, wanting to know how her little girl was coping with the death of her friend. "It must be frightening for her to know she might end up like Ashley."

"Not really, just how sad it was, but not much more," he answered.

They stood there in awkward silence until she gained strength to talk again.

"Let's talk later this week. There are a lot of calls and arrangements that need to be made."

Grant nodded, and then he did something he hadn't done in more than two years: he hugged her.

Wednesday, October 9

Walking his mother through the townhouse, Grant smiled as he watched her face light up. It was evident that she approved of his choice.

"Oh, Grant! It's beautiful," she gushed. She had wanted him to move out of the apartment since the moment he moved in. She didn't want her son wasting time in limbo. His marriage was over, and it was high time he accepted it and moved on.

Dorothy Adams knew all about moving on. Tom, her husband of almost forty years, had died of a heart attack six years earlier. It had been sudden. People always asked her if it was harder that way, without having the chance to say good-bye. Dorothy didn't feel that way at all, and was certain that, had it been the other way around, Tom would feel the same. They had told each other how they felt every day, and followed the rule about never leaving or going to sleep angry. Their marriage had been a happy one, and Dorothy couldn't have asked for anything else, except for more time together.

They had raised two wonderful children, Grant, the older, and a daughter, Anne, who was a schoolteacher just outside of Chicago. In her mid-sixties, Dorothy was an attractive grandmother, with stylish silver hair and kind blue eyes. Because of her fair complexion, she stayed out of the sun, and as a result looked ten years younger than she really was. Her friendly personality made her popular with the gentlemen in her church group and among her circle of friends. Last year she even went on a "Silver Singles" cruise. Grant was the first to admit that it was embarrassing that his mother had a more active social life than he did.

"It will make quite the bachelor pad, dear," she said with a mischievous twinkle in her eye. "I'm sure I won't even be able to hear you from my bedroom on the lower level."

"Oh, no," Grant teased back. "Remember, Ma, you aren't moving in with Anne or me. We're sending you to the home." They had a running joke about her moving into a nursing home. It was funny because she was still in her prime, sharp as a tack.

"Thanks a lot! What did Katie think? I'll bet she just loved the view from her room!"

"She did. And how do you know which room is hers?" he asked her.

"The one with bigger closet, of course. A girl that age needs her space," she said, smiling. She already had some decorating ideas and was sure her son wanted her help. She loved him dearly, but his sense of style needed a woman's touch. *Thank God*, she thought, *I am that woman, not Elizabeth.*

Dorothy had never liked her daughter-in-law. Of course she loved her granddaughter dearly, but she had known that her son's marriage was doomed from the start. He had been a twenty-five-year-old graduate student, and Elizabeth Murray only a college sophomore, when the two met. They had dated a short time, just a few months, when Elizabeth got pregnant. Then Grant asked her to marry him and she accepted. Elizabeth seemed eager to play house, become a wife and mother. But she was so young, and Dorothy feared it wouldn't last long. She and Tom gave their blessing reluctantly. Elizabeth's parents, on the other hand, had been thrilled with the idea of their only daughter starting a family early. In addition to throwing a large, beautiful wedding, they put a substantial down payment on a charming home in a quiet neighborhood in St. Paul. Dorothy couldn't deny that the Murrays were good to her son. Too bad Elizabeth wasn't. When Katie started first grade, Elizabeth went back to school herself to finish her paralegal degree. After graduating, she got a job working for an attorney named David Hughes. Two years later, before their twelfth wedding anniversary, Elizabeth broke her son's heart. She was having an affair with her boss and wanted a divorce. Dorothy looked at Grant now. Although he would turn forty next year, he was still her little boy, and she wanted him to be happy.

"Good riddance, Beth Murray," she muttered. Her son was finally ready to move on.

"What are you plotting, Mother?" Grant asked.

"Never you mind. I was just getting some ideas for the family room. That is, if you want my help," she teased, fishing for an invitation from him.

"I was thinking, if you wouldn't mind staying with me for a few weeks, you could have free reign while I'm at work all day. We can hire the painters the builder used in the model, and you can shop to your heart's content at all of your favorite stores. Just get whatever you think will look good—and masculine," he added.

"Oh, I think I can manage. It's always fun to spend someone else's money."

"Mom, I also want you to know that I spoke with Beth last Sunday when I dropped Katie off, and it looks like she'll be coming to live with me, at least for awhile."

"Who, Beth?"

"Bite your tongue! Mom, Katie is going to be with me from now on," he told her. He knew she would be thrilled. His mother absolutely adored Katie, her only grandchild. His sister Anne had been married for five years and was now expecting her first baby in February. But until then, it was all Katie, and to say she was spoiled didn't even scratch the surface.

"Oh Grant, what wonderful news! Now I really do want to move in! Sit down and tell me everything. How did Elizabeth Murray, formerly Mrs. Grant Adams, and soon-to-be Mrs. David Hughes, take it?"

They sat down on the only two chairs in the room and he relayed the story, as requested, in full detail.

~

James watched as Steven paced back and forth across the Persian rug in his office. They were scheduled to meet with Will in fifteen minutes. They had come straight from the Minneapolis/St. Paul International Airport where their flight had landed less than two hours before. Both brothers had attended a weekend conference hosted by the University of Arizona and had decided to stay a few extra days. Paula and Audrey had joined them. Originally Will and Barbara had planned to go as well. But Will couldn't leave his work, not even for a few days, so neither he nor Barbara went. That morning Will had sent them an e-mail about the final results of his project. The message was marked urgent, but didn't really give them any details. He only said that he wanted a meeting with both of them as soon as possible.

"Couldn't this have waited until tomorrow, Will?" James asked his partner calmly as he entered the office. The flight and the rainy weather had given him a dull headache.

"No, I wanted you to see this right away," Will stated as he slid a red folder across the desk toward the brothers. Then he stood back in order see their reaction.

"We agreed to shut that project down months ago," snapped Steven. It was exactly the reaction Will had expected. "It's costing us thousands—no, tens of thousands of dollars!"

"I admit these results aren't what I was expecting, but don't you see how close we are? This could help us find what we've been looking for, Steven. James, you realize that if we keep at this, it could mean—"

"It *could*," Steven interrupted. "Will, do you hear yourself? You're spending a lot of time and money, which may I remind you isn't all yours, on something that *could* be. But what if it's not? How do you get off deciding on your own which projects are worth more than others?

"Remember, it was James and I who studied respiratory diseases back at the U of M in the first place. We spent four years on that research. That knowledge finally paid off. That's how we discovered the treatment compound now being tested in the trials. It's showing excellent results," he concluded, his voice rising in pitch and volume. "And what does all your work show? Nothing! What do your results indicate? Nothing! Stop searching for something that isn't there, Will! You're a gifted scientist, but you're also arrogant and stubborn as hell. Not every theory you have will prove true. Move on to something else, for Christ's sake. There's a world of diseases out there."

"Will, I'm sorry your work didn't yield more positive results," James said, trying a more supportive approach. "I know that this project meant a great deal to you and you were confident the compound would be successful." He could tell Will was at the breaking point. Will had believed the compound would work, and now, in black and white, the data proved otherwise. "I know you're disappointed ..."

"Disappointed? Disappointed? That doesn't even come close to how I'm feeling. The compound worked before—I just don't understand. All of the early experiments, even up until last week, showed it *was* effective." Will sighed. Then his expression changed, as if he had thought of something. "Perhaps if we just try a few more arrangements, even the most minute change in structure could mean—"

"Will, you know we don't like to play this card, but James and I control two thirds of this company. I demand that you end your research—*effective immediately!*"

"So it's the old two-against-one, Steven? What are we, in the third grade?" Will was on the defensive.

"Just stop wasting our resources, Will. Take an objective look at your results and admit defeat."

"I'd like to take some time off and clear my head. This whole thing has really taken it out of me. Oliver can handle the lab while I'm gone," he suggested. *Oh you'll love being the one in charge,* he thought, *won't you Dr. Klein?*

"Under the circumstances, I think that's a very good idea," Steven agreed. His tone sounded less hostile now.

"I think it'll be good for you to get out of the lab for a while. Like you said, Oliver can run things while you're away. I'll talk to him before he leaves today," James said, standing up from his chair. He handed Will the folder and left his two partners alone.

"For the record, Steven, I guess I owe you an apology for going behind your back," Will said dejectedly. "But this issue has come up before. We just don't see things in the same light. Maybe it's time for me to move on."

"MacPhearson wouldn't be the same without you, Will," Steven admitted.

"Thanks." Will turned and walked out the office door.

At that moment, Steven would have given almost anything to know what Will Adison was really thinking.

~

Barbara knew something was wrong the second he walked through the door. The first thing he did when he arrived that evening, something he hadn't in such a long time, was kiss her. Then, without a word, he walked up to his bedroom and began to pack his suitcase. She followed. As she stared at him, she was certain that he had finally decided to leave her. It was something she had been expecting since overhearing his conversation at the country club, and yet she found herself shocked that it was actually happening.

"Where are you going, Will?" She asked a simple question for such a complex situation.

"I've decided to drive to the cabin and stay for a few days, maybe as long as a week. I need a break from everything, Barbara. Things are falling apart and I've got to figure out some sort of plan for holding it all together." He sounded tired.

"Are you going alone?" She couldn't help asking. She knew Jessica had been to their cabin before.

He looked at her as though the thought of bringing someone else had never occurred to him. "Yes. I need time to think, to clear my head. I don't want you to come down or even call, unless there's an emergency."

So he is going alone, thought Barbara. She believed him, for the moment. *Maybe he's finally decided to leave Jessica.* Barbara had always thought of it as a fling, a mid-life crisis, but never a relationship that would last. *A little more fishing won't hurt.* "Will, what's wrong with you?"

"The compound failed. Everything was going perfectly, and then all of a sudden it failed. I don't know. I guess I might have misinterpreted the earlier results. Nothing has worked out the way I had planned. Our marriage, my job, everything. I don't have anything left," he stated flatly. There was no emotion in his voice. He had no energy left for emotion.

"Are you sure? But you were so certain that this final run of tests would confirm the earlier data. Will, you said—"

"Whatever I said was wrong. It's not going to happen. James and Steven and I met today and I officially ended my research on this compound, for real this time. I just can't figure it out, and I'm too tired to try anymore."

"But there will be other projects. It's not as if this is the only one," she offered.

"When I get back, we need to talk, Barbara. You know why. For what it's worth, I do love you. I've always loved you," he told her. Then, for the second time that day, he kissed her on the cheek. He walked out the door five minutes later.

Even though Barbara Adison watched Will pull his car out of the parking lot and drive down the street, she couldn't believe he was gone. Turning away from the window, she looked around the condo with an objective eye, as if to see what it said about the people who lived there. It was spotless, no children around with their messes. The decorating, modern and elegant, suggested the owners had money. It struck her that, although there was a fire lit and the table was set with a tossed salad and pasta, there was nothing in any of the rooms that conveyed the warmth of family. There were no photos around. No toys to clutter the rooms. The steel and glass of the tables had severe lines. Everything was in its place, almost as if real people didn't even live there. It could have been one of those homes featured in a magazine. Despite all the beautiful furniture, expensive art, and designer fabrics, the room was cold and impersonal.

Even though it had been slipping away for years now, her marriage, Barbara realized, was more than likely over. Her life, like the things around her, felt as though it belonged to someone else.

But Barbara Adison was not one to wallow. She didn't want Will to have the upper hand again. This time she wanted to be ready for him with a plan of her own. She refilled her glass of wine, sat down in Will's black leather chair, and picked up the phone. The first step in that plan was to call her lawyer.

Tuesday, October 15

Grant's first few days at MacPhearson were completely uneventful. There were the usual forms to be completed. He was introduced to countless colleagues, and was given a guided tour of the entire complex.

Grant's personal tour guide was James MacPhearson, and the two spent the morning walking the grounds and the building. MacPhearson Pharmaceuticals had a beautiful campus. The three-story building was surrounded by woods of tall pine trees, separating it from both the highway and surrounding farmland. Land in this area was being developed quickly and it had been Steven's idea to buy more than they needed in order to maintain a serene atmosphere. "The last thing I want to see when I leave work," he had told his brother, "is another one of those goddamn strip malls."

As they headed inside and passed through a tiled lobby, with its comfortable-looking couches and chairs, several plants, and small fountain, James kept up the commentary. "The building was designed for us. Steven, Will, and I hired an architectural firm out of Seattle that specializes in laboratories and businesses in the biotech industry." It was clear he was proud of not only the building, but also what it stood for. They walked down a long hallway, with several closed doors on either side. About halfway down, James opened a door on their left. "We aren't large, but what we lack in quantity we more than make up for in quality. This is one of our in-vitro labs. Look at it, Grant. State of the art equipment, designed to promote efficiency and safety. I'm not sure if you are aware of our impressive safety record."

"So far, everything I have seen far exceeds my expectations. It's not surprising that the company is well respected in both the scientific and business worlds," Grant said as he followed James's lead into another, smaller laboratory. Unlike the room from which they had come, where Grant estimated about twenty-five researchers were working, this room was empty.

"Grant, you've got the job, remember?" James laughed, "But I do appreciate and accept your compliments."

"Where are the in-vivo labs?" Grant asked. As a research scientist, testing drugs and compounds on animals like mice and ducks was his least favorite task. Although he knew many leaps in science could not have been made without the sacrifice of animals, he could never get used to doing it himself. He considered it a necessary evil.

"Down that hallway," James answered, pointing. "But we'll skip that end of the building, if you don't mind. And this is Will's personal lab. He has no desire to run the business side of MacPhearson. Of course, we all started out that way. At first, Steven, with his business background, was able to handle that side of things. But then, with two drugs approved by the FDA in a relatively short period of time, we grew. The profits from those drugs—especially the first—funded several other projects. Will didn't want to give up the lab—it's where his real passion lies—so I moved upstairs and traded in my lab coat for a suit," he told Grant, still walking.

"So do you miss it?"

"At times, but I'm smart enough to realize when I'm not the best. Will is an absolute genius, and it would not have benefited MacPhearson or me to have his talents wasted upstairs," he continued. "And back there is Will's office. He has one upstairs as well, but that's really just for meetings. In fact, he uses it so infrequently, we've actually started storing some records in there."

As they reached the hallway, James and Grant turned to the left, and after a few paces stepped into another lab, where Grant recognized Oliver Klein leaning over a tray of test tubes. Oliver nodded in greeting and kept at his work.

"Not much of a socializer, that one, at least not in the lab. Catch him at lunch, though, or worse yet, at the bar, and you'll never get free," James whispered as he held up a hand to his employees. Grant recognized a few people from the party the other night and hesitantly raised his hand as well. This lab was smaller, with ten or so scientists looking busy. Grant had spent enough time in the lab to wonder if this was an act purely for the benefit of their boss. Lab work was funny that way. Some days there wasn't enough time to get things done, and other days you felt stranded, waiting for a project to finish or data to be run.

They walked through more laboratories, each one similar to and yet different from the one before, and then up the stairs to the second floor. James explained to Grant that this was where most of the administrative work took place and clinical documents were kept. This floor reminded Grant of Webber Scientific, offices along the perimeter and large interior rooms filled with endless files and a sea of cubicles.

"MacPhearson now employs about two hundred fifty people. At first it was just the three of us, literally working out of Steven's unfinished basement. But then we got some private funding, took out second mortgages on our homes, and jumped. For a few years, we had a very small lab in Minneapolis with about forty employees. It was there we designed Alerzan, a drug designed to treat domestic allergies. It was our first drug approved by the FDA. It did well on the market, and still does, although when the patent runs out there will be competition from other labs that will produce generic versions of it. Then there was Respara, an asthma medication. Anyway, success, as you know, leads to expansion, and here we are." He paused at the stairway leading to the third floor. For Grant, it was refreshing to work for someone who spent his own sweat and blood to succeed. Webber was owned and run by Charles Wright, grandson of the founder, Henry Wright. Henry named the company for his first wife, Mae Webber, who died of scarlet fever shortly after the birth of their child, a son. Unlike his grandfather, young Charles lacked any business insight, was rumored to have practically bought his MBA, and spent more time on the golf course than in the office. But Webber Scientific was a powerhouse. With so many successful and lucrative drugs on the market, even Charlie couldn't kill it.

"Webber and MacPhearson are like night and day," Grant mumbled to himself.

"Pardon?" James turned around halfway up the stairs.

"Oh, nothing, James. I was just taking it all in," Grant replied.

The third floor was the most familiar to Grant. It was where he had spent his time waiting for the interview to get started, and where he completed most of his paperwork and general company training the day before. It also held all of the offices of the clinical research associates, including Grant's. Because Grant had already seen most of this level, James suggested they end the tour. It was after eleven o'clock and he was late for a meeting with his brother and the legal team.

"Thank you again for showing me around personally, James. I wanted some time to meet with the other clinical research associates, and Diane Norton said I should stop by her office before lunch," Grant informed him.

The two men shook hands and walked away in opposite directions, Grant looking forward to his meeting, and James dreading his.

～

Robert Dawson checked his watch for the third time. James was usually quite punctual. Robert was the head attorney for MacPhearson Pharmaceuticals and carried a full schedule that day. He had graduated from William Mitchell Law School in St. Paul and had been in practice for almost twenty-three years. He had been retained both by well-established companies and younger, start-up companies—like MacPhearson—when they hired him eight years ago. After two years, when Alerzan was moderately successful on the market and Respara was in the process of FDA approval, they offered him a full-time position. He now had two staff attorneys and an assistant in his legal department. Having made only average grades in law school, he later earned the reputation of being a shrewd corporate attorney because of his abilities in the courtroom.

Robert ran a hand through his thinning, grayish-blonde hair and straightened his suit. It, like the rest of his wardrobe, was expensive—with custom tailoring. He always had champagne taste, and would settle for nothing less. That explained why he was still unmarried at the age of forty-eight. No one could live up to his high expectations.

He looked over at Steven and finally broke the silence. "He does know we have a meeting today, right?"

"He knows, Rob," Steven answered.

"Well, I hope he gets here soon. I only have another thirty minutes or so before I have to leave. I have another meeting in Minneapolis at twelve-thirty," he stated. At that moment, James breezed in through the door and sat down across from Robert. He briefly apologized, explaining that he had been giving a tour to Grant Adams, the new CRA they just hired.

"Steven told me about him last week. Sounds like a good fit," offered Robert.

"Look, let's get this started since we're running short on time as it is," Steven said, taking over. "Let's start with new business. James, why don't you bring Rob up to speed?"

"The compound Will was developing was shown to be a failure in later tests. As you know, it was a derivative of B319, the drug currently in clinical trials for the treatment of bronchiosclerosis. Those trials are showing excellent results. We plan to submit the data to the FDA and, pending approval, it could be on the market some time next year. We think this is the best time to go public. We want you to start researching and drawing up the necessary documents. That is, if you think we still can in light of the Jacobs situation." James leaned back in his chair with his hands clasped behind his head. It was a favorite position of his. His daughters even joked that if there ever were to be a statue made of him, it would have to be in that very position.

"When exactly are you thinking of doing all this?" Rob asked. These transitions, even under normal circumstances, needed to be planned very carefully and usually took months.

"We were hoping to have everything laid out by the end of this year. We'll present the information to the employees after the first of the year, giving them the option to buy in first, with a profit sharing program," Steven added.

"I don't think that timeline is unreasonable. And you'll go public when?"

"After B319 hits the market, hopefully sometime next summer or fall at the latest," James interjected.

"Again, seems reasonable. Anything else on that issue?" Rob asked. When both brothers shook their heads, he went on to the real reason for their meeting. "I've been reading over the case file. It seems he had no other health factors, aside from the asthma, and the only medication he was taking was Respara. If they do in fact sue, I would advise you to settle the case out of court and pray it doesn't happen to anyone else. Now this is just a possibility, but the FDA could pull Respara from the market in order to conduct additional safety studies."

"Shit!" Steven slammed his fist down on the table, then covered his face with his hands. James was motionless. *Cool as a cucumber, like always,* thought Robert. In the eight years he had known the MacPhearsons, he had never once seen James lose his temper.

"Well, think about what I said about settling out of court. I'll keep you informed of the FDA's decision," Robert said quietly, getting up to leave. He hated being the bearer of bad news, and this was potentially very bad news for these two men.

"We'll let you know what we want to do when Will gets back," James said, taking off his glasses. He suddenly leaned forward. "Rob, just how badly might this affect our plans about going public?"

"If it's only one case and goes away quietly, I don't think it will do much damage, especially if B319 is approved and goes to market. The public and media will forget that Respara was pulled—*if* it gets pulled—as soon as they start hearing the buzz about a wonder treatment for bronchiosclerosis. People have incredibly short memories. We'll just have to wait and see, gentlemen. I'll be in touch," he said as he gathered his papers, closed them in his briefcase, and left the brothers alone.

"We need B319 to get approved, James." Steven sounded determined.

"It will. Everything will be fine, you'll see. If Respara does get pulled, there's nothing we can do about it. I'm not even convinced it was the cause of the Jacobs kid's death anyway. As Robert said, we might have to do some additional studies to prove it's safe, but that's happened before. None of this is new. Steven, it will be fine," James said, his voice stronger now. He needed Steven to keep it together. Any financial hit they took from Respara could be more than replaced with the profits they stood to gain from B319.

After Steven left the office, James fixed himself a drink. He needed one after this day. As he sipped, he thought about the boy. Kyle Jacobs was an eleven-year-old who had been prescribed Respara by his doctor to treat asthma. Five weeks ago he was playing soccer and suddenly dropped to the ground. An ambulance was called. The boy's father performed CPR at the scene, but Jacobs was pronounced dead upon arrival at the hospital. There were, of course, several theories proposed by the local media. It was an extremely hot weekend, in the upper nineties and humid. The boy had been in a soccer tournament, playing four games in three days. He died on Sunday afternoon. Many speculated he died of heat exhaustion or complications due to dehydration. As soon as the news reported the boy had asthma, James began tracking the story. A few days later it was reported in the St. Paul *Pioneer Press* that Kyle Jacobs was taking Respara and the medical examiner was trying to determine if it could be linked to the young boy's death. The link garnered media attention on both a local and national level, as Respara was a widely prescribed medication for asthma sufferers. There were emotional stories in the *Pioneer Press* and the Minneapolis *Star Tribune*. All mentioned Jacobs had been taking Respara. James felt terrible for the family. He had two daughters of his own and couldn't imagine the pain of losing a child. But he still didn't believe it was the drug. There were other factors that may have contributed to the boy's death. Then, after only a few days, Kyle Jacobs's story was replaced by more current news stories.

James rubbed his eyes. He finished his drink and poured another. He had to do what Rob told them to do—wait. James MacPhearson hated waiting.

~

Outside Steven's office, Jessica Monroe was packing her bag and getting ready to leave for lunch. She had classes that afternoon at the University where she was earning her degree in business administration. All three of her bosses completely supported her decision to go back to school. They even let her take an afternoon or morning class one day each week so she could complete the program more quickly. Her job's flexibility wasn't the only benefit, however. MacPhearson offered tuition reimbursement. If she kept her grades above a B average, and stayed with the company for at least three years after earning her degree, they would pay for half the cost of tuition and books. Although it kept her busy and she felt like dropping out more than once, it was an opportunity she couldn't pass up. She was in the home stretch, and had expected to finish her classes the following June.

But now, with the baby due in the spring, she would have to either arrange to miss class for a few weeks or wait until fall semester to finish her classes. Both plans were severely flawed, and Jessica reprimanded herself as she walked out to her car. How could she have been so stupid as to let this happen? What had she been thinking? Now she was more than likely about to become a single parent, and she knew the challenges that faced her were going to be difficult at best. Will was either too busy to talk to her, or was making a conscious effort to avoid her. They had hardly spoken since she told him about the baby. He was either still in shock, or wasn't sure what to say to her. *Maybe he just needs time to get used to the idea*, thought Jessica, trying to convince herself. She wondered if Will had told Barbara by now.

Although Jessica was tired, stressed, and felt sick most days, she was already falling in love with her baby. Being pregnant was such an amazing experience. She knew, according to the books she bought, she probably wouldn't feel the baby move for a few more weeks at the earliest. But even though she was only fifteen weeks along, it was as if she could sense the tiny life developing inside her. Jessica had this wonderful secret, and yet she couldn't share it, at least not yet. Of course she'd have to tell her family soon, before she started really showing. Eventually they'd accept the situation. And she'd tell Amy. She'd need both her family and her best friend by her side. Will would come around; he always did. He thought about breaking it off before, but he always came back. *Because he loves me. And he'll love you, too,* she said as she patted her stomach. *The three of us will be together and we'll be so happy.*

Friday, October 18

Grant pulled into his new garage, stopping just short of a stack of boxes that still needed unpacking. The garage was solely his responsibility, so it was the most disorganized part of the house. As he walked into the townhouse, he looked around the first level. The hallway was painted a soft taupe and his mother had found a long wool rug to run the length of the hallway. It was colorful, just the right amount to hide any dirt he tracked in, she had told him. He passed the small laundry room to the right and ignored the growing pile of dirty clothes sitting under the chute. Grant was the type to let chores go for as long as humanly possible. Only when he finally ran out of the last pair of dark socks or clean boxers would he surrender and take an entire day to do laundry. He knew this drove his mother absolutely crazy. *That's one thing my mother and Elizabeth have in common*, he thought, smiling to himself. The office, on his left, was almost finished. The pale orange walls brightened the windowless room and complimented his espresso-stained office furniture. His job with MacPhearson meant he could do some of his work at home, so having a private office was essential. He still needed to set up his equipment. The computer was up and running, but the fax machine, scanner, and mini copier would have to wait. On the walls hung some black and white photos and a large map. Ever since he was a little boy he had a map of the world hanging somewhere. In the apartment, it had been pinned up in his bedroom. It was obvious his mother had sprung for a new one. This version was completely updated, as far as a map could be, anyway, but looked like an antique. The effect was nice and Grant made a mental note to thank his mother for this personal touch.

As he climbed the stairs to the second level, he felt the soreness in his knees again. He first noticed it a few years before, and knew it was just another sign that he was getting older and out shape. Now that he had lost some weight, it just meant he was getting older. He could already smell something wonderful coming from the kitchen. For a moment, he paused at the top of the stairs and watched his mom.

She was listening to the radio, an afternoon news program, and humming to herself as she finished chopping peppers for their salad. Grant was instantly a boy again, watching his mom cook a family dinner. He could almost see his father reading the paper in his old club chair, and then getting up to go into the kitchen to steal some food. His mother would scold her husband, but in a teasing way. Grant knew his parents' marriage had been a happy one, and it made him envious that his own hadn't turned out the same way.

"Are you going to stand there all day, dear, or are you going to give me a hand in here?" His mother's voice brought Grant suddenly back to the present.

"I was just thinking about Dad," he admitted. "I miss him."

"I miss your father every day," she said, with a hint of sadness. She had healed from, but not forgotten, what she had lost. "You said Katie would be moving in next Saturday, right? Does that mean she's not coming tomorrow?"

"Yeah," Grant sighed. "Beth wanted them to spend the weekend together. I think they were going to drive up to Duluth, do some shopping, and maybe walk through Gooseberry Falls State Park, if the weather is nice." Although he would rather have had Katie move in sooner, he knew he should give Beth the weekend; it was the least he could do.

"Alone? Or is David going along, too?"

"David is in the middle of preparing for a big case and thought it should be a girls' weekend. Apparently he was very supportive of the idea of Katie coming to live with me. I don't know if I should be grateful to him, or assume that he just wanted my kid out of the house."

"Either way, you got what you wanted, and Katie did, too," Dorothy reminded him. "Stop worrying about his motives. Who cares? Now tell me, how is our girl feeling?"

Grant and Beth had told his mother. Unlike Beth's parents, who were overly dramatic, she would be strong, and might be needed for things like taking Katie to doctor's appointments and staying overnight with her. Although concerned for her granddaughter's health, Dorothy handled the situation well. She knew Katie didn't want to make a big deal about it, so she only discussed it with her son in private.

"Beth seems to think she's doing really well. I think she's still holding out hope that Katie's been misdiagnosed."

"That would be wonderful news, wouldn't it?" Dorothy asked cautiously. "Even if she does indeed have bronchiosclerosis, perhaps hers is a milder case and won't be more than a mere annoyance to her from time to time." Like her son, she had done some research about the disease. Even the experts admitted there was still much to be learned.

Grant listened to her as he opened a beer and sat down at his new dining room table. The natural maple table and chairs were a drastic improvement over the card table he had used for eating meals in the apartment. "Well, there is one other thing I've been wanting to tell you. I haven't told Katie yet, but MacPhearson is currently running clinical trials on a new treatment for bronchiosclerosis. So far, it's been effective,"

"And safe? Is it safe, Grant?" his mother asked, stepping into protective mode.

"Only very minor side effects have occurred in patients so far," he answered. When he saw her skeptical expression he added, "Minor side effects as in nausea and drowsiness."

"Will they even let her into a study, what with you being an employee? I would think that might cause a problem."

"Well, I was upfront with them during the interview. I told them their research on bronchiosclerosis was one of the major reasons I was interested in coming aboard. I explained about Katie and they said it was a possibility."

"A possibility, but not a definite yes?" she asked.

"Because I'm not assigned to that particular study, there wouldn't be a conflict of interest. They just have to clear it with the legal department, and Dr. Adison, the other partner," Grant offered confidently. It really shouldn't be a problem. He wasn't monitoring the studies for B319, the drug used to treat bronchiosclerosis, and if they preferred, he could even have Beth bring her to the clinic. That way, he wouldn't have any contact with the site.

Dorothy, her initial questions answered, felt hopeful. "That would be wonderful, Grant. Just think if your company was the one who cured bronchiosclerosis? How exciting!"

"It's just a treatment, Mother. But even so, it would be an incredible feeling, knowing that I was involved with the people who could save Katie and countless others. They could all lead normal, healthy lives," he said, his throat tightening. It would be amazing. His mother sensed the emotion in his voice. She stood behind him and wrapped her arms around her only son. She was so proud of him.

"Now," she said, wanting to lighten the mood, "get off your butt and help me. Oh sure, you can save the world, but you can't give your own mother a hand with dinner?"

Dinner was even better than those he remembered his mother making when he was a child. Along with the salad, they had stuffed pork chops, butternut squash, and fresh green beans. Dorothy was an excellent cook and she found it so much more fun to cook for two than for one. At home, she would make stews and soups, freezing portions to reheat later. But a dinner like this just wasn't worth the effort for just herself. After they cleared the table, she poured them each a cup of coffee and showed him her latest buys and additions to the townhouse.

The main level, was mostly a large, open L-shaped room, which incorporated a sitting area, the dining area, the kitchen, and a family room. The townhouse was actually a row house, the front and back of the unit having windows facing north and south. Dorothy had succumbed to the new trend in decorating and painted only the west and south walls a dark red. The other walls were now the pale color of vanilla ice cream. The sitting room sported two comfortable, brown club chairs, each with ottomans, which could also be used for seating. In front of the window was a square table with a chess set. Katie and Grant both loved to play, and she wanted them to have it available whenever they wanted. The dining area, besides the new table, also housed a small buffet for storing liquor and wine glasses. Grant had always wanted a home with a bar, so she thought this might be a nice touch. As she suspected, he was thrilled.

The kitchen consisted of earth-toned counters along the cranberry walls and a rectangular island. The kitchen opened up to the family room, which was Dorothy's favorite. In the corner was a stone fireplace with a maple mantel. She put family photos and a few vases with flowers there. She purchased two moss green loveseats, along with a set of nesting tables. There was a hutch to hide the television, although she had a feeling her son would never close the doors, and an entertainment center for his stereo and vast CD collection. She could imagine Katie having her giggly teenage friends over, maybe even for a slumber party. The bathroom, at the end of the hall, was now painted a dark wheat. She had added a glass shelf, a few candles, and thick towels in slate blue.

"Now, the upstairs isn't done yet, but give me a few more days. It will be all ready by the time Katie moves in next weekend. I'm using her furniture from the apartment, but I got her a new duvet, and framed posters from her favorite movies, and ... well, you'll see." She knew Katie would love it. Grant's bedroom, they had decided, would be painted green. He wasn't that particular, and probably would have been fine if Dorothy had taken over, but she insisted that he make the final decisions. She earmarked a few catalog pages with things she thought he might like. In the hallway, just outside the two bedrooms was a loft area that overlooked the open stairway. It was now filled with a long bookcase and the large rocking chair that had once been Grant's father's. She loved that chair. It reminded her of when Tom would read to the children when they were young, rocking them until they could barely keep their eyes open. She had given it to Grant when Katie was born.

The only other room on the upper level was the master bath. It was now the color of eggplant, with fluffy cream towels and a painting of African violets. It was pretty, without being too feminine. After all, it was Grant's bathroom, too.

"Mother, you have really outdone yourself," he said, putting his arm around her shoulder. She had managed, in just a few days, to create a home for him and his daughter. He couldn't wait to show Katie.

"Well, hiring the professional painters from the developer was what saved me. That alone would have taken us a month. Remind me never to paint more than one room by myself ever again," she said laughing. "And the shopping was my pleasure—all the fun and none of the bills."

"Well, it looks absolutely perfect, Mom." He complimented her again.

"Just remember that when the next credit card statement comes," she called over her shoulder as she headed down the stairs.

Saturday, October 19

Will Adison stared out of the cabin window, looking at the cold, gray river. He finished the last of his coffee and pulled on his heavy, brown barn coat, turning up the collar. He thought about grabbing some gloves from the closet, but then changed his mind. He opened the back door, crossed the small deck that offered a view of the river, and climbed down the stairs, his boots breaking the morning silence. The wind was strong, and he soon regretted leaving his gloves back at the cabin. It had turned chilly this week and the grass beneath his feet was covered in frost. The cloudy day was just beginning, but Will had always been an early riser. Especially when he had something on his mind.

He still couldn't believe the data. It couldn't be right. He had been so sure of himself, so sure that the drug would work. He wasn't used to being wrong, and the fact that Steven had been right made this an even more bitter pill to swallow. As if the drug wasn't enough, he also had the situation with Jessica—and Barbara for that matter—to deal with. A father? Now? He would turn fifty next year, making him sixty-seven when the baby graduated from high school. *Oh God*, Will thought, *people will think I'm his grandpa. Or her grandpa. What in the hell am I going to do?*

As he walked toward the shore, he wrapped his mind around the idea of becoming a father and the impact it would have on Barbara. It would kill her to find out that, after she couldn't give him a baby, another woman could. *She's put up with so much; will she forgive me for this?* Affairs could be discreet, but a baby couldn't be kept quiet. No, the only thing to do would be to break things off with Jessica. He would provide more than adequate financial support, and would spend as much time with the child as she would allow. He could not picture himself leaving Barbara to start a new life with Jessica and the baby. Will realized how this would look from Jessica's point of view. He loved her enough to carry on with her behind closed doors, but he didn't love her enough to stay when she needed him the most. *She's young, though,* he reasoned. She would find someone else and they'd build a life together. *A life with my child,* he reminded himself. Jessica was a young woman, but a capable woman. She would be able to give the child a good life. She had family nearby, was finishing a degree, and had a stable job. The job! *Would she stay at MacPhearson now?*

It stunned him to realize that he hadn't asked *her* any of these questions. He had just left her there in the coatroom at the party, with some excuse about having to get back to his colleagues and wife. Then, with everything going on at work, he hadn't even bothered to call her or stop by her desk. *I'm such an asshole!* He needed to call her. He needed to find a way to tell her that he wasn't going to leave his wife.

Even though he had known it all along, Will felt some sort of relief making this deliberate decision. He was still worried about the baby, how it would all work out, and how Barbara would react. But he knew where he stood. Even if Barbara left him, it would be a mistake to stay with Jessica. She'd see that—eventually. Feeling as though a weight had been lifted from his mind about his personal life, he was able to return to assessing the weight of his professional life.

Now that he was away from the lab, he could see the situation from both sides. He should never have gone off and continued the experiments alone, without telling his partners. But, on the other hand, what if the drug had worked?

Will skipped a stone across the surface of the water, something he'd enjoyed doing with his grandfather, at this very spot, forty years before. It helped him to concentrate. The cabin had been built by his grandfather and he had spent many summers there as a boy. The river, the woods, the whole place calmed him. *It was the right thing to do, to come here now,* he thought.

After a while Will came to his second major decision of the day. Next week, he would drive back into town, to his office, and collect the data. Maybe if he looked it over and compared it with the notes on his laptop here at the cabin, something might jump out at him. It would be on his personal time, so no harm to the company. Maybe he'd missed something; maybe he had made a mistake. His persistence had paid off before, and he felt like he had to at least find out *why* it went wrong the second round of testing. Will laughed at his obsession with this research. There was something special about this project. As another stone danced across the chilly water, he finally resigned himself to the fact that he just couldn't let it go.

Monday, October 21

Grant settled into his office chair and began looking over documents from the two studies to which he was assigned. One involved a topical cream used to treat cystic acne and the other study dealt with an oral medication that helped type 2 diabetics produce insulin. Both were effective in the in-vitro and pre-clinical animal testing stages of research. New drugs are not easy to get approved. After the initial stages of research, MacPhearson had then filed an Investigational New Drug Application with the FDA. Because both were approved at this point, the drugs went on to the clinical stage of research, involving human subjects. During these phases, regulations are very stringent to ensure the safety of the subjects and yield reliable test data. Both compounds showed excellent results in Phase I, when each drug was tested on healthy human subjects for toxicity and dosing levels. A257, the acne cream, was currently in Phase II. Here the number of subjects increased and the population contained more variables, people of different ages or gender. Studies in this phase were being run to determine if results varied according to different populations. Of course, they were studying safety and unwanted side effects, known as adverse events, as well. Grant's other assigned study, S320, was already in Phase III. This study had an even greater number of subjects involved, almost six hundred, and long-term effects and product efficacy were the focus. If S320 were clinically proven to be safe and effective after Phase III, then MacPhearson would submit a New Drug Application to the FDA. The FDA would then review the data gathered during all trial phases and approve or deny the product to go on the market. In pharmaceuticals, the primary goal is to develop a drug that is proven to be safe, effective, and marketable. The thick binders, several for each drug, were physical proof that the process could be long, complicated, and even sometimes political.

Grant looked over the information for both studies. As a study manager, he would be ultimately responsible for monitoring the data for A257 and S320. The clinical research associates working with him would visit their assigned sites, the clinics or hospitals where the studies were conducted, to monitor. The sites for these two studies were located throughout the United States and ranged from a tiny clinic in rural Iowa to a prestigious hospital in New England. At Webber, Grant had traveled to the sites to ensure the protocol was followed, the data collected was accurate, and the subjects were protected. Safety was of the greatest importance when testing with human subjects. Now he would only travel to sites to assist and train new or otherwise inexperienced study monitors. He was relieved that his travel was expected to be less than ten percent.

Although the compounds and therapeutic areas were different, clinical research was fairly standard from one company to another. All had to adhere to the same FDA regulations. Since Grant had earned a master's degree in clinical research and had a strong management background, he felt pretty confident about being able to step in and hit the ground running.

Grant thought back to his meeting the previous Wednesday with the study monitors on his team. Diane Norman was the most experienced of the group. She had been at a large pharmaceutical company for thirteen years before moving to MacPhearson. Apparently she held Grant's position first, but stepped down after only a few months. She wanted to cut back on her hours and responsibilities in order to help care for her mother, who was ill. Diane was sharp, with blunt-cut, silver hair and fashionable, rimless glasses. If he had any questions about the studies or anything at MacPhearson, she would be the person to approach.

There were three other study monitors on the team, all younger than Grant. Tracy Whitman had been with MacPhearson the longest after Diane, with her third anniversary coming in November. She was petite, with short, dark hair and a crooked smile. To Grant's surprise, she also had the mouth of a sailor. Derek Rodine was a tall, articulate intellectual type. He had been a biochemist at the University of Wisconsin before coming to MacPhearson a year and a half ago. His personality was subtle compared to Tracy's, but Grant discovered during their conversation over lunch that Derek had a pleasantly dry sense of humor. The last member of his crew was Allen Jennings. Allen was only a few inches taller than Tracy and very outgoing. He shook Grant's hand firmly and was personable from the moment he met his new boss. Grant liked him instantly, although a quick take of Allen's muscular build made Grant promise himself to start hitting the gym again. He had scheduled one-on-one meetings with all four for the next day, and was looking forward to learning more about each of them and their assigned sites.

Grant closed the files and let his head rest on the back of his chair. A look at the clock shocked him. He had been reading the study files for almost three hours. He and Beth had agreed to meet at the clinic for Katie's appointment at four-thirty. If he left now, he would have just enough time to get there during rush hour traffic. He grabbed his coat, closed up his office, and, even though Grant Adams was not a religious man, said a prayer for his little girl.

Grant was fifteen minutes late for the appointment. But Dr. Billings was also running behind schedule and Grant arrived just as Katie's name was being called out in the waiting room. Beth had brought her in last week for some tests, but both wanted to be here for the results.

"I apologize for the wait, folks. How is everyone?" Dr. Billings reminded Grant of a turtle, with his round glasses and small frame. Grant had to bite his tongue each time they met to keep from laughing. Beth knew what was going through her ex-husband's mind and shot him a disgusted look as if to say, *how can you possibly laugh at a time like this?*

"We're fine, Dr. Billings. Just a little anxious to get the test results, I guess," she said as she sat down in the chair closest to the doctor. Katie sat quietly between her two parents. Grant could tell she was nervous. *You poor little thing,* Grant thought. *You shouldn't have to go through this.*

"I'll get right to the point then. These additional test results confirm that Katie does in fact have bronchiosclerosis," stated Dr. Billings without emotion. He forged right ahead, ignoring Beth's audible gasp. "Right now, the key is to keep it under control. She can help by exercising—but nothing too strenuous—getting enough sleep, and minimizing stress."

And how exactly is she supposed to do that after what you've just told her? Grant wondered. Aloud he asked, "So what else can we do? What does this mean?"

"There isn't really anything else to do. Her condition is mild right now—presented symptoms so far are wheezing, fatigue, and loss of appetite. It will worsen, but that can happen over months—possibly even years. Unfortunately, Katie, we just don't know a lot about this disease. We do know that it causes hardened deposits in the bronchial tubes, which constrict the airways. That is why it might sometimes feel difficult to breathe, much like when someone experiences an asthma attack.

"The first case was diagnosed only twenty years ago in England, but the incidence rate, or number of new cases, has increased dramatically in the last few years, especially in kids your age." Grant also knew it had become one of the most deadly diseases in children and adolescents. He was relieved the doctor did not state the grim facts.

"While we still aren't certain what causes the disease, the risk of developing bronchiosclerosis increases in urban areas, which may mean air quality plays a role. The doctor who first discovered the condition is a pediatrician in a hospital on the east side of London. He noticed a large number of children from that area were suffering from a respiratory condition he hadn't encountered before. He felt the disease was linked to the extremely poor air quality in the most industrial sections of the city. Your father has told me that you'll soon be living with him in Hudson instead of St. Paul with your mom. As crazy as it sounds, that might make a big difference for you.

"You need to stay positive, Katie. A good attitude is more important than anything I can do for you. Things in medicine are changing every day. You just need to take care of yourself so that you're ready when a treatment becomes available," he said, patting her shoulder. "Can I talk to your parents for a few minutes, Katie? It's about insurance and I don't want to bore you."

"Sure. Mom, Dad, I guess I'll just wait for you outside," she told them. Her voice was wavering and Grant's heart broke. He knew how much she wanted to believe that the diagnosis had been wrong. And now her hope was gone.

Dr. Billings watched her walk to the lobby before he turned back to Grant and Beth. "Katie's condition will get worse. I want to prepare you for that. She's got to maintain a healthy lifestyle, as much as possible, to stay strong. I was being honest when I said that it could be years before things get really bad."

"Or months. You said it could also be a matter of months!" Beth had lost control. She spat out her words, tears running down her face.

"Beth, get it together for Christ's sake!" Grant scolded her like a child. "Do you really think seeing you like this is going to help her? We're her parents. She needs us to be strong for her. You heard what the doctor said. It could be years. Let's try to focus on that and not scare her any more than she already is."

"You're right, I know. But when I think about …" Beth was trying, Grant could see that. But trying wasn't good enough. He was growing impatient with her.

"Go splash some cold water on your face and wait with Katie. I have to talk with the doctor about something," Grant ordered.

"What? Why do you need to talk with him? Is there something you aren't telling me?" she asked, truly frightened.

"Beth, I'll tell you later. Go be with Katie. I'll be out in a minute," Grant said more softly this time. It worked. She nodded and asked Dr. Billings if there was an open exam room where she could freshen up. He called a nurse to take her out and then closed the door once more.

"I'm so sorry, Grant. Now, what's on your mind?"

"Well, as you already know, I'm a CRA. But now I'm with MacPhearson Pharmaceuticals," Grant began. Dr. Billings obviously recognized the local company because he nodded. "I went to them because they are currently running clinical trials on a treatment drug for bronchiosclerosis. I explained our situation with Katie and they said it might be possible to get her in one of the upcoming studies."

"And you want my opinion?" asked the doctor.

"Yes," Grant responded.

"If she were my daughter, I'd do anything I could to get her into that study. You must know that once a patient is diagnosed, there is an extremely high mortality rate within a two-year period of time. As I said, Katie's case is mild right now, but the progression of bronchiosclerosis can be very rapid. I think it would be very advantageous if she could begin receiving treatment, even an experimental one, while she is still strong. From the journal articles I've read, the earlier trials were shown to be effective for most patients. But studies on bronchiosclerosis aren't common and the waiting lists are usually long. So there is a new trial? Do you know anything about the doctor or clinic yet?"

"No," Grant answered honestly. He wanted to get Katie's doctor's opinion before asking anyone at MacPhearson. "But I know there's going to be at least one site here in the Twin Cities. Thank you for your time, Doctor." The men shook hands and Grant walked out of the office with a glimmer of hope. He knew what he needed to do. He needed to get his daughter into that study. It could be the only thing that could save his little girl.

Tuesday, October 22

Steven MacPhearson walked into his brother's corner office without knocking. James looked up from his computer, clearly annoyed. Steven ignored his brother's expression, knowing that as soon as James heard the news the rude entry would be forgotten.

"I just heard from Dawson," he opened.

"And?"

"Sarah and Mike Jacobs have decided not to sue," Steven blurted. "Apparently the medical examiner didn't find enough evidence to pinpoint Respara as a contributing factor to the kid's death."

"Thank God," James whispered. He knew the Jacobs family could have filed a wrongful death suit. Even though Dawson said it was unlikely the Jacobs would win, the bad press could have really hurt MacPhearson's reputation. Even their successes thus far might not have been enough to survive the negative publicity.

"Their attorney called Robert earlier this morning," Steven explained. "They are dropping the whole thing. They said they just want to move on. They were only pursuing the case in order to make sure Respara was safe and prevent the same thing from happening to another kid. Since it doesn't look like it was Respara, they don't want a long, drawn-out battle in civil court."

"I really feel for them. I can't even imagine what it must be like to lose a child, but I'm glad they aren't willing to sue when it isn't warranted. We should prepare a statement for the media. Can you get Robert to get something together and we'll look it over later today? I think it would be best if it could be ready in time for the five o'clock local news. If they get wind of this story, I want to be ready," James suggested.

"Good idea. I'll talk to him right now." Steven was already heading out the door.

"Wait a second, Steven. There's something else I want to discuss with you." He indicated that Steven close the door. Steven did and then sat on the edge of James's desk. Even after all these years, Steven liked having the height advantage over his older brother. It made him feel superior.

"Will called me last night at home. He'll be coming in tomorrow morning to meet with us, and then he'd like to go back down to his cabin for another week. What do you think?" he asked, although he had already told Will it would be fine.

"I don't see a problem with it. In fact, I think it's better if he's away right now. It makes it easier for us, and Oliver is doing just fine handling everything in the lab," Steven replied. It was true. Things were running smoothly with Will away. Oliver was more than competent, and Steven was well aware of his future goals of running the laboratory division one day.

"That's what I told him. I think it might be a good idea for the three of us to talk about upcoming projects for his return. He's really out of sorts right now, and I think if we get him going on something new, he'll get excited and—"

"And forget this other mess. I completely agree. The sooner he moves on, the better it will be, for all of us," Steven added. He straightened himself and smoothed his dark blue suit. He had a lunch meeting with the marketing department and wanted to look put-together. In truth, he hadn't been sleeping very well lately and the stress he was under was showing. He had dark circles under his eyes and his skin looked sallow. But now that everything seemed like it was going to turn out okay, he felt better. Maybe tonight he would actually be able to sleep.

"Didn't I tell you to trust me, Steven? Didn't I tell you all of this would blow over? And I was right, wasn't I? You should always trust your big brother," James told him as Steven opened the door leading to the hall.

While Steven admitted that James had been right, he also knew that trusting him was a separate issue entirely. He had barely stepped out of James's office when Grant Adams touched his arm.

"Steven, I was wondering if you and James might have a minute?" he asked.

"Can James help you, Grant? I'm on my way to a meeting right now," Steven answered curtly. He made a mental note to tell Grant that all meetings should be scheduled through Jessica. She kept his meetings and appointments in order, and handled a few tasks for James as well. Most mornings he had no idea of his daily schedule until she sent him his itinerary.

"If I could just have a few minutes. It's very important that I talk with both of you," Grant pleaded. Steven sensed Grant's urgency and decided to see what he had to say. Clearly this was more important than arriving at his lunch meeting early.

"Alright. After you." Steven opened the door to James's office for the second time that morning, again without knocking.

"What did you forg—oh, Grant, good morning. I thought it was just Steven again," James stammered, standing and walking out from behind his desk.

"I'm sorry to barge in here and interrupt your day, but I really need to speak with both of you about an urgent professional and personal matter," Grant began in an unsettled tone. Steven and James sat down next to one another on the small sofa near the window. The comfortable seating arrangement was where James conducted many of his meetings. Both he and Steven had large offices to accommodate such conferences. Grant sat in a wingback chair facing them.

"It's my daughter, Katie. I mentioned at the interview that she has been diagnosed with bronchiosclerosis and that I am very interested in getting her enrolled in the upcoming study," he continued, his voice tense. Both brothers nodded, so he went on. "Well, she had another appointment yesterday. We, my wife, my *ex*-wife, and I thought perhaps the doctors were mistaken, because she's been feeling fine. Unfortunately, it turns out they were correct. Her x-rays show greater levels of blockage in her lungs. I'd like to get her into the study over at the University of Minnesota. I asked the study manager assigned to that trial and learned enrollment is almost closed. Please, is there any way you can help me? It might be her only chance."

James observed Grant quietly. It was obvious he was desperate. He wanted their help and James could easily see the fear in Grant's eyes. This was a man who would stop at nothing to save his daughter.

"To be perfectly honest with you, we've never had a situation like this before. As you know, we don't control who does or does not get into our studies. In general, having a CRA's family member involved in one of our studies is probably not the best idea. But since there's no guideline set by the FDA and no company policy in place to prevent her from getting in, we'll do what we can. Otherwise I have the feeling we'd lose you before we even got to put you to work. With that said, I do happen to know the investigator over at the U—"

"Golf buddy," Steven interrupted.

"Yes, Doctor Carruthers and I go way back. I spoke with him last week. I recall him saying that they have two spots left to fill, that a few subjects are still in the screening phase to see if they're eligible." He saw the change in Grant's expression, and wanted to caution him. "You know that if those patients qualify, she'll have to wait for a future study, Grant. We won't remove a subject who is already on the list and eligible for treatment. We'll also need to clear it with Will. He'll be in tomorrow and we're having a breakfast meeting here at nine o'clock. Why don't you join us for the first part and we'll see what he has to say," James offered.

"Do you think he'll have any objections?" Grant asked, the worry again apparent in his deep voice.

"Probably not. But Will does like to play by the rules where the FDA is concerned. If the subjects have qualified since I spoke with Carruthers, and their randomization numbers have been assigned, there's no way he'll let her in. It could mean a major setback or even a shutdown of the study if the FDA found out we had cherry-picked one of the subjects," James explained.

"Officially, we would never break, or even bend, any regulations," Steven added, wanting to make their position clear to Grant.

"And unofficially …?" Grant had to ask.

"We'll see you tomorrow morning, Grant. Why don't you leave a little early today and spend some time with your family?" James suggested. His tone indicated his sympathy for Grant's situation, but also effectively communicated that the meeting was over.

Grant thanked both men for their time. As he walked down the hallway toward his office, he decided Will Adison would not prevent Katie from getting into the study. If he had to drag Katie here and play on Will's sympathy, he would do it. Regulations wouldn't prevent Katie from getting into the study. If he had to bend or break the rules, he would do it. He would do whatever it took.

～

Jessica stood up as soon as she saw her boss enter the waiting area outside his office. Steven should have been in the conference room, but he was heading right for her desk. He hurriedly told her about the meeting with Will, James, and Grant Adams. He knew he might miss his late morning tee time; would she call the club and have the time rescheduled? As he turned to leave, she assured him she would make

51

the call and sat down, relieved she hadn't done anything to upset him. He seemed so tense lately, even more than usual. At first she thought maybe she was being overly sensitive. The pregnancy had made her very emotional. But after more than a few days of getting barked at for nothing, she was sure there was something wrong with Steven. Usually he treated her well, but lately he didn't even say hello to her. She had also considered the possibility that he had found out about her relationship with Will, but as time passed, she dismissed that idea as well.

Will. He had been gone for almost two weeks. If she hadn't overheard Steven on the phone with his wife, she wouldn't even know where he had gone. But she'd heard Steven clearly tell Mrs. MacPhearson that Will was licking his wounds down at the cabin. She also heard something about how Will had gone behind Steven's back, continuing to work on an experiment that was supposed to be shut down. That must not have gone over very well. Steven, who enjoyed being right, seemed angry, but also a bit relieved that Will was away. And Will took failure hard. But maybe there was another reason he was away. Maybe he was figuring out a way to leave Barbara. Maybe that was why she hadn't heard from him in so long. He didn't want to talk to her until he had ended things with his wife. *That has to be it*, she thought. Jessica closed her eyes and imagined them holding their baby at this time next year. Maybe things were going to work out after all.

～

Oliver Klein took a seat at an empty table in the cafeteria. He was looking forward to a nice, quiet lunch by himself. He loved running the lab, loved being in charge, but today had been stressful. Two tests had to be rerun due to carelessness. In the pre-trial phase of research, any mistake is costly. Lab supervisors and directors are ultimately held responsible for the costs of their testing and experiments. Oliver couldn't afford errors. He wanted to be the director of the laboratory division at MacPhearson, and he wanted it sooner rather than later. With Will gone, it was finally his opportunity to step out from Will's shadow and prove to James and Steven that he was more than qualified for the job. Will could work on his research all day and Oliver could take over for him as the head of the lab. He already did most of the duties Will was supposed to do, and he was hungry for both the title and the recognition.

"Do you mind if I sit with you, Doctor Klein?" Grant asked, although he was already halfway seated.

"Please, join me, but call me Oliver. This gives me the chance to actually talk to another human being," Oliver lied. He would much rather have headed back to the lab where he could finish planning his rise to the top.

"So, I hear you're in charge while Will's away."

"Yeah, I am. Although most of the things I'm doing now I do even when Will is here," Oliver admitted. It was true. He didn't see why he should hide it from Grant or anyone else.

"So Will is pretty much into the research end of things?" Grant asked.

"You could say that. When he gets into a project, he can't do anything else. He's been so isolated lately; there are days when I don't even see him. But I keep everything on track," Oliver said. Grant could sense a bit of resentment in his voice. It was clear Oliver felt he got stuck with all the work in the lab, and got little credit. It made Grant uncomfortable to learn of this dynamic. He felt it was dangerous to get involved in office politics, especially when he didn't know either candidate. After an awkward silence, he decided to play it safe and changed the subject.

~

Will Adison turned on the radio about halfway into his drive back to the Twin Cities. It was a gorgeous drive along the highway: trees, farmland, and quaint towns. He was still forty minutes from St. Paul. He planned on spending the night at home and going into the office the next day for his meeting with James and Steven. Of course, he would also have an opportunity to pick up his notes on the project he was supposed to forget. He also hoped being home in the evening would give him a chance to talk to Barbara. He spent the first part of his drive rehearsing what he would say to her.

The affair with Jessica, the only indiscretion he ever had in their eighteen years of marriage, was something he completely regretted. He would spend the rest of his life trying to make that up to her. With a baby, though, he knew he wouldn't be able to end things with Jessica cleanly. They were connected now for the rest of their lives. He wanted to provide for the baby and be as involved in its life as both Jessica and Barbara would allow. Things would be difficult, but it could work.

The harder part would come the next morning when he would finally have to face Jessica and tell her that it was over. She was an emotional girl to begin with, and now being pregnant, she was likely to be fragile at best. He didn't even want to think about that conversation until he had talked with Barbara. In a blatant attempt at distraction, he turned on the local news on the AM dial.

After a few reports—one about a city council member accused of accepting bribes, another about a proposed school referendum, and then the weather—Will was hardly paying attention. But then he heard the word "Respara" and turned up the volume.

"In a news conference held just moments ago, Miles Winslow, Chief Medical Examiner for Hennepin County, announced that no definitive link could be made between the use of Respara and the tragic death of eleven-year-old Kyle Jacobs. All pathology and toxicology tests were inconclusive," the reporter stated matter-of-factly. She gave a brief background of the story, including the suggestion by Kyle's doctor that perhaps the asthma drug Respara had caused the boy's death. Of course, the reporter included the name MacPhearson Pharmaceuticals, reminding viewers that the company who produced the drug was local. It amazed Will that she could sound so removed from such an emotionally charged case. But, then again, that was her job. He stared at the highway ahead as she continued, "Malcolm Delaney, attorney for the Jacobs family, announced that his clients, Sarah and Michael Jacobs, will not take on the pharmaceutical company in civil court.

"MacPhearson attorney, Robert Dawson, also present at the conference, provided a brief statement as well, offering condolences to the family and expressing confidence that Respara is still, in fact, one of the safest asthma drugs on the market. Caroline Edwards, reporting live from Minneapolis."

"For more information on this story," transitioned the news anchor, "visit our Website."

Will turned the radio down as he heard the sports reporter begin a new story. He couldn't believe James had not called him about the Jacobs case. They had been worried about it for weeks now. But maybe James *had* tried to reach him. He had turned his cell phone off while walking through the woods and realized that he had forgotten to turn it back on again. It was a terrible habit that Barbara nagged him about. Sometimes he would miss an entire day's worth of calls. He pulled his phone from its case. Sure enough, there were three messages from James's office number.

At least he tried to reach me before the conference, Will thought. Although he was a full partner, Will could never compete with the close relationship between the two brothers. And now, with the two of them heading up the business end while he was down in the lab, the distance was even more pronounced. Will had known James for almost twenty years, and trusted his judgment implicitly. But Steven was different. Will liked him and respected him, but he just didn't trust him. He always got the impression that Steven would walk over his own mother to be successful.

Which was why Will was so distraught after the failure of this latest project. If his lab showed positive results, his position was secure. Clinical research was a painstakingly slow business. Any company had to accept the high cost of research and development, but it had to be countered with some success in order to maintain balance. Will knew this latest project was a very expensive error on his part. He went behind his partners' backs and the risk hadn't paid off. Steven always spoke very highly of Oliver Klein, and Will had no doubt that, if it weren't for James, Klein would one day take over the lab.

Feeling stressed, he decided to again turn up the radio. This time he chose classical music, which always helped him relax. As he drove north, crossing over the Mississippi River toward the messes he had made in his life, he watched the trees blur into streaks of color, his mind emptying of all thought.

～

Just as Will was passing through the city of Hastings, Grant Adams was dialing the home number of his ex-wife.

"Elizabeth? Hello, it's Grant. How are you?"

"I'm fine—still a little shaken by the appointment yesterday, but otherwise okay. I suppose you want to talk to Katie," she responded. Her voice sounded tight.

"Actually, I wanted to talk with you for a minute first. Yesterday, I asked Dr. Billings about a study being done by MacPhearson for B319, a drug they're developing to treat bronchiosclerosis." Grant launched in, not wanting to give her a chance to comment. "I spoke with two of the partners today and it looks like Katie might be able to get into a study at the University of Minnesota. The drug is in the last phase of development, and looks like the FDA could approve it as early as next year. What do you think?"

It was not her opinion, but rather her permission, he needed. Because they shared legal custody and Katie was a minor, participation in the study required consent from both parents. Grant prayed she would agree.

"Are you sure it's safe, Grant? I don't like the idea of my daughter being a human guinea pig," she said.

"*Our* daughter would have an opportunity to get a drug that has been shown to be very safe and effective in treating bronchiosclerosis. Look, Elizabeth, this was one of the reasons why I signed on with MacPhearson. They have been studying asthma for years and so far are the only company even close to finding a treatment for bronchiosclerosis." Hearing only silence, he went on, "This is the only way for her to get this drug now. She might not be able to wait until it's approved. I think we need to give her this chance."

"Do you think it could cure her?" she asked. Grant could tell he had convinced her.

"It's not a cure, just a treatment. She would probably have to take the medication for a long time, maybe even for the rest of her life. But in studies conducted so far, patients taking this pill have shown no signs of their condition worsening. Think, Beth; Katie barely shows any signs of the disease. What if taking this pill could keep her where she is right now? What if she never has to get really sick?"

"Are there any side effects?" Beth's skepticism was resurfacing.

"Some patients were nauseous and others experienced headaches. A few reported drowsiness. But other than that, nothing major," he stated.

"And it's safe for children? Dr. Billings recommended it for Katie?"

"Yes, he said if Katie were his daughter, he would do everything in his power to get her into this study. The University of Minnesota Children's Hospital is highly respected and he thought it would be advantageous to get her started on the treatment as soon as possible," Grant explained, adding his own spin on Dr. Billing's words. Beth was not an easy sell and would place more value on the advice of the doctor than that of her ex-husband.

"Well, when should we tell Katie?" Beth asked.

"I thought I could take her on a tour of MacPhearson later this week and explain how clinical research works. I don't want her to be scared. I'm meeting with the higher-ups tomorrow, and it looks like I could get her into the clinic conducting the study by the end of the week for testing to see if she qualifies. But I'm telling you now because I need your consent."

"You're sure about this, Grant?"

"Katie is going to beat this thing. She'll grow up to be strong and healthy. Trust me, Beth. We'll dance at her wedding," he said quietly. He heard the click on the other end, knowing Beth wasn't able to say anything else. And at that moment he realized that, after everything that had happened, he forgave Beth. The past was over, and they both needed to focus on their daughter's future.

Wednesday, October 23

Will turned the alarm clock off before it even had a chance to sound. He hadn't slept well after his conversation with Barbara. She told him she had already contacted her attorney, Rebecca Sinclair, about starting divorce proceedings. She just couldn't take the humiliation of his affair with Jessica becoming public knowledge. The baby, she said, was an innocent victim in the whole situation. For the baby, she felt deeply sorry.

Will explained that he was going to tell Jessica things were over, that he would be part of her life only as the father of her baby. He apologized and asked Barbara to give him another chance. He was still in love with her, and wasn't that what mattered most?

Despite his pleas, Barbara remained strong and stubborn. In fact, Will had been genuinely surprised she didn't scream at him. He almost wished she had; her reserved tone was even more unnerving to him. She seemed so calm. Could anyone really decide to end a marriage in such a tranquil state?

Will asked her to hold off on filing for a divorce for six months. He pleaded with her to give him more time. They could go to counseling, take a trip together. He even offered to take a leave from the company in order to spend more time with her. She must have known that was a sacrifice for him, but she didn't agree. She said only that they had wasted too much time already. And then she casually brought up the fact that in six months, he would have a son or daughter with another woman.

Will closed his eyes again and pushed the palms of his hands into his temples. His head, from the lack of sleep and the pressure of the last few weeks, had steadily developed a throbbing ache. He wanted to go back, do everything over again. He had somehow managed to destroy three lives, and now a fourth, all because he was flattered that a young woman had noticed him. *How pathetic is that?*

He heard the door to Barbara's room open, then his own. They had been sleeping in separate bedrooms for the last few years. She came in and sat on the edge of his bed. She had been crying.

"Will, we used to be happy. *I* used to be happy. I don't even know who I am anymore. This whole thing has turned me into someone I don't even recognize, someone bitter. I'm just tired of it all. I believe and appreciate everything you said last night. But I can't ignore the fact that you are going to have a child with that girl. An affair can be forgiven, and I might have been willing to do that. But now that a child is involved, I just can't. That baby will be a constant, living, breathing reminder for me. I want us to end things now, while there are still some good feelings left between us. If I stay, it will eat away at me and I'll end up leaving anyway. In a few months or years, I'd still end up leaving. So I'm going to do it now, while I still have some dignity."

"I am so sorry," Will said feebly, without opening his eyes.

"I know. I am too," she said softly. Will felt her get up from the bed and heard her close his bedroom door. She was gone.

~

James opened the newspaper to the article about Respara and Kyle Jacobs. The story, only six paragraphs long, was on page four, following several other local stories in the metro section of the St. Paul *Pioneer Press*. James read the article and shook his head. *Typical*, he thought bitterly, *when it's bad publicity for us we're on the front page, but when we're cleared the story is practically hidden.* His mind wandered back to yesterday's news conference. He and Robert had anticipated correctly; the statement they prepared had had just the right tone. Hopefully the public's confidence in Respara would return. If not, sales would be impacted drastically.

James knew Respara was safe. His own granddaughter, Jenna, was on the medication, a fact he mentioned in several interviews. He would never put a drug on the market that wasn't proven to be completely safe. Thinking of Jenna reminded him of Grant's daughter, Katie. James had already placed a call to Dr. Andrew Carruthers, the investigator at the University of Minnesota Children's Hospital. He and Dr. Carruthers were friends—and Carruthers had headed up several studies with MacPhearson Pharmaceuticals.

James loosened the knot of his tie and sighed. As they'd told Grant, if the subjects ahead of Katie turned out to be eligible and randomization numbers had been assigned, it would be a problem. Getting Katie Adams into the study at that point would be in clear violation of FDA regulations. But if no data had been documented for those patients, it left some room to maneuver. No one would ever have to know. Dr. Carruthers said he hadn't even met with the last two subjects. It would be easy to tell one that he or she didn't qualify. James was willing to bend the rules, and this would be a severe bend. He knew Steven would agree, and Carruthers was not going to be a problem. MacPhearson had given his clinic generous budgets for studies over the years, and would continue to do so in the future. Many doctors saw their role as investigators as a way to increase revenue. Carruthers was a reputable doctor who cared for his patients. But he also liked to make a profit.

James knew Will would be the one who needed convincing. If he thought bending the rules for the Adams girl would in any way jeopardize the study, he would absolutely refuse. James had considered getting her in and not telling Will, but something like that would be difficult to keep quiet.

He picked up the phone and dialed Carruthers's number at the clinic. Grant Adams was desperate to get his daughter into that study. Now he and Carruthers needed to figure out exactly how they would make it happen.

$\sim$

When Grant walked into the conference room, all three men were already seated around the table. It was hard to believe that only a few weeks ago he had been in this very room, interviewing for his job. So many things had happened since then, it seemed unreal.

"Thank you, James, for scheduling this meeting. I know how busy you all are. And Will, I really appreciate you driving in today," Grant said as he sat down across the table from them.

"I was coming in anyway, so no problem. Now what's this all about?" Will asked directly.

For the second time in as many days, Grant explained his daughter's diagnosis and condition. He was sincere and somehow managed to keep his composure. James and Steven, already aware of the situation, looked sympathetic. Will listened intently.

After Grant finished, ending by expressing his desire to get his daughter involved in the study with Dr. Carruthers at the University of Minnesota, Will shot a glance toward his partners.

"I spoke with Carruthers yesterday to find out where exactly they were at as far as subject enrollment was concerned," James admitted; it was evident he felt no regrets for his actions.

"They're already going to meet their goal—enrollment is closing. I know because I checked in with him a few days ago. There's not really anything we can do on this one, Grant. But there is another study starting in a few months with a site in St. Paul. You could try to get your daughter into that study," Will offered.

"I understand, and if it comes to that, it comes to that. But Katie's feeling good right now. If we could get her started on treatment soon, her chances of staying at this stage are much, much better." Grant's voice rose with emotion. It was taking every ounce of energy to stay in control.

"Will, it wouldn't be hard to get Katie in by assigning her one of the numbers reserved for the last two subjects. Carruthers hasn't met with them yet, and still doesn't know if either one will even qualify," James countered.

"That doesn't mean it's *right* to remove a subject now. Those two patients are ahead of Katie on the list. Bumping one or both to make room for someone else is not ethical. Grant, I completely understand your desire to help your daughter. If I were you, I'd do the same. But we've got to play by the rules or the entire study could be shut down. If that happens, many more parents will have sick children," Will argued.

"Will, the chances of anyone finding out are zero. And even if the FDA did somehow find out, you know they wouldn't shut down the entire study. We'd get audited, but once they found out everything else was accurate, they'd think it was a mistake and probably just give us a warning," James reasoned. Grant felt relieved that James was on his side, and even though Steven hadn't spoken at all, Grant could sense that he, too, was willing to help him.

"It doesn't matter if the FDA knows or not. *We* would know. We would know that someone else's kid got bumped. Grant, you said yourself that Katie's symptoms are mild. She could wait for the next study. And the drug will hopefully be on the market some time next year anyway." Will was not backing down. Grant could feel his heart pounding, like it might burst any second.

"By then it may be too late! A few months could make all the difference!" Grant shouted in disbelief. "You're willing to let my daughter die?" *How could anyone be this cruel?*

"Will ..." Steven said cautiously, finally speaking.

"Grant, I am truly sorry, but I refuse to go along with this. And I can't believe James and Steven thought I would. It's wrong," Will said. He pushed his chair back, got up, and walked out the door.

"Grant, maybe Will is right. She'll be fine. You said so yourself, her symptoms are mild," James said.

"For now," Grant sighed.

"If she gets any worse, we'll handle it then," James tried to placate him. It wasn't working.

"What do you mean, 'we'll handle it then'?"

"Let's see how Katie does over the next few months, Grant," James told him, standing up from the table. Grant was barely listening. "We manufacture the drug right here in our laboratory. Things always have a way of working out. Now, why don't you get back to work?"

Grant nodded, barely able to comprehend. He was totally devastated by the decision. *How am I going to tell Beth?* He was the one who managed to convince her that Katie needed treatment now, before her sickness got any worse. She wouldn't take the news well, Grant was sure of that. Objectively, he could see Will's point. He didn't feel exactly right getting Katie into the study at the expense of someone else's child. But he was beyond the point of being objective. Someone else's child, without a name or a face, didn't matter to him right now. The only child that mattered to him was his own.

~

"What the hell are you doing, James?" Steven yelled as he slammed the door of the conference room. "Have you lost your goddamn mind?"

"I didn't say anything, Steven. All I did was let him know we are willing to help him help his daughter," James replied.

"How? By destroying the whole damn company? By telling him that if his kid *does* happen to get worse, we'll get her the drug some other way? Now that would be illegal, James, and you know it. At that point, we would have to falsify documents or get her treatment outside of a controlled study. How would we explain needing doses of the drug? And someone would find out if we just took it—there would be a discrepancy in the inventory. We'd be convicted of fraud, and it could destroy MacPhearson. We wouldn't be able to dance around the regulations for something like that. There would be no 'gray' area. Jesus, James! I can almost feel Dawson's blood pressure rising from here. If the FDA—"

"Steven, will you sit down and stop ranting? It will never come to that. We don't have to do anything. But if Adams thinks we will, it gives him hope until the next study begins. He knows she'll get treatment at some point, and has the security of knowing that if she does happen to get worse, we might be able to help her out. *Might*. He gets peace of mind, and we get an employee who is very, very grateful—and loyal. Loyalty is a valuable quality in an employee."

"You're playing with fire, James," said Steven.

~

Oliver Klein was startled to see Will walk through the laboratory door that morning. Will had been gone for two weeks and no one had mentioned to him that Will was coming back anytime soon. Maybe Will was checking up on him, making sure things in the lab were on track.

"Good morning, Klein. How are things going here?" Will asked as he looked around with an observant eye.

"Everything has been just fine since you've been gone. Are you enjoying your vacation?" Oliver asked. He was glad nothing major had happened in Will's absence. It only made him look better in the eyes of Steven and James to have a clean record while he was in charge of things.

"Well, I'm glad to hear it. James told me you were keeping the ship afloat." Will sounded as though it actually pained him to hear that Oliver was doing well. "I'm just back for the morning. I had one meeting already and came down here to pick up some things."

"I'll get out of your way then. I'll see you ..." he let his sentence trail off, forcing Will to complete it.

"I'm guessing I'll be back next week, two at the latest. I'll be doing a little work from my cabin," Will answered, disappearing into his office.

Oliver shrugged and turned back to the data on his computer. He couldn't help but peer over the screen in the direction of Will's office. Through the industrial blinds covering the office window, he saw Will load his laptop and several thick files into a large crate. The fact that he was taking his computer and files with him to his cabin didn't strike Oliver as odd. What did, however, was *which* files Will was taking. Although the distance from where Oliver sat to the office window was close to fifty feet, he was certain that Will was taking the files of his failed project, the same project that was supposed to be terminated. Twice, in fact. Oliver watched him lay some other papers on top of the crate and switch off the light. Once outside, Will looked around while he locked the office door. Oliver quickly dropped his head to make it appear he was concentrating on his computer screen. He didn't want Will to know what he had seen. He looked up just as Will was leaving the lab. He waved his hand politely. He even smiled. *Why is he taking those notes?* Oliver asked himself. Steven and James would probably be just as curious as he was. Maybe he should tell them. No, he decided, that little piece of information might become more valuable later.

Oliver thought back to that night in the lab. Almost three weeks had passed. *I wonder if he'll be able to tell what I've done.*

〜

Jessica brushed her blond hair away from her face and leaned back against the seat of Will's car. They were parked at a picnic area five miles from the office and her car was at the other end of the lot, the far end. There was a park and a lake, but both were usually quiet, making this the perfect spot for them to meet unseen. They'd been there before. Lunches, before work, after work. It had seemed so romantic at the time. But now everything had changed. Turning her head to look out the window, she watched a few kids playing at the park. They seemed so happy, so free. She thought of her baby and wondered if her child would ever be that happy. It was already coming into the world with a huge disadvantage.

She was still processing what Will had said to her. Something about not being able to leave Barbara, that he still loved his wife, that Jessica had her whole life ahead of her. He made it seem as if she was lucky to be rid of him. He did want to be a part of the baby's life, of course, but just not a part of hers. Not that way, anyway. He had asked her if she was okay. Feeling numb, she couldn't even answer.

Words were not coming to her mind. All she felt was the sting of rejection and then the fear that she and the baby were on their own.

Will started to say something else, but she held up her hand to stop him. She didn't want to hear his reasoning. This was her life, not some problem to be solved.

She reached up and wiped her eyes with the back of her hand. Without saying a word she opened the door of the car. Then she hesitated and turned back to face him. Jessica Monroe, twenty-seven and pregnant, was devastated, but not defeated. With her last ounce of strength she slapped Will across the face, got out of the car, and ran to her own. Will let his head fall into his hands. His cheek burned from where she had struck him. He heard the squeal of her tires as she tore out of the parking lot, causing the children at the park to turn and look.

Thursday, October 24

James MacPhearson walked downstairs to the lab. He needed to talk to Oliver Klein. Oliver had submitted a request to begin a new study. James was here to tell him that his request would be put on hold. They had so many projects going on that all three partners yesterday decided to wait. Steven knew how Oliver would react, which was why James was the one going to the lab this morning.

"Hi, Oliver. Mind if I come in for a bit?" James asked. Oliver looked up from the microscope and motioned for James to sit on one of the lab stools. James stood.

"What brings you down here so early, James?"

"I just wanted to see how things are going, what with Will being gone and all. Steven said you are doing an excellent job running the lab, so I just wanted to see for myself."

"First Will, now you. Do I really need to be checked on? At any other company I'd be a lab director. I wouldn't be filling in for Will Adison. I'd *be* Will Adison." Oliver was annoyed. It was one thing to put in your dues, but being checked on like this was insulting.

"I wasn't checking up on you, Oliver," James started. "Did you say Will was in here? When?"

"Yesterday, late morning. He came in to get a few things and left. Said he was going to be doing some work at the cabin. Wasn't here more than ten minutes," Oliver responded. *Should I tell him about the files?*

"Oh, I didn't know he even came down here. Did he say what he was going to be working on?" James tried to sound to casual, but his voice wasn't very convincing.

"Not really sure. You know Will, James. He's always got something in the fire," Oliver replied. James stared at him, saying nothing.

"Is that all then? I've really got a lot to do this morning."

"Yes, yes, get back to what you were doing. Sorry to bother you. Oh wait, Oliver?"

"Yes," he answered, already looking back into the microscope.

"We decided to put your proposed project on hold for now. The timing just isn't right. We'll see if we have the resources for it when some of our current projects have finished, maybe in the spring," James stuttered. He knew this would be a blow to Oliver. Surprisingly, Oliver didn't even look up. He simply mumbled something indiscernible and nodded to indicate he heard what James had said.

When he heard the lab door close, Oliver looked up. He had done an outstanding job of remaining calm with James here, but now he was fuming. He was sick of coming in second place. With his experience and qualifications, *he* should be running a lab. *I should be the director, not Will.* Will was too obsessive, too isolated. Oliver knew everything going on in all the labs. He had been patient, but his patience was wearing thin.

Friday, October 25

Grant looked over the files piled on top of his desk. He was reading them, but not comprehending much of anything. He was distracted. Katie was moving in tomorrow, and that meant Beth and David were going to be there. Beth told him on the phone last night that Katie had been coughing a lot lately and seemed tired. She admitted she was relieved that Katie would be participating in the study. He replied with something noncommittal, not yet knowing how he was going to tell her that Katie might have to wait to begin her treatment. She would break down, especially if she thought Katie was getting worse. But Beth was known to exaggerate at times. Maybe she was wrong. Maybe she just *thought* Katie's symptoms were getting worse. So far, Katie hadn't said anything to him about not feeling well. He could kick himself for mentioning the study to Beth before getting the final word from the partners. But sooner or later he'd have to come clean with her. Grant opted for later.

He closed the file he had been looking at for the last thirty minutes. Allen Jennings, a young CRA with only a year of experience, had been complaining about one of his sites. According to Jennings, the study coordinator was behind in entering the data for many subjects, and had made numerous errors in the early stages of the study. Since study monitors were held accountable for the accuracy of information being submitted to the FDA, they tended to be extremely detail-oriented people. Experienced monitors could look through data binders and find missing or suspect information quickly. They needed to be fast, because most monitoring visits lasted, on average, for only one or two days and took place only every four to eight weeks, depending on the nature of the study. Every piece of information reported to the sponsoring pharmaceutical company needed to be derived from source documents, which included each subject's medical history and data obtained at visits throughout the study. If any unintended side effect occurred, it was critical to have all the data related to that subject updated and accurate for review. Adverse events or serious adverse events, known in the industry as AEs or SAEs, had to be documented and reported. The event needed to be investigated in order to determine if it was related to the study drug. The FDA approved very few drugs. If side effects did occur, the FDA wanted to know. It was a complex process designed to prevent unsafe drugs from reaching the market. The FDA regulations were some of the strictest in the world. With the litigious nature of the American public, neither pharmaceutical companies nor the FDA could afford to put a drug on the market that hadn't been extensively tested.

Finally able to concentrate, and fully absorbed in Allen's notes from the site, Grant didn't hear the knock on his partially open office door. He looked up to see Diane Norman. Wearing a chocolate brown suit and muted silk scarf, she was the image of professionalism.

"With your head down like that, I thought you might have fallen asleep," she teased. "These files can do that to you, you know."

"Sorry, Diane. What can I do for you?"

"Well, it sounds like you are going to be heading out to Dr. Spencer's office in Seattle with Allen, is that right?" she asked. Allen had apparently shared his concerns about the site with her as well.

"Yeah, I plan to go out with him in early November for his next visit. I agree—the site is a disaster. He's got flags on practically every document for one subject. The FDA would have a field day if they audited the place." Grant's voice sounded as frustrated as he felt.

"It amazes me how some people take such little pride in the work they do," she said, agreeing.

"Well, hopefully they're not all this bad," he sighed.

"Fortunately, they aren't," she said. "Most coordinators realize the importance of accurate documentation. When I was acting as the study manager before you came, we got most of the sites cleaned up. It's just that we need to get all the data in by the first of the year if we want to submit the new drug application to the FDA in February."

"What about A257? How does that study compare?" Grant asked. The study he was currently reviewing was S320, the type 2 diabetes medication. A257, the cystic acne topical treatment, was only in Phase II, so it would be several more months before that study would end.

"It's better."

"Anyway, you came to see me. What is it that I can do for you?" he asked her again.

"I was really just checking to see how you're settling in," she replied and smiled, knowing she was probably coming across as too motherly.

"I appreciate it, really," he admitted. He already felt more at home here than he had after years at Webber. And someone like Diane was a very valuable resource. "Just trying to learn these protocols."

"Give yourself some time. It will likely take six months to a year before you're completely comfortable with everything. Remember, you can always call on me if you have any questions," she offered. She had seen too many CRAs burn out over the years. In clinical research there was a fine line between ensuring accuracy and getting caught up in perfectionism. It was their job to decide what was important and what was trivial. Focusing on the trivialities of a vast amount of data could be a never-ending task.

"Oh, I'm sure I'll need to bend your ear now and again," he admitted, "but only if you'll let me buy you a cup of coffee as compensation."

"Agreed," she said over her shoulder. She smiled as she took one last glance at the mountain of paperwork on his desk. She was so glad it was his job to manage these studies, not hers.

~

Barbara Adison slammed down the telephone receiver so hard she was surprised it didn't smash into pieces.

"Goddamn you, Will Adison," she yelled. She had just spoken with her attorney, Rebecca Sinclair. Rebecca informed her that if she divorced Will now, she wouldn't gain nearly as much as she had thought. Apparently, most of their assets were tied up in MacPhearson. But if she could wait until the company went public, her portion of the stock would be worth substantially more.

Just my luck, she thought sarcastically. I finally, *finally,* decide to leave him and now I can't. She remembered Steven's announcement at the party. They planned on going public sometime in the next several months. Will had asked her to give him six months to prove himself. Maybe if she agreed he would merely think she had decided to give him a second chance after all. That seemed reasonable. Ironically, finding out she had to stay married to her cheating husband in order to collect what she rightfully deserved wasn't the most disturbing part of their conversation.

Rebecca had also mentioned, in complete defiance of lawyer-client confidentially, that she had seen an appointment scheduled for Will the following week with Frederick Lewis. It was all she said, but it had been enough. Lewis was a senior partner at Jones, Lewis, Sinclair, & Associates. He had handled all the estate planning for Will and Barbara a few years ago. An appointment with Lewis could only mean one thing: he was planning on changing his will. Will had told her he would provide financially for the baby Jessica was carrying. Was he planning on changing his will already? Barbara imagined so. It was amazing that this little creature, someone she had never met, was solely responsible for what was happening to her life. She was no longer in control. Things were merely happening *to* her.

Barbara Adison had had enough.

Saturday, October 26

Grant opened the door expecting to see Katie, but instead David Hughes was on his doorstep. In his arms he carried a crate full of Katie's clothing. Beth and Katie stood just behind him, also loaded down with boxes and bags.

"I thought you said she didn't have that much stuff." Grant greeted them and stepped out of the way to let them all in. The weather that morning had decided not to cooperate. A chilly drizzle fell steadily from the dark gray sky and Grant noticed he could see Katie's breath in the air as she said good morning to him. They made their way past him and Katie directed the two adults to her room. They decided that a lot of Katie's things would stay in her room at Beth's, to keep it the same when she visited on weekends and for breaks and holidays. When Grant caught sight of the rest of the boxes in the back of their sport utility vehicle, he could only shake his head. "Women," he muttered.

"What was that, dear?" Dorothy asked her son. She was in the kitchen, still at the table sipping coffee and reading the entertainment section of the local newspaper. It was the only part of the paper Grant had ever seen her read.

"Nothing, Mom," he said as he pulled on his shoes. The sooner he got started the sooner David and Beth could leave. He wasn't thrilled about inviting the man who broke up his marriage into his home. Neither Beth nor David had made it much past the front door of the apartment.

"I may as well head upstairs and help Katie get some things put away," Dorothy called as she got up from her stool.

"Mother, behave," Grant warned her.

"Who me?" she asked innocently, but Grant caught the glint in her eye. She never missed an opportunity to spar with her former daughter-in-law.

As Grant was tucking another box under his arm, David stopped him by the rear of the truck.

"Grant, I just want you to know I think this will be good for all of us."

"Well, thanks for your approval, David. It means a lot to have your permission." Grant couldn't believe his nerve.

"I didn't mean—look, I just think it's great that you and Katie can spend more time together, that's all," he countered, attempting to explain. Grant gave him an insincere smile and started back to the house.

When he walked into Katie's bedroom, his bad mood lifted immediately. She was so excited to see her new room. His mother had really outdone herself.

The walls were painted celery green and the striped duvet cover had thin, dark red and pale green stripes. Over the maple daybed hung a framed poster of Georgia O'Keefe's *Oriental Poppies*. The sheer drapes were cream-colored and were held back from the window with dark red ties. To the right of the window was a large maple dresser next to a small dressing table with little drawers and a mirror. Dorothy had painted it a deep crimson color. The room looked gorgeous, and Katie was overwhelmed.

"Oh, Grandma, it's just beautiful!" She hugged her tightly.

"It really is lovely, Dorothy," Beth said from the hall. Grant wondered where she had been. He didn't like the idea of her looking around his place on her own.

"Well, a beautiful girl like you deserves a beautiful room like this," Dorothy said, clearly pleased her granddaughter was happy. "Why don't you and I let the others carry the rest of your things and I'll help you get settled?"

Everything was in place by noon. Grant, to be polite, offered to order a pizza for lunch, but Beth and David declined. They had plans for later in the afternoon and wanted to get home. Grant was relieved they didn't accept his invitation. David gave Katie a quick hug and left to wait out in the car, giving Beth a chance to say good-bye to her daughter in private. Grant, however, had to practically drag his mother into the living room in order to give them privacy. When he walked into the kitchen a few minutes later, he saw the two of them sitting on the steps near the door. Katie had her head resting on Beth's shoulder and Beth was gently stroking her hair. Grant, for the first time since the divorce, saw Beth not as his former wife, but just as Katie's mom.

The two got up quickly when they saw him and Grant chided himself for intruding on such an emotional moment. Both wiped away tears and Beth gave him a sad smile before walking out the door.

From the small window on the landing of the stairs, Katie watched their car pull away. Grant wanted to go over and hold her, but knew she needed space.

After lunch, Katie and Dorothy watched a movie on television while Grant got dinner ready. He wanted Katie's first real meal in her new home to be a special one. He was making his dad's signature spaghetti sauce. It was so nice to look out into the family room and watch them together. It felt good to have people around, he decided. After only a few weeks in the townhouse, it had become more of a home than the apartment had ever been.

By eight o'clock, Katie decided to get ready for bed. Grant had rented a new movie, a cheesy teenage romance he knew she wanted to see, but she said she was just too tired.

"You mean I humiliated myself at the video store for nothing?" he teased. He had gotten a few smirks from the clerks at the counter, all teenagers themselves.

"Sorry, Dad. The move really took it out of me. How about tomorrow?" she suggested.

"Deal. I'll be up in a minute, okay?"

"Okay. Goodnight, Grandma. Thank you again for my room. I just love it," she said as she threw her arms around Dorothy's neck.

"Goodnight, honey. Get some rest. I'm making French toast in the morning," she said.

Fifteen minutes later he went into her room to kiss her goodnight. She was already asleep. He went to move her blanket to cover her and noticed a tissue near her pillow. There was blood on it. He thought back on the day and realized that she had been coughing a lot. But they all had, and Grant had dismissed it at the time as due to the weather. Now he wasn't so sure. She had gotten so tired, and there really weren't that many things to unpack.

Was she just worn out because the day had been so emotional? Or was she getting worse? Grant leaned over and kissed her on the forehead.

"I love you, my sweet girl," he whispered. He watched her breathe, like he had done so many times when she was a baby. He had no idea how much time had passed before he was finally able to leave her.

Sunday, October 27

Jessica Monroe called her mother early on Sunday morning to cancel their plans. The Monroes ate brunch together most Sunday mornings at her parents' house in south Minneapolis. But this morning, Jessica wasn't up to seeing her family. The day before she had finally told her brothers about the baby. They were angry with Will and blamed him for ruining their little sister's life. After dealing with her brothers' reaction, she needed more time, and courage, to face her parents.

After hanging up the phone, she immediately picked it back up. There was one more person she wanted to call.

"Amy, hi. It's me. Do you think you could come over, right now? I really need to talk," she said, her voice weak. The tears had already returned.

An hour later, the two girls sat in Jessica's apartment, curled up on the sofa.

"Wow, what a bastard." Amy didn't hide her feelings about Will, after she heard the details from her best friend. "He's staying with her even though you're pregnant with his kid?" If Amy was anything, she was blunt, and blunt was what Jessica needed at this point. "Well, I think you let him off too easily, that's for sure."

"What else could I do?" Jessica felt like her life was spinning out control. She had to get a handle on things, for the baby's sake. Talking with Amy made her feel better. She had kept everything hidden for so long; it felt good to finally tell people.

The girls spent the morning together, with Jessica crying and Amy trying to comfort her friend. They decided that Jessica should see Will one more time to make sure things were really over. Later that day, she would drive to the cabin where they could talk, undisturbed. They still had decisions to make about the baby. No matter what else happened, the baby had to come first.

$\sim$

Grant checked the alarm clock again. It was after nine and he heard nothing to indicate that Katie or his mother were awake. Although he was by nature a late sleeper, the two of them were usually early birds. He rolled over and then an overwhelmingly bad feeling came over him. It took only a moment for him to remember.

Last night he awoke more than once to the sound of Katie coughing. It was enough to make him get some medicine from the kitchen. It seemed to help a little, but each cough sent a chill through Grant's body. Lying in bed across the hall from her, surrounded by darkness, was one of the most frightening experiences he ever had. After seeing the bloody tissue, he couldn't help but draw the conclusion that Katie's symptoms were getting worse. Thoughts rushed through his mind as he realized he was living every parent's worst nightmare.

Oh, God, he pleaded, *please no. Don't do this to her, she's just a baby. I have to do something to help her. I can't just stand by and watch her get worse. I'll go talk to Will and convince him that he has to let her in the study, that she can't wait any longer. She seemed fine just a couple of weeks ago. Who knows what could happen to her in a few more months?*

He had overheard Diane Norton mention that Will had a cabin on the Mississippi River, in the town of Red Wing.

~

Will Adison looked again at the computer screen. He was comparing the data entered on the spreadsheet to his handwritten notations. It was monotonous work, but if he found what he was looking for, it would all be worth it. The problem was, after three days of reviewing the data, he still didn't know *what* he was looking for. He was just hoping something would jump out at him.

He tried to stare at something across the room to rest his eyes. He needed a break. The headache that began as a dull throb had now graduated to persistent pain. Will pushed back his chair and walked to the medicine cabinet in the bathroom. Hopefully Barbara had left something he could take. Unfortunately, the only bottle he found had expired two years ago. Shrugging, he decided to give them a try anyway and he tossed two pills to the back of his mouth, washing them down with tap water and rinsing away the bitter taste they left behind. He had never been good at swallowing pills. In fact, he would never have been able to swallow these pills a few years ago. He had to crush or at least break pills in half in order to get them down, something he had done since he was a child.

Will stared at himself in the dusty mirror. He hadn't bothered with the switch, so the only light in the tiny room came from the hallway and the small window in the shower. The day was cloudy and the inside of the cabin was dark as evening settled in. He cringed at his dim reflection. He looked like someone else. In the past months he seemed to have aged ten years. He gently touched the lines around his eyes. Faint only a year before, they now were deep creases. His hair needed a trim, but he had been so busy lately he hadn't had time to make an appointment at the barbershop. The last time he had been there had been well before Labor Day. Will had imagined himself as the distinguished type. He always looked the part of the intelligent scientist. Now he just looked old. He couldn't bear looking any longer.

He slowly made his way back to the sofa where his work was spread out, covering almost every surface in the living room. He pushed aside a heavy file, not caring that the movement caused several papers to fall and scatter on the floor. What did he care that they were out of order? What did he care about anything anymore? Will Adison lay down on the couch and buried his head in one of the pillows, finally letting the stress he was feeling rise to the surface. He hadn't cried at his mother's funeral, or for any of Barbara's miscarriages, but he cried now. Maybe he was crying for all of it, making up for lost time. Then, spent and exhausted, he fell asleep.

Hours later, in a deep sleep, Will was unaware that he was no longer alone in the cabin.

PHASE II

Monday, October 28

The cottage was located on a wooded lot on the western bank of the Mississippi River, just within the city limits of Red Wing, Minnesota. What would normally be a serene setting was exactly the opposite on this particular Monday morning. Sergeant Pat Donnelly slowed his unmarked sedan and parked on the grass just behind two Red Wing squad cars. He ran a hand through his dark brown hair and zipped up his coat. In his late forties, he had been with the department for fourteen years and was finally promoted to sergeant last winter. He grabbed his coffee and closed the car door as he took in the scene.

This cabin was nicer than the home he shared with his wife, Christine, and their two children. After a rather long, paved driveway shaded on both sides by mature Norway Pines, the house came into view. The two-story Tudor had a white stucco exterior and exposed brickwork, giving it charming curb appeal. The windows were framed with dark green shutters and flower boxes, now empty, hung below each. The yard was immaculate, and Pat could see the river behind the house. *No one on a cop's salary could afford a spread like this*, he thought as he crossed the yard. The morning frost had already begun to soak through his shoes. Christine had warned him last night about the forecast, but he had only been half-listening.

A few Red Wing firefighters and deputy sheriffs from Goodhue County were standing in the front lawn. As soon as the Red Wing police had established that the scene would need more than just a routine investigation, they had called Pat. As sergeant, Pat was in charge of all investigations for the city, but he often called on the county for help. Because the case involved a death, Pat had also called in the

Goodhue County coroner, George Woods. Woods, Pat reasoned, must be inside. His van was parked off to one side of the long driveway, but he was nowhere in sight. Three of his own uniformed officers were visible outside the cottage as well; two were talking quietly as they looked over the front entrance and the third was standing at the end of the driveway with an older woman who held a small terrier in her arms. Pat could hear her providing the requested information: name, date of birth, address, and telephone number. She was clearly upset, and Pat assumed she was the neighbor who had placed the emergency call.

"Mrs. Anderson?" he said as he walked toward the pair.

"Yes, I'm Marvel Anderson," she answered, tucking the dog under her left arm and holding out her right hand. Pat shook it even though the dog started to growl at him.

"Hush, Ivy," she whispered harshly, and the dog quieted down.

"I'm Sergeant Donnelly with the Red Wing Police Department." He identified himself and held up his badge. She studied it closely, which surprised him, and then returned her gaze to his eyes, apparently satisfied. He could tell she was rattled, but hoped she could provide some valuable information. "Can you tell me what happened this morning, Mrs. Anderson?"

"Well, Ivy and I were out on our morning walk. We left the house a little later than usual this morning. We were up late last night watching that made-for-TV movie about Princess Diana. By we I mean my husband Herb and I were watching television, not Ivy here, although she probably caught more of the show than Herb. He always falls asleep after a heavy dinner and yesterday I made a pot roast," she said. Pat suspected her rambling wasn't due to nervousness. She was clearly enjoying the attention. Pat knew she was going to be a tough one to keep on track.

"You mentioned you were running late. What time did you and Ivy leave the house this morning, Mrs. Anderson?" he asked, bringing her back to the subject.

"Oh, please, call me Marvel. We left around six-thirty. It was still fairly dark so I grabbed my flashlight." She pulled it out of her pocket for Pat to see. "We passed the Adisons' on our way back. The sun had started to come up so I wasn't using the flashlight anymore. I remember talking to Ivy about the beautiful sunrise, and how it was such a pretty morning, with the frost." She shivered and Pat nodded at Officer Daniels to give her his coat. She shifted Ivy to the other arm and thanked the policeman.

"So what exactly happened when you walked past this cabin?" Pat prodded.

"Well, I didn't notice anything at first, but then Ivy decided she needed to make a stop right over there in the yard," she said, pointing to the mailbox on the right-hand side of the driveway. "But don't worry, Sergeant Donnelly, I always carry a baggie with me." She smiled and reached into her pocket once again, this time pulling out a steamed-up baggie that confirmed her story. Pat nodded and tried to hide his smile. She was so sincere and he didn't want her to think he was being rude.

"So while Ivy was, was … doing her business, something happened?" he asked her.

"Well, I was looking around—Ivy likes her privacy and gets nervous if someone is watching her—and I noticed what looked like smoke coming from underneath the garage door. Well, I thought maybe the place had caught on fire, although the house seemed to be fine. I knew Mr. Adison had been down here lately—I saw him just the other day over at Bonnie's Diner. Herb and I were there, eating an early dinner—Herb likes to miss the crowds—and Mr. Adison came over to our table, just to say hello." She was about to add something else, but Pat cut in. *At this rate, we could be here all day*, he thought. He felt bad for Marvel Anderson, but he couldn't afford to spend time on anything unrelated to the case.

"When you noticed the smoke, what did you do, Mrs. Anderson?"

"I said to call me Marvel, Sergeant," she scolded, shaking a finger at him. It was difficult for Pat to remain calm, but he swallowed his frustration and nodded, encouraging her to continue. "I used my cell phone to call 911. Herb insists I take it with me whenever I'm alone. And I sure am glad I had it today. Is everything okay, Sergeant Donnelly? Is everything all right? None of the officers here have told me anything and I'm worried," she said, looking past him in the direction of the garage.

"I'll probably need you to come down to the station later, Marvel, but for now why don't you head home. You have been a tremendous help to me this morning and you did the right thing by calling us. I promise to call or stop by later this afternoon when I have more information. Herb is probably wondering why you haven't gotten back yet," Pat told her.

"Oh no, he's probably still snoring away. Herb never gets up until after eight o'clock. Well, except when he has plans to go golfing. When he has an early tee time he can always get up, even without the alarm," she continued. Pat knew he needed to end the conversation or he would never get free. He made eye contact with Officer Jim Daniels, who smiled in return. Pat endured a lengthy minute hearing about Herb's golf game until Jim finally rescued him.

"Sergeant Donnelly, we need you over here right away," he called, from behind Mrs. Anderson, still smiling.

"Thank you very much, Marvel. Now I want to make sure you get home safely, so I'll have Officer Daniels walk you home." Jim's smile faded immediately.

As he heard her launch into conversation with Jim, Pat turned back toward the house. The garage door was now open, and whatever Marvel Anderson thought was smoke had dissipated. George Woods walked out of the front door toward Pat. Ironically, he was anything but the picture of good health. Pat thought seeing all those people who died from poor lifestyle habits would serve as a warning to him, but clearly George ignored them. He weighed at least two hundred fifty pounds, and was more than a few inches short of six feet tall. His face was often flushed and his thinning hair was worn long and brushed over to one side in an apparent attempt to conceal his prominent bald spot. No one was fooled. He greeted Pat and asked if he was ready to head inside. Pat glanced down the road. When Marvel was out of view, he followed George's lead, and the two men walked inside.

The only car in the double garage was parked on the right side, with the passenger door tight up against the east wall. Pat guessed the person who parked the car was probably used to parking in a small garage. The car was a dark green wagon, the sporty kind, and looked like a newer model. In the driver's seat was a man slumped over the steering wheel, leaning slightly toward the window. He appeared to be tall, with slightly graying, dark hair. According to Greg Mattson, the deputy sheriff, the man fit the description of the homeowner, Will Adison.

So far, Pat knew there were three possible causes of death.

It could have been due to an accident. Too many people make the fatal error of leaving their car running with the garage door closed. Pat had worked a case several years ago, as a patrol officer, of a young woman who was going to visit her boyfriend after an evening of drinking with her roommates. When her friends passed out she decided to spend the night at his place. She never made it. The evidence suggested she had passed out in the front seat of her car after turning the key in the ignition. The medical examiner found her blood alcohol level was more than twice the legal limit. It was a cold night, and the investigator surmised she wanted to let her car warm up before driving. She was overtaken by the fumes and never regained consciousness. Her body was discovered the following morning when one of her roommates heard music coming from the garage. As sad as it was, Pat remembered hearing the sheriff say it was lucky that no one else died that night. Her roommates could have easily died if the deadly fumes had leaked into the house, or the girl could have killed someone while en route to her boyfriend's.

Another possibility was that this was a suicide. Pat asked Officer Mattson, the first person to arrive at the scene, if anyone had found a note. At the time they hadn't, but they would all be looking for one in the house and especially once they were able to get inside the vehicle. Poisoning by carbon monoxide was a painless way to die, making it a very appealing method for some. Pat would want to talk with family members, close friends, and coworkers to determine Adison's mindset in the past few weeks. Most victims of suicide have histories of previous attempts or recent changes in behavior. Many even discussed their suicidal thoughts with others who often don't heed the warning. It was also possible that Will Adison had intended on taking his own life but had changed his mind too late.

Pat would, of course, let the evidence tell the story of what really happened here, but he already had a strong gut feeling. The last scenario, the one Pat instinctively felt applied to this case, was that this man whom he assumed to be Will Adison had been murdered.

Several hours later, sitting in his tiny office at the Red Wing Police Station, which was housed in the Goodhue County Law Enforcement Center, Pat Donnelly poured himself a third cup of tasteless, black coffee. It was the only thing his stomach could handle at this point. The truth was, he had never gotten used to seeing a dead body. Some of his colleagues made it seem like nothing. He could still do his job, of course. But it affected him. He had tried to hide his feelings when he telephoned his wife. His daughter, Kelsey, had a soccer game later that day, but he had already called to cancel. He wasn't even sure if he would make it home at all that night.

The crime scene technicians had been called in, at his request, from the Minnesota Bureau of Criminal Apprehension. They were also sending two agents to assist him with the investigation. Pat wanted everything done by the book with this case, and he knew the BCA had state-of-the-art equipment and facilities. His city police department, which had jurisdiction, would work in conjunction with both county and state officials. The man had been officially identified as William Adison, and Pat was keenly aware that Adison's death would be big news, locally and possibly beyond. The death of an owner of a pharmaceutical company, one that had been in the news recently, wasn't going to go unnoticed. The media would be all over this case. He didn't want them to spin the story, making it look like his people were in over their heads. He'd also get heat from the county, whose attorney, Debra Mason, would demand a clean investigation. Potential homicide cases weren't common in a community like Red Wing, and handling such a case correctly would go a long way toward advancing her career.

From the window, Pat could see a domestic model sedan pull into the small parking lot. *Well*, he thought, *here we go*. He glanced at the clock above his office door. It was almost eleven-thirty. He watched as the two BCA agents stepped out of the car into the cold, dreary day. The male agent looked older, with weather-worn skin and lots of silver in his dark hair. He was tall, but not quite as tall as the woman walking next to him. She had striking, reddish brown hair, cut just above the shoulder, which was whipping around in the wind. She held it back from her face with one hand, while the other clutched her black trench coat.

Moments later they were inside the main entry of the county government center. Pat, whose office was in the west wing on the first floor, met them there and the three exchanged introductions.

"Agent Sam Davis, BCA," said the male agent as he crisply shook Pat's hand. "This is Agent Melinda Hendrickson." Pat shook her hand as well. She had the firmer of the two handshakes and, Pat guessed, she was only in her early thirties. Davis looked to be about Pat's age, which was forty-nine. He led them into his office where he had already begun to write notes on a board hanging on the wall. Being a visual person, he appreciated having the details of a case laid out clearly; it helped him see how the pieces fit together.

"Our crime scene techs just finished up at the house. So, what else have we got?" Agent Hendrickson asked.

Pat brought them up to speed, which didn't take long at all, since the body had been discovered only four and a half hours earlier. They called in the St. Paul Police Department to give notification to Adison's wife, Barbara. Before they could even ask, he told them she reacted as expected when given the news by the officers. She was on her way now, insisting that she drive herself, and was expected to arrive within the next few minutes.

George Woods came into the office and more introductions followed. Pat let the Goodhue County Coroner describe the initial scene investigation. To Woods, this was an open and shut case of suicide, although he would not state that officially until he had performed the autopsy, scheduled for the following morning. Unofficially, it appeared Adison had died from asphyxiation, likely caused by carbon monoxide poisoning. He was found in a vehicle, garage door closed. The gas tank was empty and the engine had died before the police arrived at the scene. Dispatch had received a call from one Marvel Anderson, a seventy-four-year-old neighbor of the deceased, who had noticed what she mistakenly thought was smoke coming from the garage while walking her dog. According to Marvel and two other neighbors, Will had been staying at the house for the last few weeks, without his wife. Agent Davis raised his eyebrows at that piece of information. Adison lived in St. Paul with his wife—no children—and was part owner of MacPhearson Pharmaceuticals, a small but successful company located just east of St. Paul. He held the title of Director of Laboratory Operations, and was, by all local accounts, brilliant.

"It seems like either an accident or a suicide," said Agent Hendrickson, looking at both Pat and George Woods. "We know there must be something else, or we wouldn't have been sent down."

"A neighbor of Adison's saw a car driving down the street last night with no headlights on. It's a very quiet road, only a few houses. This other witness, Herb Anderson—"

"Any relation to Marvel?" Sam recognized the surname.

"Her husband," Pat affirmed, nodding. "He fell asleep in his chair in front of the television. When he woke up, his wife had already gone to bed. As he walked across the living room, he heard a car coming down the road, from the direction of Adison's house. He only saw it briefly, so he wasn't able to give a good description. But he noticed the car was driving with its headlights off."

"And this was last night?" Melinda asked.

"Yes, although Herb was unable to provide an exact time for us. I think, and your superiors agree, this warrants more investigation. We haven't officially ruled out anything," Pat added.

"We just want to make sure we're covering all of our bases. This is going to be a very public case," Woods explained and then repeated that he would like to perform the autopsy before going into any details. He felt comfortable talking theories with Pat, someone he'd worked with for years, but didn't want his assumptions to drive the case, especially in the early stages.

As far as he and Pat were concerned, it was going to be an uphill battle keeping the details of this case private. But he knew the state workers weren't the only potential problem. It wouldn't be hard for a reporter to start chatting it up with an officer or to sit in the local diner until harmless gossip made its way around. No, it was human nature to talk about scandal, and a suspicious death in Red Wing was about as much of a scandal as the town had seen.

George also wasn't thrilled about the fact that Pat had called in the BCA, although he knew it was standard procedure. While he couldn't deny that the BCA had one of the nation's best forensic crime labs, he didn't appreciate the arrogance that sometimes went with that reputation. Over the years, he had teamed with some very good agents from the state, but also had his fair share of cocky investigators who thought they were better at their jobs than they really were. Most of the younger agents didn't know he had worked in the Hennepin County Medical Examiner's office for fifteen years before moving to Red Wing. His wife was from the area and had wanted to raise their children away from the fast-paced lifestyle of the city. George didn't like the stereotype that local law enforcement was a step below.

Pat, wanting to establish his authority in the case, suggested interviewing Barbara Adison right away.

"Agent Davis, I'd like you and George to observe the interview with Mrs. Adams from the room adjacent to my office. I thought maybe Agent Hendrickson and I could interview Mrs. Adison when she arrives. She might open up more if questioned by a woman," Pat stated. He knew his words could be misinterpreted, so he clarified. "Women generally respond well to other women, especially in a time of crisis." Having Barbara Adison feel comfortable was advantageous for many reasons. Although he hadn't shared his theory with his colleagues, if Pat's instincts were right, she would be a suspect. It was unfortunate that spouses were automatically considered in homicide cases, but statistics show that most homicides are not stranger-on-stranger violence. People are usually killed by someone they know: someone they live with, work with. Someone they like, even love. On the other hand, if it was a suicide, Will Adison's wife likely saw signs of his depression in recent weeks. She would also know the car well, whether or not it had any maintenance problems. Pat knew they would need everything they could get from her.

Yes, Pat thought, *this is going to be a long day.*

Pat was about to take the first sip of his fourth cup of coffee when his assistant announced her arrival. He stood up quickly and walked toward the police reception desk to greet her.

Barbara Adison was a very beautiful woman. He had assumed she would be more of a plain-Jane type, and it amused him that nothing could be farther from the truth. She had wavy, shoulder-length, dark brown hair, the long legs of a model, and was dressed in what was clearly a very expensive suit. It was the kind of outfit that his wife, Christine, would save for something special—a wedding or a party. Pat was almost certain Barbara Adison dressed this way as a rule. She smiled faintly when he held the door for her as she stepped into the west wing of the government center. It was the strained, weak sort of smile Pat had seen too many times during his career.

"Hello, Mrs. Adison. I'm Sergeant Patrick Donnelly. I am very sorry we have to meet under such circumstances," he said gently.

"Thank you, Detective," she responded absently. Pat observed she had been crying. Her eyes were red and her make-up was slightly smudged, but she seemed determined to appear under control.

"We can talk in my office," he said, slipping his hand under her arm and leading her around the corner.

"This is Agent Melinda Hendrickson of the Minnesota Bureau of Criminal Apprehension." The three found places to sit, and the already small room seemed to shrink in size. It made for an uncomfortable environment and even Barbara Adison seemed anxious to get started. It was she who spoke first.

"I know, from the officers who came to the condo, that my husband is dead. Will someone please tell me exactly what happened to him?"

Pat explained that a neighbor had spotted fumes coming from the garage and how, at least for the time being, the most likely theory was that Will had died from carbon monoxide poisoning in the garage of their river cottage. He had been found inside the vehicle, key in the ignition, gas tank empty. Barbara put a well-manicured hand to her mouth, and closed her eyes.

"Oh my God! Was it an accident?" she asked unsteadily.

"Our initial investigation has just gotten underway, Mrs. Adison. We don't want to make any premature statements at this point in time," Pat said as he glanced over at Agent Hendickson, communicating that he wanted her to take over the interview.

"Mrs. Adison, while we know this must be a very difficult time for you, it is imperative we gather all the information we can immediately so we can find out what happened to your husband," she explained in a soothing voice. "We'd like to ask a few questions today that might help us get started with our investigation." Barbara nodded and straightened herself in the old leather chair next to Pat's desk. He couldn't help thinking she looked completely out of place in his drab, cramped office.

Barbara confirmed much of what they already knew of Will Adison, and then the interview turned to the specifics, the kind of personal information only someone very close to a victim could provide. Will Adison led a very complicated life. When they asked why Will was staying at the cottage alone for the last few weeks, Barbara explained that he had been very stressed lately, even depressed, due to recent events in both his professional and personal lives. She told them that Will had been working on a treatment for a deadly disease that had turned out to be a failure and he was devastated that the drug didn't work. He was a very talented, dedicated scientist. He had gone behind his partners' backs to continue work on the project, she went on, and there was still some tension at the office. At that point, the only time during the interview, Barbara broke down.

"I'm sorry, but I just can't believe I am referring to my husband in the past tense." After she regained her composure, they had discussed Will's personal life. Barbara admitted that she and Will were having problems in their marriage, stemming mostly from the fact that Will had been having an affair with another woman.

"Her name is Jessica Monroe," Barbara informed. "She also works at MacPhearson. And she is carrying Will's child."

Pat had checked his watch. They had been at it for thirty-five minutes.

"He said he was going to end things with her," Barbara continued, "because he wanted to make our marriage work. He offered to go to counseling, begged me to stay, saying he'd do whatever it took."

"How did you react?" Melinda pushed carefully.

"I won't lie and say I wasn't furious with him. I had known about Jessica for quite some time, but the baby was what I couldn't get over. I felt humiliated; everyone would know my husband was cheating on me! And then, to bring an innocent child into the situation," she said, shaking her head. "But Will came home to the condo last Tuesday night. We talked. He asked for six months and I reluctantly agreed. He was going to come back down here to the cabin for a few more days, to do some work, and I was to join him later this week."

That was the last time she had seen her husband, but she had spoken with him by phone on Saturday evening. She said he had seemed distracted, which wasn't unusual when he was working.

At the end of the interview, Agent Hendrickson asked where Barbara Adison had been on Sunday evening and early Monday morning.

"Why? You, you can't possibly think *I* had anything to do with this?" she stammered in disbelief.

Pat assured Barbara Adison they were only being thorough, gathering as much information as they could. He did not, however, share with her the fact that he was not convinced it was suicide. She said she understood, but her tone was much cooler when she stated she had been at her monthly book club meeting on Sunday evening until nine thirty. After the group broke up she'd returned home, got ready for bed, read part of a novel, and went to sleep. She did not leave her condo until her drive down to Red Wing after the officers told her about Will. She provided the names of the women at the book club meeting, but admitted there was no one who could verify her whereabouts after nine thirty. She had neither made, nor received, any calls at her home phone number. She hadn't seen any neighbors when arriving at her condo, and assumed no one had seen her in return.

"One last question, Mrs. Adison, and then we will let you head back home," Pat informed her. He took her raised eyebrows as acceptance and asked something that had been bothering him since one of his officers found it that morning. *It might be nothing*, he told himself, but somehow he felt it was important to the case. "Does the name Katie Adams mean anything to you?"

"Katie Adams? No, why?"

"Just asking. Thank you for all of your help, Mrs. Adison." Pat held out his hand, which she shook halfheartedly. She nodded at Melinda before walking out of the tiny office. Pat noted how she looked as she left—her hunched shoulders seemed to bear an enormous weight. His train of thought was broken upon hearing his name.

"Pat? So, what's your take on her? Do you think she was honest with us?" Melinda asked as George and Sam returned to his office.

"I don't know. She was up-front about their marriage and the affair. But she did seem nervous when we asked her where she was last night," he added, thinking aloud.

"I thought the tears came on a bit strong," Melinda commented.

"And then she got real cool when she realized we might consider her a suspect, even if only for the time being. Too bad for her that no one saw her after nine-thirty," George said gruffly. "I also don't think she's telling us the whole story."

"I agree. I'll bet she was a lot angrier with her husband than she let on today. You don't get over an affair that quickly. You'd have an emotional reaction, not a logical, detached one," Melinda said, perched on top of a two-drawer, metal file cabinet. "She said he was going to leave his mistress, even though she's pregnant. That's also a lead we've got to pursue."

"It looks like I'll be spending some time up in the Twin Cities," Pat told them. "I'll head home for the afternoon and pack. Tomorrow morning, I'll drive up early and we can interview people from MacPhearson at their offices." He wasn't looking forward to being away from his family, but he had to admit that this case was intriguing. Will Adison was a well-off, intelligent scientist. He had a marriage on the rocks, a pregnant mistress on the side, and an expensive project at work that had recently been proven to be a failure. Just one of those things could make someone depressed. All three could easily make someone have a nervous breakdown. *But,* Pat thought, *did Will Adison really kill himself, or was someone trying to make it look like he had?*

～

Forty miles north of the Red Wing Police Department, Steven leaned against the doorframe at the back of the largest conference room at MacPhearson Pharmaceuticals. There was a considerable amount of chatter, although most people were whispering. Ever since he and James had sent out an urgent e-mail asking everyone to gather upstairs at four o'clock sharp, the rumor mill had started. Some were sure the company was going to go public sooner than expected, now that the Jacobs case involving Respara was dropped. Others thought Will Adison had decided to quit. The lab workers especially knew how hard his failed experiment had hit him. A few even threw out the idea that MacPhearson was going to be bought out by a larger drug company. Steven looked at them speculating, whispering, wondering.

He was almost enjoying himself. That feeling immediately disappeared, however, when he saw James at the opposite end of the room. The group grew quiet with anticipation, no one wanting to miss what James was about to say. Steven made his way over, and stood just behind his older brother.

"Thank you for being here. I know you are all busy and ready to get home for the evening, but I have a very important announcement that Steven and I wanted to tell you in person. I am sure it will be all over the news this evening and for quite some time, I expect.

"Our own Dr. Will Adison died sometime last night or early this morning at his river cottage down in Red Wing," he said, his voice almost breaking. He waited for the room to quiet again before continuing. "I spoke with Barbara this afternoon. She said they found his body this morning. He died from carbon monoxide poisoning."

Diane Norman was the first to break the silence. "It happened while he was asleep? Didn't he have detectors installed at the cottage?" she asked, visibly shaken by the news. She had worked with Will for years and had a tremendous amount of respect for him.

"I spoke with a Sergeant Donnelly of the Red Wing Police Department. The initial evidence suggests Will's death was most likely a suicide. He and his people are coming by tomorrow to talk with some of you. He assured me it would just be for routine questions. I—well, Steven and I that is—would like it if everyone could be here by eight o'clock tomorrow morning. If you had planned to be out of the office tomorrow, please make it a point to come in anyway. It's very important the police have the opportunity to talk with you. We need to cooperate and help them in any way we can. The sooner we have answers, even painful ones, the sooner we can take care of our family here at MacPhearson."

"James, I think it might be a good idea if we had a moment of silence to honor Will, our friend and colleague," Steven suggested. People around the room bowed their heads. A few sobs were audible and several people held hands.

After a few minutes, James thanked everyone for attending and asked his employees to go home and spend time with their families. He held back tears as everyone offered condolences as they left the room. James noted two people he had seen earlier were no longer there. He had made deliberate eye contact with both of them during his announcement, but now Jessica Monroe and Oliver Klein were gone.

$\sim$

Jessica slipped into the ladies' room at the opposite end of the building. She couldn't breathe and felt like she could faint at any moment. *They found Will!* James's words swam in her head and she couldn't keep any of them straight. It was all happening so fast. She leaned against the wall and tried to steady her breathing. All of this stress couldn't be good for the baby.

What am I going to do now? Oh my God! Will, what if they find out what I've done? Think, think, dammit! Oh, God, what if someone saw me? What if the police find out I was there? She knew someone might have seen her in Red Wing. It wasn't that big of a town and the locals might have noticed her with Will before: they had gone to the cabin together a few times over the summer. If the police were coming all the way up to St. Paul to ask questions, maybe they weren't convinced it was a suicide. Of course they would focus in on her. The jilted lover—how obvious. It was as if she were a character in a novel. She needed to call Amy. She pulled her cell phone from her purse. She was shaking so badly that she needed to dial the number more than once before she got it right.

"Amy, oh my God! I've got to talk to you, but not here," she whispered into the cell phone. She hadn't heard anyone open the door, but checked under the stalls to be sure she was alone.

"Jessie? What is it? Where are you?"

"I'm at work."

"You sound awful. Are you okay? Is it the baby?" Amy's voice was full of concern. She knew Jessica had been at the breaking point since Will told her things were over between them. She had convinced her friend to go see Will at his cottage, but hadn't heard from her since. *Things must not have gone well,* Amy thought to herself. She felt guilty about giving Jessica such poor advice.

"Can I come over, Amy?"

"Sure, right now?"

"Yeah. I need your help. You have to help me figure out what I'm going to say to them when they ask me about Will and Red Wing," she hissed. She sounded hysterical.

"Who? Jessie, what are you talking about?"

"The police. They found his body, Amy. Will's body …" her voice trailed off as her throat tightened.

"Jessie?"

"Amy, you have to help me figure out what I'm going to tell the police."

~

Oliver was already on his way out of the parking lot by the time the meeting was officially over. He turned up the heater in his car. Even though the afternoon sun was warm, he felt chilled and sick to his stomach. The police were coming tomorrow. That was the last thing he had heard as he'd headed down the hall away from the conference room. He would have to think carefully about exactly what he would say to them tomorrow. He needed to go back to his apartment and concentrate on getting his story straight. He wanted to sound natural when he answered their questions. Sounding natural, and not rehearsed, would take practice.

Should I tell them about the phone call? They could probably trace the call anyway, so it would do him no good to lie. He didn't see the harm in them finding out about it. Will could have called him to check on things at the lab. Will was still the director and Oliver was filling in for him, after all. No, that wasn't too out of the ordinary. Oliver also thought it might be a good idea to make it seem like he was annoyed Will was checking up on him. The two were not friendly and everyone at MacPhearson knew it. It would seem more believable if he said he was irritated that Will had called him, even insulted. He felt his hands shaking as they gripped the steering wheel. *I have to get a hold of myself by tomorrow*, he thought, *or they'll see right through me. It'll be fine. A phone call isn't enough to arouse any suspicion.*

But something else was making him nervous. As he sat in the afternoon rush hour traffic, he thought about what was inside his apartment. *If the police find it, it won't look good*, he thought. *But it's just a routine investigation. They have no reason to search my apartment. I'll just have to be very careful about what I tell them.*

The unusually long commute afforded him time to formulate a plan. By the time he reached his apartment, Oliver Klein had created the story he would share with the police if they questioned him. It made sense to tell them about the phone call, but he would tell them nothing else.

~

"So, how do you think it went?" James asked as he leaned back against the sofa. He had decided to go over to Steven and Audrey's after the meeting. He stared at his brother across the room, which was painted a stark white. The black leather sofa, as well as a matching loveseat and two club chairs, were seated in a grouping near the fireplace, which was currently unlit. Brightly colored pillows and a geometric-patterned floor rug broke up the contrast and breathed life into the room. Behind Steven was an archway leading into the kitchen. Paula and Audrey were there, calling the local florist, ordering sprays of flowers for Barbara and the office. Paula had come over to see Audrey as soon as she heard the news.

"I think you were very good. No sense in any of them having to learn about it from the television or radio. I'm sure it will be one of the lead stories this evening," Steven told him, using the remote control to turn on the television. Sure enough, the local news anchor was covering the story.

"… was found in his family's cottage in Red Wing, just south of the Twin Cities metro area. Chief of Police Pedersen is expected to make an official statement sometime tomorrow. Adison, age forty-nine, was partner and chief laboratory director of the Afton-based MacPhearson Pharmaceuticals. MacPhearson's asthma drug, Respara, which made headlines this summer, was linked to the death of eleven-year-old Kyle Jacobs. Last week, the Hennepin County Medical Examiner's office released results which determined Respara was not, in fact, the cause of Jacobs' death. Adison, a graduate of the University of Minnesota, is survived by his wife Barbara. Stay with Channel Eleven news for more on this tragic story as it unfolds."

Steven snapped off the television.

"Why do they always have to bring Respara into it? Isn't Will's death awful enough without having to drag something else into the story?" he asked. Paula and Audrey had caught the last part of the news story and both took seats on the chaise.

"How is Barbara?" Paula asked her husband. James sighed and lowered his head.

"I tried calling her again on my way over here, but got their voicemail. She must be making calls or have the phone off the hook. It was so strange to hear Will's voice on the recorded greeting. I just can't believe he's gone," James said, letting his head slip into his hands. He felt exhausted. These last few hours had been just about unbearable.

"How did people react at the office?" Audrey asked.

"How do you think they took the news?" Steven shot back sarcastically.

"I'm sorry, I just—"

"No, I'm sorry, honey. I shouldn't take it out on you. I'm just feeling guilty about everything that's happened. I was the one who was so hard on Will when his project failed. I kept reminding him of all the resources he had wasted. After all the wonderful research he did for us, I didn't even give him a break," he said quietly.

"But you were only protecting MacPhearson. Will kept his research going without your knowledge. You did the right thing to question that. You had no idea all this was going to happen." Audrey walked over to him and held his hand in hers. She had never seen her husband this upset before.

"We were both angry with him, Steven," James offered, "and I came down on him just as hard as you did. I should have seen how upset he was. I've known him for years, best friends since college. When he came back from the cabin, he looked awful. I knew he was depressed, but had no idea it had gone that far. I should have talked with him. I should have helped him."

"Stop it, both of you," Paula scolded gently. "Neither of you could have known what was going on inside Will's head. He had been gone for weeks. And both of you had every right to disagree with how he went behind your backs and continued to work on a project he was supposed to end. There's nothing you can do about that now. He's gone. All you can do is try to help Barbara."

James nodded, unable to speak. He looked over at Steven. Paula was right. They needed to go see Barbara.

～

Grant went to bed early that night, the stress catching up with him. From his room, he could hear Katie's radio playing softly across the hall. Ever since she was a baby she liked to have music on as she fell asleep. Beth had put a radio in her nursery and would play music to quiet her down. It soon became habit. Grant had been thinking a lot lately about when Katie was a baby. They had been so happy then, a family of three. Beth had been a good mother. Nervous, of course, Katie being their first. But she seemed genuinely happy. It wasn't until Katie was older that Beth got restless.

Grant rolled over onto his side and his thoughts drifted to Will Adison. Adison had been the only thing keeping Katie out of the study. Now that he was no longer an obstacle, Grant was growing impatient. He wanted to go into the office tomorrow morning and talk with James and Steven. Neither of them had a problem with her getting into the study before. Grant closed his eyes even though he knew sleep was a long way off. He didn't want it to look bad either, by going to them too soon, like he wanted to benefit from Will's death.

I'll wait a few days. Then it won't look so opportunistic. Just a few more days.

Tuesday, October 29

Grant was surprised when it was James and Steven who approached him about the study. He had gotten to the office before eight, as they had requested the day before. Grant had a lot of work to get done before his first co-monitoring trip to Seattle the following week. He had no idea if the police would talk to him or not, but he knew having them around would make it harder to stay productive.

When he pulled into the parking lot, several other cars were there already. He wondered if the others were following orders, or if their curiosity had just gotten the better of them. The first and second floors were unusually busy, with more people standing in the hallways talking than working in their labs or offices. When Grant reached the top of the stairs on the third floor, he heard his name being called from below.

"Grant. Grant." Steven was climbing the open staircase, a flight below Grant, trying to get his attention.

"Oh, Steven. What can I do for you this morning?" Grant asked.

"Let's talk in your office. I'll walk with you," Steven answered. He wanted their conversation to be private. They walked the fifty feet to Grant's office in silence. To Steven, Grant looked uncomfortable, even nervous, but he supposed that wasn't unusual considering what the day had in store for them. There was a news crew filming the outside of the building. So far, they hadn't let any reporters inside, but that, too, would probably change. James and Robert Dawson were formulating a strategy at that very moment.

"Grant," he began, closing the door of the office while Grant took off his coat and hung it on the coat stand near the window. "James and I were discussing your situation last night." He didn't want to go any further just yet.

"My situation? I thought you two had enough going on for one day," Grant said honestly. He was surprised they would think of him, considering everything that had happened.

"Well," Steven continued, "your name came up when we were rehashing the events of the last few weeks, trying to get a better picture of everything. Of course, our meeting with you and Will last week came up. He felt badly about your daughter and the study. I spoke to him about it later that day and he said he wished there was something more he could do." Steven took a seat across from Grant, who was now sitting at his desk.

"I didn't talk with him about it after the meeting," Grant explained. "I figured the decision was made. The current study is still going to happen, isn't it? I mean, with everything … well … nothing is going to change it, right?" Grant couldn't help but worry that Will's death might cause a delay in the study. He hoped his concern for his daughter was not interpreted as a lack of concern for Steven's partner and friend.

"Grant, what I'm trying to tell you is that James and I think Katie should have an opportunity to get into this trial, the one starting now. I want to make it clear that no rules or regulations will be broken by her participation, only slightly bent. There's enough gray area to leave us a bit of room to maneuver. Will thought it would be unethical to get her into this study so late in the game, but sometimes ethics can get in the way. We think Will's judgment was clouded on this one. We were going to try to talk to him this week when he got back, to see if we could change his mind," Steven explained. He knew he had Grant's attention now. "Since Will was the only one who had reservations about it, James and I think you should go ahead and meet with Dr. Carruthers."

"Are you sure?" Grant hated himself for even asking the question.

"Yes. No one even has to know Will didn't agree with her participation in the study. We haven't told anyone. Grant, Will may have changed his mind anyway; we'll never know. We think helping your daughter is the most important thing at this point, the right thing," he said quietly. It was true, every word. Will *might* have changed his mind. And what difference did it make now anyhow? "This is by no means a guarantee she'll get in. But at least she might have a chance. I took the liberty of scheduling an appointment for Katie with Dr. Carruthers tomorrow morning at eight-thirty. We'll see what unfolds," Steven said.

"I don't know what to say, Steven, except thank you. I know this must be a very difficult time for you and James, and I truly appreciate your concern for my daughter. It means a great deal to me," he said, trying to keep his voice steady.

Steven nodded a few times, stood up, and walked out of the office. Grant sat there, stunned by the conversation that had just taken place. They had called Carruthers. He didn't even have to ask them. They *offered!* It couldn't have gone more smoothly.

~

When the police arrived, Jessica was already feeling sick to her stomach. She was nervous about having to answer their questions. The flicker of hope that they wouldn't need to talk with her was quickly snuffed out when James called her into his office just after eight fifteen. They decided to conduct the interviews in the owners' offices. Both afforded privacy, with thick doors, and were virtually soundproof. Jessica walked slowly over to James's office. It seemed like an agonizing distance, each step drawing her closer to the place she least wanted to be. She tried to keep herself from breaking down, but if she did, she and Amy had planned she would use the baby as an excuse. They couldn't fault a pregnant woman for being emotional.

Once inside the office, she was ushered onto the sofa by James, who then left her alone with the police. The officers were dressed in street clothes. Jessica had pictured them wearing uniforms. Both seemed pleasant enough, but Jessica was still guarded.

"Good morning, Ms. Monroe. I'm Sergeant Patrick Donnelly with the Red Wing Police Department and this is Agent Melinda Hendrickson from the Minnesota Bureau of Criminal Apprehension. We'd like to ask you a few questions."

"Alright." Jessica knew her voice sounded hesitant.

"Are you aware how Dr. Adison died?" Melinda questioned, starting the interview. The story had been played on all the local news programs, both radio and television. They were aware the MacPhearsons had made an announcement to the employees the day before. Pat and Melinda thought it would be best to see how much people knew. Sam Davis was conducting his own interviews across the hall in Steven's office, and the three would discuss their notes over lunch.

"Mr. MacPhearson announced yesterday that Will died from carbon monoxide poisoning. People here at work want to believe it must have been some sort of accident, but James said yesterday it looked like a suicide." She couldn't keep her voice from breaking.

"Our initial investigation points in that direction, but we still have some unanswered questions. That's why we're here—to find out more about how Dr. Adison was behaving in the months, weeks, and days prior to his death," Pat explained. She looked so young and frightened, and Pat couldn't help but think she was just a child. If Barbara Adison hadn't told them yesterday about the pregnancy, Pat would never have guessed this woman was going to have a baby.

"I see. Well, what would you like to know?" she asked.

"What was your relationship with Dr. Adison?"

"We were close. Actually," she said, leaning forward on the edge of the couch, "our relationship was closer than that of a boss and employee." She and Amy felt it would be better to be honest about the affair. Barbara knew, and she would more than likely tell the police about it anyway. And there was also the chance that someone else had knowledge of her relationship with Will.

"If you've talked to Barbara Adison, then you already know that Will and I were involved. In fact, I am four months pregnant with his child." She patted her stomach as she spoke and Melinda believed her actions were more subconscious than dramatic. She had seen many expectant mothers touch their stomachs without even realizing it, as if already protecting their baby from the outside world.

"Was Will aware of the baby?"

"Oh yes, I told him a few weeks ago, when I was sure," she answered.

"What was his reaction?"

"He was … surprised. I think he was starting to get used to the idea, though. He had always wanted children—he and Barbara couldn't have any," she said looking downward. "He said he wanted to be a part of the baby's life, to be a real father."

"And what about his relationship with you?"

"Right after I told him about the baby he said he thought we should end things. He gave me all these reasons for how it would be better for me, being so young and everything. But I think he may have changed his mind while he was staying at the cabin."

"What made you think that?" Melinda asked.

"He called me from the cabin this past weekend and said he wanted to see me. We had spent some time there over the summer, away from the city," she explained. "It kind of became our place. He wanted me to drive down on Sunday afternoon so we could talk."

"And did you?" Pat wanted to know. "Did you drive down to see him in Red Wing?"

"Yes, but I was only there for about an hour. He asked to see pictures of the baby. You know," she said, looking at Melinda, as if she might understand things better than Pat, "pictures from the first ultrasound. He seemed really happy when I showed them to him. He said I'd be a good mother. I thought things were okay with us again."

"What time did you arrive in Red Wing, Ms. Monroe?"

"About four o'clock," she responded. "Traffic was light and I made good time getting down there."

"And you stayed for how long?"

"Like I said before, only about an hour. I left the cabin just a little after five."

"And you stayed at the cabin the whole visit? You didn't go anywhere else?"

"No, we were at the cabin the whole time. We walked down by the river, but other than that, we were inside the house," Jessica told them.

"How did Dr. Adison seem to you?"

"What do you mean?"

"Well, could you describe his emotional state?"

"He seemed happy about the baby," she said.

"Did the two of you discuss work?"

"No. He just said he was looking forward to getting back. I think he was going to be starting a new project."

"Alright, Ms. Monroe, thank you for answering our questions today," Pat said, ending the interview.

"That's it?" Jessica sounded surprised.

"That's really all we need," Melinda assured her. Jessica stood up, her face wearing an expression of relief. She was just about to leave the office when Pat stopped her.

"Oh wait, Ms. Monroe, one more thing. When you were with Dr. Adison, did he say anything about the two of you getting back together? Anything specific about the baby?"

"No, not really. He just said he was happy he was finally going be a father. He didn't say anything about us, and I didn't want to push it—things were going so well, you know."

"Okay, thank you."

Melinda walked Jessica out of the office and informed her that they probably wouldn't need to speak with her again. Jessica smiled and said she was glad to help and they could talk with her at any time. Agent Hendrickson congratulated her about the baby and then left her alone.

Jessica dropped into her office chair once Agent Hendrickson was out of sight. She could only hope they wouldn't find the truth. The police would have no way of finding out that Jessica hadn't returned to her apartment until almost ten o'clock the night Will died.

She was shaking so badly she thought about having a cigarette, but knew she couldn't. Instead, she opened her purse and looked again at the ultrasound photo of her baby. Will's baby. Just seeing that black and white image calmed her. Ignoring the pile of work on her desk, Jessica turned on her computer and started an online search for baby names.

~

Across the hall from where Melinda and Pat were interviewing other employees, Agent Sam Davis waited for Dr. Oliver Klein. They were to meet in Steven's office at nine thirty, but Klein was already five minutes late. While he waited, Sam looked around the office. He smirked at the contrast between the office of a corporate executive, like Steven MacPhearson, and that of a government worker, like himself. His own office at the BCA was the complete opposite of this suite. Where he had a banged-up metal desk, MacPhearson had a walnut beauty. Sam sat in a swiveling office chair; MacPhearson's was made of fine Italian leather. Decorating Sam's walls were bulletin boards with information about current cases, maps, photos, and faxes. On MacPhearson's walls hung tasteful, and what appeared to be expensive, pieces of art. And of course, MacPhearson had a window, whereas Sam's light came from the fluorescent fixture on the ceiling.

"Pretty impressive, isn't it?" Oliver Klein had come in while Sam's back was turned. Sam smiled and sat down behind the walnut desk, trying it out. Dr. Klein was not what Sam had been expecting. He would look more at home in a football jersey than the white lab coat he was wearing.

"I'm Agent Sam Davis from the Minnesota Bureau of Criminal of Apprehension. I trust you know why we're here today."

"Yes. James mentioned you guys were investigating what happened to Dr. Adison down in Red Wing, but I'm not sure if I know anything that will be of help to you," Klein stated.

"It's amazing how the smallest pieces of information can be incredibly useful," Sam explained. "How well did you know Dr. Adison?"

"Well, I guess, at least professionally. Will is, rather *was*, the lab director here at MacPhearson. I am sort of the second-in-command, so to speak. He oversaw all of the current lab projects and was also responsible for a large part of the research and development side of our lab. I manage the research assistants and oversee established projects," he began.

"So, was Will considered your direct supervisor?" Sam asked.

"I guess you could say that. He was one of the owners and he, more so than James or Steven, was directly involved with the laboratory. But often he got real wrapped up in certain projects and pretty much left me to handle the day-to-day operations."

"And how long have you worked for MacPhearson?"

"Just about seven years," Klein answered. "After the first drug, Alerzan, hit the market, they decided to expand and added what amounted to an assistant lab director position."

"You said Adison was involved in research and development. We understand he had been working on a project that failed. Can you tell me more about that?" Sam coaxed.

"Well, any time you put in a lot of effort, only to have the results slap you in the face, it's tough. I think Will took it harder because he hadn't had many failures before. Will was an excellent scientist, but he was also very lucky. Very lucky. To develop two drugs that make it through clinical trials, hit the market, and actually do well is an amazing feat. I guess you could say he had just the right combination of hard work and luck." Klein's response revealed a touch of envy, which Sam picked up on immediately.

"So he was taking this recent failure pretty hard, then?"

"Yes, you could say that. That's why he went to his cabin, to take some time off."

"And who was in charge of the lab while he was away?"

"I was. I am. I still am," Oliver clarified.

Sam asked a few more routine questions and then informed Oliver the interview was over. He hadn't found anything particularly interesting in this first interview, but knew he had a long way to go. So far, however, he had this case pegged as a suicide. Intelligent, successful scientist, perhaps a little on the arrogant side, sees his project go down the tubes, along with his marriage. *Add to that a pregnant girlfriend and even I'd think about calling it quits,* Sam thought.

Sam's next three interviews, with Tara Wolfe and two other lab technicians, confirmed what Dr. Klein had told him. Will Adison had been spending the majority of his time on this special project that no one else knew much about, often in his office behind closed doors. He let Klein run the show, and had been keeping long hours for months. To his staff, he seemed preoccupied and agitated.

Tara Wolfe even recalled one night in the lab when Dr. Adison had stayed late again, waiting for some very important results. The next day he looked horrible. Word had spread that the project was a bust and that the MacPhearsons had found out about it.

According to all three, Will Adison did not seem like the type to commit suicide, but he was under tremendous pressure. Each one, when asked if it were possible, said Adison was on the edge, and yes, it was entirely possible he had taken his own life.

The diner, on St. Paul's Grand Avenue, was just starting to get busy with its daily lunch crowd. Located near upscale shops, offices, a few private colleges, and a well-established residential neighborhood, it was a local favorite. Melinda, Sam, and Pat were seated in a booth at the back of the restaurant. They had just placed their orders and started to discuss the busy morning.

Sam shared notes from his four interviews. Then Melinda filled him in on Jessica Monroe and two other employees, one from human resources and the other, Robert Dawson, head of the legal department. So far, the investigation was favoring the suicide theory. Adison was clearly having more than his fair share of problems. Sam and Melinda were discussing their report, thinking they might have the case closed by the week's end. Pat remained quiet.

"Something about this just isn't sitting right with me," Pat said, tapping a straw against the table. Moving helped him think. "I get that he was at the end of his rope. I can see how it wouldn't be unreasonable that the guy decided he just couldn't take it any more. But something still bothers me."

"The baby," Melinda nodded. "I thought the same thing when I heard Jessica Monroe talking about the baby."

"It just doesn't seem right that a guy who's finally going to be a father and is excited about a baby who will be born in a few months, goes into his car to take a carbon monoxide nap," Pat said, shaking his head. "I don't buy it."

"I agree, but what if he *wasn't* happy about the baby? All we have is the Monroe girl's word for it, and what if it was just wishful thinking on her part?" Sam replied.

"Have the forensics results come back yet?" Pat asked.

"The crime scene techs said the house looked clean; no sign of forced entry, nothing looked out of place, no sign of a struggle. How about the autopsy? I thought Woods said he'd be done with it by now."

"If he hasn't called me by this afternoon, I'll call him. I know he was going to start last night or early this morning. I asked him to put a rush on it, with the media attention and all," Pat told them. He had leaned on Woods to get things going. He was impatient with this one.

"If the house is clean, we have even more reason to go along with the theory he did it himself." Sam didn't see the need to make it more complicated than it was.

"But what if it was just an accident?" Melinda conjectured. She, too, wasn't convinced it was anything more than a suicide, but wanted to hear what Sergeant Donnelly had to say. She knew from the moment they met he was good at his job, and he definitely had more experience than she did.

"So you think it was an *accident*?" Sam didn't hide his view on that theory.

"I'd like to see the toxicology report first," she shot back. She didn't like the sarcastic tone in Sam's voice.

"I agree. The tox report may be valuable. But accidental death is still not the only other possibility," Pat suggested, testing the waters. Sam leaned back and let out a not-so-subtle sigh.

"But our guys said the house was clean, Pat," he repeated.

"See, all that says to me is that no one *broke* in. It doesn't say Will Adison didn't *let* someone in."

The car ride back to MacPhearson Pharmaceuticals was uncomfortably quiet. Pat sensed he and Sam were at odds over this case, and that Melinda would rather not be placed in the middle. She had listened to his theory at the restaurant, but

Sam was her partner, and even Pat realized his hunch was little more than just that. The car driving without its headlights still bothered him. He wasn't sure why he had such a strong feeling about Will Adison's death not being a suicide. He looked at his watch: one fifteen. They had scheduled interviews with James and Steven MacPhearson at one forty-five. If Pat still hadn't heard from Woods by the time the interviews were over, he would call in. He wanted the results from the autopsy.

This time, when they were admitted into the building, all they had to do was show their visitors' badges. That morning it had taken them almost fifteen minutes to fill out the proper forms, receive the badges, and be assigned a company escort. Pat nodded at the security officer who had helped them as he walked past the lobby.

Both James and Steven MacPhearson were already in the office when Pat, Sam, and Melinda arrived. James was seated at his desk, but rose when he saw them come in. He invited them to take seats in the area at the back of the office, near the window. As she made her way across the room, Melinda explained that she would speak with James while Pat and Sam were interviewing Steven in his office. After the three men left, the interview was underway. Melinda's conversation with James focused on his relationship, both professional and personal, with Will Adison. James told her that he had spoken with Adison on Saturday afternoon and said he had seemed depressed. James admitted he felt responsible for what happened to his friend. If he had perhaps seen the signs sooner, he might have been able to help.

Across the hall, Steven's interview pursued a similar line of questioning. At the end of the discussion, when Pat asked about Will's personal life, Steven told them Will had been having an affair and that his wife was threatening to leave him. "To top it all off," Steven explained, "his mistress is now pregnant. So yeah, I'd say the guy was under a bit of pressure." He then added that Adison's problems went beyond the company and that James, who felt some responsibility, should not blame himself. Steven went on to say that James was feeling guilty about his friend's apparent suicide. He had always been a good friend to Will. When Sam asked if he and Will were as close, Steven laughed, telling him they got along just fine, but that James and Will were friends first. Steven, being two years younger, was kind of like the tag-along little brother.

While Pat caught every word Steven said, he watched Sam intently. Sam was tapping the front of his notebook with a pen; clearly he was ready to wrap up the interview and get home to his family. The gesture, although slight, infuriated Pat. They would still need to file a report, and Pat wanted to be thorough, to leave no stone unturned. Although he wasn't ready for the interview to be over, there wasn't anything he had yet to ask.

The men returned to James's office together just as Melinda was finishing her conversation with him. As the group stood, there was a knock on the open office door.

"Sergeant Donnelly, sir?" Sheila, an administrative assistant, poked her head in. She looked hesitant, and Pat wondered how often she dared interrupt a meeting.

"Yes?"

"There's a George Woods holding for you on line two," she stated.

"Thank you," he answered, looking at James who pointed to the phone sitting on his desk.

Pat had no idea why George would call him here instead of on his cell phone. The rest of the group was now talking at the other end the office, but Pat didn't like the idea that he would be talking to George in front of an audience.

"Sergeant Donnelly," he said quietly, his back turned to the group.

"Pat, why in the hell haven't you returned any of my messages?" Pat wouldn't be surprised if the group could hear George from across the room.

"What messages? Hold on, George," he said unclipping his phone. Sure enough, the battery was dead. Pat couldn't even get his phone to turn on. Damn! Of all days for this to happen. He must have grabbed the wrong battery that morning when he left.

"Battery's dead, George," he replied. "What have you got for me?"

"Well, I think you'll be very interested to hear what I found today."

"Go ahead," Pat said, glancing over his shoulder at the group. They were still chatting away and Pat wanted this conversation to appear casual.

"Sergeant, your boy had methanol in his bloodstream. Not a lot, but enough to make him very, very sleepy."

⁓

The last interview for the day, the one scheduled with Grant Adams, was rescheduled for the next morning. Pat didn't tell Melinda and Sam his reasons until they were in the parking lot outside the building. He wanted to head back down to

Red Wing and meet with George. Tomorrow they would have to come back to question more people, and could talk with Adams at that time. Sam and Melinda agreed Pat would go down alone and the three of them would meet for breakfast early the next morning.

On the drive, Pat was full of nervous energy. He couldn't wait to get to the coroner's office and find out exactly what George discovered. Methanol! When he told Sam and Melinda about it, Sam, sticking to his theory, commented that Will might have taken the methanol himself, as part of the plan.

But why would someone take methanol and then go sit in a car full of carbon monoxide fumes to finish the job? Carbon monoxide poisoning wasn't painful, so why go through all the trouble? And to plan and carry out a suicide, Adison would need a clear head. Methanol would get in the way.

Two hours later, just after five o'clock, Sergeant Patrick Donnelly finally had good reason to treat the case as an official homicide investigation.

George Woods had found ethyl alcohol and small traces of methanol in Will Adison's bloodstream. Once this piece of information was discovered, the crime lab returned to the cottage. After only an hour, the crime scene technicians informed George that there was one small thing missing from Will Adison's house. Something so insignificant that it might not be missed, unless a person was looking very carefully.

In the glass-recycling bin in the pantry, there were seven empty, imported lager beer bottles. There were four left in the refrigerator. A complete search of the cottage, including outside and in the trash, turned up nothing. What was found was a folded cardboard carrying case for the twelve-pack and a receipt from Lennie's Liquor on Seventh Avenue. The bottles had been purchased with a credit card the day before Will Adison died.

"Where's the twelfth bottle, Pat?" George asked, the question rhetorical. "Normally, on its own, I wouldn't think too much of it. There was no bottle inside or outside the cottage. No broken glass in the trash. In this day and age, you aren't likely to give someone a beer for the road. So there's one beer bottle that's unaccounted for. So what? Strange? Maybe. Intriguing? Not really. But when you combine that missing bottle with the traces of ethyl alcohol and methanol found in the victim's body, that's a little too much to consider a coincidence for me. What about you?"

Pat was well aware that, for the first time since the body had been discovered, George Woods used the term "victim." The two men, both experienced in their respected fields, spent the next hour developing a new theory about how Will Adison had died.

Wednesday, October 30

The University of Minnesota Children's Hospital stood on the East Bank campus. Most of the rooms afforded a beautiful view of either downtown Minneapolis or the Mississippi River with the St. Paul skyline in the distance.

Dr. Andrew Carruthers finished his coffee and set aside the sports page. He had gotten to work early, knowing that his schedule was packed. He had back-to-back appointments until two thirty, when he would leave for the day. Although the weather had recently been on the cooler side, Andrew had a three o'clock tee time with a few doctor friends. They were trying to squeeze in as much golf as they could before the snow came. The weather looked like it would cooperate.

His first appointment of the day, Andrew noted as he looked over his schedule, was with a MacPhearson employee and his sick daughter. James MacPhearson, a friend of Andrew's, had called to personally request she be seen as soon as possible. Instead of coming into the clinic at nine o'clock, Andrew scheduled them for eight-thirty and arrived an hour early. According to James, Katie Adams seemed like an excellent candidate for the bronchiosclerosis study for which he had been screening subjects. James reminded Andrew his site was to enroll thirty subjects. In fact, Andrew had met with a patient who qualified for the study just the day before. There was now only one spot remaining.

Andrew was still waiting on results of the final laboratory tests to determine whether or not another patient would qualify to participate in the study. Andrew was scheduled to meet with this other patient's family later in the week. If Katie Adams qualified for the study, and was given the sole remaining spot, it would mean the other patient would not be allowed to participate. According to James, Katie Adams had only a few, mild symptoms. Andrew's other patient, who was technically next on the list, was at a more critical stage in the disease. The treatment was his last chance. But a personal request from James MacPhearson was not to be taken lightly.

MacPhearson Pharmaceuticals had used his clinic for several studies, which had proven to be very lucrative. Andrew was developing a solid reputation in the medical field, was recently featured in the *Journal of the American Medical Association,* and the extra revenue it sent his way was welcomed. Andrew and MacPhearson Pharmaceuticals had a mutually beneficial relationship. He just hoped helping the Adams girl wouldn't be a mistake.

~

Grant and Katie sat patiently in the waiting room of the clinic. Katie was thumbing through a teen magazine with articles that were much too mature for her, but Grant let her look anyway. He wanted her to have a distraction before the appointment. Last night he had explained to her how clinical trials work. He stressed the importance of making sure drugs were safe for patients. It helped that he worked in the field and could answer her questions as more than just her father. She trusted his opinion. Once she understood that at this stage in the research process the drug was proven to be safe and had been shown to slow bronchiosclerosis, she was completely on board to be a participant in the study.

But Grant had also tried to caution her against getting too excited. She would have to have some tests done to make sure she qualified, but Katie wasn't listening to him. She was beaming and talking about how next year at this time she would consider trying out for the basketball team. In addition to soccer, Katie was a pretty good basketball player, quick and aggressive on defense. They had all agreed she needed to sit this season out, just in case her symptoms acted up. Recently, she hadn't talked much about things in the distant future, perhaps not wanting to make plans when so many things were unknown. Grant had noticed even in the last few days that she had started taking naps when she got home from school. The coughing at night kept her awake and she was exhausted. *Hopefully that will all end soon and she can just get back to being a normal teenager. If there even is such a thing,* Grant thought as he glanced at her magazine. There was an article about body piercing that nearly took his breath away.

"Adams, Katie?" the nurse called from an open doorway to the right of the check-in desk. Grant and Katie stood up and Katie gave him an excited smile that made his heart melt. He hoped he had done the right thing by telling her about the study. He didn't know how she would handle it if she didn't get in now.

After she was weighed and measured, Katie and Grant were shown into a small, brightly painted exam room. Unfortunately, the hue did nothing to lift his spirits. Grant was frightened, and it took a concerted effort to conceal that fact from his daughter. It all came down to this.

Dr. Andrew Carruthers came in a few minutes later and talked with both Grant and Katie, gathering information for her medical history. Normally, he would have a nurse perform such a time-consuming task, but if they were going to push her tests through, Andrew wanted to collect the data himself.

After fifteen minutes of questions, he felt she was likely to qualify. There was no family history of cancer, diabetes, or other chronic illnesses. Katie was of healthy height and weight, and her blood pressure was normal. She looked fatigued, but other than that, her color was good and she only coughed a few times during the meeting. If Andrew didn't know she had been diagnosed with bronchiosclerosis, he would have guessed she was suffering from a virus and would have told her to go home to rest for a few days.

"Well, from everything you've told me, you look like a good candidate for this study," Andrew told them. "But, we have to run some tests first and see how the lab work comes out."

"What kind of tests, Doctor?" Grant asked.

"Nothing major; a little blood work, x-rays, a urine sample." He grinned in response to the look on Katie's face. "Just the basics. We want to rule out anything that could complicate the situation." He wanted to keep it as simple as possible with Katie in the room, knowing that Grant, a professional in the field, understood the process well.

He shook Katie's hand and called for the nurse to escort her to the lab area.

"I really appreciate this, Doctor," Grant said in a grateful tone once Katie and the nurse were gone.

"Well, let's see how her lab results turn out, Mr. Adams. I'll put a rush on them."

"Call me Grant, please."

"Listen, Grant, I feel like I need to say this. I would never do anything to jeopardize the reputation of this clinic and hospital, or the University. James called and put some pressure on me to give your daughter a chance. This is definitely not how I like to run my practice. The only way Katie will be able to participate in this study is if another patient, a patient much sicker than your daughter, does not qualify. In fact, I am expecting that patient's lab results any moment. You know enough about clinical research to know how all of this works." Dr. Carruthers was interrupted by a knock on the door.

"Here are the lab results you were asking for," whispered Tania, although Grant could hear every word clearly. Then her voice became inaudible as she said something else to the doctor.

"Grant," Carruthers said, setting the folder down on his desk, "please excuse me. I have an urgent phone call. You may wait for Katie here or in the lobby, if you prefer." He was about to close the office door when he turned and added, "If Katie does get into this trial, how she was placed stays with the MacPhearsons and the two of us."

"I understand and completely agree," Grant concurred.

As Andrew had predicted, Grant elected to wait for Katie in the exam room.

After the appointment, Grant dropped Katie off at school for the rest of her classes. He and Beth had decided they would try their best to schedule Katie's appointments outside of school hours so she could maintain good attendance. Today's appointment, however, couldn't wait. But against Katie's protest, neither Grant nor Beth saw any reason to keep her home all day. She could still make five of her seven classes.

On the way over to the middle school, they talked about how her classes were going and the other kids. Katie seemed to enjoy her new teachers. That didn't surprise Grant; Katie had always done well in school. She was making some friends, too. There were a few girls she had more than one class with and two of them played soccer. Katie had recognized them from teams she had played against in the past.

"If you'd like, maybe you could ask a few of the girls over on a weekend, for movies or something," he offered. This was definitely uncharted territory for him. Grant knew all of Katie's friends from her old school but, with the rare exception of bringing one of them along to a movie or to a restaurant, Grant was a newcomer to the concept of teenage girls hanging out.

"Thanks, Dad. I'll see how it goes," she responded. Grant couldn't tell if she was quiet because of the appointment, or if this was the beginning of the stage where his teenager would rather stare out the window than discuss her social life with him. He hadn't yet broached the subject of boys. He didn't think she was interested, but after seeing the magazine at the clinic he knew he better start communicating about things like boys and dating soon. When she leaned over to kiss him good-bye before getting out of the car, Grant breathed a sigh of relief. His thirteen-year-old daughter still loved him enough to kiss him on the cheek in the parking lot of her school. Grant etched the scene into his memory. He knew his little girl was growing up and she probably wouldn't be doing things like that for much longer.

~

Pat Donnelly, Melinda Hendrickson, and Sam Davis were waiting outside Mac-Phearson Pharmaceuticals. Grant noticed them as soon as he pulled into the lot, and when he saw Donnelly hold up a hand, he knew they were waiting for him. He looked at the clock on his dash. Only a quarter of ten, and his clock had been set ten minutes ahead. It was something Beth always did. Both of them constantly ran late and she thought it might help them to be on time. It wasn't particularly successful, but Grant still stuck to the old habit.

He parked and walked slowly toward the building. He had to admit it was a bit intimidating to see three officers waiting for him. *Just keep calm; you'll be fine.*

"Mr. Adams, good morning." Sergeant Donnelly seemed cheerful. "With this beautiful, warm weather, we decided it was just too nice to wait for you inside."

Once the foursome entered the building, Melinda left the men in order to follow up with other employees; Sam and Pat would talk with Grant Adams. Grant offered his office for the questioning and Donnelly accepted. The size and furnishings of Grant's workspace reflected his rank at MacPhearson. The small room provided just enough chairs for all of them to sit comfortably. It was also obvious that Grant had only recently come to MacPhearson. Partially unpacked boxes littered the floor and the only personal item in view was a framed photo of a young girl.

"My daughter, Katie," Grant informed Pat. "She's thirteen now, but that picture is still one of my favorites." It showed a girl of about nine or ten sitting in a field of wildflowers. She was wearing a sundress and her hat was lying in the grass beside her. Pat noted she had the same warm smile as her father.

Sam felt impatient. After Pat had briefed them that morning over breakfast, both Melinda and he were ready to devote all their energy to this case. Sam felt like he had something to prove. Not only had he been wrong about the case, but he'd been rude to Pat Donnelly as well. He still had no idea how Pat had it pegged as a homicide from the beginning. There hadn't been much to go on, and Pat had even admitted to them that it was just a gut feeling, a feeling that could just have easily been wrong.

The three, along with George Woods, had decided they would not release the results of the autopsy to the media just yet. So far, the only news conference held had been vague, stating the death was an apparent suicide, but a routine investigation was still pending. Keeping details of the investigation a secret could prove to be difficult, but might provide them with the edge they needed when questioning people, people who were now considered suspects. People like Grant Adams.

After leading with a few general inquiries about Grant's career and his position at MacPhearson, Sam hit him hard with the question they all wanted answered. It was a strategy they had agreed on. Get him talking, get him comfortable, and then hit him.

"Mr. Adams, why would Will Adison have your daughter's name written in a notebook at his cabin?"

"What? I have absolutely no idea!"

"Did Will Adison ever meet your daughter?" he asked.

"No, as I said before, I just started with MacPhearson and the only company function I've attended was a cocktail party. I went alone." He was visibly shaken by this line of questioning. Sam took advantage and kept going.

"So, if he never met Katie before, had the two of you ever discussed her? I mean to the point where he would know her name?"

"Oh, I think I might know what this is about." Grant nodded and seemed to relax. He needed to stay calm. "My daughter has bronchiosclerosis. It was one of the reasons I came to MacPhearson in the first place. We—James, Steven, Will, and I—had talked about getting her into a clinical study, sponsored by MacPhearson, for an experimental drug that treats the disease. Maybe he was thinking about her down at his cabin. I'm not sure what else it could be," he offered smoothly. It seemed logical enough.

"So you all agreed to get her in?" Pat asked, firing his first question of the morning.

"Well, I asked them if it would be possible. Her symptoms have been getting worse lately. I was open with them when I interviewed, and when I asked, they said it would be okay," Grant lied. He was sitting here, calm as could be, lying to the police. *Can they tell?*

"So has she started treatment?" Pat asked again.

"She met with the doctor conducting the trial—over at the University of Minnesota. But we won't know for sure if she'll be eligible to participate until later this week."

"I'm sorry to hear about the situation with your daughter. I hope things go well for her." Sam's voice was sympathetic. His daughter Brittany babysat for a little boy in the neighborhood who had recently been diagnosed with bronchiosclerosis. Sam and his wife knew the family on neighborly terms, but his daughter was taking it pretty hard. She had come home from their house crying the last time because she said it was so sad to see him getting sicker. Sam's wife suggested she stop babysitting, but Brittany wanted to continue. Learning that Adam's daughter had the same disease made him regret being so hard on him earlier. But he also got the feeling Adams wasn't coming clean with them.

"Have you ever been to Will Adison's cabin, Mr. Adams?"

"No," he replied.

"Just out of curiosity, where were you on Sunday evening?"

"Why?"

"We just want to be thorough," Pat assured him. "My boss is always getting after me about having complete reports." He played it off as routine—just another day on the job.

"Well, my daughter was spending the evening with my ex-wife for her birthday," he explained.

"Your daughter's?"

"No, my ex-wife's. They went out to eat downtown, and then Katie spent the night at her house in St. Paul. I was alone, so I took advantage of the peace and quiet and got caught up on some work."

"So you didn't go out at all? You were home the whole evening," Sam questioned. Grant nodded.

"Did anyone happen to see you?" Sam asked.

"No. I don't have any neighbors yet," he explained. "My townhouse is brand new and the other units in my building aren't going to be ready until after the first of the year."

"Thank you for your time, Mr. Adams. We'll be in touch," Pat said.

Unbeknownst to Pat, Sam had the same feeling about Grant Adams. He was hiding something.

~

The afternoon at the office was completely non-productive. Grant managed to look over a few reports, but spent most of his time staring out the window. He left for home at three thirty, but made sure to carry files with him, making it seem like he was going to do more work that evening.

The files never even made it out of his car. Instead, he invited his mother over for dinner.

A quiet evening at home with his two favorite ladies was exactly what Grant needed. Only when Dorothy asked about the doctor's appointment was Grant reminded of everything. But Katie's response was brief and, to Grant's relief, his mother let it rest at that. After dinner, they watched television together in the family room. Grant kept his uneasy thoughts in the back of his mind. Nights like this were the reason why he had taken the risk in the first place.

When Dorothy left, declining his invitation for her to stay the night, Katie went up to bed. Grant was suddenly aware of the silence in the house. He tried to read from a novel he had started, but couldn't concentrate. He finally gave up and went to bed.

There, alone in the dark, his thoughts won the battle. He couldn't hold them off forever. His emotions were so conflicted. He felt hopeful about Katie getting into the study, but also guilty for what he had done to get her there.

Grant fell into a restless sleep. He had always considered himself to be a good person. He never thought himself capable of deliberately causing harm to another human being. But that was before.

Thursday, October 31

Pat Donnelly placed an early morning telephone call to Barbara Adison. His intention was not to wake her, but to talk with her before she had any chance of turning on the morning news. In a voice that conveyed sympathy and yet was direct, he informed her there was about to be a news conference down in Red

Wing regarding the death of her husband. When she asked why, Pat explained, carefully omitting several details, that the investigation was now being treated as a homicide.

"Oh my God," she said quietly. Pat couldn't be sure if her voice suggested sadness or fear, or perhaps a bit of both.

After a few more minutes of conversation, with her asking and him skirting questions about the case, Barbara hung up the phone.

She lay in bed trembling. She looked over at the slightly open window on the far side of the room. She liked keeping the bedroom cool and sleeping under layers of blankets and down comforters. The room seemed very cold now, the covers unable to keep her warm any longer.

She looked at the clock. The conference, according to Sergeant Donnelly, was scheduled to start in forty-five minutes, at nine o'clock. That would give her enough time to take a hot shower and make a pot of coffee. God knows she was going to need it to face this day.

Thirty minutes later, her wet hair was wrapped tightly in a towel and the pot of coffee was brewing. She still had fifteen minutes until the conference, but turned on the television anyway. With the traffic reporter shouting his report from a helicopter high above the freeway, Barbara stared at the television. Her eyes dry, she waited anxiously for the segment about Will.

The news conference, which aired on all four local morning news programs, was held by the Red Wing chief of police and the Goodhue County attorney, Debra Mason. Chief Pedersen, a pleasant-looking man in his early sixties, with thick, white hair, opened with a brief statement announcing that Dr. William Adison's death was now being treated as a homicide. He was careful not to make any mention of the fact that Will had methanol in his system. He only spoke of the carbon monoxide. He requested information from anyone who might know anything about the case, even something that might seem insignificant.

County Attorney Debra Mason fielded questions from the media. She looked at home in front of the camera, her sandy blonde hair, cut just above the shoulder, held in place by a band, and her cream-colored suit well cut and flattering. Small, dark-framed glasses completed the look of a professional young woman who was determined to make her mark.

She deftly answered questions in vague but accurate terms, giving away only what was necessary. She also remained calm as her responses caused the reporters to get aggressive. Eventually, she ended the conference and walked into her office. The Channel Five news anchor team provided a review of the facts of the Adison case.

~

Robert Dawson snapped off the television in James's office. He dropped his head and felt his pulse quicken. Last month his doctor had advised him to take a vacation and consider working fewer hours. *That's not going to happen anytime soon,* he thought bitterly. *Not after what I've just seen.*

"I don't have to tell either of you that this is not the kind of publicity Mac-Phearson needs right now," Robert said sternly. They had survived the Respara issue with little repercussion, but another hit of bad press was the last thing the company needed while trying to restore public confidence.

"This is not the kind of news that makes an investor want to back a company," he went on, glancing at his watch. It was only nine thirty, but he wanted a drink.

"Even though it's unrelated to the company?" Steven demanded. Usually he was the one to overreact.

"Steven, an owner of MacPhearson Pharmaceuticals has been killed. How can you possibly think this is unrelated to the company?"

"I just meant that—"

"Robert, let's talk damage control," James recommended.

"For now, we should wait. If it turns out to be some random act of violence or something, we might be able to actually gain from the situation. You know what I mean. The local news will be sure to do some in-depth stories, and you two can talk about how much he'll be missed at MacPhearson," Robert said, thinking aloud. *It might not be so bad,* he reassured himself.

"I also don't think it's a good idea to let the police talk with people here."

"Sergeant Donnelly already left a message this morning on my voicemail. He said he and the other two agents will want to do some follow-ups, but they'll be at the BCA offices in St. Paul," James reported.

"Good, you don't want camera crews hanging around," Robert agreed.

"So we wait?" Steven asked.

"We wait. I know it's not the answer you're looking for, but it's the only one I have for you right now."

~

Pat slipped into his office just as the news conference was wrapping up. He didn't want to face reporters armed with cameras and questions. Both Pedersen and Mason had done exactly what he told them to do. It was important that details about the case not be leaked to the media. At least not until they were ready.

Sam and Melinda were checking on results from the cottage at the BCA lab. George Woods was meeting with a medical examiner from the BCA at the Goodhue County morgue. Sam recommended someone from the state go over the autopsy results with Woods, just so there would be better communication between the agencies involved. Pat knew George was a little put out, but had agreed without much of a protest. He was a good coroner and was confident his work would stand up to any other examiner.

The three had decided to conduct the bulk of the investigation in the Twin Cities, where their primary suspects were located. If anything broke down in Red Wing, Pat would make the drive to cover things at that end. He could see his family once in a while. When he'd left the house that morning, packed for a week's stay in a hotel, Christine had kissed him on the cheek, but Pat knew she wasn't thrilled with the idea of him being gone so much. She understood this was an extremely important case, perhaps the most important of his career, and Pat knew she was proud of him. Although she had been a cop's wife for many years, she couldn't hide the fact that she was worried about him. It also meant she would have to shoulder the responsibilities of the house and kids while Pat was away. She was more than capable, but it was a lot for anyone to handle. Tonight was already Halloween, and the holiday season was just around the corner. *Should be home long before then,* he thought as he settled into his desk chair.

He wanted to be around for Halloween. It was a busy night for the police, even in a community like Red Wing. There were always kids playing pranks, some innocent and others not. *Let it go,* he reasoned, *the rest of the force can deal with anything that might come up while I'm away.* He'd reminded Christine to keep an eye on Kelsey and Danny. Both were going to a Halloween costume party at the community center. It was a great way for the kids to have fun, and it kept them off the street and out of trouble. Leave the trick-or-treating to the little ones. Pat had reassured his wife that everything would be fine, that hopefully they'd get some breaks in the case soon. With any luck, they might have the answers within a few weeks, he'd said. Her eyes told him she didn't believe that any more than he did.

~

Grant sat at his desk and stared at the computer, his eyes dry and sore. He had come into work early, knowing he had a lot to accomplish. He knew he had been distracted since starting at MacPhearson and wanted to prove he had a strong work ethic. At Webber, they knew he was a hard worker. For years he had been consistently one of the first to arrive and one of the last to leave. He had excelled and moved up the ranks quickly. He wanted to provide for his family. *How ironic,* he thought, *since all those hours at the office is what Beth claims ruined our marriage.* It was just like her to lay the blame on someone else.

Water under the bridge, he told himself. But maybe that's why he wanted Katie to come and live with him so badly. Maybe he wanted to make up for not being there for her as much when she was little—make up for lost time—because he didn't know how much time she had left.

The loud ring of the telephone startled him.

"Mr. Adams?" The voice at the other end of the line sounded familiar to him, but he couldn't quite place it.

"Yes," he answered.

"This is Tania, Dr. Carruther's nurse. I wanted you to know we have the results of your daughter's lab tests." That's where he had heard her voice before.

"Already? We were just there yesterday. Does she qualify for the study?" Grant asked. He doubted if she could provide an answer over the phone, but thought he'd give it a try anyway.

"I'm sorry, sir, but you will have to discuss that with Dr. Carruthers. He wanted to know if you would be able to come into the clinic around three o'clock this afternoon."

"Three o'clock will be just fine. We'll be there," he told her.

It wasn't until he hung up the phone that he remembered it was Halloween. Since there was no school the next day due to a teachers' workshop, Katie was going to Beth's for the long weekend. Their old house was in a nice neighborhood filled with kids. They always got dressed up and handed out candy to the trick-or-treaters. This year Katie was going to be a soccer player. Not very creative, Grant had told her.

"At least this way you don't have to go shopping with me for a costume. Remember last year?"

"I think a soccer player is a brilliant idea for a costume," he said in agreement.

He promised she would be at her mother's in time for the first trick-or-treater.

As he watched the hands of the clock at the clinic, Grant wasn't so sure he would able to keep his promise. By three thirty, Katie's name had still not been called. He checked with a different nurse at the desk. All she would tell him was Dr. Carruthers was running a little behind.

Katie, who had discovered the same magazine she had been reading before, was deeply absorbed in an article about girl athletes. At least it was sports and not boys. Grant set down a *Sports Illustrated* magazine from last spring, and looked around the almost-empty waiting area.

There were only two other people in the room. The little boy, Grant guessed, was about six years old, and was dressed up in a Spider-Man costume. His mother was trying to stop him from running around the room, shooting imaginary webs. The nurse shook her head and muttered something under her breath from behind the counter, clearly disapproving of the behavior.

"Tommy," the mother coaxed, "why don't you come and sit down by me and I'll read to you."

"I'm not Tommy," he replied.

"Thomas Michael, come over here and sit down. I know you had candy all afternoon at your school party, but you need to rest."

Grant smiled to himself. He watched Tommy continue to shoot his webs on to chairs, doors, and the nurse's desk, all while singing the theme song from the Spider-Man cartoon show. By now, Katie had put down her magazine. This was far more interesting.

"I'm not Thomas Michael. I'm Peter. Peter Parker," he said as he narrowly escaped her clutches. She looked over at Katie and Grant, embarrassed, as she got up and moved toward her son.

"Well, if Peter Parker wants to go trick-or-treating tonight, he needs to sit down next to his mother." Peter Parker was sitting quietly in less than five seconds.

"Katie Adams," the nurse called.

"Well, Dad. I guess this is it!"

~

Katie arrived at her mother's house before dusk or any trick-or-treaters had arrived. Grant spoke briefly with Beth, explaining Katie would be participating in the study, and her first treatment would begin on Monday afternoon. He invited her to go along before she even had a chance to ask. He knew it would be good for Katie to have both of them there. They would be given special instructions, and Beth would want to hear them firsthand. He kissed Katie the soccer player on the head and then left, just as he saw a princess and a dinosaur toting plastic jack-o'-lantern buckets walking up to the door.

~

Across town, Trish Garrett waved to her five-year-old son, Tommy, as he and her husband, Scott, walked down the driveway to begin trick-or-treating. When Scott had arrived home from work, Tommy had been so anxious to go out that they barely managed to eat dinner. She still hadn't told Scott about the doctor appointment. *Maybe it is for the better*, she thought. *At least this way he can still enjoy the night.* Tommy was so excited to be Spider-Man this year. The costume that her mother-in-law had made was just perfect. He had worn it all day; the school he attended still had a Halloween celebration for the kids. Setting the camera on the kitchen counter, she realized how glad she was that, even though Tommy had complained, she had taken so many photos before they left. She had been with Tommy since she got the news, and had somehow managed to keep herself together, for his sake. Now that she was alone, she finally let the tears come. The disappointment was overwhelming. She had allowed herself to believe the drug would save Tommy, that everything would be fine. He had been diagnosed with bronchiosclerosis when he was just four, practically still a baby. She had to stay strong, for her husband and her son.

That afternoon she had been told that Tommy's last set of lab tests disqualified him from participating in the study.

She couldn't help wondering if this would be his last Halloween.

Friday, November 1

Although Grant had a mountain of paperwork on his desk waiting for him Friday morning, he passed the door to his office and walked straight down to the owners' offices. He was grateful, and wanted to thank them first thing. When he approached Jessica Monroe's desk to inquire about Steven's schedule, he couldn't help but notice how awful she looked. Normally, she was a very pretty girl. On that particular morning, however, her hair was mussed, her eyes swollen, and her skin blotchy.

"Jessica, are you okay?" he asked, even though he didn't know her very well. She seemed like such a nice kid.

"Oh yes, Mr. Adams, I'm fine. Just a little under the weather, and I guess stressed out because the police are going to be questioning people again today. Not that I mind, but it makes it so tense around here," she explained, fending off his concern.

"I heard they'd be calling people to the BCA offices throughout the day. Have Steven and James arrived yet?"

"Yes, they're both inside." She nodded toward Steven's office. "They have a nine o'clock meeting with Oliver Klein. But he's not even here yet, so I'm sure you could catch them before it starts," she suggested. Grant glanced at his watch. Eight forty-five. That should give him enough time. He knocked three times on the closed door. Everything about this building seemed so solid, so strong.

Steven opened the door just as Grant was about to knock again, his hand midair.

"Hello. Jessica said I might be able to catch you both before your meeting with Dr. Klein," Grant said as Steven invited him to sit down. On the table were the remains of a breakfast consisting of bagels and coffee. Grant wondered how two siblings could spend so much time together and not go completely crazy. He loved his sister, but didn't think they could work together for more than five minutes without getting on one another's nerves.

"I spoke with Andrew Carruthers last night, Grant. He told me the good news about Katie," James said. Grant was surprised. It seemed like James was always a step ahead of everyone else. Maybe that's why he was so successful.

"That's actually why I'm here, to say thank you in person. I can't tell you how much I appreciate all you've done to help us," he said sincerely.

"Her treatment starts on Monday, right?" Steven asked.

"We have an appointment Monday afternoon," Grant told them.

"Well, we're just glad we could help," James said, taking a sip of his coffee. "How's the work going for you?"

"I'm getting up to speed on the protocols for both studies, and I'll be co-monitoring out in Seattle with Allen Jennings."

"Seattle? Is that Dr. Spencer's site?" Steven asked.

"Yes. Allen said it's a messy site—some potentially major data discrepancies. He's worried about them getting audited," Grant explained. The FDA has the authority to audit records and documents any time during the course of a study. Violations of regulations could result in delays, fines, or even the shutting down of a site or, in extreme cases, an entire study.

"Well, he has a new study coordinator. Kelly, I think her name is. Go easy on her if she's new, Grant. She's just learning," Steven joked. Grant's supervisor at Webber had told them what a detail-oriented CRA Grant was before they hired him.

"I will, boss," he assured him. "Well, I'll leave you to your meeting then. Again, thank you very much, for everything."

"You're welcome, Grant. On your way out will you send Jessica in?" Steven requested.

"No problem. Is she feeling okay? Not to be insensitive, but she wasn't looking very good a few minutes ago," Grant said quietly. He didn't want Jessica, who was sitting at her desk, to overhear him. "Looks like she has the flu or something."

"Oh, she has something all right," Steven chuckled. "But it's not the flu."

"I'm sorry?" Grant asked, missing the joke. Steven looked at James, who indicated he could share the gossip.

"Everyone is going to know soon anyway. Jessica Monroe is pregnant," Steven smiled.

"Oh, I didn't know she was married," Grant said before he could stop himself. It was really none of his business.

"Oh, she's not married. The baby's father is her boyfriend. Or was her boyfriend." Steven was talking in riddles.

"*Was* her boyfriend?"

"Grant, you haven't been here long enough to know this, and they did a pretty good job keeping it quiet, but the father of Jessica Monroe's baby is Will Adison."

Grant absorbed the surprising information as he told Jessica they wanted to see her. Watching her walk into the office, Grant could see why Adison would be attracted to her. Young, pretty, seemed very sweet. But Will had been married. And married to a very attractive woman. But Grant knew firsthand not everyone stays true to promises like wedding vows. He wondered if Barbara Adison had known about the affair. Grant remembered how much it had hurt to learn Beth had been cheating on him. *But at least she'd had the guts to tell me.* He couldn't imagine finding out another way. Office romances are especially hard to keep secret. Had Will told his wife about the baby? Grant wondered how she might react. Barbara Adison did not seem like a pushover. Then he remembered what Jessica had said about the police questioning people. Surely Barbara would be considered a suspect. She definitely had a motive if she knew about the affair. Will Adison and Jessica Monroe. *I guess I'm not the only one with the proverbial skeleton in my closet.*

~

Tara Wolfe and Jessica Monroe ate lunch at an Irish pub in downtown St. Paul. Both girls had been called in for questioning that morning and had decided to drive together. They were friendly at the office, but had never spent time together socially. When Jessica learned Tara had to go down to the BCA headquarters, she called her in the lab and offered to give her a ride. The questioning only took an hour, but both girls were starving by the time it was over. Melinda Hendrickson recommended the pub. A good place to grab a burger, it was only a few miles from the BCA building. As promised, the food was excellent. They enjoyed their lunch and chatted away, getting to know each other better. None of the other patrons at the pub would have ever guessed these two young women were part of a murder investigation.

~

Oliver Klein walked down to his office, his step a bit lighter than usual. It had finally happened. He had just come from a most satisfying meeting with Steven and James MacPhearson. They had offered him the Laboratory Director position. Will's position. They told him they hadn't even considered looking for anyone outside. Klein was the only man for the job, Steven had said.

And he was. Oliver had the experience and the expertise to run the lab as well as, if not better than, Will Adison ever had. He told them so at the meeting. He wanted to make it clear to them they could trust him to do the job. After returning to his office, he glanced at the phone. He decided the news called for a celebration. Even though he had an afternoon appointment with the police, he didn't want that to put a damper on the day. He placed a call to a young artist he had dated a few times and made reservations at an upscale steakhouse in downtown Minneapolis. With the promotion, he'd receive a substantial increase in pay. Maybe down the road, he'd be running the whole company. Oliver Klein was a realist, but why not? He'd been patient, patient until he saw an opportunity. Will Adison gave him that opportunity and Oliver wasn't going to blow it. This was the chance of a lifetime. He just had to be careful. He didn't want them to get suspicious. Finally things were going right for him. Finally.

~

Feeling full but satisfied from her lunch, Jessica peeled off her coat and sat down at her desk, finally having the energy she needed to work. She felt warm hands run across her shoulders and looked up to see Steven MacPhearson. His hands lingered for only a moment, but even so, it made her feel strange.

"Sorry, Jessica, but you looked so tense. If there is anything I can do for you, please just let me know," he offered.

Jessica sighed. He was just being supportive. He really was a great boss. "Thanks, Steven. I appreciate that very much," she said, smiling up at him.

"If you need some time off for an appointment, or you need to leave early because you're tired or not feeling well, that's fine by me. You could even work from home—as long as nothing restricted leaves the office."

"I might take you up on that," she responded gratefully. Both he and James had been very understanding when she'd told them about the baby. They said Will was like a brother to them and they would do anything they could to help her out. They offered to give her a twelve-week maternity leave after the baby was born, claiming they needed to make their employee benefits package more attractive. James even mentioned they might look into a small daycare program. She was definitely blessed.

"Jessica?"

"What, oh, I'm sorry, I was just thinking about how great you two have been to me," she admitted.

"I asked if you've told your family," he repeated, concerned. She had mentioned to him on several occasions how strict her father was and how he and her brothers were overly protective of her. *Men and their daughters,* he thought. *So glad I have sons.*

"Yes, I've told them. No sense putting it off. I'm actually going over to my parents' house tonight." Her parents had been disappointed but accepted the situation. Jessica had not shared with anyone, even Amy, how angry her brothers had been when they found out. "They, of course, want to know what's going on with the investigation. It's been all over the news."

"How did your meeting with the police go?" Steven asked, hoping he didn't sound too anxious.

"Fine. They just asked more questions about Will, you know. And about other people around here," she added, immediately wishing she hadn't.

"Oh?"

"Yeah, but it was all pretty basic," she answered nonchalantly.

"Anything I should know about?" he asked point-blank. "Be careful not to get too friendly with them. That might just be one of their strategies. As Will's friend and owner of this company, I have a right to know if there's anyone they are focusing in on."

"No." She did not look him directly in the eye.

"Let me know if that changes. And Jessica, be sure to take care of yourself and that baby. It's all we have left of Will, and I think he would want me watching out for you," he said quietly. He touched her hand lightly and then turned and walked back into his office, closing the door behind him.

The police did seem different toward me today, Jessica thought. Not exactly friendly, like Steven had suggested, but different somehow. Their questions focused more on what was going on at MacPhearson, rather than on her relationship with Will. *And they didn't even ask about my trip to Red Wing on Sunday.* She just confirmed the time she arrived and left. Were they going easy on her now so she'd get comfortable? So comfortable that she might say more than she should?

Jessica couldn't help wondering if she should tell Steven more about her interview with the police. She glanced at the clock. If she was going to make it to her parents' house across town, through rush hour traffic, in time for dinner, she needed to leave right then. Grabbing her purse, keys, and jacket, she decided there wasn't anything that couldn't wait until Monday.

Saturday, November 2

The morning sun shone brightly in the eastern sky. It was warm for early November, a perfect day for golf. But instead of teeing off on the course, Steven was being escorted through a dreary hallway to be questioned by the police. Why couldn't they have called him in yesterday? He wanted to be cooperative, but for Christ's sake, Saturday?

He swore under his breath as the agent showed him into a small room, furnished with only a rectangular table and four folding chairs. The contents of the room were reflected in a large mirror. Steven was certain that people were watching him from the other side.

Two of the chairs were already occupied. Steven sat down across from Sam Davis and Pat Donnelly. If Steven's instincts were right, Melinda Hendrickson was watching as well. He saw the agent turn and leave, closing the door behind him.

"Thank you for coming down this morning," Pat opened.

"Of course, I'll do anything in my power to help you, but do you have any idea how long this meeting will take? I told my wife I would able to make an early lunch with some friends," he stated.

"This shouldn't last more than an hour. We actually have your brother coming in later," Sam said evenly.

"Great, then let's get started," Steven replied.

"Where were you last Sunday evening, between the hours of five o'clock and midnight?" Sam questioned. The medical examiner had placed the time of death between eight and ten o'clock.

"I was actually at home watching a couple of movies," Steven answered. They certainly weren't wasting any time this morning. As they fired direct questions at him he thought of what they were really trying to get at.

"Was anyone there with you, or were you alone?" *Do you have an alibi?*

"I was with my brother, James."

"Was anyone else in the house with you? Your wife? Kids?" *Is there anyone else who can corroborate your story?*

"Both of my boys are away at college, and my wife went to dinner and a movie with James's wife, Paula."

"For how long were the ladies gone?" *How long were you and James alone?*

"Let me think. I remember them leaving the house around six thirty. They wanted to try out a new Thai place over in Edina, and needed to leave early. I think they were trying to make the nine o'clock—or maybe it was the nine thirty—show. Anyway, they got home around midnight. James was asleep on the sofa; he can never make through a movie if it starts past ten," he said, shaking his head.

"You said you watched two movies that night." Pat wanted the details. *Can you please be more specific?*

"Yeah, actually Sergeant, I still probably have the rental receipt." He pulled out his wallet and extracted a receipt from a local video store. Two movie rentals, both action movies, were rented on Sunday afternoon, paid for with cash. "We thought we'd watch some the wives didn't want to see," he explained.

"And that was the entire evening? You didn't leave your residence?" Sam questioned. *Did you take a drive down to Red Wing?*

"No, all we did was watch the movies. Oh, and the news. James was awake at that time still and I stopped the movie so we could catch the local ten o'clock news."

"I always watch the news just before going to bed each night," Pat prompted, encouraging Steven to elaborate. "A habit of yours as well?"

"We caught the story about that merger between those two powerhouse pharmaceutical companies out East. You know, keeping an eye on the competition," he said with a smile.

"No, I actually don't know. I think that will be all, Mr. MacPhearson," Sam informed him, "for now."

"That's it? Well, okay. Let me know if you need anything," he offered.

"We will," Pat said evenly.

As MacPhearson left, Sam turned to the glass and waved Melinda in. She appeared moments later and the three of them sat down at the table. They wanted a chance to talk before James MacPhearson arrived. He was scheduled in twenty minutes.

It came as no surprise to any of them when James MacPhearson's story matched that of his brother, down to the last detail.

"So, what's your take on the suits?" Sam asked, leaning forward, drumming his fingers on the table. Over a pot of bad coffee, Pat, Sam, and Melinda were discussing the facts of the case thus far. The only interesting piece of information that had come to light in the last twenty-four hours arose during their interview the day before with Jessica Monroe. When asked why Adison would have the name Katie Adams written in his notebook, she had looked puzzled.

"Isn't that Grant Adam's daughter?" she had asked.

"It is. Do you know of any reason why Will would have that name?"

"Well, the only thing I can think of is that it might be related to the study they were talking about last week," she had reasoned. Pat's gut told him Ms. Monroe really didn't know anything more than she was telling them.

"Go on," Melinda had encouraged, knowing that Jessica responded better to her than to either of the two men.

"Well, Grant asked if his daughter could be part of new study on bronchiosclerosis—she has it," Jessica had said, thinking back to that day. "I could hear them talking because Steven hadn't completely closed the door to the conference room. At first things were pretty quiet—not that I was deliberately eavesdropping. But then it got a lot louder."

"What do you mean? Were they shouting?" Melinda had asked.

"Not really shouting, but talking loudly," she clarified.

"Heatedly?" Sam pushed. Melinda had shot him a look. She should be handling this girl.

"Please don't put words in my mouth, Agent Davis. They were talking loudly. I could tell Will was upset, and Mr. Adams seemed angry."

"Do you know exactly why Will and Mr. Adams were upset, Jessica?"

"Yeah, Mr. Adams was mad at Will because he said Mr. Adams's daughter couldn't be in the study."

They agreed that, according to the evidence, Will Adison was most likely killed by someone he knew, possibly someone he knew well. Because the crime scene unit had not found any evidence of forced entry, it was probable that either he had let the killer into the cottage himself or the person had a key. Of course it was also possible Adison had left the door unlocked. Nothing of value had been taken from the cottage and Adison was found wearing a fairly expensive watch and his wedding ring. There was no sign of a struggle. And the use of methanol reflected careful planning. This was clearly not a case of burglary gone awry. Will Adison was killed for another reason, and it was their job to find it. Adison certainly had his fair share of people who would benefit if he were no longer around. Pat definitely wanted to talk to one of those people in particular. He wanted to talk to Grant Adams.

Monday, November 4

Grant couldn't believe the day had finally arrived. Katie, like all the other participants in this study, was going to receive the drug containing treatment for bronchiosclerosis. Since this was a trial in the third phase of research, there was a fair amount of data, gathered from earlier trials, to show the safety and efficacy of the drug. They could expect to see significant improvement within two to four weeks. Her coughing should decrease, she should have more energy, and her lung function should increase by anywhere from fifty to eighty percent. She might experience some minor side effects, but the benefits far outweighed any potential adverse events. Beth looked at him and, even though she said nothing, Grant could tell she was grateful.

When Katie returned to the exam room, both Dr. Carruthers and his nurse Tania explained the details of the study and the medication. Grant knew the background about clinical trial procedure, but Beth wanted to hear it from the doctor. Satisfied, Beth then asked about the specifics of this drug.

Katie would need to take two pills each day, with or without a meal, for the entire length of the study. Dr. Carruthers said the study was expected to last for twenty-six weeks. Half a year, Grant thought. Dr. Billings had told us that might be how long she had left to live. He looked at Katie and a wave of emotion swept over him. She was getting a chance.

Katie would be responsible for taking the pills herself, and she would fill out a chart with her parents as a reminder. The pills came with reminder stickers for the house and Grant had two sets already, one for his townhouse and one set for Beth's place. Katie would also be required to keep a medical journal, to record how she felt each day and if she noticed any side effects. Grant had worked on studies with similar procedures.

Grant was actually glad Beth was there. It was good for Katie to have both her

126

parents' support, and this way Beth had direct access to Dr. Carruthers. She never asked how Katie got into the study so shortly before it began. Neither Grant nor Dr. Carruthers offered that information.

They left the office just after four thirty and the three of them, at Katie's request, went out for pizza. Grant enjoyed himself more than he thought was possible, considering he had spent almost three hours with his ex-wife. It made Katie so happy. They managed to have a pleasant conversation, actually getting along, and not just for their daughter's benefit.

That night, when Grant and Katie got home, she gave him a long, tight hug. When she finally let him go, they walked into the kitchen, hand in hand. Grant poured her a glass of ice water and Katie Adams took her first pill containing the experimental drug to treat bronchiosclerosis.

After Katie went to bed, Grant cracked open a beer and sat down in front of the television. He wanted to see if there were any updates on the death of Will Adison. The police had questioned him again that morning. He was sure they considered him a suspect. They asked him again about Katie's name being written down in Adison's notebook and his whereabouts last Sunday night. He told them the same thing he told them before. They probably would have left him alone, too, if someone hadn't told them about Will not wanting Katie to be in the study. *It had to have been Jessica,* Grant thought. *She was the only one around when we had that meeting. She probably overheard me. I was so stressed that day; I was practically yelling at Will.*

"You told us earlier, Mr. Adams, that all four of you agreed about your daughter getting into the study, but we have a witness who says otherwise, says that Will Adison was against the idea," Sergeant Donnelly had told him. "Why did you lie?" he'd demanded.

"I know I shouldn't have lied, but I knew it would look bad if you thought Will didn't agree. The truth is, he changed his mind the next day. That's what he told James. Ask him," he had said, feeling beads of perspiration soak through his shirt.

"Oh, we will, Mr. Adams. We will."

Even though James would back him up, Grant knew the police probably wouldn't believe either one of them.

Tuesday, November 5

Christine Donnelly sat across the table from her husband. She was happy he was able to come home, even though it was just for the night. In her eighteen years of marriage to him, she couldn't recall another time when she had seen him looking more run-down.

"So, how did it go?" she asked cautiously. Pat had come back to Red Wing for a meeting with Chief Pedersen and the county attorney, Debra Mason. From his mood, it was clear things hadn't gone well.

"They want this case solved—yesterday—and yet they waste my time sitting in a stupid meeting," he said tensely. "Why aren't the lab reports in? Why haven't we been able to focus our investigation on one suspect? Why aren't we ready to arrest someone?" Christine let him continue, knowing he didn't expect answers from her.

"And yet, they stressed that in such a high-profile case, they want to make sure everything is done by the book. 'We want everything to hold up in court, Donnelly.' Who do they think I am? We're doing everything we can. Even the BCA says we're handling it fine. But Mason wants results—and fast. She's up for re-election next year. Wouldn't it be great for her campaign to have a murder trial under her belt? Putting a killer behind bars. It just doesn't get any better than that," he said bitterly.

"So you go back to the Twin Cities tomorrow?"

"Yeah, and it looks like I might be there awhile. We have to talk with a lot of people. Melinda and Sam have offered to bring in a few other agents from BCA for some more manpower and I think I'm going to take them up on it. There's just no way the three of us can cover this one," he sighed. He was exhausted. The initial adrenaline rush from the case had faded. Now the lack of sleep and the sheer stress were catching up with him. He wanted to spend some time with his family, but all he could think about was taking a long, hot shower, and crawling into bed. Hopefully Christine and the kids would understand.

The shower turned out to be much shorter than he would have liked. After only a few minutes of standing under the scalding spray, he heard a knock on the door. Christine came in holding the phone and told him it was urgent.

"Pat Donnelly here," he said as he turned off the water.

"Sergeant, sorry to bother you at home. I thought you might want to hear about this." It was Officer Scott Bailey, a rookie.

"Well, what is it?" Pat hoped he hadn't sounded too harsh. Bailey was a good kid.

"A call came in today from a man who claims to have seen a dark-colored sedan the night of Adison's murder," Bailey said.

"The car driving without its headlights?" Pat asked. Aside from Herb Anderson's statement, they had no leads on the mysterious vehicle.

"No, he said the car was parked outside Adison's cottage," he explained.

"Why did he wait so long to come forward?"

"Well, the guy saw the car from Adison's neighbor's window."

"So?"

"The neighbor is Mrs. Austin Greene. We spoke with her last Monday, to see if she had seen or heard anything unusual at the time of the incident."

"Yes, I remember, Bailey. There was nothing of significance in her statement. If I remember correctly, she said her husband was out of town." Pat was starting to put things together.

"Sir, the guy who called in, the guy she was with that night, wasn't Mr. Greene," Bailey said, confirming Pat's suspicions. "Seems Mrs. Greene has been having a little fun on the side."

"Did you run a vehicle search?"

"Yep. We already ran a check on the DMV records for our list of suspects," he said.

"I think I know where you're going with this, Bailey. I saw her pull into the parking lot at MacPhearson. Jessica Monroe drives a black sedan. She said she had left the cottage by then, but of course she could have been lying."

"Yes sir, she does. But there are two other people on the list you gave us who have registered vehicles that also fit the description."

"Who?"

"Barbara Adison and Dr. Oliver Klein."

Wednesday, November 6

The unexpectedly blue Seattle sky was just what Grant needed. His flight had landed at two forty-five in the afternoon, but he didn't need to report to the clinic until the next morning. He was monitoring with Allen Jennings. They had planned to meet in the hotel lobby and go out for dinner together. Grant would have preferred to eat on his own, but going out with Jennings would be a good way for him to get to know one of his direct reports better.

It still bothered him that he actually needed to get permission from Pat Donnelly for this trip. James and Steven had told him not to worry about it, but it couldn't look very good to have a new employee being watched by the police.

At five o'clock, as agreed, Grant and Allen met in the hotel lobby. They went out to a trendy Chinese restaurant for dinner. Jennings was good company. He kept Grant entertained with stories from his college days, which weren't that long ago. Grant shared a few of his own, and the two realized they both enjoyed tennis.

"Maybe we could play sometime after work," Allen suggested. "There's a park not too far from the office with decent courts."

"Now, you know, you'd have to let me win," Grant joked. "I'm one of the people who decides if you'll get a raise."

"Don't worry about it. I'm already in the hole for next year as far as MacPhearson is concerned," said Allen, shaking his head. "I'll play you to win."

"What do you mean, you're in the hole?"

"Oh, you'll like this one. I'm pulling into the parking lot one morning for work not too long ago and I can't see, because the sun is coming up and is right in my eyes. Well, I end up bumping the boss's car—his Beamer," Allen told him.

"Oh, no; I've heard that car is like a baby to James."

"You have no idea," Allen continued. "So he offers to not report it to the insurance agencies because it would make my rates go up, right? All I have to do is pay for the repairs. Which is fair because, like I said, it was totally my fault. And there was only this little dent and a few scratches. Guess how much it cost me?"

"No idea."

"Fifteen hundred dollars! Man, can you believe that shit? He's probably got a couple of million and I make peanuts." The beer was loosening him up.

"Yeah, I guess I won't hold it against you if you manage to beat me on the court. Just don't park next to me," Grant said dryly.

Grant watched as Allen ordered them both another round of drinks.

Thursday, November 7

Dr. Spencer's office was located in a private clinic on the east side of Seattle. The building was very modern, with massive windows and copper siding, and housed several private practices. Spencer's office was on the fourth floor, which meant a ride on the elevator. Grant tried to steady himself by leaning against the rail. His head was pounding and his stomach felt even worse. He was never going to drink again. Jennings, on the other hand, seemed totally unaffected by the night before. He had talked almost non-stop on the ride from the hotel to the clinic. Grant was already dreading their tennis match. Looking at how one night on the town affected him, Grant felt old. He used to be able to drink without consequence in college, but now his body just couldn't take it.

Monitoring was a detail-oriented task. It consisted of hours spent staring at files and going over medical records and documents in patient files. It could cause a headache on the best of days. Grant thought he would never make it through the day. He could barely stand on his own, he felt so weak. He looked at the clock when he felt like he couldn't take it anymore. It was nine o'clock.

After lunch, Grant reviewed the files of all fifteen patients. Just familiarizing himself with the site, he assured Jennings. Of the fifteen files, several contained errors. Dates were missing on some forms and a few patients had not been seen within the required time frame between study visits. Jennings knew that following protocol was extremely important in clinical research. But with studies involving hundreds of subjects at multiple sites, mistakes did happen.

Sunday, November 10

Pat felt refreshed after spending the weekend at home with his family. It had been just what he needed to maintain his sanity. This case wasn't going to be one of those open-and-shut deals.

Over the weekend he had been in contact with the officers and agents who were placing calls and interviewing people who had seen or heard anything in connection with the list of suspects in the case. Pat had a feeling they were looking in the right direction. They just needed to look harder.

So far, the only suspect who had a decent alibi was Barbara Adison. But even her whereabouts were only established for a portion of the evening. Several members of her book club verified her attendance at their meeting, which ended around nine thirty. Adison was most likely killed between the hours of eight and ten o'clock. If Barbara drove directly from the meeting to the cottage, she could have gotten there as early as ten thirty. George Woods felt Adison had died earlier than that, but he couldn't be absolutely certain. So while it wasn't likely that Barbara Adison would have had enough time to carry out her husband's murder, it was possible. She could not yet be eliminated as a suspect.

Jessica Monroe admitted seeing Adison on the day he was killed. She claimed she returned home in the early evening, but there were no witnesses. Her apartment did not use security cameras.

Oliver Klein had an alibi, but had no one who could back him on it. Apparently, he had gone on a date last Sunday evening with a woman he had met in a bar the previous weekend. They went to a nightclub and danced for an hour, two at the most. Her name was Jenny Johnson and Klein didn't know much more than that. All he knew was she lived in the Twin Cities and was a waitress. He couldn't even remember the name of the restaurant where she worked. She had called him for the date, and since he wasn't all that interested in her, he never bothered to ask for her number. Klein claimed he paid for their drinks with cash all night. None of the staff at the club remembered seeing him there.

And there was still Grant Adams.

Monday, November 11

Melinda Hendrickson shuffled through the pile of papers on the table in Sam's office. She had obtained a warrant for the release of phone records of calls made to and from Adison's cottage. On Saturday, October 26, the day before Adison was killed, he had placed three calls, one to his wife, another to James Mac-Phearson, and the last to a local pizza joint in Red Wing. The call to MacPhearson was placed at five fifteen and lasted twelve minutes. This evidence corroborated MacPhearson's statement that he had spoken with Will the day before he died. According to MacPhearson, Will seemed depressed during that conversation.

On Sunday morning, a call was placed from the cottage to the cellular phone of Dr. Oliver Klein. In his statement, Klein told them Adison had called him to check on things at the lab. He said it was not unusual for Will to check ongoing projects, even on the weekends. A handful of lab workers came in during weekends to run tests and maintain experiments. Will, himself a workaholic, saw no difference between calling Klein on a Sunday and on a workday. Will wanted updates on all the major projects, as well as results from some recent animal testing. The men also discussed upcoming projects and the supplies they'd order to initiate those jobs. Klein's cell phone records matched those of Adison's phone company. The call lasted twenty-two minutes.

She leaned back and closed her eyes. *Someone went down to that cottage for a visit. The only person we know was there,* she thought, *was Jessica Monroe. Obviously, someone is lying. Or,* she thought, *there's another solution we haven't even uncovered yet.* She checked her watch. Only eight thirty. It promised to be a long day of questioning witnesses, to check out alibis and hopefully gather new information. Melinda had her first appointment at ten o'clock at the law offices of Jones, Lewis, Sinclair, & Associates. Frederick Lewis handled estate matters for the firm's clientele. Information indicated Adison was in the process of changing his will; only he never had the chance. It was Hendrickson's job to try to find out what changes Adison was trying to make before he was killed.

∼

At the end of the afternoon, Grant picked up Katie from school and drove her to his office. Over the weekend she had convinced her dad to bring her to MacPhearson. She wanted to personally thank James and Steven for helping her get the treatment for bronchiosclerosis. Of course, she had no knowledge of everything that was done to enroll her in the study. Grant was reluctant, with all of the negative goings-on at the office, but she had insisted. And, just as when she was younger, she was able to get her way.

She clearly charmed them both. They talked and joked with her easily, not at all like two powerful corporate executives. *But they're family men, too*, Grant reminded himself. Steven had two sons and James, two daughters and a granddaughter.

As they were about to leave, Barbara Adison walked into the office. Grant knew Katie recognized her picture from the news, but his daughter was, thankfully, polite enough to not say anything. Grant thanked them once again and he and Katie left. They had another appointment with Dr. Carruthers.

"Seems like a sweet girl," Barbara Adison commented after they left.

"She is. We're so glad you could come in this afternoon, Barbara." James took her coat and offered her a seat. "We have much to discuss."

"The authorities have finally released Will's body. You should both know I have scheduled the visitation for Wednesday evening at Murphy & Sons' in St. Paul and the funeral service will be on Thursday, at eleven at St. Vincent's. We won't be going to the cemetery," she informed them. James understood. He knew Will had wanted to be cremated.

"Is there anything we can do for you?" Steven asked gently.

"Actually, my mother and sister are in town and Audrey and Paula have been kind enough to offer their help as well, but thank you." Will's mother had died just after college and he wasn't at all close with his father. He had no brothers or sisters.

"I don't have much time, so let's get down to business, shall we?" she suggested.

Her directness took Steven by surprise, but he was willing to honor her request.

"As you must know, Will's assets have been frozen during the course of the investigation. As his sole benefactor, however, I am able to act, in his place, as full partner at MacPhearson."

"You don't need to worry about that, Barbara. With all you've been through? We can take care of everything on the business end. Let us handle it," James offered. *God knows the woman has been through enough these last few days.*

"I'll probably take you up on that, James. For now. But eventually I want to get involved in the company. I want to make an informed decision when the time is right."

"A decision?" James asked.

"To decide whether I want to come on board or sell Will's portion of the company to both of you," she stated flatly. James glanced at his brother. They both knew that the value of the company would increase substantially when the treatment drug for bronchiosclerosis was approved and hit the market. If the company went public as planned, that would have tremendous impact on Will's share as well. Neither knew how much Will had told Barbara of their plans. Both of their wives were happy to spend the money without taking any interest in business matters. But Barbara was different. She was intelligent and had earned, although never utilized, some sort of business degree. James couldn't recall if it had been marketing or management. Either way, she was sure to do her homework before handing her share of the company over to them on a silver platter.

"Steven," she added, "I noticed Jessica Monroe wasn't at her desk."

"She's ... at an appointment," he stammered. How embarrassing for Barbara. Jessica was at one of her prenatal appointments.

"Please tell her to call me. There are a few things we need to discuss. Well, as I said, I do have to get going. I have been so busy these last few days. I think that's the only thing keeping me sane," she said as James helped her into her coat. He gave her a warm hug to let her know he meant what he said about being there for her.

"I'll have Jessica call you. Stay in touch, Barbara. And let us know if you need anything," Steven said gently, grabbing her hand. He wasn't usually an affectionate person, but she seemed almost vulnerable standing there. She had come to the office numerous times before, although the visits had decreased in the last few years, to see Will. She would laugh and talk with the employees and everyone had always taken an instant liking to her. Today she didn't seem like the same woman. As he watched her walk down the hall toward the stairs, Steven noted that she didn't speak to anyone.

∽

When she got into her car, Barbara Adison lit up a cigarette. She hadn't smoked since college, but had bought a pack earlier in the week. If ever there was a time for cheating, now was it. She had promised herself that as soon as the whole mess was over she would stop again. But for the time being, she needed something to help calm her nerves. It had been harder going to see them than she had anticipated. James and Will had been best friends at one time. She found herself expecting to see Will around every corner. It was hard to imagine the company without him.

She knew that she wanted to hold on to Will's share of the company for several more months. From what Will had told her, MacPhearson was on the brink of becoming a major player in the pharmaceutical industry. Why should she miss out on all that? She had certainly earned it.

Tuesday, November 12

Pat Donnelly sat in his hotel room, the contents of the case file spread out all over the bed. He was going to head to the BCA building, but wanted some time to sort things out on his own first. There was something bothering him, but he couldn't quite put his finger on it. The ringing phone broke his train of thought. And if that wasn't enough to irritate him, the call was.

Pat spent the next fifteen minutes getting chewed out by County Attorney Debra Mason. She wanted a progress report and was immediately frustrated the focus of the case was widening as opposed to narrowing on one or two suspects. She had to face the reporters, not Pat. Her office had to issue statements, not his. She made it seem as though hers was the toughest role to play in this whole case.

She wanted to give the media more details about the cause of death. Maybe if they appealed to the public, they might uncover some useful information, she reasoned. Pat was adamant about keeping certain aspects of the investigation quiet. It could be used as leverage when they got closer to breaking the case. Thankfully, Chief Pedersen was on Pat's side. Both men agreed the information obtained by forensics should not be made public for the time being. Pat was in charge of the case and nothing could be issued in a statement without Pat's consent. And, Pat reminded her, if there were any leaks, he would know exactly where to look. If she or any member of her office leaked information that jeopardized the case, he would make that information public. And that might not be the best publicity for her, considering her upcoming election. He knew it wasn't wise to make an enemy of her, but he didn't care at this point. He had a case to solve and didn't have the time or energy to play political games.

The day before, the crime scene technicians submitted a report with information Pat thought might be useful. Adison had been found fully clothed inside his vehicle. He wasn't, however, wearing any shoes. And even more intriguing was the fact that the soles of Adison's stocking feet were clean.

Woods's report suspected the amount of methanol in Adison's body was enough to render him unconscious, but not enough to kill him. There wasn't any reason they could gather why his shoes would be removed after he was killed. None were found in the near vicinity of the vehicle. And the missing beer bottle led them to believe the killer had spiked his beer with the methanol. Therefore, the clean socks suggested two key pieces of information: Adison passed out from the methanol in the cabin, and he hadn't walked to the car in his stocking feet.

Evidence gathered at the scene, from the flooring surfaces in the cabin—starting in the living area and bedrooms, through the kitchen, and out to the garage—was not consistent with dragging. Carpet fibers were undisturbed, and there were normal soil, hair, and dust patterns on the hardwood floors and kitchen tile. Whoever killed Adison had carried his body out to the garage and placed it in the vehicle. So either the killer was strong enough to carry Adison's one-hundred-seventy-five-pound body from the living room to the garage, or there was more than one person involved in Adison's death.

Unlike the cottage, the garage was not well kept. Dust and dirt on the floor could have revealed valuable information about the events of that night, but any footprints or other patterns had been compromised, if not intentionally by the killer then unintentionally by the officer responding to the scene. In his report, Officer Daniels stated that he had approached the vehicle to ascertain the condition of the person inside. His footprints alone had destroyed, or at least disturbed, crucial evidence. Pat knew it was in no way the officer's fault. The safety of the person inside the vehicle was top priority. If Adison had simply been unconscious, Daniels might have been able to save him. He did exactly what he was trained to do.

There was one other finding. After the witness came forward with the information about the dark sedan in the driveway, Pat, Sam, and Melinda had reviewed all of the notes and official reports gathered at the scene. On one page of handwritten notes from the morning Adison's body was discovered, a technician had jotted down information about a small stain in the driveway, about three inches in diameter. The technician indicated the fluid was most likely antifreeze and commented there was no other observable evidence in the driveway. There was no way of knowing if the stain was significant to the case, but it was possible it came from the car parked in the driveway the night of Adison's murder.

Pat ordered further tests from the BCA. Small chips were removed from the driveway and sent to the lab for analysis. Laboratory tests determined the fluid left on the driveway was antifreeze, but could not ascertain how long the stain had been there. Adison's car had no leak. Now that they had a list of vehicles matching the description given by the witness, they could check them for leaks and compare antifreeze concentrations. It was a long shot. Any vehicle, even the pizza delivery car from the night before the murder, could have left the stain. And the car in question could have already been repaired.

As in many cases, even the smallest amount of physical evidence could tell them the story about what happened in the last hours of Adison's life. Pat, Sam, and Melinda all agreed the murder was played out in several carefully executed steps. Because there was no evidence of forced entry, Adison must have let the killer into his cottage or left the door unlocked. Will was given the methanol, most likely in his beer. Then, once he lost consciousness, his body was carried out to the garage and placed in his vehicle. Adison's car was turned on and left running with the garage door closed. The killer probably went back into the house, waited until Adison was dead, and left once the job was done, creating the perfect illusion of a suicide.

Now that they had pieced together the *how*, they needed to find the *who*.

Wednesday, November 13

Barbara Adison looked as well as could be expected standing near the back of the gathering room at Murphy & Sons' Funeral Home. She was dressed in a long, flowered skirt and black jacket. Her mother and sister were on either side of her, as if standing guard. The room was crowded and the mood subdued. Will had died young, and many people had turned out to show support for his grieving widow.

Three people in the room, however, had never met Will Adison, at least not while he was alive. Sam Davis, Melinda Hendrickson, and Pat Donnelly asked Barbara if they could come to both services, to observe the mourners. The majority of the people in the room were Will's friends from MacPhearson. Pat Donnelly recognized several of them on sight. He was waiting for one particular guest. Approximately twenty minutes after Oliver Klein arrived, Pat gave the signal. He chatted with Klein for a few minutes to ensure Melinda and Sam an unnoticed exit. Barbara Adison, he observed, was busy talking with guests.

Outside, Melinda spotted Barbara's car immediately. Hours earlier she had watched as Barbara, her sister, and mother arrived at the funeral home. The two women had flown in from out of town, but it was a stroke of luck that they chose to drive Barbara's car instead of their rental. She looked around casually and then dropped to her knees. On the ground she laid a plain gold ring, which was actually Sam's wedding ring, in case anyone questioned her actions. The car had been parked for just over two hours. There was no liquid on the pavement beneath her vehicle, and the underside showed no visible leaks.

Sam, on the other end of the lot, performed the same act, using his keys as the dropped object. While they checked Barbara's vehicle to be thorough, Oliver Klein's was their main target. Someone Klein's size could easily have carried Adison's body. Sam dropped to his knees and, grasping the keys in his hand, looked under the dark blue sedan. Nothing.

Pat himself had checked under Jessica Monroe's Honda Accord earlier that day on the street in front of her apartment building. Her car had been clean as well.

It was important to check the vehicles on public property, since they could look without obtaining a warrant. Pat wanted to keep this piece of information quiet for the time being. Although any connection between the residue left at the scene and a leak from a suspect's vehicle would be purely circumstantial, it could point them in the right direction. Any lead was worth pursuing.

But in this case, the pursuit led to yet another dead end.

~

Later that afternoon, Melinda Hendrickson met with Frederick Lewis to discuss Will Adison's estate. Adison had called him the third week in October to discuss changing his will. Adison wanted to name his unborn child as a benefactor. Lewis had drawn up the papers himself, but Adison never made it to the appointment. It was scheduled for the thirtieth of October, three days after Will Adison's death.

The meeting with Lewis gave Melinda Hendrickson one other interesting piece of information. Barbara Adison had called her primary attorney, Rebecca Sinclair, several times in the last few days. She wanted to know how fast she would be able to access Will's assets. Since the newly drafted version of the will had never been signed, Barbara Adison remained the sole beneficiary of her husband's estate.

Thursday, November 14

Thursday morning seemed to reflect the emotion of the day. The sky over St. Vincent's was cold, gray, and depressing. The wind was sharp and leaves blew across the city in swirling, dancing patterns. Winter was making its presence known; a few feathery snowflakes drifted toward the ground during the midafternoon. It felt like a day for a funeral.

Because Adison had wished to be cremated, the service at the church was immediately followed by a luncheon at the country club. Will loved the club and Barbara had many fond memories of him there. The manager had arranged a buffet of hors d'oeuvres, fruit, vegetables, and salads. The tables were simple but elegant, with flowers and a white candle on each to warm the room.

Jessica stared out the window of the club, looking at the gray waves of the St. Croix River crashing against the banks below. These last two days had been the worst of her life. Now everything seemed so final. Will was gone. The man she loved and the father of her baby—gone. Her child would never have the chance to play catch in the backyard or go on family trips. Not with Will. Now all she and the baby had were each other.

At first Jessica hadn't planned on going. She tried to tell herself it was out of respect for Barbara that she wouldn't attend, but the truth was, Jessica hated funerals.

In fact, her grandfather's funeral, almost twenty years before, was the last one she had attended.

But then Steven had given her the message that Barbara wanted to talk with her. She had been terrified as she dialed the phone. She and Barbara had not spoken since Will confessed their relationship to his wife. Barbara was not friendly on the phone, but she was cordial. She thought it was important Jessica be there for the services. She admitted it was not her preference, but Jessica was carrying Will's child and he or she should be there. For Will, she had explained.

There was no way for Jessica to back out. And so she attended both services, ignoring the stares and the whispers, ignoring the gossip and the scornful looks. She was there for Will and for their baby.

She turned away from the window just in time to see Agent Sam Davis quickly turn his gaze. She had seen Davis, as well as Melinda Hendrickson and Pat Donnelly, last night as well. They were there as part of the investigation, watching, waiting for someone to make a mistake. It made her angry. They weren't there because they cared about Will. They were like vultures, circling and waiting.

$\sim$

Oliver Klein wanted to leave. He had gone to the visitation the night before and made an appearance at the service. He was sitting at a table with Tara Wolfe and a few other researchers. All were busy sharing stories of Will, talking about his brilliant career and wondering how MacPhearson would fare in his absence. Oliver could hardly stand it. Only a funeral could make people forget about how flawed a person was in real life. He swallowed his comments along with another sip of wine. *At least there's alcohol here,* he thought. It was about the only thing helping him get through the day.

"So when do you think they'll hire his replacement?" asked Stephanie Fields, a researcher in the animal lab. Only Tara knew of Oliver's appointment as lab director. He had to tell someone about his promotion and she had been in the lab just after his meeting with James and Steven. Tara was on her third glass of wine and Oliver could tell she was feeling the effects. He anticipated what was coming, but was helpless to stop it.

"Oh, they already have the position filled," Tara said, forgetting the information was privileged. There it was. It was only a matter of time. Why had he told her?

Realizing what she had done, she tried unsuccessfully to change the subject, but her efforts were too little, too late. Oliver leaned forward and rescued her.

"I will be taking over as the new lab director," he stated without emotion. This was not the way he had envisioned spreading the word of his promotion. Not that day. Not at Will's funeral.

The employees at the table all started talking at once, asking questions and offering congratulations. Oliver was quickly caught up in the moment and slipped easily into accepting their compliments. He never noticed the person sitting behind him, one table away.

Pat heard every word. It made sense. Oliver Klein was strong enough to carry Adison's body. Oliver Klein drove a blue sedan. Oliver Klein didn't have an airtight alibi for the night of the murder. And now he knew Oliver Klein had a motive for killing Will Adison.

Friday, November 15

Pat Donnelly shared what he had overheard at the luncheon the day before. He also voiced his contention that Klein appeared to be their strongest suspect. Neither Jessica Monroe nor Barbara Adison could have carried the body without assistance. Unless they were working with someone else, or new evidence proved otherwise, it looked like they could be ruled out at this point.

"Unless one of them hired someone to do it," Melinda said aloud. So far they had assumed the individual responsible had committed the murder. But there was an outside chance the killer paid someone else to do the dirty work.

"True. We haven't considered a murder-for-hire scenario yet," Sam contemplated.

"I just don't think that's the case here. It seems too personal. And don't forget about the missing beer bottle," he reasoned. "Why would Adison have drinks with a stranger? No, I think we were right when we said Adison knew his killer."

"Yeah, I agree," Melinda nodded. "Adison wasn't the type to just invite a stranger into his home to knock back a few. He seemed too private for that."

"Pat's right. Unless the ladies weren't in it alone, I think they are at the bottom of the list. And Klein's at the top—for now. And we still have Adams, and James and Steven MacPhearson. I think we should focus our efforts on those four men," Sam said, leaning back in his chair. It was only ten o'clock and already his back was sore.

Without warning, the list of four men suddenly grew to six. At ten minutes after ten, a young male agent informed them a call had come into the St. Paul Police Department, which was then relayed to the BCA.

"An anonymous caller said he was in a bar in St. Paul the Saturday night before the murder. He was hanging out with friends, shooting some pool. Anyway, he and a friend played a game against two guys who had been playing at the table next to him. According to this witness, they're brothers—clean-cut, upper-class. And both were drinking a lot. Apparently during the game they started talking about this other guy. They said he deserved to be beaten to a bloody pulp for what he had done. The caller couldn't be sure, but he thinks he heard them say the guy's name was Adison.

"When he saw the news the caller started to put the pieces together. He thought we should check it out, but didn't want to give his name."

"Brothers? James and Steven MacPhearson," Pat concluded aloud.

"No. The names of these two guys," the agent informed them, "are Jason and Randy Monroe."

~

That evening Grant and Katie went out for dinner. They went to one of their favorite places to eat, one famous for its gigantic burritos. They were celebrating the good news they received at Katie's appointment. The drug appeared to be working already. After just eleven days of treatment, the swelling in her bronchioles had noticeably reduced and her lung capacity had increased by almost twenty percent. Dr. Carruthers said her system was responding well to the medication.

She even looked healthier, Grant thought as he watched her take an enormous bite out of her burrito. She smiled, trying to keep her mouth closed and chew at the same time. It was so good to see her happy again. And she didn't seem to mind the idea of having to take medication for the rest of her life. She said it was just like taking vitamins. One of her new friends from school, she told him, was diabetic and had to give herself shots every day. Compared to that, two little pills were nothing to complain about.

On the way home, they stopped for hot chocolate and a walk along the river. Katie was going to be spending Thanksgiving with Beth, so she was staying home for the weekend. Grant was going to miss not having her around for the holiday, but even with that, he had a lot to be thankful for.

Saturday, November 16

Just as she was stepping out of the shower, Barbara Adison heard a knock at the back door of her condo. Her mother and sister had gone for a walk on the trails just behind the complex. One of them must have forgotten to bring along a key.

She quickly wrapped herself in her thick, white, cotton robe and ran to the door. When she opened it, she was completely surprised.

"What are you doing here?" she asked curiously.

"Just let me in before anyone sees me," he snapped at her.

She stepped back and let him in, looking around to make sure no one was in sight.

"I thought we agreed we weren't going to be seen together for awhile," she said harshly. "I'm alone right now, but my mother and sister could be back any minute."

"Things have changed."

"What, what's happened?"

"Will's project. From his notes I was able to figure it out. This is it!" he said excitedly.

"Are you sure?" She couldn't believe it. This was all happening much faster than she thought it would.

"Absolutely," he said. "Do you understand what this means? This is going to change everything."

Sunday, November 17

Sergeant Pat Donnelly slowed the car as he neared Lake of the Isles. Most of the houses were set back from the street, with beautiful views of the lake. This Minneapolis neighborhood was quite exclusive, according to Sam Davis. After the officer's news, they had done some digging on Jessica Monroe's two brothers, Randall and Jason.

Both men were successful and highly educated. Randall, age thirty-three, was engaged to be married the following summer and was employed as a financial analyst with a firm in downtown Minneapolis. Jason, two years younger, also unmarried, was an advertising executive. Both brothers, along with their father, Richard, were known to be protective of the only girl in the family, Jessica. In fact, although neither young man had a record, both had been picked up in college for getting into a fight with a student outside the community high school. According to the police report, the student had been spreading rumors about their sister.

Pat was interested to find out if they were still protective. How would they react to the news that their little sister was pregnant with the child of a married man?

This was a completely new angle and one Pat hadn't anticipated. He thought Adison's killer was somehow connected with MacPhearson. Could they have been looking in the wrong direction all along?

Pat shook his head as he walked along the stone path leading up to the house. Jessica Monroe came from a very wealthy family.

"Come in, Sergeant." Richard Monroe, tall and strong featured, opened the door just as Pat stepped onto the front porch. He was an intimidating presence. Pat suddenly felt sympathetic toward any boy Jessica Monroe had dated in high school.

"Thank you, Mr. Monroe," he answered as he stepped inside. He took off his hat and coat, which Richard Monroe took and hung inside a nearby closet. He led Pat into a small sitting room just off the foyer. The room was cozy, with comfortable leather chairs and a small fire inside a stone fireplace. It was exactly the kind of room, Pat thought, for sipping a good cup of coffee and reading the newspaper.

"Would you like anything to drink, Sergeant?"

"No," he said, shaking his head, "no, thank you. I'll just wait for Randall and Jason to arrive."

"They should be here shortly. Randy was going to pick up Jason on his way over. Both boys live here in Minneapolis. You said on the phone you're from Red Wing. Are you familiar with the Twin Cities?" Mr. Monroe seemed nervous. Pat could tell by the way he spoke and noticed that his hands, holding a drink, were unsteady.

"Somewhat. I'm staying at a hotel in St. Paul. But I make it up to the Cities a few times each year—museums, sporting events, theater. Come up for dinner sometimes," he answered. Christine loved coming up to Minneapolis to see plays, attend art exhibits, and go shopping. Pat wasn't as interested in the arts as he was in sports, but it made her happy. It gave them a chance to spend time alone together. A few times, for a birthday or anniversary, they would leave the kids with Christine's parents and they would stay overnight or for the weekend.

"And here they are," Richard said, looking over Pat's shoulder out the window.

Pat turned and saw a car pull into the driveway. A few minutes later they came into the house and stepped into the sitting room. During introductions Pat noted both young men resembled their father.

"As I said on the phone, I'm investigating the death of Will Adison of Mac-Phearson Pharmaceuticals. We know he was involved with your sister, Jessica," he began. He watched their faces carefully for any signs of reaction to the mention of Adison's and Jessica's names. So far, there were none.

"And how exactly can my boys help you, Sergeant?" Pat was surprised it had taken him that long to ask the question. When he had called Jessica that morning, she had said her brothers and father were planning to watch the Vikings game at her parents' house. Pat had called Richard Monroe to confirm that both Randy and Jason would be there just before noon. Richard Monroe had simply said Pat was welcome to come to his home to talk with his sons. He didn't ask why, leading Pat to conclude Richard Monroe knew exactly what this was about.

"On the evening of Saturday, October twenty-sixth, you were both at a bar in St. Paul called the Ninth Avenue Tap, is that correct?" he asked.

"Yeah, that sounds about right. An old friend from college was in town and he called up some guys we hadn't seen in a while. We all decided to go out, shoot some pool, catch up, you know," Randy said. His manner was calm, collected, and very professional. Jason nodded, but said nothing.

"At this bar, you were overheard discussing your sister's situation with Adison." It was a statement, not a question. "Can you tell me what was said during that conversation?"

"Well, Jessie had just told us she was seeing this married guy from work. If that wasn't bad enough, she then told us she was pregnant. You can understand why we'd be a little upset." Randy's composure was slowly unraveling. It was exactly what Pat wanted.

"How could he do that to her, and then not stand by her?" Jason had finally found his voice. It was much higher than Pat had anticipated, making him sound young.

"You know what it's like to want to protect your children? Do you have any daughters, Sergeant?" Richard Monroe asked. Pat ignored the question.

"I understand why you might be concerned about the situation. I'm just trying to do my job. Randy, Jason, where were you on the evening of October twenty-seventh?"

"Sergeant, this doesn't sound like the kind of conversation you described when we spoke on the phone. It sounds to me like my boys are being questioned, and if that's the case, I would prefer it if my lawyer were present." Richard Monroe stood up abruptly, but his son stopped him.

"No, Dad, it's fine," Randy said. He turned to Pat and leaned forward, as if about to share a piece of very important information. Pat was listening. "On that evening, I was at my church." He sat back with a look of smug satisfaction.

"Church? On a Sunday evening?" Pat asked. He found the expression on Randy's face irritating.

"I'm on the church finance committee. With my background, they asked me to help out with the budget and the books for this year. At St. Michael's over in Richfield. We meet once a month on Sunday evenings. At least ten people saw me there, two of whom are priests." The expression remained unchanged.

"And at what time did this meeting end?"

"They usually go pretty late, and that one was later than usual because we had the school budget to go over. I'd say I got home around eleven forty-five, but you could call the church and have the secretary give you a copy of the minutes."

"I'll have an agent go over to the church in the next day or two," Pat said. *An alibi doesn't get much more airtight than that*, he had to admit. But Jason had yet to answer. Pat looked at him expectantly.

It turned out Jason's friend had gotten tickets to see a play at the Guthrie Theater in Minneapolis. They had met several friends from work there and went out for a late dinner after the show. He didn't arrive home until after eleven and his two roommates could verify that he stayed at his apartment for the remainder of the evening.

Pat thanked the Monroes and left. What had seemed like an interesting angle on the drive over had now been only a diversion. But he still put in a call and requested an agent check out witnesses to corroborate the alibis of both Randy and Jason Monroe. They seemed privileged and arrogant, yes, but not killers. But Pat had been an investigator long enough to know some of the most brutal murders were committed by people whose neighbors and friends thought of them as friendly and kind. "Oh, no, Sergeant," they would say, "he would never hurt a fly!"

And so, Pat thought with frustration, *I'm right back where I started.*

Monday, November 18

Oliver Klein settled back into the black leather chair that had just been delivered to his new office. The police had searched Will's office and seized his files, but returned them shortly after. Oliver had Will's things boxed up and placed in storage on the second floor, keeping only the desk and file cabinets. Of course, most of the files would remain intact, but Oliver wanted nothing of Will's that wasn't MacPhearson-related. James and Steven offered to purchase all new office furniture, but Oliver actually liked the heavy, oak desk, matching file cabinets, and worktable. Only the chair he wanted new.

It was still stiff and smelled strongly of leather. Oliver was testing it out, leaning back and swiveling, when Tara Wolfe surprised him.

"Dr. Klein?" she said from behind him. He nearly fell out of the chair.

"Oh, ah, yes, Tara? What can I do for you?" he stammered.

"There are some old files of Will's out here, too. Mostly notes on older projects. What do you want me to do with them?"

"Is there anything we might need?"

"To be honest, most of it looks pretty old and Will's handwriting was so bad, I don't think we could make anything out of them anyway. I know all of his important notes on projects were put into the computer, so we could all read them," she smiled, "so the paper notes are just back-ups, really."

"Put them in one of these boxes," he said, handing her a cardboard carton, "and I'll send them upstairs with the rest of his things. I'll have personnel call Barbara Adison to see if she wants us to store his personal things here, or if she wants to come and pick them up."

"They should all fit in here. I'll just bring them back when I'm done."

"Thank you, Tara. I'll see you at the meeting?" he asked. He had scheduled a meeting with the entire laboratory staff to explain his role as the new director. He wanted them to know that their positions and primary responsibilities would not change, but he planned on taking a more active part in the day-to-day operations than Will had. He also wanted them to know he was going to ask James and Steven for an increase in wages. It was a constant complaint in the lab that researchers at MacPhearson had salaries below industry standards. Oliver knew the announcement would not only help his direct reports get fair compensation for the work they performed, but would also paint him in a very positive light with his new team of employees. He was no longer their colleague or supervisor. He was Director of Laboratory Operations.

No matter how many times he said it, he couldn't help but smile.

Tuesday, November 19

Jessica Monroe shrank back. The gel for the ultrasound scope was colder than she had expected. The technician smiled as she turned on the monitor to the right of the examination table.

It was nothing short of amazing. This ultrasound, unlike the first, provided a clear image of her baby. Jessica could see the tiny hands and one of the small feet. The tech slid the scope across her belly and pointed to the outline of the baby's head.

"Does everything seem to be okay?" Jessica asked. She was worried somehow the past weeks might have had an effect on the baby.

"Everything looks just fine," the tech reassured. Her soothing voice helped Jessica relax a bit and enjoy seeing her baby. She could now see the second foot. The baby was so active, and Jessica could see it moving on the screen as she felt the tiny flutters in her stomach. She spent the next few minutes absorbed in the experience. She was going to have a baby. All of a sudden it seemed very real to her.

"Would you like to know the sex of your baby?" the tech asked.

Jessica answered without moving her eyes from the screen. "Yes, I would," she said quietly. She always thought she would want to wait until her babies were born to find out. Better to be surprised. But for some reason, with this baby, she felt she had to know.

Later, in her apartment, Jessica's eyes filled with tears as she looked at the photos of her son. She had already chosen a name for him: Liam, the Scottish version of Will.

Friday, November 22

It had been a long week. At least they were getting some answers, Pat thought as he drove south on Highway 61. He was heading home for the weekend. He needed the break and Melinda and Sam had agreed they all needed to take some time to process the information they had. It was the same advice Pat gave his daughter, Kelsey, when she would struggle with a problem in her algebra class. She would defeat herself by giving up in frustration. Pat always told her to step back from the problem. After a few minutes, she would be in the right mindset, able to see things clearly. The solution seemed obvious. Pat was hoping that would happen in this case.

The week had yielded some valuable information. Agents from the BCA had checked out Randy and Jason Monroe. Both alibis were confirmed by several reliable witnesses, which was no surprise to Pat. And they weren't the only ones who were now officially crossed off the list.

Until this morning, Pat thought Oliver Klein could be their guy. He had both motive and opportunity. He was now the director of the lab at MacPhearson, he was strong, and he drove the right kind of car. But Klein had lucked out when Jenny Johnson called him for another date. This time he made certain to get her number, which he handed over to the authorities. She confirmed he had been with her on the night in question. Oliver Klein was dancing and drinking in St. Paul while Adison was being murdered in Red Wing.

Pat still had a feeling about Grant Adams. Adams knew something, he was sure of it. The way he avoided looking Pat in the eye and how his manner fluctuated between nervousness and confidence was suspicious. When he got back on Monday, he planned to follow up on his instincts. Grant Adams was hiding something.

Saturday, November 23

Trish Garrett was growing impatient. They had been sitting in the Urgent Care lobby of Regions Hospital for almost an hour. Tommy was curled up on the vinyl seat next to hers, his head in her lap. He had finally fallen asleep. Scott was on the other side of him, trying not to look worried. But Trish knew better. She had seen the look in his eyes when he came in, holding Tommy. Blood stained the front of his t-shirt.

They left in a rush, Trish even leaving behind her purse. Speeding along the residential streets, she felt the drive to the hospital lasted far too long. *What's happening to him?*

And now they sat here waiting? For what?

"Mr. and Mrs. Garrett?" A young woman in scrubs came over to where they were sitting. She gave a sympathetic smile toward Tommy.

"We have an exam room ready for Tommy. Do you want to carry him back?" she asked.

"Yes, yes. Is there a doctor who can see him right away?" Scott didn't bother to hide the frustration in his voice.

"Actually, we've called in Dr. Fischer, who specializes in bronchiosclerosis. When your wife told me about Tommy's history, we had him paged. He's waiting for you inside," she explained as they walked. She stopped and showed them into a small triage room, closing the curtain as she left.

Dr. Fischer was a gentle-looking man with kind blue eyes and dark hair just beginning to show strands of gray. He helped Scott lay Tommy carefully on the examination table. The change in position woke Tommy and he rubbed his eyes, squinting from the bright light above his head.

"Hello, Tommy. I'm Dr. Fischer. I understand you've been coughing a lot this morning. Is that right?"

Tommy looked at both his mom and dad. When they nodded he answered, looking at the doctor. "Yes, I've been coughing a lot today."

"Does it hurt when you cough, Tommy?"

"A little."

"Is it hard for you to breathe?"

"Yes," Tommy nodded, looking as if he were about to cry. "It feels like it does when I run too hard. My chest hurts."

"Tommy, I want to listen to you breathe and I'm going to put this stethoscope on your back so I can hear your heart and lungs working, okay?" Dr. Fischer looked at Tommy's parents. They were frightened.

"You noticed the blood earlier this morning?" He directed his question at Scott. Of the two, he seemed more stable.

"Yes. Is it his bronchiosclerosis, Doctor?" Scott didn't know why he even asked. He already knew the answer.

"That's my thinking, but let's see," he said, holding the stethoscope against Tommy's pale skin. Tommy looked up at Trish with wide eyes. He was scared. She couldn't bear to see her son that way.

"The doctor is trying to help you, honey. It won't hurt, I promise," she whispered, reaching for him. She stroked his little fingers and squeezed his hand, hoping it might help.

After only a few minutes, Dr. Fischer ordered an x-ray of Tommy's chest and back. He was certain Tommy's lungs were blocked with plaque caused by the disease, but needed the x-ray to determine how far it had progressed.

"I think the images will show partial blockage of Tommy's lungs, in the bronchioles. As you already know, bronchiosclerosis causes deposits to form which then create a coating on the interior lining of the bronchial tubes. This coating then picks up any debris entering the area and eventually hardens, resulting in a narrowing of the tubes.

"Listening to Tommy's labored breathing, I can tell he has at least some blockage already, but I want more tests to see how severe his condition is. We need to see how the disease is progressing before we can decide a course of action. Unfortunately, we're very limited as to what we can do at this stage. There are treatments being tested, but none are available at this point in time. I want you to prepare yourselves," he said quietly. After nineteen years in medicine this was the part of his job he hated the most. Even without seeing the test results, he knew Tommy Garrett was dying.

Sunday, November 24

The plane had been warm and stuffy, but now Barbara Adison pulled her coat across her lap. The cabin temperature must have dropped ten degrees since take-off. In wool pants and a jacket, she was probably dressed too warmly for Florida. But the chill and dampness of the Minnesota fall had settled in and she couldn't bear to leave the house with only a lightweight jacket. Will had always joked she would never make it in a survival course. She wouldn't be able to leave anything behind.

Will. Thinking about him made her feel alone. Where had things gone so terribly wrong? How had everything spiraled out of control before she even realized what was happening?

It probably started when they found out they couldn't have a baby. They both wanted one so desperately. Most people just assume they will get married and raise a family, but it doesn't always work out that way. She had spent more than a few years in a depressed state, neglecting herself and Will, not wanting to go out or see friends or family. Everything reminded her of the child she would never have. Commercials on television, movies, even books seemed to revolve around children.

Yes, she thought as she leaned her head against the back of the seat, *it was probably then that our marriage began to unravel.* She began taking anti-depressants and saw a therapist, but she was never the same. She felt like a failure. Will had asked her if they should think about adoption. But Barbara knew that was a long journey with no guarantees, and her heart couldn't handle any more disappointments. No, she had decided that she would rather accept the fact she would never be a mother, and try to move on with her life.

And she did. She took classes, learned to cook, traveled, and played a wonderful Auntie Barb to her sister's daughter and son. They adored her, and somehow they helped ease her pain until gradually it faded.

She hadn't known about the affair until Will's confession. He didn't have to tell her, but couldn't take the guilt. It had come as a complete surprise to her until she thought back to all of the subtle hints he had left for her.

She hadn't even asked for any details. She simply said she understood and did not want a divorce. She just wanted him to leave her alone.

But when she found out about the baby, it crushed her. *How could he have done this to me?*

Her mother was right. Some sun and rest would be good for her. Her family was meeting at her mother's condo in Boca Raton for the Thanksgiving holiday. She would spend a week there, playing on the beach with her niece and nephew, reading, sleeping, and recovering from the events of the past month.

It angered her that she had to notify Sergeant Donnelly about her plans. He made some calls to verify where she would be staying, but had given her the green light the day after she called. She asked if there had been any new information about the case. "Still working on it," he had told her. "Following up on several leads in the case, Ma'am."

She wondered how long it would take for them to find the truth.

Monday, November 25

Pat smiled to himself as he drove north along the highway. An offhanded comment, dropped during an interview almost one month before, became salient the night before in the calm of his living room.

As usual, he and Christine had watched the ten o'clock news together before going to bed. Poor weather conditions were expected and Christine was concerned about his drive. Channel Five, in an attempt to entice viewers to watch key segments, announced the times certain reports would air during the program. The complete weather report aired at fourteen minutes past ten. After watching several stories, the weather segment finally set his wife's mind at ease. The worst of the snowstorm was supposed to stay to the south. Christine went to bed, but Pat had decided to catch the rest of the program. Every single segment involved news at the state or local level. It dawned on him that the ten o'clock news wouldn't air a report about a business merger of two companies with no local ties.

Most people are not good liars, and those who are usually become overconfident at some point. In either case, errors are made and cases are solved. The guilty party offers too much information, adds too many details in an attempt to make the lie sound believable.

That one innocuous remark could be the very thing to help Pat catch Will Adison's killer.

Sunday, December 1

The Thanksgiving holiday had given skiers and snowboarders one more reason to be thankful. A snowstorm, much worse than had been predicted by the weather forecasters, dumped almost nine inches of snow on the Minneapolis-St. Paul metro area from early Friday afternoon through late Saturday night, causing hazardous roads and an incredible number of traffic accidents.

By Sunday, however, the roads were clear and the only reminder of the storm was a beautiful blanket of pristine snow. Oliver loved the first snowfall of the year. Everything looked so fresh and clean, unlike later in the season when the plows and traffic turned the snow a filthy gray. An adept skier, he usually hit the slopes as soon as the season began. But this year was different. This year, he had to focus on his work.

Not wanting to face the crowded airports and the holiday bustle, Oliver opted to stay home over the long weekend. His sister had invited him to her house in Michigan, but he was going to be seeing his family at Christmas, so he decided not to accept.

The four days were well spent; he accomplished even more than he had intended. Things were going much better than expected. It had been a long time since he actually enjoyed what he was doing. With only a few researchers in the building, he could focus on his projects, instead of babysitting the staff. He liked working in Will's lab. It was private and well designed. It was amazing how much he could complete when his time was uninterrupted.

If things continued to go as they had the last few days, he might have the experiment concluded by early the following week. It was invigorating for him to be part of a company with such exciting projects in the works. No wonder Will had stayed away from the management part of the lab. The science side was much more appealing.

He was about to unpack a fresh tray of tubes to use later when his cell phone rang.

"Hello?" he answered gruffly. He was not in the mood to be disturbed.

"We need to talk. Can you meet me?"

"Now?" he asked. He looked reluctantly at the tubes on the counter.

"Yes. You know where. I'll see you in half an hour." He heard the click before he had a chance to respond.

Ten minutes later, Oliver Klein switched out the light and locked the doors to his office and the adjoining lab.

Tuesday, December 3

Steven MacPhearson's morning had not gotten off to a good start. He had been out of the office since the previous Wednesday, and his workload had increased substantially judging by the look of his desk. His voicemail was even worse; he had twenty-eight new messages. He sat down and started to sift through the piles: documents for him to review and sign, minutes from meetings he had missed the day before. He absently pushed the speaker key on the desk phone so he could listen as he worked. Most were routine, but one in particular, left at eight thirty the previous morning, caught his attention.

"Hello, Mr. MacPhearson. This is Sergeant Pat Donnelly. I spoke with your assistant, Ms. Monroe, but she wasn't able to help me. I just had a few more questions for you. Give me a call when you get back into the office."

So the police wanted to talk with him again.

Without listening to the last two messages, Steven walked to his brother's office.

~

Pat Donnelly sat in Sam's office with his arms folded across his chest. Just when he thought he had a good lead, the case took an unexpected twist.

Yesterday, Melinda Hendrickson had gone over to MacPhearson Pharmaceuticals to talk with Jessica Monroe. Jessica was very upset her brothers had been questioned as suspects, and to keep her receptive to talking with them, they figured an apology from Melinda would go a long way. It did.

Jessica was skeptical at first, but Melinda had explained the police were just trying to find the person who was responsible for Will's death. Didn't she want the person who killed her baby's father to be brought to justice?

Jessica nodded and showed Melinda the pictures from the ultrasound. Jessica carried them in a folder inside her purse. Melinda knew her ruffled feathers had been smoothed. They chatted for a few more minutes. Before she left, Melinda told Jessica they would still be in touch. Jessica again offered any help they might need.

That exchange was not all that significant in and of itself, but what happened just after was critical.

As she was walking across the parking lot, Melinda had noticed Grant Adams pulling away from a parking space near her car. She couldn't be sure why she even looked. But she did.

On the pavement, under the spot where Grant Adams's car had been parked, there was a small puddle of fluid that appeared to be antifreeze. She immediately collected a sample to compare with the substance found at the scene.

The list of vehicles matching the description given by the witness in Red Wing was narrowed only to dark sedans. The officer had excluded vehicles of other colors. Grant Adams drove a sedan that was registered as red with the Department of Motor Vehicles. In reality it was a deep red, flecked with black. It could easily have been mistaken for dark blue or black in poor lighting conditions.

"How does Grant Adams fit into all of this?" Pat asked, shaking his head in frustration.

Wednesday, December 4

The police were handed an opportunity. The lab results comparing the antifreeze from Adams's car to that found on Adison's driveway were delivered first thing that morning, enabling Sam, Melinda, and Pat to formulate a plan for their interview with Grant Adams. It had to be executed perfectly.

"Oh, Mr. Adams, come in." Sam greeted Grant as he approached the doorway from the hall. "We've been expecting you."

"Good morning," Grant said hesitantly. Sam Davis and Pat Donnelly smiled at him and offered him a seat. This was the last place he wanted to be.

"Our investigation has taken a rather interesting turn of events recently, Mr. Adams. And I have to admit, things aren't looking very good for you."

"I don't understand."

"Let me fill you in then." Pat was sitting on the corner of the desk. He leaned back, appearing relaxed. Pat's confidence only seemed to make Grant more agitated. He was bouncing the foot of his right leg nervously and the color had drained from his face. "We don't think Adison changed his mind about your daughter getting into the study. You say you were alone at your home during the time of the murder—no witnesses to support that, however. Am I right so far?"

Grant said nothing.

"So you're on a list of suspects. We conduct our investigation, following up on leads and tips, when *wham!* a key piece of evidence falls right into our laps. Wouldn't you say that's about how it happened, Sam?" Sam Davis nodded.

"So, Grant, here's the story. A certain ... *stain*," he paused and stressed the word for maximum effect, "was left at the scene by some mystery car which was, oddly enough, seen by a witness. No kidding! According to this witness, a dark sedan was sitting in the driveway of Adison's cabin on the night of the murder. Your car would look dark in color from a distance in low light, don't you think? Do you want to know what that stain was, Mr. Adams?"

Again, Grant remained quiet. He didn't move his eyes from Pat Donnelly's intense stare.

"Antifreeze. Can you believe that? Of all things to come along and wreck someone's perfect plan. Antifreeze. And do you know what else, Mr. Adams," he said, now leaning forward, his face not more than a foot from Grant's. This time Grant responded.

"My car is leaking antifreeze," he said matter-of-factly.

"Bingo!" Pat slapped his hands loudly and hopped off the desk.

"But my car just started leaking—I mean, I only noticed the mark in my garage yesterday," he said defensively. They had no proof his car had been leaking three weeks ago.

Sam Davis seemed to read his thoughts. "How convenient for you, Mr. Adams. Amazing that this leak, the same kind left by the car belonging to the person who killed Will Adison, just started now. But do you have any proof that your car *wasn't* leaking antifreeze on October 27th?"

"I think," Grant said, "I'd like to call my attorney."

~

Pat and Sam joined Melinda in the room next to Sam's office.

"So," she said curiously, "I couldn't catch everything. How did he react?"

Pat smiled. It wasn't often he had the chance to play bad cop in Red Wing. Too many people knew his character. He was enjoying himself.

"We've got him. Now let's let him sit in there and sweat."

~

"Miller, Hughes, DeLisi, and Associates, may I help you?" A pleasant voice greeted Grant from the other end of the phone line.

"I need to speak with David Hughes please. It's urgent," he said.

"And whom may I say is calling?"

"Grant Adams. Tell him it's an emergency." He wasn't sure if David would take his call unless he knew it was important.

Grant waited for what seemed like an eternity before he heard David's voice.

"Grant? My secretary said it was urgent. Is Katie okay? Is it Beth?"

"No, no. Katie and Beth are both fine. I really didn't mean to scare you, but I didn't know if you'd take my call."

"What can I do for you Grant?" Under normal circumstances, Grant would never think of calling David Hughes for help. But these circumstances were anything but normal. David Hughes was the only attorney Grant knew.

"I need you to come down to the Bureau of Criminal Apprehension headquarters right away. I'm being questioned about Will Adison's death. Can you do that?"

"What's this about?" David sounded skeptical.

"I'll explain everything when you get here. Just please come," Grant begged. "And David? Please don't tell Beth."

"I'm on my way. Don't say anything more until I get there."

"Thanks."

~

Pat Donnelly walked back into the office just as Grant was hanging up the phone.

"Your attorney coming?"

"Yes, and he's advised me not to say anything until he and I have had a chance to talk," Grant said stiffly. He felt sick to his stomach.

"Fine. I'll be back in half an hour," Pat said as he closed the door. Grant looked around the small office. He felt claustrophobic, like he couldn't breathe. The air was stale and the room seemed warm. He loosened his tie and undid the top button of his dress shirt.

He was scared.

"Hello, David. Thanks for coming," Grant said. It had taken David forty-two minutes to arrive. Grant must have checked his watch during every one.

"What? No lawyer jokes this time?" David said to break the ice. He wasn't especially pleased about coming. Not only was Grant his fiancée's ex-husband, but he also didn't like keeping things from her. "Uh, what's going on here, Grant?"

"They think I killed Will Adison," Grant said, unable to look David in the eye.

"Did you?"

"How can you even ask me that? Jesus, David! No, I had nothing to do with it. I have no idea who killed Will Adison. All I know is that it certainly wasn't me." Grant was immediately on the defensive. David wasn't sure how to read Grant's strong reaction. Was it a good sign that he vehemently objected to being involved, or was it like that old saying about protesting too much?

"Why don't you tell me what's going on," he said as he sat down.

Grant explained what had happened, having to backtrack several times because he was so upset. When Grant finally finished, David turned away from him and looked out the window.

"Wow," he finally commented.

"Wow? I tell you they think I killed a man and all you can say is wow?" Grant cried. Maybe calling David had been a huge mistake.

"Well, you know this isn't my area of expertise, but I'd say it sounds like they have only circumstantial evidence. Have they made any mention of filing charges yet?"

"Filing charges? No. Do you think it's really going to come to that?" he asked, stunned. This was all happening so fast.

Neither heard Sam Davis's knock before he entered the room.

"Grant, that depends on you," he said as he walked slowly across the office, holding an envelope in his hand. "Now Sergeant Donnelly thinks you're his guy. He's got pressure on him from the county attorney and the Red Wing chief of police. They're breathing down his neck to get this case solved. The county attorney wants to prosecute the bastard. You know how those folks can be? But me, I just don't know. Something more to this whole thing, I think."

Grant opened his mouth but stopped when he saw David's hand.

"I've got my own little theory about what went down in Red Wing. Grant, I don't know if you had a part in this whole mess, or if you just got dragged in by pure coincidence. But until I find out, I think you're stuck." Sam smiled as David Hughes and Grant Adams listened. "Now, here's what I think happened to Will Adison."

"That's quite a theory, Agent Davis," David said aloud.

"Thank you. I've been working on it for a while. You see, I was wrong about this case in the very beginning and I don't like to be wrong. So Mr. Adams, are you willing to cooperate?"

"I'd like a few minutes alone with my client," David replied.

"Take all the time you need." Sam strolled out of his office, leaving the two of them alone.

"What do I do?"

"What do you mean 'what do I do?' You help them. If you don't, it makes it seem like you have something to hide," David said evenly.

Grant didn't respond.

"*Do* you have something to hide, Grant?"

"No," he said reluctantly, "not exactly."

"What the hell does that mean?"

"Are you going to act as my attorney?"

"I'm here, aren't I?"

"And you won't say anything to Beth. I don't want her or Katie to know about any of this," he sighed.

"Well, I'm bound by attorney-client confidentiality once you retain me. You know that, Grant."

Grant reached into his pocket and took out a black leather wallet. He threw what amounted to seven dollars on the desk, tossing in a few quarters for effect.

Then he managed a weak smile and said, "Consider yourself retained."

When they left the BCA building an hour later, Grant, upon the advice of his attorney, had agreed to cooperate with the police. A mole. It was up to Grant to get information from the inside. To build a case, they needed evidence. Hard evidence. The search of Will's office and files had yielded nothing. The authorities couldn't gain access to all company property, private property. But an employee could. Grant had access to all sorts of files, including e-mail. The police could use anything that was voluntarily turned over to them by Grant. *Although*, he thought bitterly, *it doesn't feel voluntary.*

"You're doing the right thing, Grant. Think about it—small town jury, murder case. They've got a guy with no alibi, who drives the right kind of car that has a leak, who was arguing with the victim the week before the murder. Motive? You killed him to save your daughter's life. Case closed," David said as Grant opened the door of his car.

"What would you think if you were on the jury?" he dared to ask.

"You want the truth?"

Grant nodded.

"Guilty."

"You do believe that I didn't do it, don't you, David?" Grant was in shock that this was really happening to him. It all seemed surreal.

"It doesn't matter what I believe, Grant. I'm going to help you because you happen to be the father of a little girl who I love. A little girl who has had too much to deal with in the last few years. And Beth would never forgive me if you asked for my help and I refused. So here we are, Grant. I'll do whatever I can because I love those girls, but don't ask me anymore what I believe. It doesn't matter."

Friday, December 6

Without having much of a choice, Grant paid closer attention to what was going on behind the scenes at MacPhearson Pharmaceuticals, but not enough to arouse the suspicions of those around him. While he was willing to cooperate, he was not willing to take unnecessary risks. Grant, who usually kept to himself, started up conversations with people he barely knew. He lingered at the water cooler and took leisurely lunches trying to learn anything useful he could for the police. Why obtain a warrant when the police could get stuff handed to them by an insider? *An insider they put the screws to.*

The study. It was something he knew he couldn't dismiss. In fact, that was what worried him the most. If the police found out about what he'd done, they could make trouble by going to the FDA. If fraud was suspected in any way, the FDA would want to investigate the site, which could, depending on their findings, result in the study being put on hold. Katie's treatments would be delayed. In fact, any site participating in the study could be audited, delaying treatment for all the subjects involved. If only Katie could get in at least thirteen weeks of treatment before anything happened. But eight more weeks was a long time for him to hold off the police, or for them not to find anything on their own.

When he arrived home from work that evening, there was one message, a hang-up. That meant that the police had called. They had agreed that all calls would be conducted from Grant's home line. His cell phone and work phone were out of the question. If the police needed to contact him, they would hang up before leaving a message on his voicemail. Grant walked quietly over to the stairs and listened for Katie who was upstairs doing homework. He heard her radio playing softly through the closed door to her bedroom. Then he walked back to the kitchen and made the call he was dreading. *Might as well get it over with*, he thought.

～

Pat Donnelly knew it might take awhile before Grant would find what they needed, but he was still impatient. So far, Adams said, he had nothing.

"Keep digging, Adams. Remember, I got the county attorney breathing down my neck and I don't know how much longer I can stall her. You've got to give us something to change her mind."

He put down the phone without giving Grant a chance to respond. He wanted Grant to feel the pressure. He wanted Grant to think they'd settle for him. The truth was, he was just a pawn. But with Adams's eyes and ears at MacPhearson, they might be lucky enough to catch a break.

Saturday, December 7

The small café was almost thirty miles north of the Twin Cities, far enough away that she'd avoid running into someone she knew. But Barbara Adison caught herself looking around nervously anyway, just in case.

It was dangerous to meet, but she had to see him. She knew someone would eventually notice the files missing from Will's office. Will hadn't been the most organized man, and while it had plagued her during their marriage, it was a blessing to her after his death. His random system was probably the only reason their secret hadn't been uncovered. At least not yet. But they were running out of time. He told her it would be over by now, but things were taking longer than expected. Wasn't that always the case?

"Hello, Barbara," he whispered in her ear, causing her to jump.

"You scared me half to death," she said catching her breath. The lies, secrets, and sneaking around were getting to be too much for her. "Is it ready?"

"Almost," he said, signaling the waiter. "Honey, these things take time."

"Do you think anyone knows about us? I'm starting to get paranoid."

"No, we're fine. By the way, you were brilliant last time at the office. Very professional. I don't see how anyone could know what's going on between us," he whispered calmly as the waiter approached. He ordered two cappuccinos and informed the waiter they were in a terrible rush. Trying to catch an early movie, he explained.

They were at the café not more than twenty minutes, making arrangements to meet again, next time at a motel just few miles from the café. There they could have more privacy.

"Barbara, I know this has been hard on you, but it's the way it has to be right now. Just hold on a little longer for me, okay. By the time we see each other again, it will almost be over. No more sneaking around. We'll be free," he promised her. He sounded so convincing.

Monday, December 9

James MacPhearson's morning was off to an excellent start. He and Steven were meeting Robert Dawson at the country club for a working breakfast. Dawson said he had good news about MacPhearson going public. James knew the seasoned attorney was cautious. A green light from him was very promising news indeed.

"Morning, gentlemen," he greeted them as he sat down. "As I told James last evening, I think you two will be very pleased with what I have to say."

"Go on," Steven urged. He didn't have the patience this morning for one of Dawson's long, drawn-out discussions. "Get to the point."

"Well, it seems the best time to go public with MacPhearson is after the first of the year, as we had planned. I know the drug for bronchiosclerosis won't get approval until later in the year, but I think that's beneficial. Just after we go public, a new wonder drug hits the market."

"The value of the stock skyrockets. Our stockholders and employees turn a rather nice profit and have a valuable investment in a company on the rise. I like it, Robert, I like it," James said evenly.

"So what do we do now? What's the next step?" Steven asked.

"Just let me handle it. I'll take care of everything. We should have some sort of press conference. I was thinking late January or early February," Dawson suggested.

"It sounds excellent," James replied, a subtle smile playing across his lips.

"Gentlemen, you two men are going to be very, very rich," Dawson said brightly. Suddenly his brow wrinkled as if he had only just remembered something. "Adison. What about Will Adison's share? Have you spoken to Barbara about her plans yet?"

"No, not yet. We wanted to meet with you first so we could provide her with the most current information," Steven explained.

"Is she thinking of selling?" Dawson looked astounded.

"We're really not sure of her plans." James looked down as he unfolded his napkin and placed it on his lap. "After everything she's been through, I think the company is the last thing on her mind."

"Well, I think we have something to celebrate," Steven told them. "Bellinis all around."

~

He hadn't been expecting it. He had innocently gone to the office housing the clinical documents. Rose Hilmer, with her librarian glasses and serious expression, ran the records office. She informed him, in a tone suggesting he should have already known, that records from closed studies were kept in storage.

Tracy Whitman, one of the study monitors under Grant, had asked a question about a protocol from a study that had ended three years before. He offered to look up the information for her; it would be helpful to know the system of record keeping at MacPhearson for future reference.

Because the MacPhearson Pharmaceuticals building was new, there was still more than adequate storage. In fact, the facility had been designed to accommodate future growth. As such, several rooms on the second floor were unused. One large room on the east side of the building was devoted entirely to storage. It was a well organized home for a variety of materials. Old files and records no longer in use were kept along the back wall in monstrously oversized metal file cabinets. The rest of the room contained odds and ends: laboratory equipment, reference materials, supplies, computers, and even office furniture.

It was as Grant was making his way to the file cabinets along the back wall that he noticed the boxes. They were neatly stacked in one corner, set apart from the rest of the supplies. Marked clearly, in thick black marker, was one word: Adison.

Grant knew the police had seized Will Adison's files during their initial visits to the office. But what if they had missed something? Will was a scientist. Maybe there was information someone outside the industry wouldn't think was useful.

Grant looked around the room. He was alone. It wouldn't be too hard to come down here and look through those boxes. But how would he explain it if someone came in and he was caught looking through Will's things. It would raise questions and that was the last thing he wanted to do. Since it was his first visit to the storage room, he had no idea how often people came and went. For all he knew, it could be busy during office hours.

If he really was going to do this, and he was far from decided, it would be better to come back before or after regular office hours. Coming in on a weekend might look suspicious, since that wasn't typically done by study monitors. He didn't have any current projects that would warrant coming in on the weekend. But he could come in early, or stay late, claiming he had to catch up on work. He had missed some office hours for Katie's appointments and she had another scheduled later this week. It wouldn't be unreasonable for him to want to make up that time.

Finding the file he needed for Tracy Whitman, he closed the cabinet drawer and gave one last look at the boxes in the corner. It would be pretty easy for him to take a look. Especially now, while there was no one around. One of the boxes wasn't sealed at the top. He could easily reach inside …

Just as he was about to open the box, the door to the room swung open and two lab assistants walked in. One of the women let out a startled scream when she saw Grant. Then they both burst into giggles.

"Oh, God, Mr. Adams, you scared me," she explained. Grant remembered her name as Stephanie, but couldn't be sure. He didn't recognize the other young woman.

Grant withdrew his hand naturally and neither of them seemed to notice. He smiled and held up the thick file in hand as explanation for why he was in the storage room.

"Now you won't have to work in the dark," the unfamiliar woman said. She walked over and flipped a switch, instantly brightening the room.

"Oh, that's okay, I've already found what I was looking for, but I'll keep it in mind for next time. Stephanie, right?" He took a shot. She nodded, clearly surprised he remembered her.

"And I'm Heidi, from down in the lab. I don't think we've met before." She held out her hand in a brisk professional manner that contradicted the immature behavior she and her friend had just displayed.

"Well, it's nice to meet you now," he said warmly.

"We've got a ton of work to do. See you around, Mr. Adams," Stephanie said, shifting her weight. She brushed her dark bangs out of her eyes as she smiled.

"Call me Grant, please," he requested as he walked past them toward the door. *She's flirting with me!* Before closing it behind him, he took one last look back at them. Neither could be much older than twenty-five. As he walked back to his office on the third floor, Grant Adams couldn't help but feel flattered.

Wednesday, December 11

E-mail at MacPhearson Pharmaceuticals was much like that at any other company. Employees relied upon it to communicate with other companies, clinics, and contract organizations, as well as with others within the company itself. In fact, a significant portion of interoffice mail was transferred electronically, reducing paper waste and increasing efficiency. People could communicate with virtually any associate from the comfort and privacy of an office or lab. Workaholics could check messages from home, at any hour, or while on vacation a thousand miles away from the office.

While the majority of e-mail was professional in nature, a sizeable amount was considered junkmail. Grant had faced worse at Webber, because it had a larger number of employees, but wasn't surprised after only a few weeks at MacPhearson to see his in-box contain at least a few dozen messages on a daily basis. Usually, he tried to delete those that clearly were not work-related. He had no interest in going to happy hour, and didn't have time to sit around reading jokes or looking at pictures of co-workers' kids or vacations.

Grant was in a hurry on Wednesday morning, and in his rush he didn't think of the significance of one of the many e-mails he skimmed over before heading off to yet another meeting.

He was about to move on to the next message when he read the invitation a second time.

You are cordially invited
to attend the sixth annual
MacPhearson Pharmaceuticals
Holiday Party,
which will take place at
company headquarters
at seven o'clock in the evening
on Friday, the twentieth of December.

RSVP – regrets only – to
Steven MacPhearson

It took Grant a few moments to realize this party would provide the perfect opportunity for him to stay late at the office. It wouldn't make sense for him to drive to the townhouse, only to have to turn around and drive back again. Most employees would want to go home and change for the party; the office would probably be deserted. Anyone helping to set things up for the evening would most likely be on the first floor, where he heard previous parties had been held. The second floor, and, more importantly, the storage room, would be abandoned.

The only problem was the party wasn't until the end of next week. Grant wasn't sure if he could stall the police for that long. Maybe he should start looking through the files held in storage, but only a few. He would claim he needed additional time to look more thoroughly. By then Katie would have received nine more days of treatment. That might work.

Hold on, Katie, he thought. *Just a couple more weeks.*

Friday, December 13

On Friday afternoon, an unanticipated opportunity presented itself. Tracy, finished with the file Grant had gotten for her, left him a voicemail telling him she would return the file on Monday, but wasn't sure exactly where it needed to go. Immediately after receiving her message, Grant walked down to her office. It was late afternoon, and like on most Fridays, a large portion of the staff had already left the building.

"Tracy, I'm glad I caught you," he said, looking over the wall of her cubicle. He was glad he had an office that afforded at least a little privacy.

"Hi, Grant. I was actually about to head out," she explained, pulling on her coat.

"I just wanted to get that file from you," he said evenly. "I actually have to go down to the storage room myself now to get some other documents, and figured it would be easier for me to return the file instead of trying to explain to you where it goes."

"That would be great. Thanks." She handed Grant the thick folder and grabbed her purse from under her desk.

"So any fun plans for the weekend?"

"Actually, yes. My boyfriend and I are going shopping tonight," she said with excitement. "I'm buying a new dress for the party next week. You're going aren't you?"

"I wouldn't miss it," he said with a slight grin.

Ten minutes later, one floor below, he carefully placed the file back where he had found it. He had already pulled a thick section of papers from one of Will's boxes and slipped it into an empty folder. If anyone happened to see him coming out of the storage area, it would look like he had an ordinary file. He planned to take it home with him for the weekend where he could examine it more closely.

Grant hoped the police were wrong in their suspicions. Maybe, somewhere in these papers, was the answer to what really happened to Will Adison.

He never noticed the security camera, mounted close to the ceiling, near the door, that had recorded his every move.

That evening, alongside a tall glass of dark beer on the dining room table, Grant spread out the contents of the file. Katie was staying at Beth's for the weekend, so he had the townhouse to himself for the next two days.

Adison may have been a brilliant scientist, but his handwriting left much to be desired. The fact that most of his notations contained scientific symbols and his own private shorthand didn't help.

The papers contained a substantial amount of information. Most of it amounted to notes about different projects he had started. Grant remembered James telling him on his tour of MacPhearson that Will was the mastermind of the lab. He often worked alone to develop new drug treatments, or adapt current MacPhearson compounds, improving upon them or finding new uses for them. James had said some of the research assistants had to transcribe Will's erratic notations, putting the data on computer. Grant didn't envy them the job. Will's notes were hard to follow. Although his eyes grew weary and his head pounded, he continued, not wanting to stop until he turned the last page. Tempted to finish in the morning, he couldn't help but wonder if something important, something critical, was waiting for him on the next page. After nearly four hours he stacked the papers neatly, careful to keep them in the same order, and placed them back into the folder.

So far, he had found nothing.

Monday, December 16

Barbara Adison looked at them blankly. James and Steven seemed to be hanging on her every word. When she had called James over the weekend to suggest they meet to discuss the future of MacPhearson Pharmaceuticals, James had practically begged her to come in right away Monday morning. He sounded crushed when she explained that she had an appointment scheduled for the morning and wouldn't be available until the afternoon.

"Well, have you come to a decision, Barbara?" James asked gently. It really would be in everyone's best interest for her to sell Will's share of the company. She knew nothing of the industry and James and Steven would be willing to help her out by taking it off her hands for a fair price.

"I think I'd like to retain Will's share—my share," she corrected herself, "and remain a full partner with the two of you."

They both looked stunned. Barbara had anticipated they would be.

"Are you certain that would be best, dear?" James got up from his chair and took a seat next to her.

"Well, I want to give it a try at least. You know I do have some business background. I know I'm not the scientist Will was, but I hear Oliver Klein is doing a wonderful job as lab director. Maybe I can help out as a manager or work with the marketing department," she suggested.

"But James and I have that all under control, Barbara. We really don't need any help, but it's so kind of you to offer," Steven said, trying to maintain his composure.

"Well then, I could just be a sort of silent partner for a while. I could learn about the company's operations and things and sit in on meetings, just to keep informed and maybe help out with smaller projects as they come along. Who knows, maybe one of you would like to get back into the lab someday. By my coming on board, you'd be free to do that, if you wanted."

"Yes, but are you sure? I spoke with Robert Dawson just yesterday, and we are prepared to make you a very generous offer," James coaxed.

"Well, I guess I should at least hear what you had in mind," she agreed. Steven exhaled loudly, looking every bit as tense as he felt. *She has to accept.*

After James revealed the amount of money they thought was more than fair, Barbara sat quietly for a long moment. The figure was a reasonable price for one third of MacPhearson at its present market value, but Barbara knew it would be worth much more in a very short time.

"Thank you both very much. This offer is more than I expected," she sighed.

"So you'll sell?" Steven hovered over her like a bird waiting to descend on its prey.

"Sorry guys, but no. I want to hold on to Will's share for now. I feel like it's keeping me connected to him somehow. This just seems right, and I know it'll be good for all of us."

She stood up, smoothed her skirt and jacket, and walked out the office door. Neither James nor Steven said anything to her as she left.

Friday, December 20

The night of the big party. Grant had been waiting for more than a week. He knew he had to get some information for the police during the party. They were growing impatient with him. Donnelly was angry when Grant spoke with him on Thursday morning and threatened again to turn over what he had to the county attorney. Grant assured him if there *were* something to be found in the office, he would find it that night.

Donnelly was interested in the contents of the storage boxes, any information pertaining to Will that might strike Grant as odd. But he made another suggestion as well. During the party, he wanted Grant to go into one office in particular. Reluctantly, Grant agreed. He knew there was no turning back.

The majority of the employees had spent the workday talking about the party. Grant overheard and participated in several trivial conversations about clothes, food, dancing, and drinks. It seemed to be the event of the holiday season. Steven MacPhearson sure knew how to throw a party.

But Grant was distracted. He knew what he had to do, but dreaded it. As always, when something dark was looming on the horizon, the day passed quickly. Before he knew it, his office clock showed the hour of five.

Grant decided to look through the records in the storage room before the party started and check the office once the party was well underway. Since the guests would be on the main level, he decided it wouldn't be too difficult to disappear to the third floor.

He knew the alarms would be turned off all evening, at least until the party was over. Apparently a few years ago, two colleagues had decided to step out to get some air and had set the alarms off. The police responded and were not amused. They had parked their squad cars at the end of the driveway for the remainder of the evening to discourage anyone from driving home under the influence. Keeping the security system off during party hours was to prevent such a thing from happening a second time.

He'd only need about ten minutes. Twenty at the most. He changed clothes in his office and ran his fingers through his hair. Looking in the mirror, he studied himself. He only hoped the police were wrong. And that he wouldn't get caught.

The search in the storage room yielded nothing useful. Grant made his way down to the party unnoticed just as the first guests started to arrive. He saw Allen Jennings and Tracy Whitman wave him over. They were standing near the bar, talking with Oliver Klein.

When Grant walked over to them, Oliver Klein immediately offered to get him a drink. Grant accepted a beer, only to keep up appearances. It would be his only one; he needed to have a clear head.

Time seemed to stand still on one hand, and rush by on the other. Grant, in the middle of a room full of people smiling, laughing, and celebrating the spirit of the holidays, had never felt so alone.

~

Finally, at eight o'clock, James MacPhearson took the microphone and greeted his guests. He and Steven agreed to share the good news about MacPhearson going public as the highlight of the evening. Tonight was a night for celebrating the accomplishments of the employees at MacPhearson. They were about to become a major player in the fast-paced world of pharmaceuticals, not just some upstart company from Minnesota. The mood around the office had been subdued since Will's death. They needed to improve morale. As James addressed the crowd, he noticed someone toward the back of the room, moving in the shadows, toward the door. When the door was opened, the light from the hallway illuminated the figure leaving the room. *Where is Grant Adams going?*

~

The third floor was dimly lit; only the energy-saving safety lights were on at this hour. There was no indication that a party, with well over two hundred guests, was taking place two floors below. Grant walked quietly down the hall, stopping in front of the last office on the right-hand side. James MacPhearson's office. He took a deep breath and opened the unlocked door. It was now or never.

The only light in the office came from the computer monitor on Mac-Phearson's desk. It was just enough to navigate the room. Grant crossed the office swiftly, not wanting to spend any more time than necessary. His heart raced and he could feel it beating with every breath he took. Perspiration started soaking through his shirt.

MacPhearson wasn't the type of executive to have his office cluttered with unnecessary files. The room held only one large file cabinet, to the right of the window. Grant was grateful many of his meetings had taken place in this very office. He headed straight for the cabinet and was both surprised and relieved when he found it unlocked.

He opened the top drawer but swung around immediately as he heard someone enter the room behind him. He contemplated dropping to the floor to conceal himself behind the desk, but knew it was too late.

A long, dim stream of pale light shone into the room from the hallway. James MacPhearson was smiling at him. An odd sort of smile, like the smile of a parent who discovers a child misbehaving but is amused rather than angry. He walked toward Grant and sat down in his chair. The two men looked at one another in the silence of the shadows and distant music found its way into the room from far below.

"James, ... I ..." he stumbled. *Can James not hear my heart beating?*

"Grant, Grant," James said graciously. "I know why you're here. I was expecting you to come, and you didn't disappoint me. Please, sit down. We have a great deal to discuss."

PHASE III

Barbara Adison watched as James made a curious exit just after finishing his announcement. The news that MacPhearson was going public made the crowd excited and talkative. Every employee would stand to make money from the move. Barbara noticed James had a hard time looking at her during his announcement, even though she had been standing just in front of him. It must have killed him to know how much profit he could have made if she had sold him Will's share. In a few months, it would be worth twice as much as the amount they had just offered her.

But things weren't over yet. James wasn't happy with her. When she had arrived at the party, he had greeted her coolly and excused himself right away. Steven hadn't spoken to her at all that evening, which didn't surprise her. He wasn't as good an actor as his brother. Maybe she should try to catch James.

Maybe the time had finally come.

～

Jessica had seen Barbara Adison from a distance. The two hadn't spoken since the call just before Will's funeral. Jessica contemplated going over to her, but decided against it. There had been rumors about Barbara coming to work at MacPhearson. If that were true, Jessica wondered how long it would be before she lost her job.

"Hello, Jessica." Tara Wolfe was making her way across the room. *She looks gorgeous*, Jessica thought, looking down at her own thick middle and swollen ankles. Pregnancy had not been kind to her in recent weeks.

The two chatted for a while and were soon joined by other researchers from the lab. It was nice for Jessica to think of other things. Will and the baby had been on her mind constantly. Studying had been almost impossible for her. But she had managed, somehow, to complete the semester, and even though her grades would be lower than usual, she was relieved to be done. She was taking the next semester off and wouldn't have classes again until the fall. Only three more courses and she would have her degree, graduating next year.

She relaxed and enjoyed listening to the gossip and conversation of Tara and her friends. They included her in the discussion, making her feel welcome. It was nice to have friends again. It was nice to not feel so alone.

～

Oliver Klein was just polishing off his fifth drink of the night when his date tugged on his sleeve, indicating she was ready to leave. He would have rather stayed longer and closed the place down, but she was persistent. *And very young and very attractive,* he reminded himself. He probably would have a better time with her back at his place than here anyway. He ordered a quick drink for the road while she went off to the ladies' room. No sense wasting an opportunity to get in the last scotch of the evening. When she returned, he retrieved their coats and helped her into hers. It wasn't an easy task for him and she had to help him along. More than one person saw her taking his car keys from him. He was clearly in no condition to drive. She guided him out of the door, struggling to keep him headed in the direction of his car.

～

"So what do you think, Grant?" James asked. He seemed different somehow, more serious. *No, that's not the right word,* Grant thought. *Sinister was more accurate.*

"I don't know what you mean," he answered honestly.

"Well, you're in my office, in the dark and uninvited, so you must have some motivation for wanting to look through my private files," James said calmly.

Grant took an uneasy breath. He knew it was no use to lie. At this point, James would never believe it if he gave some innocent excuse about needing to see a file without permission. He had no choice but to tell the story. Not the whole story, but at least part of what was happening.

"The police think you might be involved in Will Adison's murder." There. He said it. Now there was no going back.

James cracked a smile.

"Really?" James looked amused, as if he were merely playing a game. "And what do you think? Do you think I am capable of murder?"

"No, of course not," Grant replied, treading cautiously. He had to let James take the lead.

"Then what were you doing in here?"

"The police have no proof for their theory—probably because it isn't true—but asked me to look around."

"And what have you told them so far?" James's face remained cold as stone.

"Nothing. Which is true. I have found nothing so far that would implicate you, and that much I *have* told Sergeant Donnelly." *Careful, careful.* He steadied himself.

"That's good, Grant," James said, nodding. "But what I am having such a hard time understanding is why you would help the police in the first place."

"I really didn't have a choice. They said they would try to pin it on me. All they have is circumstantial evidence, but the county attorney down there is willing to take her chances with it. It doesn't look good for me." He had to convince James he was helping the cops to keep them from pinning the murder on him, not because he actually thought James was responsible. "I told them you would never do such a thing to your partner, to your friend. They said I had no choice but to cooperate. And so I looked around, if only to prove to them they were wrong about you," he continued, not knowing if James believed a word. He couldn't read his expression.

"I'm disappointed in you, Grant," James said, shaking his head slowly. "I thought I could trust you—"

"You can, James, you can," he reassured him, trying to sound convincing.

"Especially after all I have done to help your daughter."

Grant felt an icy chill shoot down his spine.

"Grant." James came closer to him and Grant could feel the warmth of his breath. "I helped your daughter when no one else could. She's being treated, and from what I hear, she's doing quite well."

Grant said nothing.

"And you were grateful to me for that, remember?" he continued.

"I still am grateful," Grant said hesitantly.

"You should be. I helped you, Grant, and now it's your turn."

He was trapped. There was no way out. He listened as James MacPhearson explained.

"I want it back, Grant."

"What back? I don't have anything. I told you," Grant responded sincerely. He had no idea what James meant.

"I know you have it!" James shouted at him. "I saw you take his things from the storage room."

"I don't have anything," he repeated.

"When is Katie's next appointment?"

"Leave my daughter out of this!"

"See, I just can't do that, Grant." James's voice was barely above a whisper. Grant could smell the sour sweetness of the champagne. "You bent the rules to get her into that study, and now I'm feeling pretty guilty about it. Aren't you starting to feel guilty about that, Grant? I'm wondering if maybe it was a mistake." He shook his head.

"No, please. She hasn't done anything wrong."

"But you have. I know it doesn't seem fair for her to pay for your mistakes. Do you know what would happen to her, if she doesn't get her treatments? What if Dr. Carruthers removed her from the study? If I asked him to, he would, you know. He's a good friend—and well compensated for his efforts."

"He wouldn't. It would be unethical," Grant reasoned.

"Unethical? Unethical like committing fraud? Unethical like changing the medical records of a young boy to keep him from getting into a study with a drug that could treat him? You altered little Tommy Garrett's lab results, which disqualified him from the study. Don't look surprised; I know all about that. And that's the only reason your daughter got in. One call to Carruthers and she'd be out."

Grant dropped his head. He couldn't bear to look into James's cold eyes any longer.

"But that doesn't have to happen, Grant. Katie can still get treatment, and everything will be just fine. But you'll need to work with me here, help me from time to time. Fix some data. Keep our records clean. You'd be surprised at how much better our results could be, how much more effective our drugs could look, with a little help from you. It could be a very nice arrangement."

Grant said nothing. All he could see was Katie's face. Hear her voice. Her laugh.

Breaking the agonizing silence, James finally spoke. "You know, Grant, when I have a decision to make, I usually try to sleep on it. Why don't you go home, get some rest, and we'll meet tomorrow. We can talk more then. Right now, I have a party to attend. And I'm not a very good host if I leave my guests alone all night, am I?"

"How do you know I won't go to the police? How do you know I won't tell them everything?"

"I don't. At least not for sure, Grant. You can never know exactly what someone will do in any given situation. All you can do is rely on past behavior to predict future behavior. From what I have seen of you, you are a man who loves his daughter. If you go to the police, there is nothing I can do to stop you.

"But every choice has consequences. If you, or anyone else for that matter, go to the police, your daughter will be immediately removed from the study. She'll no longer get the treatment her poor, diseased, little body needs. How long do you think she could last, Grant? Based on earlier trials, without the B319 drug, I'd give her a few weeks at most," he added. "I'm sure you already know how painful bronchiosclerosis is in its final stages—like slowly suffocating. Poor kid. I wonder what she would think if she knew her dad could have saved her life, but chose not to."

Grant tried to block the image of Katie suffering.

"And even if you did take the high road and help the cops, don't you worry about me, Grant. They won't have enough to get a conviction. Any defense lawyer fresh out of law school could win that case. Katie would be the one to lose."

He walked out of the room and left Grant alone in the dark.

Saturday, December 21

The café where James wanted Grant to meet him was crowded. The streets and shops were bustling with people in a rush to finish their holiday shopping. Grant was already late, having had to park six blocks away. He bent his head downward to protect himself from the biting wind. Since the sun had set, the temperature had dropped well below freezing.

When Grant finally stepped inside, James waved him over like an old friend. Sitting there in a long, wool coat and cashmere scarf, he looked like any distinguished man, taking a break from shopping for expensive Christmas gifts for his wife. Grant hated him.

"Well, Grant, have a seat and join me," James invited. "Can I order you a coffee, or anything?" James offered. It was as if the purpose of the meeting was a social visit.

"I'm not going to Donnelly," Grant said quietly. The café was loud and their table was isolated from the rest, but he felt the need to be discreet.

"Good decision, Grant." James sipped his coffee and carefully dabbed his mouth with a napkin. Ever the gentleman. "Just go about your business as usual. I know you may not see it now, but it's better this way." He was smiling. He had Grant right where he wanted him.

Grant wanted to jump across the table and strangle him with his bare hands, but instead he sat quietly. He knew he was in no position to go on the attack.

"Business as usual," Grant repeated. He sounded very unconvincing.

"And don't try to get clever, Grant. I'll be watching you—closely. Keep telling Donnelly you're looking into it, but can't seem to find anything," James instructed. His expression was pleasant, but his eyes were cold and dark. Grant wondered when he had sold his soul to the devil, and what payoff he had gotten in return.

"Already done. He called me this morning and I told him I thought they were on the wrong track, but that I'd keep looking," Grant told him. Donnelly had not been impressed. He had said if Grant couldn't come up with something soon, the county attorney might want to move ahead. She might charge Grant.

"And if you don't find anything for them?" James asked, eyebrows raised with curiosity. This game was entertaining for him.

"They'll let me take the fall, charge me with Will Adison's death," he said evenly.

"I wouldn't let that happen, Grant," James consoled him. "I won't let anything happen to you. You are very important to me."

Grant's only response was a deep sigh and spiteful look.

"Now Grant, Christmas is just around the corner. Try to get into the spirit of the season a little." James finished the last of his coffee and stood up. He was almost to the door of the café when he turned around suddenly, as if he had forgotten something.

"Oh, Grant? Remember to say hello to Katie for me."

~

Grant had only been gone for a few minutes when Katie Adams returned to the townhouse. She and a friend had seen a movie in the afternoon and had planned to go out for pizza with the girl's parents, but her friend started to feel sick, so Katie was dropped off two hours earlier than expected. She had no idea her dad wouldn't be home. He hadn't said anything about going out.

Katie turned on the hall light and tried to set the code for the alarm. After a few unsuccessful attempts, she gave up and walked up to the second floor. She was starving. The only thing she had eaten since breakfast was popcorn and soda. She opened the refrigerator and was delighted to see her dad had ordered pizza for himself for lunch. Grabbing a few slices, she settled herself on the couch and turned on the television.

Maybe she should call her dad's cell phone. But what if he was on a date? He hadn't told Katie about anyone special, but what if that was just because he wasn't ready to tell her. *They could be having dinner right now*, Katie thought hopefully.

She was probably the only teenager with divorced parents who didn't want them to get back together. A few years ago she had wanted nothing more. Every penny tossed into a fountain, every birthday candle she blew out, and every first star accompanied the same wish. But then she realized her mom and dad were better people apart than they were together. Her mom and David were happy; Katie had never seen her mom smile so much. Her dad had taken a little longer to come around, but ever since they moved into the townhouse, he seemed like he was ready to move on, too.

She looked at the soft blue light of the clock on the microwave. Almost eight. If he really *was* on a date, he might not get home until late, when she was expected to return from her night out. *Or*, Katie thought switching from her romantic daydreams to self-serving ones, *maybe he's out Christmas shopping for me*. She didn't know how much money her dad made, but judging from the townhouse, his new job probably paid pretty well. And he always spoiled her at Christmas. Her mom did, too. Sometimes being the kid of divorced parents had its advantages. And this year would probably be even better, since she was sick.

Katie yawned, realizing how tired she was. The day had really drained her. She turned off the television and climbed the stairs. A hot bath sounded really nice. And since her dad was gone, she wouldn't have to worry about him yelling up to her that she had been in there for twenty minutes and wasn't it time she got out.

The bathtub in the new townhouse was perfect for soaking, with jets on three sides. Katie loved sitting in the tub. The steam seemed to clear her lungs. She ran the water and poured in some of the bubble bath her grandma bought for her. It smelled like flowers. She climbed in as the tub began to fill with warm water.

She never heard the sound of breaking glass.

⁓

Two floors below, a gloved hand reached past the jagged pieces of glass and turned the bolt on the door. The information was correct; the door led through a hallway, right into Grant Adam's office. The separate entrance was designed for someone who had a home business. *How convenient.*

The office was small and organized. The files were easy to go through. The desk took only a minute. *Nothing, nothing!* It had to be there, somewhere. Even his briefcase was clean. *Where could it be?*

The only other place that would make sense would be his bedroom. Maybe there was a safe. Up the stairs, one at a time. The house was new, and none of the boards creaked. *Lucky.* The second floor was empty, as expected. Up to the third floor.

Wait! What the hell was that?

The sound of water splashing was unmistakable. *Someone is in the house!* It couldn't be Adams—he was meeting with James right now. It had to be the girl.

A sliver of light escaped the bathroom just below the heavy wooden door. It wouldn't take more than a few minutes to check his room.

A few more footsteps, past the bathroom door. *Still splashing.*

The flashlight was cold and hard. Its beam split the dark of the room like a spotlight. The dresser first. Just across the room. The first three drawers opened smoothly. Unexpectedly, the top drawer stuck, causing the dresser to shake. One bottle of cologne fell to the floor.

⁓

Katie sat motionless in the tub. She turned off the jets, certain she had heard something. She looked at the knob on the bathroom door. It was unlocked. She sat there for what seemed like an eternity. Her dad would have greeted her by now, knocking on the door and asking why she had gotten home so early. Her grandma was visiting friends up north. No one else, as far as Katie knew, had a key to the house.

Panic raced through her. Someone was in the house. They had to know she was there. She hadn't been quiet. All they had to do was try the bathroom door and …

She looked over at her clothes, lying in a heap on the floor. Her cell phone was in the pocket of her sweater. Trying to move as quietly as she could, Katie stepped out of the tub. With a towel wrapped around her, she pulled the phone from her pocket and stared. Tears welled in her eyes and she fought the urge to scream. The battery was dead.

She heard footsteps coming from another room. Someone was coming toward the bathroom door.

~

Irritated, Grant turned off the radio. He was definitely not in the right mindset to listen to holiday music. *What in the hell am I going to do?*

He could never have imagined being in a situation like this. He wasn't the type to take chances; he wasn't one to break the rules. He was Grant Adams, Mr. By-the-Book. Beth used to tease him that he was too good to be true. But now, within a span of only a few months, he had committed fraud by falsifying the medical records of a sick child; he was a suspect in the murder of his employer; and he knew the identity of the guilty party, but could do nothing to stop him.

After the conversation in the office, Grant knew for certain James MacPhearson had killed Will. Any hope the police were wrong was gone. The casual manner in which he had threatened Katie's life revealed his darker side.

James had been manipulating him for months. Grant thought back to that day in Carruther's office. The doctor had given Grant the bad news. According to her medical history, Katie would likely qualify for the B319 study. However, there was another patient, one ahead of Katie, who might also qualify. Carruthers had made it a point to tell Grant that the patient's parents had not yet been notified of the results. The data for that patient was in a folder Carruthers had placed on the examination room desk. He told Grant the only way for Katie to have a chance was if the other patient's results showed some sort of problem. And then Carruthers left the room, leaving the folder behind.

Katie would only be enrolled in the study if the results in that folder were changed to show that the other patient did not qualify.

Grant knew enough about clinical research to know what would make a subject ineligible for a study. It only took a moment to open the file and make a few subtle changes. Carruthers never mentioned anything.

It was all such a nightmare.

But what would James gain by getting rid of Will Adison? Maybe if Grant could find the answer to that question, he could find a way out of this whole mess.

In order to keep Katie safe, he had to play the game, at least for a few more weeks. Six more weeks of treatment to be exactly halfway through the treatment schedule. After that, her system would be stronger. Maybe he could go to the police then—tell them everything. He'd explain that James threatened the life of his daughter. He might be thrown in jail, for the fraud or obstruction of justice, but the study would continue. The doctors, having seen such promising results in earlier and current studies, would want to keep their patients in the trial.

Grant knew that in the real world, unlike on television or in movies, a court case like this could last for years. He could talk to Barbara and Steven. They would want to keep the company profitable. Assuming James pled not guilty, they would have no reason to pull B319. It was so close to being approved by the FDA, it might be available by the time he faced a jury. Katie could receive treatment from any physician in the country. James would have no hold over him.

It's a long shot, but it could work, Grant thought. *With everything that has happened to me lately, anything is possible.*

~

Katie turned her head. *Is that the garage door?* It was difficult to hear anything over the sound of her blood pounding in her head. But ... yes! It was. *Dad must be home!* She looked at the base of the bathroom door. She saw nothing. Whoever had been standing there must have heard the garage door, too. She hoped the sound had scared whoever it was away. If not, her dad was walking into a very dangerous situation. Three floors below, he would never hear her if she screamed. She had no way to warn him.

∿

Get out! Get out! Get out! The stairs seemed to be much longer than before. *Turn the bolt on the front door. Get outside. Close the door. Stay on the sidewalk—the wet concrete won't show any footprints. Around the house. Good—garage door is closed. Quickly; down the road to the car. Close the door. Start the engine. Drive!*

"It's me. His daughter was there! And then he came home! Why didn't you call me? I could've been caught!"

"Don't panic. You didn't get caught and that's what's important. Did you find it?"

"No."

"What?"

"You heard me. It's either not there or he was telling the truth and doesn't have it."

"Or you just didn't find it."

"I'm not going back."

"You're not in any position to refuse."

∿

"Dad! Daddy!" Grant wasn't expecting anyone to be home, but he heard Katie's voice coming from the upstairs. She sounded frightened.

"I'm coming, Katie! I'm coming!" He bounded up the stairs, nearly tripping on the rug in the entry. He opened the bathroom door and saw Katie huddled in the corner, her hair wet and a towel wrapped around her. She was shaking, and Grant could see the tears streaming down her face.

"Katie, what is it? What happened? What are you even doing home?" He rushed over to her and threw his coat around her shoulders. *Oh God, please don't let her be sick!*

"Dad, there was someone in the house. Just before you came home. I heard him. He was in your room. I heard him! And then he must have heard me because he came toward the bathroom. And it wasn't locked, Dad. But he must have heard

185

the garage door open, because then he ran out. Didn't you see him?" She spoke so fast it was hard for Grant to process what she was saying. *Someone had been in the house?*

"Katie, stay here and don't move. Lock the door behind me and take my cell phone. Call 911 immediately." He got up and closed the bathroom door.

"Dad, don't!" Katie screamed, but she already heard him going down the stairs. She locked the door and called the police.

Grant opened the front door. It was unlocked. Whoever was in the house must have run out the front, which was why he didn't see anyone when he got home. The front entrance and the garage faced opposite directions. Grant stepped out into the dark night. He saw no one. The other townhome units, still in various stages of construction, were dark, and the dead-end street was deserted. He caught his breath and walked a few paces from the door. In the distance, he heard the high-pitched wail of a police siren.

Grant thanked the officers from the Hudson Police Department and closed the door behind them. A search of the house yielded physical evidence that there had been an intruder. The glass from the lower-level entrance door was broken and the bolt had been turned. No alarm had sounded, since Katie hadn't reset it when she arrived home. His office was a disaster. Someone had been looking for something. The officers were curious why his office was the focus. Grant shrugged and said he had no idea what anyone might be looking for. His bedroom had also been hit. Perhaps the robber was looking for valuables, he suggested, although nothing appeared to be missing. They dusted for fingerprints, but were not optimistic. The robber had most likely worn gloves. The sidewalks were wet with sleet; any footprints left by the intruder were lost. They secured the door and said they would call him in the morning to finish the report. If he noticed anything missing, or had any other trouble, he shouldn't hesitate to call them.

He had gotten Katie to bed with a mug of hot chocolate to help her sleep. He turned on one of her latest favorite CDs—some obnoxious boy band singing about love and loss. Grant wondered how boys that age could claim to know about such deep feelings. But it seemed to help her calm down. She finally drifted off to sleep, with him sitting on the edge of her bed and the nightlight from the bathroom shining dimly into her bedroom. As he watched her sleep, he silently apologized for putting her in harm's way. All he wanted to do was protect her, and tonight she could have been killed. Her world, her safe haven, had become the scene of a nightmare. He couldn't imagine how frightened she must have been, knowing there was someone in the house, coming for her.

Grant knew who was responsible. It had to be James. He had gotten him out of the house in order to send someone in to look for whatever it was James thought he had. But they didn't find it. And he didn't know if that made him feel safe or even more at risk.

Monday, December 23

The day before Christmas Eve, the laboratory was very quiet. Christmas Eve and Christmas Day were both paid holidays at MacPhearson Pharmaceuticals. Only a skeleton crew was needed to keep the lab running. The few employees who were required to come in were paid overtime wages and would work staggered, four-hour shifts so their lab duties wouldn't interfere with family plans. The MacPhearsons were all about family. Most researchers had decided to take vacation during the holiday week, so things were calm for a Monday morning.

Oliver Klein entered the building through the back door and was able to get to his office unseen. He was taking a risk, but needed more time to continue the project. An unauthorized project. He was planning on coming in over the holiday as well, when the results would be ready for analysis. So far things were looking promising, and Oliver was confident he was on the brink of his first major success as Laboratory Director.

If all went as well as he hoped, it would make quite an impact in the medical world. And Oliver Klein would be part of it all. It was exhilarating. It had been a long time since he felt truly passionate about a project. He wanted to think his motives were altruistic, but he knew better. He wanted the recognition he deserved. He wanted to see his name printed in medical journals. But his road to glory was a very dangerous one.

The danger only made Oliver want it more.

$\sim$

"Grant, come in, come in." James ushered him as though he were a special guest. Grant thought about not coming in to the office at all, but wanted to keep an eye on him. It took the greatest effort not to accuse him of setting up the break-in. Grant already knew the answer, but he wanted confirmation anyway. Maybe he could convince James whatever it was he was looking for, he didn't have it.

"I wanted to give you an early Christmas present. Just in case you weren't feeling confident in your decision, I wanted to give you some peace of mind," James said sincerely. "Have you seen today's paper?"

Grant, looking stoic, shook his head. He had been too distracted that morning to sit and read the paper.

"Why don't you turn to the obituaries," James prompted.

Grant turned to the back pages of the local section of the *Pioneer Press*. He scanned the articles in tiny print, not knowing where all of this was leading.

Then, toward the bottom of the first column he saw it.

Garrett, Thomas Michael, 5

Tommy Garrett, of Roseville, died Friday afternoon after a courageous battle with bronchiosclerosis. He is survived by his mother, Patricia, and father, Scott, as well as his best friend, a Cocker Spaniel named Dutch. He is also survived by grandmother Sharon Garrett and grandfather Sam Michaels, great-grandmothers Anna Garrett and Marie Williams, aunts, uncles, and many cousins. Tommy was preceded in death by his grandmother Anna Michaels and grandfather Thomas Garrett. Tommy attended kindergarten at Springdale Elementary, where he made many friends. His smile and laughter will be greatly missed.

Services will held at Garrison Funeral Home Friday, December 27ᵗʰ, 5:00-8:00PM and Saturday, December 28ᵗʰ, 11:00AM at St. Mark's Catholic Church in St. Paul. Luncheon to follow. In lieu of flowers, the family requests that donations be made to Springdale Elementary School in Tommy's name.

There is no gift more precious than the gift of a child.

"You see, Grant, every choice has a consequence. Remember that file you altered in Carruthers's office that day? It belonged to Tommy Garrett. Poor Tommy. The medicine Katie has now should have gone to him. It would have saved his life. But instead of you, it's Mr. and Mrs. Garrett who are grieving. It's their child who will be buried." James's voice was low, but his words were sharp. "I wonder what Sergeant Donnelly would think if he knew the whole story. You're a murderer, Grant." He took the paper back and carefully folded it again along its crease.

"I was trying to save my daughter's life! You killed Will out of greed or profit, or …" Suddenly weary, he let his voice trail off, unable to continue. It was all so impossible. Could this really be happening?

"I did what I did out of necessity, Grant—same as you. This runs so much deeper than you and your damn daughter. Adison wasn't as innocent as you might think. If he had lived, it may have cost your Katie her life, and the lives of thousands, even millions just like her." James glared at him.

"What in the hell are you talking about?"

"Go home Grant. Kiss your little girl. Enjoy the fact that she lived to see another Christmas. Sergeant Donnelly won't hear anything from me, Grant. I'll keep your dirty little secret."

Tuesday, December 24

Christmas Eve. Grant could hardly believe how quickly time had passed. He awoke early, his head aching. He had only slept for a few hours the night before. The little sleep he did get was plagued with nightmares. Katie dying. Arranging her funeral. Burying her next to his father. The picture in the paper haunted his thoughts. He had recognized the boy immediately. It was Spider-Man from the clinic. Grant and Katie had watched him happily bounding around the office, so full of life. And now, only five years old, he was gone. And Grant was directly responsible. He had killed that little boy as sure as if he had squeezed the life out of him with his own two hands. Grant had thought about going to the police after leaving the office yesterday. But it wouldn't change anything. It wouldn't change what he had done. It wouldn't give the Garretts their son. James and Steven would pull Katie out of the study and she would die, just like Tommy. And then everything would have been for nothing. Katie had to live.

And so he got out of bed and made breakfast for his daughter. He knew she was feeling much better after her terrifying experience Saturday night. She was going to spend Christmas Eve with Beth and David, and they would bring her back the next day, when Grant's mother was coming over to make them dinner. Grant's sister, Anne, and her husband were staying home for the holiday because her doctor had advised against traveling in her last trimester. But Dorothy was flying down to Chicago a few days after Christmas and would stay until after the New Year, only to return a few weeks later when the baby was born.

After breakfast, he helped Katie pack and gave her an early present.

She tore at the paper, but opened the small velvet box carefully. She delicately held up a beautiful gold locket on a rope chain and smiled up at him. Inside were two pictures: one of Katie when she was a baby and the other was of Beth and him on their wedding day. He wanted her to know they would always love one another because they both loved her so much.

"Oh Dad, it's perfect. I love it. Thank you," she said, her eyes glistening. She hugged him tightly and told him how much she loved him.

And in that moment, Grant was able to accept everything he had done.

Beth came by around noon to pick up Katie, and lingered at the door while Katie grabbed something she had forgotten in her room. Grant had told her on Sunday about the break-in, and had reassured Beth he had already called a locksmith and arranged to have additional deadbolts placed on all the doors. She had taken it surprisingly well. Despite the upscale neighborhood, their home in St. Paul had seen some trouble over the years. The garage in the alley had been vandalized and the house had been broken into once while they were away on vacation when Katie was younger. She did ask again when the rest of the units in the building would be finished. She would feel better knowing other people were around.

But when Katie came back down, Beth changed the subject and told Grant to wish his mother a Merry Christmas. He said he would and asked her to do the same to David. Without Beth's knowledge, Grant had spoken to David nearly every day about his case. But he hadn't told David about James MacPhearson or Tommy Garrett. He waved as he watched Beth's SUV back out of the drive. When they had gone, he looked at the clock on the wall in the dining room. It was only twelve fifteen. Most clinics were open on Christmas Eve.

The night before, Grant had gotten an idea. Maybe he could convince Doctor Carruthers to still give Katie the treatments, even if the study shut down, even if James MacPhearson asked him to remove her. He doubted it would work, but it was worth a try.

He was dressed and out the door in half an hour. He pulled his wool scarf and coat up around his neck. The bright sunlight, reflecting off the stark, white snow, stung his eyes and made them water. Once inside his car, he put on his sunglasses. He could be at the clinic by one thirty. Maybe Doctor Caruthers could be persuaded.

~

Tania was at the front desk, now decorated with garland, ornaments, and several snowmen. Her coat and purse were already sitting near her chair. She looked annoyed at having to be there on a holiday, and when Grant looked around the lobby, he could hardly blame her. He was the only one in sight at the moment.

"Hello, Tania. Merry Christmas," he wished her, as he tried to look past her to the offices.

"Hi, Mr. Adams. How's Katie? Does she have an appointment today? I must have missed it when I looked at the schedule this morning," she said, scanning her computer screen.

"I'm actually here to see Doctor Carruthers on another matter. Is he in?"

"He was, but you just missed him," she said, checking her watch. "He left about fifteen minutes ago. In fact, you may have passed him on the road. He was heading to a meeting over at MacPhearson."

"A meeting at MacPhearson? But the offices are closed today and tomorrow," Grant said, puzzled.

"All I know is what he said. He told me he was heading over to MacPhearson for a meeting, that he wouldn't be coming back, and to have a nice holiday," she explained.

Grant thanked her and rushed out the door. He needed to get to the office right away.

∽

"Adison was right." Andrew Carruthers shook his head in disbelief. He knew Will Adison was a talented and creative scientist, but this discovery was nothing short of genius. His death was a significant loss to the medical community. No one would ever know what his career could have produced in the coming years.

"Damn clever bastard, he was," James admitted. *At least with some things,* he thought.

"What about Adams? Is he going to create any problems for us?" Andrew was paranoid. He was putting himself at risk, and didn't like the idea of yet another person knowing about their arrangement.

"We have Adams right where we want him. He can't do anything," James laughed quietly.

The men held fine crystal flutes filled with champagne and toasted one another.

"Here's to the New Year. May it be as bright as our dreams have been these past few years!" James exclaimed, drinking the entire contents of his glass instantly and refilling it just as quickly.

∽

There were only a few cars in the MacPhearson Pharmaceuticals parking lot. Grant drove around to the back entrance, the one designed for delivery trucks. He could only hope his arrival had gone unnoticed. He punched his code and the door clicked open. He was able to make his way down the hallway without seeing anyone, although he could hear voices coming from the labs down the hall. Supposedly, there were only a few experiments running today and they were confined to the labs at the other end of the building.

Grant walked silently up the back stairwell, the emergency stairwell, to the third floor. If Carruthers was meeting James, it would have to be up in the executive suites.

He felt exposed as he walked down the hall, and tried to appear casual in case he was seen. He would claim he had left behind his cell phone and didn't want to be without it over the holiday in case of an emergency. As he passed his office, he opened the door and tossed the phone onto his chair. It made no sound.

Closing the door once again, he slowly made his way down the hall, toward the MacPhearsons' offices. He paused. He could hear voices coming from James's office, the farthest room on the right-hand side of the hall.

The conference room door had been left open. It was next door to James's office, and directly across the hall from Steven's. He ducked inside and took a moment to catch his breath. The talking continued and there was no indication anyone had heard him. From behind the door, he held his ear as close to the hallway as he could manage. He had to hear what they were saying.

"How are our four patients doing, Doc?" James asked excitedly. It sounded to Grant like he had been drinking. His words were slightly slurred and his voice was loud, considering the sensitive topic. *All the better for me*, thought Grant.

"The early test results are showing the second compound is highly effective." Doctor Carruther's voice sounded relieved.

"How effective, Andrew?" James asked.

"In all four patients, there is no sign of the bronchiosclerosis, or any residual effects from the medication. It appears this compound is actually preventing new deposits from forming, as opposed to merely removing the existing plaque. The chest x-rays show all four patients are almost totally clean. It's incredible, really. Variations of this compound might even be adaptable to treat similar conditions, like arterial sclerosis," he said. "So now we know Adison did, in fact, have the cure. By giving it to these four patients, not only have we proven him right, but it will also make our clinical trial results for B319 look even better. Once the FDA sees that in some cases B319—or what they think is B319—can sometimes *cure* patients of the disease, sales will go through the roof."

"I still can't believe Will did it. Here in our little lab in Minnesota, he discovers the cure for bronchiosclerosis." James almost sounded proud of his best friend. "He could have had it all. If only he'd seen things our way, he would have been standing with us here today. He was the one responsible for discovering a cure that will eventually save millions, and yet he is the only one of us who is not going to benefit. It's almost sad when you think about it."

Grant was stunned. *They have the cure? Will discovered the cure for bronchiosclerosis and they are sitting on it! But why?* They must have moved to the sitting area at the back of the office. Their voices were muffled. He had to know what was going on.

Grant only wanted to move the door a few inches, enough so he could slide into the entryway. But the door betrayed him, creaking loudly at the change in position. Within seconds, Andrew Carruthers was standing before him, James on his heels.

"How nice of you to stop by, Grant. Care for some champagne?" James held up his glass. Even in his rush, he still had managed not to spill a drop.

"You have the cure? Will discovered the cure for bronchiosclerosis and you killed him for it? Why?" It didn't make sense. "That cure would've been worth several billion dollars. Why would you kill your partner and risk losing it all?"

"Let's sit down, shall we," James suggested, pointing to the chairs around the empty conference table. "You've had bits and pieces for so long, you might as well know the whole story. Maybe then you will realize this goes way beyond any of us, beyond the lives of Will and your daughter." He offered Grant a glass of champagne, already filled.

The men sat behind closed doors and Grant, finally, learned the truth.

James explained what had evolved over the course of the last several years. Three years after they started up MacPhearson Pharmaceuticals, Will began a new research project on asthma. He used old notes from studies they had conducted as graduate students. The compounds he cultured were too strong, often destroying healthy as well as diseased lung tissue, and causing more harm than good to healthy cells. The project was shelved.

But then, just a few years ago, there was a dramatic rise in the number of new cases of bronchiosclerosis. Like asthma, it made the simple act of taking a breath difficult, even impossible, for sufferers. But unlike asthma, attacks of which were only temporary, bronchiosclerosis left permanent damage to the body. This disease created deposits and hardened the bronchi-

oles, eventually rendering them useless. Will tried several adaptations of his earlier asthma compounds on this new disease and the preliminary results were astounding. One compound in particular was highly effective at removing the plaque deposited in the bronchioles. It was an early form of the treatment drug Katie was currently taking.

Will became obsessed. He went back to his old notes and past experiments. He was convinced that he could somehow vary the compound to cure, instead of merely treat, the disease. He needed a drug that would not only remove prior deposits, but also prevent additional deposits from forming within the lungs, all without harming the delicate lung tissue.

James and Steven were thrilled that the treatment compound was successful in early clinical trials. If the treatment drug worked as insulin did for diabetics, those affected would need to take the medication for the rest of their lives. MacPhearson would be in possession of the only patent for a drug to treat bronchiosclerosis. They would make billions. When Will came to them and requested additional resources to find the cure, they suggested it be put on hold. At first, Will didn't understand. James explained that it would be more lucrative to put out the treatment drug first. They could use the revenues from those sales to fund the additional, and expensive, research for the cure. Will was told to focus on other projects, until the patent for the treatment drug would expire. At that time, other companies would finally be allowed to market generic imitation drugs, at a significantly reduced cost to the consumer. But then MacPhearson could introduce the cure for bronchiosclerosis, again possessing the sole patent and a virtually unlimited earning potential. The generic versions of the treatment, produced by other drug companies, would be worthless.

James wanted the resources from the sale of the treatment drug to fund other MacPhearson projects. Research consumes a substantial portion of any pharmaceutical company's budget, and he thought it would be foolish to walk away from what would amount to twenty years of profits.

But Will continued his work on finding the cure. He kept it quiet, spending time in his private laboratory, while still completing his duties as lab director. James suspected what was going on and confronted him. But Will, at that time, was still unsuccessful. So James decided to let it go, always watching to see if he made any progress.

When Will began using lab equipment for unauthorized experiments, James knew he had made a breakthrough. Will confided in James, his best friend since college, thinking he could persuade him to see things his way. James knew Will had become too great a liability. Once he knew the initial experiments were complete, and Will had in fact discovered the cure, he waited until Will transferred his copious notes into his computer. There they would remain, until needed.

When the last set of tests was run, James altered the data, making it appear to Will that the compound was ineffective. Will became depressed and went to his cabin to get his head together. When he came back to the office they spoke of upcoming projects and James thought Will had finally let go of his search for the cure. But James found out later that Will had taken his notes and computer back to the cabin. It wouldn't take long for him to realize someone had sabotaged the data.

Will had to be stopped.

Only something happened James hadn't expected. The police seized Will's notes and computer from the cabin. When they were returned to MacPhearson, James looked through the data. Will's computer program indicated the electronic file had been copied to a disk. An extensive search had been unsuccessful—no disk was recovered.

So MacPhearson, who had Will's computer, work notes, and files, had the cure. But, because of the missing disk, so might someone else.

~

St. Luke's was a beautiful old church on the west side of St. Paul. The heavy stonework and intricate stained glass windows were a masterpiece of architectural design. Grant held his mother's arm at the elbow and led her into a pew toward the back of the church. The candles and low light, together with the organ, made for a gorgeous scene.

Grant, who had been raised Catholic, hadn't attended Mass in a very long time. With the exception of weddings, funerals, and baptisms, he hadn't been to church for several years.

"Remember to kneel, dear," Dorothy whispered, smiling as they walked down the row. She wished her son had stayed stronger in his faith. It might have helped him through these difficult years, and she would prefer it if Katie had some sort of formal religious education.

"Thank you, Mother," was the only reply he could muster. He was well aware of his mother's opinion, but didn't have the energy to pursue that discussion.

The truth was, he was glad to be there. Churches always made Grant feel welcome and loved. It was reassuring to know he could ask for forgiveness. It was what he needed now, more than ever before in his lifetime. But how could he be forgiven for what he had done?

Grant prayed. *What am I supposed to do?*

Grant thought back to when he was in Sunday school. He had heard the story of Abraham before. How could Abraham have been willing to sacrifice his own son for God? How could anyone sacrifice the life of his own child? And yet, that was the decision he faced: end the suffering of thousands in return for the life of his daughter. A sea of faceless, nameless others, in exchange for his Katie. She was the price he was being asked to pay.

"Grant, dear, is something bothering you? You haven't said a word since we left St. Luke's," Dorothy Adams asked her son as she took her coat off and hung it in the hall closet.

"I'm fine, Mom. Just some stuff going on at work, that's all." Grant knew she didn't believe him, but she didn't say anything. His mother was good at reading when he wanted to talk and when he needed to work something out for himself.

She put a Tchaikovsky CD in the player and poured them each a rather generous glass of Merlot.

"It will be nice when Katie gets back tomorrow. We'll have a lovely dinner. Oh, don't let me forget to call your sister tomorrow afternoon. I told her we would," she said.

"I was thinking maybe Katie and I would fly down to Chicago over her spring break from school. The baby will be a little older by then and Anne might be up to having some company. Katie hasn't seen her since last summer."

"I think it's a wonderful idea. Mention it to Anne tomorrow, though, just in case."

Grant nodded and sank into the deep, leather chair in the corner of the family room. He closed his eyes and felt the exhaustion take over his entire body. It was as if the weight of the world were pressing on him, more heavily with each passing minute. How was one person supposed to make such a decision?

Dorothy Adams looked at her son with curiosity. She wasn't sure if he was sleeping or pretending to. Something was going on with him. He hadn't been himself for quite some time. Of course, he had had a lot to deal with in the past few months. It wasn't surprising he should be on edge. But there was something else, too, she was sure of it. Her son was burdened; she could see it in his eyes. She walked quietly over to him and covered him with a thick blanket. With a quick kiss on Grant's forehead she whispered, "Merry Christmas, dear," and then turned on the gas fireplace. After checking the security alarm twice, she crept upstairs with her wine and a novel. Grant insisted she sleep in Katie's room until the door was repaired and the new locks and bolts were installed. Dorothy did not put up a fuss; she knew she would feel safer upstairs. She crawled into her granddaughter's bed and opened her book. Within minutes, she was sound asleep, like her son; only Dorothy Adams's sleep was a peaceful one.

Wednesday, December 25

Christmas morning was clear and bright. Overnight, a dusting of snow had fallen, coating the grass and trees in sparkling white. As he looked out his kitchen window, Grant was amazed at how beautiful the world could be.

His mother gave him a warm kiss on the cheek before filling her mug with the coffee Grant had just made. His neck and back were stiff from sleeping all night in the chair.

"Your bed was still made this morning, I noticed," Dorothy said as she stirred a heaping spoonful of sugar into her coffee.

"I didn't wake up until early this morning. Instead of going all the way upstairs, I just turned over and went back to sleep," he told her. "Thanks for the blanket, and for turning on the fire. It was nice."

"You shouldn't make a habit of sleeping in that chair, Grant. It can't be good for your back," she cautioned.

"If a sore back was my only concern, I'd be a happy man, Mom," he replied.

"What's that supposed to mean?"

"Nothing, nothing. Merry Christmas, Mom," he said quietly.

"Merry Christmas, Grant."

When Beth and David dropped Katie off, they both stepped inside to wish Grant and Dorothy a Merry Christmas. Dorothy was surprised at the gesture, but Grant was glad. He needed a few minutes to talk with David, alone. While the women chatted about Christmas presents, Grant offered David a quick drink before they had to leave. He brought David into the kitchen and, in a hushed voice, explained that his situation had taken a turn for the worse. David sensed the urgency in Grant's voice and agreed to call him the next morning at eight o'clock.

Thursday, December 26

It was just before seven thirty in the morning when Grant got into his car. He wanted to get to the office early. He was grateful Katie and his mother were going to spend the day together. Katie had vacation from school and Grant had been uneasy about her being home alone all day. They were planning a trip to the mall to do a few exchanges and check out the sales, and then perhaps lunch and a matinee.

As he backed out of the garage, he noticed a black car sitting at the end of his driveway. Sergeant Donnelly was behind the wheel. Grant lowered his window as he brought the car to a stop.

"I'm guessing you aren't stopping by to wish me a happy holiday," Grant said sarcastically.

"Not exactly." Pat Donnelly was growing impatient. He had gotten the county attorney to agree to a few more weeks of using Adams as a mole, but he knew her patience was wearing thin. "So what have you got?"

"Not much. So far, the files and his office haven't turned up anything important. I have been trying to pump information from everyone around me. You might be interested to know MacPhearson Pharmaceuticals is going to go public. And they've got a new drug in the works—looks like a hot one. The company's heading to the big leagues," Grant stated.

"And what about MacPhearson?"

"Some think James and Steven are the greatest bosses in the world. They pay pretty well, have good benefits, and throw nice parties. A few others think they're slave drivers, especially the research assistants in the lab. And Allen Jennings, a CRA under me, is practically afraid of James MacPhearson."

"Do you think Jennings knows anything?" Pat Donnelly asked, leaning toward Grant. Maybe Jennings could give them information.

"No, not like that. Jennings smacked MacPhearson's car in the parking lot a few months ago, that's all. He just thinks James is still mad at him for it. But I don't think Jennings knows anything about Will's death," Grant said, shaking his head.

"Murder," Donnelly corrected.

"Murder," Grant agreed. "I'll keep looking, Sergeant Donnelly, but it's not easy. The last thing I want is for them to catch me."

"We don't want that either, Mr. Adams. It could put you in a very dangerous situation."

You have no idea, Grant thought.

"I'll be in touch."

Pat Donnelly sped along the highway, the morning sun behind him, over the Hudson Bridge and into the state of Minnesota. He didn't envy Grant Adams's morning commute. He could make it from his front door to the Government Center in less than ten minutes, and there were no such thing as traffic jams along the quiet streets in Red Wing.

Adams was playing both sides; Donnelly could feel it. He was stalling them with bits of useless information that led nowhere. In nearly three weeks, they were no closer to catching MacPhearson. Donnelly knew time was running out.

～

David's call was right on time. Grant answered his cell on the second ring, turning down the news station on the radio. In a matter of minutes he told David about Tommy Garrett. Grant wanted to know if he could be brought up on charges for what he'd done. Involuntary manslaughter and fraud, David informed him, might be possibilities, but he'd have to do some legal research to be sure. He again asked Grant how he had managed to get himself into such a mess. To that question Grant had no response. He was just as perplexed as his attorney.

"I've just got to ride it out for a few more weeks, David. Then I'll come clean, about everything," he said. "But David, I swear to you I had nothing to do with Adison's death. I know James is responsible and Carruthers is involved, but I have to be careful, or they'll pull Katie out of the study. We both know what that would mean."

"I do, and I think you're doing the best you can, given the circumstances," David reassured him. Grant was relieved to hear him say it. Although he hadn't told David about the cure, just being able to share a portion of the story with someone else was a relief. It lifted some of the weight. Soon he would be able to tell David everything. David would need all the facts just to have a chance at defending him.

They agreed to talk again over the weekend. Beth had plans with a friend for lunch on Saturday. Grant remembered how many lunch and dinner dates with supposed friends she had made during the last two years of their marriage. He had found out too late most of them were with David.

Friday, December 27

The day turned out to be unseasonably warm for late December. Barbara Adison wore only a light jacket over her wool suit. She already had spring fever, but knew winter would make its return sooner or later. She wrapped up her meeting with James and Steven just before lunch. She could tell they were still bitter over her decision not to sell. It made her enjoy the meeting even more. Robert Dawson had been there, and the future was looking very good for MacPhearson Pharmaceuticals.

A phone call the night before had given her the news she had been expecting. Things were finally falling into place. But all of this secrecy had to stop. Someone else was going to get hurt. Now was the time for her to step in.

She stopped by Grant's office, but it was empty. Poking her head into Diane's office, she tried to seem casual as she asked if Diane had any idea where Grant might be.

"You know, I think he said something about going to pick up a sandwich at that deli just north of here. I guess you could try there. Is there anything I can help you with?"

"Oh no," Barbara shook her head. "It's nothing urgent. I was going to grab a bite to eat myself, so maybe I'll give it a shot. Thanks, Diane."

She headed down the stairs as quickly as her high heels would allow her. She cursed high fashion as she got to the bottom and, ignoring her aching feet, maneuvered across the icy parking lot to her car. *Clearly, Italian shoe designers and models don't spend much time walking through snow and ice. Or walking period, for that matter,* she thought with sarcasm.

When she arrived at the deli, she was grateful to see a long line at the counter. Grant was just about to be helped when she stepped up behind him and flashed a smile, asking if she could possibly get on his ticket. He accepted and invited her to join him. Most of the customers, on lunch break from offices in the area, didn't eat in, so there were several free tables.

Barbara sat down in an empty booth next to the window. The sun was shining in, making the day seem even warmer than it was. Grant, carrying the loaded tray, couldn't help but look at Barbara Adison. She was a truly beautiful woman. Her outfit probably cost more than his whole wardrobe. She was classy. He had to admit it.

201

"You're probably wondering why I invited myself to lunch with you," she opened once he was settled.

"I thought I was the one who invited you. Weren't you heading back to the office?" he asked.

"Not really," she said as she unwrapped her sandwich.

"And here I thought I was doing a good deed, saving you from that line," he smiled. He was enjoying himself. It was a nice departure from all the turmoil in his life. It almost made him feel normal again.

"Grant, there's something incredibly important I need to discuss with you," she said, her voice low. She looked around. The deli was close enough to MacPhearson that there could be other employees eating there.

"What is it?" He knew his pleasant escape from reality was about to come to a crashing halt.

"I know about Will's last project," she said evenly. She watched closely for Grant's reaction. "And I know that you know about it, too."

"I'm not exactly sure what you mean," he proceeded cautiously.

"Grant, Will talked with me about a project he was working on. An unauthorized project. Someone at MacPhearson tampered with the results of his experiment. All the early tests indicated the compound was effective. The project was a compound that could," she paused and lowered her voice even more, making Grant lean forward across the table in order to hear her, "cure bronchiosclerosis."

"Why are you telling me this?" Grant wanted to know. Could he trust her? He wasn't sure.

"Grant, did you hear what I said?" she asked, her face revealing her frustration. "Before he died, Will placed his personal notes in our fireproof safe at the house. He told me they were very important. After he died, I kept it from the police. I placed them in boxes filled with old research and other projects. The police had no idea of their significance.

"Someone at MacPhearson changed the results of Will's experiment, making the compound that could cure bronchiosclerosis look ineffective. That someone is James MacPhearson. Grant, I know he killed Will, but I have nothing to prove it. I know your daughter is in the study with Dr. Carruthers. Dr. Carruthers and James go way back. You've got to be very careful."

"So the purpose of this lunch date was to tell me you know about the cure and to warn me?"

"I think I might be able to help you, Grant."

Grant looked into her blue-gray eyes, trying to find the slightest trace of deception. There appeared to be none. If she was lying to him, setting a trap for him, she was an exceptional actress. He was going to have to trust someone; he wasn't getting anywhere on his own. She seemed genuinely concerned for both Katie and him. He decided to trust his instincts.

"I'm listening."

"You know something about what's going on, and James has threatened Katie if you expose him."

Grant gave a slight nod, but said nothing.

"What if I told you I can get Katie's treatment from another source. Then you would be free to go to the authorities with everything you know," she suggested. She prayed he would accept her offer.

"But how can you—"

"Don't ask. Just trust me. I can get her whatever she needs. She'd still see Dr. Carruthers, of course, so as not arouse any suspicion until you're ready. But she'd get her medicine from me," she whispered, waiting for his reaction. It was a dangerous plan, but right now it was their only option.

"And you're certain it's the same medication? I can't take any chances; she's my daughter," he said, tightening and loosening his grip on the paper napkin in his right hand.

"It's the exact same compound—same dosage, same pill, same everything," she promised. She didn't want to explain how she was able to get the drug. She was relieved when Grant didn't ask.

"Barbara, you know I can't go the police because of Katie." *If only I hadn't changed that data*, he thought miserably.

"Grant?"

He decided to take a risk. He told her about Tommy Garrett.

"So James has another hold over you," she concluded.

"Barbara, why aren't *you* going to the police?" he asked skeptically.

"James seemed different after Will died. He said all the right words, but they just didn't seem sincere. When I found out Will's data had been sabotaged, I wasn't sure who was responsible. Over time I learned it had to be James. He was the one person who knew enough about the experiment to alter the results in a way that wouldn't alert Will. But I had no proof. Throwing out accusations would do no good. And James would be able to cover his tracks."

Grant listened as she continued.

"Last week, when I saw James leave the party, I followed him. I overheard your conversation that night in his office. He said if you or anyone else went to the police, he'd pull Katie from the study. I know James, Grant. He'd want everyone else to go down with him—even an innocent child," she stated flatly. "But I figure if we work together we might have a chance."

"Alright. So what do we do now?"

"We'll switch the medication. Every Friday I'll give you enough pills for the following week until the end of the study. You'll need to replace the pills she gets from Carruthers at her appointments with the drug you get from me. In a few weeks, once you've had a chance to see it's working, we'll go to the police. Then, Katie will continue to get treatment—even if James and Carruthers try to stop it."

"Bring the pills to me tonight, at my place," Grant directed. "James may be watching me at the office." He scribbled directions to his townhouse on a napkin and passed it across the table to her.

"Grant, about Tommy Garrett ..." She let her voice trial off, not wanting to repeat the disturbing details of what he told her.

He nodded.

"I'm so sorry," she offered, not knowing what else to say.

"So am I."

Barbara watched Grant walk across the parking lot. They decided it would be better to leave the deli separately and stagger their entrances at MacPhearson. As far as they could tell, no one from the company had seen them together.

He had trusted her so easily. It was obvious that the man was desperate.

She pulled her cell phone from her purse and dialed his number.

"Everything went according to plan," she said, feeling exhilarated.

"Excellent work. Did he suspect anything? Did he ask about the drug?"

"Trust me, he doesn't suspect a thing," she smiled. "He just wants his daughter to be well. He doesn't care how, or by whom. I told him we'd go to the authorities within a few weeks."

"That's about all the time we should need," he said.

Barbara came late on Friday night, just after Katie had gone to sleep. She handed him the bottle quickly, as if she wanted to be rid of it. She seemed nervous to him, her eyes wide and her smile unnatural.

When Grant asked her if she was okay, she told him she was fine. She made sure she hadn't been followed, but couldn't shake the feeling that someone might be watching. She would give him the other pills, every Friday, via interoffice mail. It was clear she wanted to leave as soon as possible. She pulled her hood over her hair and brought her thick chenille scarf up to her face as she turned and walked out.

The entire exchange had lasted only a minute, but left Grant feeling apprehensive. She seemed different than she had at the deli. Why?

Please don't let this be a mistake, he prayed.

He thought once again of Tommy Garrett.

After securing the new steel door and setting the alarm, he climbed the stairs. The second floor took only a minute to check. All the windows were closed and the front door, also new, was locked and bolted.

He walked to the kitchen and picked up the Katie's bottle of medication. There were only five pills remaining, but they would have the prescription refilled at her appointment on Monday. Grant emptied the bottle and dropped in the new pills he had gotten from Barbara. He closed the lid quickly, as if that would prevent him from changing his mind.

He thought of Barbara again. He was placing his daughter's life in her hands, a woman he barely even knew. But now that he knew Carruthers was in on it, there was no turning to him for help. Carruthers would never agree to give Katie her treatments if he knew Grant had gone to the authorities. Grant had no other choice than to trust Barbara.

Saturday, December 28

The warm weather from the previous day remained for one more. Grant wore only a trench coat to the church. Two churches in the same week. He had been to St. Mark's years before, for a wedding of one of Beth's childhood friends. When he arrived, the parking lot was almost full, so Grant chose to park along the street on the north side of the church. It would allow him to enter the building just as the funeral mass started and leave without being seen.

Just before eleven, the old bells sounding the hours, he walked in and sat by himself toward the back of the church. Grant felt like a traitor, sitting there with people who had loved Tommy Garrett. But he had to come. He had to apologize to Tommy for what happened, and especially for his part in it.

He needed absolution, and attending the funeral of a five-year-old boy he had never known was the closest thing to it. He watched as Tommy's mother sobbed and leaned her head on her husband's shoulder. *Is that what it would be like for Beth and me, at Katie's funeral?* he wondered. *No, she'd turn to David, not me.*

I'm sorry, Tommy. I'm so sorry.

Agent Sam Davis had put his arm around his daughter, Brittany, when they first sat down and he hadn't yet removed it. Instead, he held her tighter, knowing this was the first real loss she experienced in her young life. She'd been to other funerals—for great-grandparents and other relatives. But they had all been older, had lived full and happy lives. As much as they would be missed, no one could ask for more out of life.

But seeing Tommy Garrett, that playful little boy who learned to ride his bike only that summer just down the street from where they lived, get sicker and sicker had hit Brittany hard. She had been his babysitter since he was only a year old and the two had gotten along well. She'd always come home from watching him with another Tommy story. Sam knew Brittany had always wanted a younger brother or sister, but she was their only child. Tommy had filled that void for her.

To be honest, it was difficult for Sam as well. He had seen some tragic stories in his career, but those people were strangers, disconnected from his personal life. His wife, Olivia, held onto his other hand as if she, too, needed protection from the sadness of it all. Life was not fair; Sam knew that. But seeing someone so young, so innocent, die—it was almost too much to take.

When the service was over, Sam turned to hug his daughter. The tears on her face were dried and she managed a weak smile for him. Someone in the back of the church caught his attention. But then Sam felt his wife tap him on the shoulder and he was distracted for a moment. As she was saying something to him, he suddenly turned away from her and, without explanation, started walking toward the rear entrance of the church.

Once outside, it took a moment for his eyes to adjust to the brightness. He heard the car start before he saw it. But there it was, on a side street, not fifty yards from where he stood. It turned the corner before he was able to get a good look. There was no way he could be absolutely certain, but Sam Davis thought he recognized both the car and driver.

"But why in the hell would Grant Adams be at Tommy Garrett's funeral?" he wondered aloud.

Sunday, December 29

Audrey MacPhearson watched as her husband poured a glass of scotch. The fact that he was drinking scotch wasn't unusual, but the fact that it was his third of the evening was.

"Steven, are you okay? You seem a bit on edge tonight, and that's your third drink," she said tentatively. She knew she had to be careful when Steven was in one of his moods. And tonight he was definitely distracted by something. He barely touched his dinner and the two hadn't even spoken in more than an hour. She put down her book, indicating to him that she wanted an answer.

"I'm fine, Audrey. Go back to your novel. Things at work are just stressful right now, that's all, okay? We're almost ready to submit a new drug to the FDA, we're getting ready to go public, and with Will ..."

"I know, honey. I'm sorry. I know how much you miss him. Do the police have any new leads?"

"No," he said shortly.

"When I think about whoever killed him getting away with it, I just get so angry. Poor Barbara. I can't imagine how she must feel. And then, to have to deal with that little slut. And now a baby. Poor thing." She shook her head and exhaled deeply.

"Audrey, you've never really been friends with Barbara Adison. All you and Paula ever did was talk about her behind her back. Why all of the concern now?"

"Steven! Just because we weren't all that close doesn't mean I can't feel sorry for the woman now. She just lost her husband. And his killer is running around, free as a bird," she exclaimed. How dare Steven throw her actions back in her face. She hadn't done anything wrong.

He'd always had a soft spot for Barbara. For some reason, both he and James did. Audrey had to admit her reluctance to get too close with Barbara Adison had less to do with her as a person and more to do with the fact that Barbara and Steven had once been lovers. But that was so long ago. It ended, badly, just before Audrey and Steven met. By the time they started dating, Barbara and Will were in a relationship, and it seemed like Steven never really got over that. He felt betrayed. How could his friend get involved with an old flame? After dating Audrey for six months, Steven proposed and his bruised ego healed over time. But it still bothered Audrey to know Barbara would be working at MacPhearson. She didn't like the idea of them seeing each other on a daily basis.

Maybe, thought Audrey, *that's what's really bothering him. Maybe he doesn't want to work with her either. I know they tried to buy her out, tried to buy Will's shares from her. But she said no. Why would she do that?*

"Just forget about Barbara, honey," said Steven. "She's fine. She has her friends and her family. I think what you and Paula did to help right after Will died was very considerate. I know she appreciated it. But let's not waste a perfectly good evening talking about her, okay? I'll pour this out and we can spend some time together, alright?"

"That sounds perfect," she agreed, setting her book on the table next to the chair. "I'll start a fire."

"I'll be back in a minute." He smiled down at her. She was jealous of Barbara. The idea of Barbara coming to work with them was driving her nuts. Steven laughed to himself as he carried his glass to the kitchen. A few nice words, a little romance; that was all the effort it would take.

Before walking back into the great room, where his loving wife waited for him, he drank the rest of his scotch, setting the empty glass in the sink.

$\sim$

Grant had watched Katie closely all weekend. Unbeknownst to her, she had been taking the new medication for two days. He wanted to study exactly how she looked, sounded, and acted, so that if there were any differences, he would know right away.

Monday, December 30

So far, there had been no observable change in Katie's condition. Even at her appointment with Dr. Carruthers, her lab work came back within normal limits. Her breathing was even and unlabored. It made Grant sick to watch Carruthers put his hands on her, but he had no choice. He had to wait and hope Barbara Adison was on his side.

Grant just needed to keep Katie healthy for another week. Then he and Barbara would go to the authorities. Even if things fell apart, Grant decided he would go anyway. Katie would be stronger by then. He couldn't face the guilt of hurting so many; he had to think of the greater good.

He didn't believe the story about James wanting to use the money for further research. If that were the case, MacPhearson wouldn't use company profits to throw lavish parties, the owners wouldn't earn such high salaries, and their wives wouldn't drive flashy cars and wear even flashier jewelry. MacPhearson wanted the recognition and the money that went along with it. Somewhere along the way, he had become greedy.

Grant couldn't bear giving in to him for much longer. He thought so many times how easy it would be to pick up the phone and give Donnelly the information he needed. But then he thought about Katie. He had come this far. He had to hold out for just a little longer. He owed his daughter that much.

When they returned home he repeated what he had done a few days before, taking Katie's new prescription bottle and filling it with the drug he had gotten from Barbara Adison.

~

Andrew Carruthers placed a phone call in the privacy of his office.

"It's been taken care of," he told James MacPhearson in a hushed voice. He was getting paranoid lately, feeling like he could be exposed any minute. But James had him—if he wanted to, James could end his medical career. Andrew Carruthers had no choice but go along with the plan.

"Excellent," James responded. "When can we expect to see any change?"

"Over the next few days, I'd say. Maybe a week. I'll know for sure when I get the lab results at her next appointment. I'm going out of town, so we'll get her in at the beginning of next week."

"Call me as soon as you have those lab results," James instructed.

Tuesday, December 31

MacPhearson Pharmaceuticals was closed at noon on New Year's Eve and all of New Year's Day. Just as over the Christmas holiday, only a few employees, laboratory researchers, were required to report to work.

Oliver Klein had a date that night. She was an instructor at a local ski resort. He laughed to himself when she had described it as a resort. It had twenty decent runs, and was conveniently located near the Twin Cities, but it paled in comparison to the slopes he had explored in Colorado and Utah. To its credit, however, it did have a lot of cute, young girls on the ski patrol. He was taking his date out for dinner and then dancing at a club.

He just had to finish some work before he could leave the lab. A senior research assistant was going to cover for him until Thursday morning. Of course, Oliver would have his beeper in case there was an emergency, but Oliver wasn't expecting to be bothered. The lab wasn't *that* exciting.

He walked back into his office and pulled the data from his project. The results were looking good, but he wanted to run it one more time, just to be sure. He didn't come this far for nothing. One minor mistake could ruin everything. He had to be certain he could replicate the results exactly before he would make his next move.

Wednesday, January 1

It was the first New Year's Day in a long time when Jessica Monroe hadn't woken up with a hangover. She had only a few sips of wine at her parents' house the night before, just enough to flavor the club soda she was drinking. Not surprisingly, she had fallen asleep on their couch at nine o'clock, and decided to spend the night. She moved into the guest bedroom, her old room, hardly waking.

In the morning the entire house smelled of pancakes and bacon. Her mother was a wonderful cook, and she was relieved the aroma didn't make her feel queasy. In fact, her morning sickness had completely disappeared.

It would be easy to have breakfasts like this every morning. It wouldn't take any effort at all to move back in with her parents as her father had suggested the night before. There was plenty of room. "Just for a little while. Until you're able to get back on your feet," he had said, trying to convince her. And her mom would be such a great help with the baby. She had already bought clothes and toys and other things for her first grandchild. Jessica had not yet shared the news that the baby was a boy. She wanted to hold on to that for a little while longer. Yes, maybe she would move back home. Just like her dad said, only until she could get back on her feet.

It's time to move on, she told herself. She splashed some cold water on her face and went into the kitchen to join her family for breakfast. Her parents would be thrilled with her decision to move back home.

~

A new year. A new beginning. Grant Adams looked at his reflection in the mirror. He seemed to have aged years in the last few months. His eyes were full of guilt and concern. He didn't even look like the same person.

They have the cure. But instead of saving lives, they're going to use it to pad the trial results of their treatment drug. They're going to hide the cure away until the profits from the

211

treatment run out. James MacPearson is willing to risk the lives of the innocent in order to benefit himself.

And I know, and yet I'm not doing anything to stop him. Not yet, he reminded himself. One more week and the police would know all about the murder, and the cure … and Tommy.

Barbara was going to contact him the next weekend and they were going to go to the BCA offices together on Monday morning. She was adamant they go together. They would meet at her condo and ride in her car.

Grant just wanted the rest of the week to pass quickly.

Thursday, January 2

Pat Donnelly lay on the bed of his hotel room and stared up at the ceiling. He had left Sam's office only an hour before. It was nine o'clock. He hadn't even realized he was hungry until he had gotten back to his room. He thought about calling for pizza, but decided to take another chance on room service. His first few meals, which looked very different from the photographs on the menu, were cold and just barely edible. He called down to the desk and ordered a bacon cheeseburger, French fries, and a soda.

After a quick shower, he called Christine. Kelsey had done well on her math test, and wanted money for a dress for the Snow Daze dance coming up at school. Pat agreed, feeling guilty about not having been home much. Kelsey was probably very aware of that as well. She hadn't said anything to him about the dance or the dress when he was home over both Christmas and New Year's. But if she played the part of the neglected child for her mother, it would go farther. Pat shook his head and smiled. She was a smart kid, that one.

In the last few minutes of their conversation, Christine mentioned that her car had gotten dented while she was in the grocery store. One more headache. Of course, no note was left. She complained, asking about what happened to the days when a person would leave a note, offering to pay for the damage.

"Should we just leave it, or do you want me to call the insurance company?" she asked him, disgusted.

"Well, how bad is it?"

"Maybe six inches long on the driver's door panel. I suppose I could call Curt and see how much it would be for him to fix. We'd be better off paying for it ourselves, instead of claiming it. I know the last thing we need, with two teenage drivers in the house, is another increase in our insurance premium," she commented. Curt, who lived one block over, had been their mechanic for years. He was fair and always looking for extra work, even bodywork.

"Yeah, do that, honey—if you wouldn't mind," he agreed. "If the estimate is too high, then we'll have to decide what to do."

"I told you we should get one of those cars with the dent-resistant side panels," she reminded him.

"You mean the ones with the plastic doors?" he joked back. "Oh, honey, my food just got here. I've got to get going."

"You mean you're just eating now?" she scolded.

"Bye, hon. Good luck with the car. I love you." He hung up before she could get in another word about his poor eating habits. Her next question would have been to ask what he had ordered. Somehow, she never quite believed him when he told her he ordered a salad.

That night Pat had trouble falling asleep. He tried watching some television to get his mind off the case, but even that didn't seem to help. Something was bothering him. He had a strange feeling all week he was missing something important, only he couldn't put his finger on what exactly it was. It would come to him eventually. He had it happen to him before. Cursing out loud at his mental block, he turned off the television set and rolled over.

After almost an hour of watching the minutes on the clock change, Pat fell into a fitful sleep, the facts of the case never far from his mind.

Friday, January 3

Grant almost didn't hear the faint ringing of his cell phone over the loud rhythmic pattern of the windshield wipers clearing away the sleet. The sound was barely recognizable, coming from the bottom of his bag that was lying on the passenger seat next to him. It was just before eight o'clock.

"Hello," he breathed into the phone, catching it on the fifth ring.

"Hi, Mr. Adams?"

"Yes, who's this?"

"This is Tania from Dr. Carruthers's office. How are you?" Her voice sounded cheerful and upbeat. Grant wished he could bottle some of her energy.

"What can I do for you, Tania?" he asked.

"I am making some calls for the doc this morning to reschedule some of his appointments next week. He has a conference in Florida," she explained. "Dr. Carruthers has to fly out early to attend a meeting beforehand. He'll be out of the office on Wednesday afternoon, which is when Katie's appointment is scheduled. I'm calling to see if you would be able to come in Monday or Tuesday for her appointment."

Grant resisted the temptation to push the appointment to the following week. The thought of not having to see Andrew Carruthers was very appealing. But Grant wanted to make certain the medication from Barbara was working. She would get a blood test. If her levels were normal, it would indicate the new medication was effective. By next week, things would be out in the open; Dr. Carruthers may not even have a license to practice medicine. Maybe he'd finally get what he deserved.

"You know, Tania, we can come in Monday after Katie gets out of school, say around four o'clock?"

"Sounds great, Mr. Adams. We'll see you both then, and thanks again for being so flexible," she stated.

"See you on Monday."

Monday, January 6

"Come on, Dad!" Katie complained as she stood with her hands on her hips in front of the bathroom mirror. "All my friends wear makeup to school. Why can't I?"

"Because that's the rule. You can wear lip gloss, but nothing else until you're fourteen," he argued back.

"Lip gloss is for babies!" she said, throwing her hands up in the air. Grant was aware that every time Katie was in a mood, she seemed more like Beth's daughter than his. It was something about her voice and the way she looked at him. Suddenly, standing there in the bathroom that morning, she looked like she was twenty years old.

"Then don't wear the lip gloss," he suggested, smiling. He knew he was making her furious, but it was better than the alternative. He had seen those girls at the mall who looked ten years older than they really were. Those girls probably had parents who caved in at moments like this. Grant and Beth agreed that Katie would not be allowed to wear makeup until she turned fourteen. There wasn't anything special about the age except for the fact that at fifteen she would be able to begin driver's education classes and get her learner's permit. With sixteen came the license. Grant shuddered at the thought of the girl standing in front of him getting behind the wheel of a car in two years. It seemed like only yesterday she was going off to kindergarten. "A girl as pretty as you doesn't even need makeup. You only have a few more months to wait, honey. Remember, your mom has big plans for your birthday."

"I know, Dad, I know. We're going to go downtown to have a day at the spa. It just seems so far away," she sighed.

"Not for me, it doesn't. And I don't think it's really fair that I didn't get invited to come along," he said, acting hurt.

"To the spa?"

"Men need pampering too, you know. And I could really use a pedicure. Just look at these feet!" Grant lifted his foot toward her and she jumped back to get away. She laughed and Grant knew he had just diverted her attention. *Score one for the old man,* he thought, feeling proud of himself.

"Say, Dad?"

"Yes, honey?"

"What about tinted lip gloss?"

The thought of their encounter that morning in the bathroom brought a smile to his face as he sat in the lobby of the clinic. Katie was down in the lab, having her blood drawn. The appointment with Carruthers had been brief—just some routine questions, more x-rays, and listening to her breathing in different positions. Carruthers had worn a strange expression during the exam, as if he'd detected something out of the ordinary. But he said everything looked completely normal. He would call them in a day or two with the lab results.

Grant let out a sigh of relief as he leaned his head against the wall. It seemed, so far, that the medication from Barbara was effective. She had delivered on everything she had promised. Next week, they would go to the police, and this whole nightmare would finally be over.

Tuesday, January 7

Pat Donnelly awoke an hour before his alarm was set to go off. In his dream, he and his son, Danny, were fixing the dent on the car. It was a far stretch from reality; neither Danny nor his father knew anything about repairing cars. It was summer. Christine called to him through the screen door and asked how much longer it would take before the car was fixed. He didn't respond and he heard her say under her breath that they should have called a professional to do the repairs.

The dream left him feeling confused until he remembered about the dent Christine's car had gotten in the parking lot of the grocery store. The dent … the parking lot … repairs …

He bolted upright in bed. *The killer's car had leaked antifreeze onto Adison's driveway.*

The other day, Adams told him that MacPhearson's car had been hit in the office parking lot. Hit by some kid employee. He said it happened a few months ago.

That's what had been bothering him all this time!

The accident in the parking lot!

The list of vehicles matching the description given by the witness contained only dark sedans. James MacPhearson drove a white sports car. What if Mac-Phearson had his car in the shop to be repaired? What if MacPhearson had driven another car down to Red Wing that night in October?

$\sim$

Melinda Hendrickson hung up the phone, shaking her head. MacPhearson's insurance company was not aware the vehicle had been involved in a minor accident.

"If it wasn't reported to MacPhearson's insurance company, then chances aren't good it was reported to Jenning's company either," Sam reasoned.

"Then we'll have to call Jennings. Since he was the one who hit MacPhearson in the first place, he probably paid for the repairs himself," Pat surmised.

~

Allen Jennings answered his office phone on the first ring.

"Yeah, I paid for his car to get fixed—cost me over fifteen hundred bucks, too."

At first, he was apprehensive about discussing the accident with the police. Jennings had pled guilty to driving while under the influence a few years back, and didn't want anything else showing up on his record. But once Pat assured him their questions had nothing to do with his driving record, he became more than willing to talk.

"Did you pay with cash, write a check, or pay by credit card?"

"I wrote a personal check," Jennings replied.

"Made out to MacPhearson or the body shop?" *Please let it be to the body shop*, he prayed.

"I made the check out to James MacPhearson. He paid the bill to the shop and I reimbursed him. I guess he felt he didn't have to worry about me stiffing him. He knows where to find me." Jennings chuckled into the phone.

"Mr. Jennings, do you remember the name of the shop where the repairs were done?" All Pat's hopes rode on the answer to this simple question.

"I think it was Davison, or Davidson, something like that," he said as he thought back to the conversations they had about the repairs. "I thought it sounded pretty pricey, but Mr. MacPhearson said his brother recommended them."

"Davison or Davidson you said?" Pat repeated the names aloud so Melinda and Sam could look up any shops in the area with that name or something similar.

"Thank you Mr. Jennings. And remember, please keep this conversation between us," Pat requested. According to Grant Adams, Jennings got along well with Steven MacPhearson. He didn't want Allen Jennings going to his boss out of loyalty.

"Won't say a thing," he promised. "Between you and me, Sergeant, I think James MacPhearson's a real asshole."

Wednesday, January 8

At eight o'clock in the morning, Melinda Hendrickson and Sam Davis stood outside the front entrance of David and Sons Auto. Oddly enough, their number was not listed in the yellow pages and they did not advertise on the Internet. They found out about the shop by pure luck. The receptionist at Davison's Auto Body on the east side told them about this small neighborhood repair shop she had heard some of their customer's mention because the names were so similar.

"So small you'll probably drive right past it," she had said. They had. Twice.

The business was located in an older home, which was in desperate need of repair work itself. The shop was actually in the garage, not more than a two-car at the most. When Melinda rang the doorbell she didn't know what to expect.

"Can I help you?" A man in greased coveralls opened the front door. He was taller than Sam and much thinner. His long hair was held back with a worn baseball cap.

"Yes, I'm Agent Hendrickson with the Minnesota Bureau of Criminal Apprehension and this is my partner, Agent Davis. We'd like to ask you a few questions about a customer of yours, James MacPhearson," she explained.

"David Farrell," he said, offering his hand to both of them. He led them into the kitchen, which doubled as the office, with piles of paper on every surface and an old metal desk sitting in the corner across from the stove.

"Does that name sound familiar to you?" Sam asked.

"I know *Steven* MacPhearson. Went to school together at Central High. I've done some work on his cars over the years," he said, lowering his voice. "Wife's not the best driver and his kids have had their fair share of fender benders, too. James MacPhearson had never been in before—said he always went to the dealer for mechanical things and maintenance, but Steven recommended me. James came in a few months ago with a nasty dent in his driver's side door, if I'm remembering correctly. Let me look in my records," he said quietly.

Melinda looked around at the piles of paper and gave Sam a doubtful glance. Sam smiled and redirected her gaze. David Farrell was opening a very expensive laptop computer on the counter.

"Yep, he came in October. Sure was a nice car, but a bitch—pardon me, Miss— but a pain to repair. Had to special-order the parts and everything. Foreign cars."

"Mr. Farrell," Sam walked over to him, "do your records show the dates you had MacPhearson's vehicle in your shop?"

"Of course my records have the dates. Here it is. The car was brought in on Tuesday, October twenty-second, and he picked it up on Wednesday, October thirtieth. I told you it took longer than usual. The parts took a long time to get here, and Mr. MacPhearson was a little impatient. Nice, but impatient. My son Jake did most of the work. Do you want to talk to him?" Farrell offered.

"I don't think that will be necessary. Do you offer rentals, Mr. Farrell?" Sam already knew the answer, but David Farrell had surprised him with the computer, so he took a shot.

"No, Sir. We're too small, but we do recommend the rental agency just a few blocks up the road. They're a big chain and they give our customers a break if we recommend them."

"Mr. Farrell, one last thing. Would you be able to print off the information about James MacPhearson's car?"

"No problem. Anything I can do to help." He whistled as he printed them a copy of the repair paperwork and the receipt.

Viking Car Rental was in every way the opposite of David and Sons Auto Body. It was big, clean, and bright, and the service people behind the counter were rude and unhelpful.

"You'll need to speak with the manager about that," said a woman with small glasses and a bad habit of smacking her gum.

"Well, Kimberly," Sam said, looking at the name on her tag, "is your manager in yet today? Could we speak with him?"

"*She* doesn't get in until ten. You can wait over there," she said, pointing her long fingernail in the direction of the waiting area. Melinda and Sam walked over and took a seat.

"She's wrapping her gum around her finger," Melinda said, looking back at the counter with disgust.

"Just don't look," he suggested. "Let's hope her manager can get us the information we need."

~

Andrew Carruthers waited anxiously outside the doors leading to the laboratory. The report he received that morning contained results he was not expecting. He asked the lab to perform the test again. They promised him the second set of results by noon. He glanced at his watch. It was now after one o'clock. He looked again at the results from the first report.

There has to be some sort of mistake, he thought.

The door finally opened. He snatched the report out of the technician's hand before she could even speak, and walked swiftly to his office. He didn't read it until he was seated at his desk.

Damn!

The results were the same as the first test. James MacPhearson was not going to be happy.

∽

"Dammit," Pat exclaimed, slamming the phone down. It was Melinda, calling from the rental agency to tell him that the manager was not willing to release any records of rentals without a warrant. It was company policy, established in order to protect the privacy of their customers.

A warrant could take a day, or more, depending on the judge. Pat sighed. Nothing about this case was easy.

∽

"Have you gotten the results back from the lab yet?" James MacPhearson cut through the pleasantries and demanded the information he wanted.

"Her levels look completely normal," Dr. Andrew Carruthers said flatly. "In fact, the treatment is still showing up in her system."

"What do you mean? Shouldn't she be getting sick by now?"

"That's what I was expecting. At her exam on Monday she seemed to be doing fine. I was waiting for her lab results because the disease would show up in her blood before she might experience any physical symptoms," he explained.

"But she isn't getting sick? That's what you're telling me, right?"

"Yes, that's what I'm telling you. There are absolutely no signs she's been deprived of the treatment."

"Did you make a mistake and give her B319 by mistake?" James's voice was filled with rage. *She's supposed to get sick! We need a tighter hold on Adams—he knows too much!*

"Of course I didn't make a mistake. The bottles I gave Katie Adams, both last week and this week, were filled with placebo tablets."

"If all she got were sugar pills, how do you explain those lab results?"

"I can't."

~

Hours later Jessica Monroe took a long drink from the bottle of water on her desk. She eyed the pile of papers awaiting her attention. She was exhausted and wanted nothing more than to go home, but the thought of leaving another task for the following day was very unappealing. She still needed to get signatures for several documents. Although she knew some of the staff had already gone home for the evening—Steven had left hours before—she decided to track down as many people as she could.

It was a decision that led to a most unfortunate consequence, placing both her and her unborn child in grave danger.

Thursday, January 9

Tania had just sat down at the computer behind the counter when she saw another patient come through the door. *Must be a walk-in*, Tania thought as she checked the afternoon schedule on the screen. With Dr. Carruthers out, there were only a few other doctors seeing patients that day. One had already left early and the other two had back-to-back appointments for the rest of the afternoon.

"Hello, may I help you?" Tania greeted the woman with a smile. "Do you have an appointment this afternoon?"

"Ah, no, actually I'm here on business," the woman explained to her. "I'm Barbara Adison, from MacPhearson Pharmaceuticals, and I'm here because I wanted to see how things are going with the B319 study. I made an appointment last month," she lied, giving Tania a warm smile and showing her the MacPhearson identification badge clipped to her black leather shoulder bag.

"Well, Dr. Carruthers is out of the office today and tomorrow. He's the investigator on that particular study. But I'm the coordinator here at the clinic, so I can try to answer any questions you might have."

"That probably won't even be necessary. I just want to look over some of your study files, just to make sure everything is in order. Is there a room I could use for a little while?"

"We have an office that is used by CRAs when they come in to monitor. I'll get you set up there. You can take a look through the files and ask me if any questions come up," Tania said, standing up from the stool behind the desk. She opened the door and led Barbara down a narrow hallway, finally stopping at a small office in a windowless room.

"All the files are located here, in these cabinets," Tania indicated with her hand. "Here is the key. Please remember to lock the cabinets when you are finished."

"Oh, I will. I don't think I'll need more than an hour," Barbara took the key and felt the cool metal in her hand. She was so close to having all the answers.

After only twenty minutes, she had everything she'd hoped to find. Tucked neatly into her shoulder bag were documents taken from Dr. Carruthers's files.

~

Tara Wolfe stopped at Jessica's desk on her way to Steven MacPhearson's office. She was dreading her meeting with him, and talking with Jessica would give her a little more time to delay the inevitable. Oliver Klein would be out all day and the next—out of town skiing in Colorado. He hadn't answered his cell phone. She didn't want to leave a message. Tara had considered waiting until he got back on Monday, but knew something like this needed to be handled right away.

But Jessica was not at her desk. *She must be out sick or have a doctor's appointment,* Tara thought. Jessica had been looking really tired in the last few weeks. Tara hoped things were going well with the baby. She wrote a note asking her to call when she got back. Maybe they could go out for dinner after work or catch a movie one evening.

After sticking the note to Jessica's computer screen, she stood up and straightened her skirt. Then she held her chin up and walked with purpose toward Steven MacPhearson's office. She may as well get it over with.

As she knocked on his door she went over exactly what she was going to tell him. As the supply coordinator for the lab, it was her responsibility. She couldn't be certain if it was just an error or if it was deliberate. But either way, according to the inventory records, there was drug missing from the storage room of MacPhearson Pharmaceuticals.

Friday, January 10

Barbara Adison hung up her office phone and checked for messages. None.

She decided to walk down to see Jessica Monroe. It was after nine o'clock and neither James nor Steven had arrived yet at the office. They had a meeting scheduled with Robert Dawson. Maybe Jessica knew if there had been a change in plans.

"Good morning, Jessica," she said politely. "I hope you are feeling better. I heard you were out sick yesterday."

Jessica nodded, but didn't say anything. She seemed very uncomfortable, tapping her foot on the floor nervously.

"I was just wondering where James and Steven are. Dawson and I were supposed to have a meeting with them this morning and so far we haven't heard from either of them."

"I don't know where they are," Jessica answered truthfully. "Steven didn't tell me about any changes to his schedule for the day. I have your meeting down for eight o'clock in the conference room, so I know he is aware of it. Would you like me to have him call down to your office when he arrives?"

She looks nervous, Barbara thought. *She'll probably always feel that way around me. Maybe both of us working here isn't such a good idea.* She couldn't help but glance down at Jessica's round belly. It still seemed unbelievable to her: Will's child would be born in a few months. She must have been staring, because she saw Jessica's hands instinctively move across her stomach.

"Yes, that would be fine. Just have either one of them call me," Barbara said as she shifted the folders she was carrying to her other arm. She turned and walked away, high heels clicking down the length of the hallway. It was then she realized Jessica had seemed much more than just nervous or uncomfortable around her. *It's almost as if Jessica is afraid of something.*

~

Later that evening, Pat Donnelly, Melinda Hendrickson, and Sam Davis stood in front of the Honorable Frederick Sloan. He was in the process of signing the search warrant that would allow them access to the records at Viking Car Rental.

Saturday, January 11

Sergeant Pat Donnelly walked into the Viking Car Rental building on Seventh Street just after eight o'clock on Saturday morning. He had watched from the sidewalk as the weekend manager turned on the interior lights and changed the sign in the window to read "Open" from the street. He seemed to be taking his time, which was especially irritating to Pat. He had spoken with the head manager the day before. She assured him the records regarding the vehicle James MacPhearson had rented the last week in October would be made available to him the following morning. She would leave instructions for her assistant, Jeffrey Callahan.

Jeff Callahan had read his boss's instructions when he arrived. He knew the cops had obtained a warrant from a judge, but that didn't mean they could order him around. Sergeant Donnelly looked impatient, and Jeff decided it would be entertaining to draw out the process as long as possible. His brother was a cop in Minneapolis, and a real jackass. Seemed to Jeff, most cops acted like they owned the world and everyone in it. He thought it might be fun to make this one learn the hard way.

"I'm coming, Sergeant, I'm coming," he smiled through the window. He played with the lock, taking extra time to open it and the outside door. "Sometimes those locks just don't want to open," he explained.

Pat could instinctively tell the guy was playing games. But he didn't have time to waste. He showed his badge and asked for any records pertaining to James MacPhearson. When Callahan started to say something, Pat pulled out the warrant and laid it on the counter. Callahan was quiet. He made exaggerated movements, walking as if in slow motion toward the file cabinet in the office behind the counter. After a few minutes, he emerged with a thin file tucked under his arm.

"When will I be getting this back," he asked, still clutching the file. "I know how sometimes things can get 'misplaced' down at the police station."

Pat ignored the cut and reached for the file.

Once Callahan finally let go of the papers, Pat hurried out to his car and headed directly for the Bureau of Criminal Apprehension headquarters. As he was exiting off the interstate, his cell phone rang.

"Hello?"

"Hi, Pat. It's Melinda."

"What's up? I'm heading into the office right now—should be there in five minutes," he stated. "I've got the file from Viking."

"Let's hope it has what we need," she said.

"I'll wait to open it until I'm back at the office. See you in a few minutes," he said, tossing his cell phone on the folder. The information inside it could blow the case wide open.

Back at the office, Pat dropped his head into his hands, covering his face. *Finally.* The rental car had been serviced for a leak in the radiator, just after James MacPhearson returned it. But they had no way to prove the radiator had been leaking antifreeze on the night of Adison's murder. And even if the concentrations of antifreeze matched, any decent defense attorney could poke a hole in that theory. MacPhearson could claim the car developed the leak after the date of October twenty-eighth. Once again, their entire case was held together by circumstantial evidence—a leak and a lie.

"Pat, I know you and Melinda feel MacPhearson is our guy. But I think Grant Adams is messed up in this somehow." Sam stood up and began walking around the small office, retracing his path as he talked. "His car fit the description of the witness. He's got a weak alibi, and I don't think he's as squeaky clean as he seems."

"But we know from the lab results that the antifreeze from his car didn't match the sample left at the scene. We just used the leak to put some pressure on him—get him to be our inside man at MacPhearson," Melinda stated, not following Sam's line of thinking.

"What makes you think that Adams is directly involved?" Pat asked.

"Well, I stumbled across something I think we should consider," he said, taking off his glasses and cleaning them with his tie. "I didn't say anything at first because I wasn't sure if or how it figured into the case."

"I thought we were supposed to be working as a team here, right?" Pat's frustration had reached the breaking point. He had been away from his family for the better part of two months. And now Davis was going off on his own? Working behind their backs?

"I only found out about it yesterday. Wanted to do a little digging on my own because it was in a much different direction than we were heading. Honestly, I didn't think it would amount to anything. So, do you want to hear what I have to say or not?" Sam asked. Neither Melinda nor Pat said a word, so he continued.

"Just after Christmas I went with my family to the funeral of a little boy who lived in our neighborhood. His name was Tommy Garrett and my daughter used to babysit for him. He died of bronchiosclerosis. Anyway, after the funeral, I thought I recognized someone at the back of the church, so I walked outside to check. I could have sworn I saw Grant Adams leave the church and drive off. But I didn't catch his license plate and I couldn't be sure. Well, we had the Garretts over after New Years, to play cards, with a few other couples we know. My wife thought they might want to get out of the house and all—I'm sure the holidays were rough for them."

He took a deep breath and continued. "A few days later, my wife, Olivia, and I were discussing their situation. Olivia said that Trish Garrett was talking about Tommy with her and the other women while they were playing cards. Tommy was being treated at Children's Hospital at the University. According to Olivia, Trish said Tommy was going to be in a study for bronchiosclerosis, and would have received an experimental treatment, but he was disqualified at the last minute. Take a guess who's sponsoring that study?"

He waited for a moment before going on.

"I asked Trish myself about this and she confirmed it. The week before the study began, Tommy was found to be ineligible. She said everything had been going along fine, but then one last test result disqualified him. It came as a total shock to them.

"I followed up by paying a visit to the clinic. Guess who was the last subject admitted into the study?"

"Katie Adams," Pat said quietly. The pieces were starting to fit together. If Adams had somehow manipulated the doctor at the clinic, getting his daughter into the study and Tommy Garrett dropped, it would mean he was indirectly responsible for the little boy's death. Maybe Adams was capable. Maybe he was pushed to the limit in order to save the life of his daughter.

"But Will Adison was murdered *before* the study began, right?" Melinda asked, leaning back against her chair.

"But, according to what Jessica Monroe overheard, Will had said no to Katie's participation. He wanted her to wait, remember? All of a sudden the two things standing in the way of the Adams girl getting treatment—Will Adison and another patient—are eliminated." He tried to read Pat's reaction, but Pat's back was to him.

"Maybe we *were* wrong about Adams," Pat admitted, staring out the window at the parking lot below. "He hasn't given us anything on MacPhearson. I wonder just how deeply he's involved."

Sunday, January 12

Grant looked at his watch and swore as he slammed the door of his car and started the engine. He was running late to pick up Katie from Beth's house. There was a wedding shower for Beth, and Grant wanted to get there before it was over so he could speak with David. He and Barbara had decided to go to the police together at the end of the week. She said on the phone she had found something. But she hadn't told Grant what it was, even when he pressed her for the information. That bothered Grant. What if she was working with them, playing both sides? James and Carruthers were blackmailing him with the medicine Katie needed. What was to stop her from doing the same thing?

He wanted David to be there when he met with the police. Once James found out he had gone to the authorities, they would pull Katie from the study and turn over the evidence proving Grant committed the fraud that led to Tommy Garrett's death. But if Barbara could be trusted, then Katie would have access to the treatment drug. And, knowing she was safe, he would be able to face the consequences of his actions, even if it meant serving jail time.

The quiet streets of St. Paul were lined with charming, older homes. He and Beth used to walk around these neighborhoods, dreaming of what it would be like someday to live in one of those big houses. So many plans they had made.

When he arrived, the shower guests were still lingering. David invited him up to the top level of the house. When Grant had lived there, the attic was a playroom for Katie, but now it served as an office for David. Grant looked around the room and was not surprised by the furnishings. The black leather loveseat, modern re-cliner, and steel-and-glass desk looked like things a high-powered attorney would choose for an office. He noticed the top-of-the-line computer and office equip-ment, and wondered just how much money David Hughes made in a year. Maybe he could afford to buy one of those houses for Beth.

"Can I get you something to drink while the ladies are finishing up?" David asked as he opened a small martini bar sitting under the dormer window. Not usually a martini drinker, Grant accepted. He took a large sip and braced for the burn in his throat.

"I plan to meet with Sergeant Donnelly on Friday and I'd like you to be there to represent me. I don't know how everything will go down."

"Have you found anything that could implicate MacPhearson?"

"No, nothing," Grant shook his head. He considered telling David the whole story, but couldn't guarantee he wouldn't tell Beth. If she got involved, it could make matters much, much worse. And he didn't want to put anyone else in danger. Who could know what James MacPhearson would do if he thought he might get caught? It was a risk Grant wasn't willing to take.

"Well, I did some checking. It looks as though the most they'll charge you with is fraud. There's an outside chance they might try involuntary manslaughter, but I don't think they'll pursue that. You'll probably lose your certification and your job, but I don't think anything else will happen—at least not criminally," he said, tossing his head back and finishing his drink.

"Criminally?"

"Well, there's always the possibility the boy's family could file civil charges against you. The burden of proof is much less than in a criminal trial. It could get very messy for a very long time."

"How long?"

"I've seen wrongful death cases drag out for years," he said quietly.

"David? Are you two up here?" Beth's voice came from the bottom of the staircase. "Your mother just left, and she was the last."

"We'll be there in a minute," he called down to her.

"Okay, I'll make sure Katie is ready to go—sorry to keep you, Grant."

"It's not a problem, Beth," he called in response.

A few minutes later they were all standing awkwardly in the foyer. Katie kissed her mother good-bye and opened the door. Grant was just behind her when he felt a tug on the sleeve of his jacket.

"Grant, Katie was coughing an awful lot today. She said she feels fine, but I think you should keep an eye on her, okay?" Her eyes revealed the depth of her concern.

"She probably just has the beginnings of a cold or something," he assured her.

"You're probably right," she said, nodding and offering a smile. "But maybe you could mention it at her doctor's appointment tomorrow. Thanks, Grant." She kissed him quickly on the cheek and took a step back, letting him out the door.

Grant looked back at David and made eye contact. The two men had agreed to meet at the Bureau of Criminal Apprehension headquarters on Friday morning at eight o'clock.

Monday, January 13

Doctor Andrew Carruthers was restless while attending to his morning patients. He wanted to get to Katie Adams's appointment, but it wasn't scheduled until four thirty in the afternoon. The hours seemed to crawl by. He was curious to see how she was feeling and wanted to get her lab results submitted before the technicians left for the evening. If he pushed it through, he might be able to have her results by the following morning.

Last week he called James and said that he wanted out. He wasn't willing to jeopardize his medical career any longer. He would never speak to anyone—about the murder, the experiments, the cure, none of it. But James wasn't willing to let him walk away.

James had already threatened to make an anonymous call to the state medical board if Andrew didn't comply with his demands. And Andrew would not receive any of the payment James had promised him. Ten million dollars in an offshore account. *And chances are,* Andrew reasoned, *Katie Adams would have died anyway.*

Tuesday, January 14

"Hello, Mr. Adams?" Tania's voice was warm and pleasant on the phone, as always.

"Yes," he answered. He was interested to see how Katie's lab tests came out. She had been coughing since Sunday, but Dr. Carruthers said he didn't think it was related to the bronchiosclerosis.

"I'm just calling with Katie's lab results. Doctor Carruthers wanted you to know that her levels are lower, but still within the normal range. The cough is most likely just a viral infection—nothing to worry about."

"Did Doctor Carruthers tell you this, or are you looking at the lab results yourself?" Grant knew Carruthers could easily lie about the tests.

"I can pull Katie's file and check myself. Hold on," she said. After a few minutes, she was back on the line. "I'm looking at the lab report right now and everything seems to be just fine, Mr. Adams."

"Thanks for checking, Tania. I just wanted to be sure," Grant said as he hung up the phone. Of course Carruthers could have altered the results. *Stop assuming the worst,* he scolded himself. *The medication from Barbara is working just fine. It's only a cold she's caught. She'll be feeling better in a few days.*

~

"I just thought you might like to know Katie Adams's lab results indicate the levels of treatment drug in her system are finally decreasing. And she's now presenting physical symptoms as well." Andrew Carruthers leaned back in the chair behind his desk.

"How long before ..." James was having dinner with his wife and wasn't able to talk freely.

"Before she gets really sick?"

"Yes, how long?"

"Because her system has become dependent on the treatment drug, I would expect her symptoms to progress rapidly."

"How long?" James repeated. He wanted to know exactly when they could make their move with Grant Adams. He felt like their hold on him was slipping.

"Only a matter of days," Andrew Carruthers said, looking at the calendar on his desk.

"Good." James MacPhearson hung up the phone and returned his attention to his wife. They were discussing her current project: planning a vacation to Italy in the spring.

"And then we could always take a week for Tuscany. Imagine the vineyards!" Paula was flipping through travel brochures and information she had printed off the Internet, unaware her husband was deep in thought. "Of course, we'll do Venice, Florence, and Rome, but let's also go to some out-of-the-way places. Jean Mitchell said the town of Sienna is just lovely. What do you think? Are you even listening to me? James?"

The sound of his own name caught his attention. He had no idea what Paula had been saying, but he could guess it was about all the places she wanted to visit. "It sounds wonderful to me, darling. It will be so nice to get away from everything here and spend some time alone with you."

"Are you okay, James? Ever since that phone call you seem very distracted," she remarked, laying her hand on top of his. He had seemed very stressed to her in the last few months, but wouldn't talk about whatever was bothering him. Maybe getting away would be good for him.

"I'm fine. Just some things going on at work. Nothing for you to worry about. In fact, according to that phone call, the problem might be resolved," he said, squeezing her hand and giving her a smile. The last thing he needed was for her to ask more questions.

"I'm glad," she said. "Now, take a look at this hotel on the Italian Riviera. Isn't it gorgeous?"

Wednesday, January 15

Heather DeMaris was just about to take her lunch into the teacher's lounge when she heard a student walk into her office. It was Katie Adams. Heather, fresh out of nursing school, was in her first year at Pine Grove. She had met with Katie's mother earlier that fall to discuss Katie's bronchiosclerosis, but so far it hadn't presented much of a problem. In fact, Heather hadn't even seen Katie for anything more than check-ins, which were done only at the request of the mother.

Heather could tell something was wrong the moment she saw Katie. The girl was clearly having difficulty breathing. If Heather hadn't known Katie's history, she would have thought the girl was having an asthma attack. Katie wheezed as she inhaled and exhaled.

"Come in and sit down here on this bed. Let me get you some water," Heather directed as she grabbed a small bottle of water from the refrigerator near her desk. Katie said nothing, but accepted the offer and opened it as soon as it was handed to her. She immediately took a long drink.

"Tell me how you feel," Heather instructed.

"Well, I've been coughing lately, but my doctor said it's just a cold," she started to explain. Heather had her doubts, but listened patiently. "And then today I started having trouble breathing. It wasn't all that bad at first, but it's gotten worse since this morning."

Heather was having a hard time hiding her concern. "You think it's because I'm sick, don't you?" Katie asked, her voice sounding fearful.

"Well, let's not jump to any conclusions, Katie. But I would feel better, because you do have bronchiosclerosis, if we called your parents so you could see your doctor today. Do you want me to call your mom or your dad?"

"My mom just started classes this week, so I guess you better call my dad," Katie answered, fiddling with the bottle of water. She took another drink and cleared her throat. Heather could tell she was trying not to cough.

Heather dialed Grant Adams's work number and was relieved when he answered on the second ring.

"Mr. Adams? Hello; this is Heather DeMaris, the school nurse at Pine Grove Middle. I'm calling because Katie came to my office a few minutes ago. She is coughing and having some difficulty breathing. I met with Katie's mom when she transferred to us, so I know about Katie's condition. I would advise you to schedule an appointment with Katie's doctor, this afternoon if possible." She knew she hadn't let him get a word in, but she wanted to present him with all of the information up front.

"Thank you for calling me so soon. Tell Katie I'll be there to pick her up in ten minutes and I'll schedule an appointment with her doctor for later today," Grant said.

Heather helped Katie lie down on the bed in her office. She noticed that the tissue in Katie's hand was splattered with blood.

〜

Pat Donnelly was not pleased with the surveillance report he received from the officer assigned to tail Grant Adams. So far there had been no suspicious activity. Sam was trying to follow up on the study at the University of Minnesota Children's Hospital, but there were now so many laws protecting the privacy of clients that it was taking longer than expected to get any information, especially about children.

If nothing in the case broke that day, Pat had planned to drive down to Red Wing the following morning and stay for an extended weekend. Kelsey was in a play and it was the last week of performances. He wanted to be at home. He wanted to be done with this case. It had consumed him for almost three months and, for the first time in his career, Pat was starting to doubt whether or not they would catch the person responsible for Will Adison's death. The trail had grown cold and they weren't even close to having enough evidence to charge someone with his murder. The county attorney called almost on a daily basis, but even that didn't bother Pat anymore. The truth was, he was beginning to feel numb. He just wanted the whole damn thing to be over.

〜

Grant waited all afternoon for a return phone call from Doctor Carruthers. At four o'clock he called again, and was told that Doctor Carruthers would get back to him as soon as possible. From the kitchen, Grant could hear Katie's coughing. She had barely eaten anything all day and her breathing seemed labored and uneven. She said she felt fine other than having those two symptoms, but Grant thought she looked tired. And there was no hiding the fact they were both scared. Grant decided if he didn't hear from Carruthers within the hour, he would call another physician. Barbara Adison said she could provide a doctor for Katie. But if the pills he got from Barbara weren't working, he had no reason to believe anything she told him.

The call from Carruthers didn't come. Grant debated whether he should call Barbara Adison or bring Katie directly to the emergency room. Everything was falling apart.

Before he made his decision, Barbara Adison called him. She was calling to confirm their plans to go to the police on Friday morning.

"I haven't decided if I'm still going to the police," he said quietly, not knowing if Katie was asleep.

"What do you mean you're not going?" she snapped. "We had an agreement."

"Well, things have changed. Katie is sick. The drugs you gave me aren't working," he hissed into the phone. If she had betrayed him and put Katie's life in jeopardy, he would make her pay.

"How can they not be working? They're the exact same drug Katie was prescribed by Dr. Carruthers in the study," she argued.

"All I know is my daughter is sick. Your drug must not work as well as the drug from MacPhearson."

"Grant, the drugs I gave you *are* from MacPhearson. They were taken out of the storage room from the lab."

"Maybe I should go to the clinic, or to the hospital with her," he wondered aloud.

"No, Grant. Look there must be some sort of explanation for this, but you know they won't be able to do anything for her at a hospital. The only drug available right now is MacPhearson's B319," she said logically.

"Well, then I'll beg James to save her life. He has the cure for God's sake. I'll do anything he wants me to do."

"Grant, before you go to James, let me try to find out what could possibly have gone wrong. I'll call you as soon as I know anything. Maybe I can get something to help her," Barbara suggested. "Please, Grant, this might be your only chance."

"I'll give you one hour."

～

"Why the hell is the drug not working?" Barbara shouted.

"Keep your voice down! The office isn't soundproof and the last thing we need is for someone to overhear us," he said, closing the blinds in the window to block the view of anyone who might still be in the lab.

"What could have gone wrong?" She looked as though she might have a breakdown.

"Are you absolutely sure she's sick?" he asked.

"Grant told me that she's coughing and can barely breathe. Why is that happening? She responded so well to the treatment drug in the study. Why now, when we gave her the exact same thing?"

"I know it's more effective in some patients than in others, but she was doing fine. I don't know what's going on, Barbara," he said quietly. "I took the treatment drug from the storage room, one bottle each week, as we discussed," he explained, letting his breath out slowly.

She wanted to believe him. After all, it was she who had approached him after Will's death. Once she was confident he was not working with James, she asked for his help and shared her theory about Will's sabotaged experiment. Oliver admitted that he had already looked at the data on Will's computer, saving it to a disk. He knew Will had been working on an unauthorized project. With the disk, and Will's notes from Barbara, he was able to replicate the experiment. Their intent was to prove Will had discovered a compound to cure bronchiosclerosis, and that he had been killed because of it.

"I just took more of the drug from the storage room. *Something* was wrong with the drug we gave her before." It was an accusation. Had she been wrong to trust him?

"What are you going to do with it?"

"I'm going to bring it to Katie Adams," she said, slipping the bottle into her purse. As she walked out the door she added, "We better pray to God it's not too late."

"Wait," he called after her, grabbing his coat. "I'm coming with you."

⁓

Grant had almost given up on Barbara Adison when she showed up on his doorstep. She wasn't alone. With her was the doctor she had told Grant about. He wasn't a medical doctor, but a PhD. He was also one of the only people with extensive knowledge of B319. With Barbara Adison was Dr. Oliver Klein.

Oliver went up and talked to Katie and tried to assess how she was doing. There was no time for Grant to be angry. He would deal with Oliver Klein later, and told him as much. At that moment, his only concern was for Katie. And he needed Oliver's help. Upon his recommendation, they brought her to the emergency room at Woodwinds Hospital. Oliver served as the consultant with the emergency room staff. Grant told them Doctor Andrew Carruthers was not to be notified regarding Katie's condition. He would call the clinic in the morning to have her records released and sent to the hospital.

Once she was in a private room, Grant made two phone calls. The first was to Beth. She and David arrived just after Grant got off the phone with his mother. Grant insisted she wait until the morning to come for a visit. There was nothing she could do for them at such a late hour, and he would need her to be at the hospital the following morning.

Thursday, January 16

Grant held out steaming cups of coffee to Beth and David. It had been a long night.

"Grant," Dorothy Adams called as she walked quickly toward the lobby of the Intensive Care Unit. "How's my granddaughter? Can I see her?"

"Right now she's sleeping, which is what she needs," Grant whispered.

"What can I do, Grant? Is there anything you need? Maybe I could bring you a change of clothes from the townhouse?" Dorothy offered.

"No, I got some things from the nurses. But maybe I'll go home this afternoon to grab a shower. Do you think you could stay here with Beth while I'm gone?"

"Of course I can, dear." As soon as Dorothy looked at her former daughter-in-law, Beth burst into tears. Dorothy set down her bag and she and Beth sat together, Dorothy holding her hand and whispering words of encouragement to calm her.

Barbara Adison came into the lobby minutes later, bringing a bag filled with bagels, fruit, and juice. Grant knew she felt responsible for Katie's condition. She and Oliver had stayed at the hospital the whole night. At first Beth had felt as if their presence was an intrusion, but once she saw the emergency room doctor talking with Oliver Klein, she realized he was a very valuable resource concerning both her daughter's condition and the drugs they were using to fight it.

Katie's x-rays showed severe blockage in both lungs.

～

James walked quickly to his office. He had just overheard someone in the cafeteria talking about Grant Adams. His daughter was admitted to the hospital the night before. He smiled as he dialed the familiar telephone number.

"It's all going exactly the way I planned it," James said as he sat down in his chair.

"So when do we finish this?"

"Not until we can get him alone. As he watches her get worse, he'll become desperate. He'll do anything we ask him," James explained, clasping his fingers behind his head. It was the first time in weeks he knew success was near. It had been such a long and complicated road.

"It was risky to keep Adams around for so long."

James sighed and loosened the knot of his tie. "We had no choice. I'll make the phone call. Tell him to meet me at his townhouse this afternoon if he wants his daughter to live. After tonight, it will be all over."

~

The sleet made it hard for Agent Trevor Camden to see. With the visibility so poor, it would have been easier to track Adams's car by staying right behind it. But of course he couldn't do that. Agent Davis was very clear Adams was not to know he was being tailed. Trevor had been with the BCA for less than a year, but had learned quickly about the pecking order. He did what Davis told him to do. But his first major assignment wasn't nearly as exciting as he had expected it to be. Watching Grant Adams was boring, at least it was until last night, when he and his daughter went to the emergency room at Woodwinds Hospital. Trevor noted in his hourly update to Davis that Barbara Adison had arrived at the townhouse with Oliver Klein, laboratory director at MacPhearson Pharmaceuticals. He and Mrs. Adison had been at Adams's home for almost an hour before following Adams and his daughter to the hospital.

He should call Davis back at the office to alert him that Adams was now traveling east out of St. Paul on the interstate, most likely going to MacPhearson or to his townhouse.

Before he was able to contact Davis, his vehicle started to slide on the ice that had formed on the roads, making them slick and treacherous. He tried to steer out of the skid but was bumped by another car whose driver had also lost control. Both cars spun out in the middle of the freeway, and were hit by traffic traveling behind them. When police arrived at the scene fifteen minutes later, a total of seven vehicles were involved in the accident. An ambulance was called.

Agent Camden was rushed by ambulance to nearby Regions Hospital. He was unconscious.

~

"Damn it!" Sam pushed his chair against the wall in frustration. "Camden was supposed to check in over forty-five minutes ago. He's not answering his cell phone. We need to know where Adams is."

"Hey guys, I just got word from dispatch that there's been an accident on the interstate. Several vehicles involved, they might have to shut down the freeway," Melinda came in, clearly out of breath. "One of the drivers was Agent Camden."

"Is he going to be alright?" Sam asked intently.

"Don't know. They're bringing him to Regions Hospital now," she answered.

"Pat, you stay here for the time being. We'll call you as soon as we find out where Adams is. Melinda, let's go," Sam said as he rushed out of the office.

Moments later Pat received a phone call from Jessica Monroe. She wanted to meet right away at the University of Minnesota bookstore on the St. Paul campus. She said she had information about the murder of Will Adison.

~

Grant saw the car parked near the end of his block. James was already there. Grant opened the garage door and pulled inside, closing it behind him. He walked upstairs and waited for the knock on the door.

"How is she?" James asked, a look of concern on his face. If Grant didn't know better, he would think James MacPhearson actually cared about his daughter. But, of course, he did know better. He allowed James to come into the house.

"I want the cure for her, James. Not B319, but the cure, and I want it now," Grant demanded. He didn't have time to play games. Katie was slipping away from him with each passing minute.

James looked out the window at the last light of the day. Only five o'clock, the dark and cold of the winter night had settled in. He held out his hand holding three bottles filled with pills. "I know about the pills you've been stealing from the storage room."

"James, I—"

"You think drugs can go missing and not show up on an inventory report? I can't believe you didn't think about that. You shouldn't have crossed me, Grant. That's why your daughter is sick right now."

Grant wasn't following him.

"As soon as it was brought to my attention that pills were missing, I knew what you were up to. I replaced the entire inventory of B319 with placebo and moved the real drug to a more secure location. From that moment on, the drug you took—one bottle every Friday, like clockwork—did nothing to help your daughter. The only thing I can't figure out is how you got access to the storage room."

"You bastard," Grant said in disbelief. *So allowing her to die wasn't enough; he was willing to kill her.*

"Grant, there is a way we can save Katie. I'll give her the cure for bronchiosclerosis. But first, you have to do something for me."

"I'll do whatever you want me to do," he pleaded. He couldn't think clearly. The adrenaline rushing through his system was fighting the fatigue he felt.

James pulled a handgun from the pocket of his coat. "I didn't want it to come to this, Grant. But you didn't play by the rules. With the amount of information you possess, you're too much of a liability. And now you'll have to pay."

"Just save my daughter, James. She's just an innocent child. Please."

"If you do exactly as I say, I'll make sure your daughter gets the curing compound tonight," James assured him.

～

Doctor Paul Nguyen walked into the family waiting room with a heavy heart. This was the part of medicine that was difficult to accept. Families could deal with the truth, no matter how grim, but the waiting that came before it was impossible, especially for parents holding on to hope, fearing the worst.

"Doctor Nguyen, how is my daughter?" Beth Murray asked.

"The disease is spreading. The next twenty-four hours will be critical. We're doing everything we can for her."

Beth nodded as tears gently rolled down her face. Doctor Nguyen told her she could go in to see Katie, but that she had been sedated to keep her more comfortable. David offered to go with her, but Beth refused. She needed to be alone with her daughter.

~

Pat walked into the bookstore at the University of Minnesota. It was crowded with students buying books for the start of the spring semester. He couldn't see Jessica Monroe anywhere. He walked up to the information desk and asked the clerk if she had seen a blonde, pregnant girl in the store. Knowing she felt more comfortable with Melinda, he hoped she would still be willing to meet with him.

"No, no one fitting that description. And you can't be in here with that," she said, pointing at his gun. "We have rules here on campus against firearms." Pat caught the glimpses of light coming from the silver ball pierced through her tongue.

"I know that," Pat told her, reaching for his badge. He never got the chance to pull it. Jessica grabbed his arm and led him into the hallway. In a corner at the other end of the student union, they sat on a bench.

"Hendrickson and Davis are responding to an accident involving one of their agents. Miss Monroe, you said on the phone you had information about Will Adison's death."

Jessica took a deep breath and told the sergeant everything she knew.

~

Oliver Klein watched as Doctor Nguyen started back down the hall to the nurses' station. They had administered the B319 Barbara had brought from the MacPhearson storage room, but Oliver could tell from the exchange with Beth things were not going well. Oliver couldn't understand why her system was not reacting to the drug. Was she too far gone? Had the disease spread so much she would never recover?

"Dr. Klein." Dorothy Adams voice was kind as she sat down next to him on the uncomfortable bench. "It means a great deal to me that you're working with Dr. Nguyen. You are a good friend to my son."

If only you knew I'm the reason your granddaughter is in this hospital, he said to himself. Aloud he replied, "I'll help her in any way I can. I feel responsible—being with MacPhearson. We thought the treatment was effective."

"Of course you did. And it really seemed to help her in the beginning. I just don't understand why the drug stopped working all of a sudden." Her eyes were brimming with tears, and she reached in her pocket for a tissue. As she spoke, Beth came out of Katie's room and motioned for Dorothy to come. "Well, it looks like I can see Katie now."

Oliver watched as she took Beth's arm and walked into Katie's room. Shaking his head, he thought of Dorothy's words. *I just don't understand why the drug stopped working all of a sudden.*

"Oh my God," he said, closing his eyes. A wave of panic rushed over him. *Somehow, James must have found out. He found out what we were up to and switched the pills. He wanted Katie Adams to get sick.*

Oliver ran to find Dr. Nguyen.

Oliver opened the bottle of pills he and Barbara had given the doctor the night before. He gently touched one of the pills to his tongue. The lack of bitter taste confirmed his fear. The pills in Oliver's hand, the pills Katie Adams had been taking, were not B319. Oliver did not know exactly how long Katie had gone without the treatment drug. If, in that time, the disease had progressed to an advanced state, the damage could be irreversible.

～

Pat Donnelly burst through the doors of the emergency entrance of Woodwinds Hospital. On the way over from the University, he had called Melinda and Sam. Agent Camden had not yet regained consciousness. Both of them would meet him at Woodwinds, and he would explain then what Jessica Monroe had told him.

"Where is the Intensive Care Unit?" he asked breathlessly. A tall medical assistant in blue scrubs instructed him go down to the end of the hall to the bank of elevators. Jessica Monroe kept up as best she could, holding her stomach as she trotted behind Sergeant Donnelly. She had insisted on coming with him, wanting to see Grant Adams and somehow find a way to make things right.

As soon as they stepped out of the elevator, Pat saw Barbara Adison talking to a woman and man in the family waiting area. He remembered the day he and Barbara had met, almost three months earlier—the day Will Adison's body had been discovered. She noticed him and then looked past him to Jessica Monroe. Confusion swept across her face.

"Sergeant Donnelly? Jessica?"

"Mrs. Adison, I know you and Dr. Klein followed Grant Adams here. Is he still in the hospital? It's imperative that I speak with him as soon as possible." Pat had no time for explanations. "It's a matter of life or death."

"Is Grant in some sort of trouble?" David asked.

"You're Adams's attorney, I remember. Do you have any idea where your client is?"

"Grant's your client?" Beth turned to David, trying to process what she had heard in the exchange.

At that point in time, three more joined the group in the center of the family waiting area. Oliver Klein had just left the nurses' station, wanting to tell Barbara Adison that James had switched the medication, resulting in Katie's current condition. Agents Hendrickson and Davis arrived moments later.

"He went to his townhouse in Hudson," David explained.

"Is he still there now?" Pat looked out the window. The sleet had turned to snow, which was falling harder now. The wind made it virtually impossible to see.

"He should be," David answered.

"What in the hell is going on?" Beth snapped.

"Sam, come with me. Melinda, stay here and take statements from Jessica Monroe, Barbara Adison, and Oliver Klein. None of them is to leave the hospital. Call for backup and send additional units to Adams's residence."

"Sergeant," Oliver Klein said, walking with him to the elevator. "I think you should know James MacPhearson has replaced Katie Adams's medication, landing her here. She may not recover."

Pat stepped into the elevator without responding.

When the elevator doors closed, Oliver turned back to the lobby and watched as Jessica spoke with Agent Hendrickson, Beth and David listening to her every word.

~

"There, Grant. You've done an excellent job," James complimented. Grant set the pen down and waited for whatever was to come next. He had just completed a letter confessing to the murder of Will Adison. He watched as James carefully laid it on the table with gloved hands. Next to it he placed a small bottle and a glass of water. Grant could only see a portion of the contents label, but that was enough. The bottle contained methanol. James MacPhearson was going to kill him.

"Please, just save my daughter. Get her the medicine she needs," he pleaded.

"Methanol is painless—just ask Will. You'll go to sleep and this will all be over."

"Why? Just tell me why you're doing this?"

"Grant, the longer you keep me here, the longer Katie waits. She's dying right now, Grant. Is that what you want?"

Looking at James, he swallowed the contents of the bottle, feeling the cool liquid rush down his throat, and waited.

~

"I had to," Jessica explained to Agent Hendrickson. "James told me if I went to the police with what I knew, he would do something to harm the baby. If he killed Will, how could I stop him from hurting our son?"

Jessica's eyes filled with tears. She dropped her head and began to sob.

"Jessica, why don't you start from the beginning and explain to me exactly what happened," Melinda demanded, taking notes as Jessica told her the same story she had told Pat Donnelly an hour before.

~

"What the hell have you been doing?" James snapped. Beads of perspiration had formed over his brow.

"Checking his office to make sure he didn't have anything that could lead to us. I also planted some antidepressants and sleeping pills in his bedroom."

"Help me get him to the car," James demanded.

Grant let out a soft moan as they moved him.

James closed the driver's side door of Grant's car. Grant was completely unconscious, the methanol working much faster on him than it had on Will Adison. He didn't even stir at the sound of the door closing. The car was running, spilling carbon monoxide into the closed garage. It was a single-car stall; James estimated it wouldn't take nearly as long for Grant to die as it had for them to kill Will.

He climbed the stairs to the first floor. The note was in plain view. In it Grant described the guilt he felt over murdering Will Adison and that he couldn't bear to lose both his daughter and Beth, one to sickness and the other to another man.

One perfect murder to cover another.

~

The St. Croix River Bridge was dangerously icy as motorists slowed to keep their cars under control. Pat and Sam inched along, aware that the minutes passing made it unlikely they would get to Grant Adams's house in time. After Pat explained what he had learned from Jessica, the two planned how they would enter the residence, both fully loaded. Hudson Police had been notified and were supposed to be sending officers, but an accident with injuries was occupying the majority of the officers on duty that night. As they crossed into Wisconsin, Pat noted they only had three more miles until they reached Adams's townhouse. He prayed they wouldn't be too late.

~

"What are you saying to me, Doctor Nguyen?" Beth choked back her tears and listened to his repeated statement.

"Katie's condition is deteriorating. The disease has caused considerable damage in both of her lungs and the surrounding tissue," he said in a clinical tone. He sympathized with the family, but knew he would serve them better if he remained professional.

Dorothy grabbed Beth's hand and squeezed it tightly. She wished Grant were here. What if he didn't make it back in time to see her? What if she …

"I think you need to prepare yourselves."

⌒

"It shouldn't be long now," James smiled as he closed the door leading to the garage. "Do you have the bottle?"

"No. I left it in the car."

"I knew it was a mistake, having you here with me," James hissed. "I should have taken care of all this myself."

"I'll go get it. You make sure everything is in order here. I'll be back in a minute."

⌒

Oliver was sitting with Barbara, listening to the doctor's report. Barbara was dozing in the chair next to his. He gently moved her hand from his arm and slowly stood up. She stirred, but did not wake.

"Beth, Dorothy, I overheard what Doctor Nguyen said to you," he began solemnly. "I want to talk with you both privately for a moment."

"This is really not a very good time, Doctor Klein," Dorothy snapped at him. Beth only stared at him with red and swollen eyes.

"Please, it's about Katie," he whispered quietly.

Ten minutes later, Oliver Klein was speeding back to his laboratory at Mac-Phearson Pharmaceuticals.

⌒

James looked around the main floor of the townhouse one last time. Nothing seemed to be out of place. *What is taking him so long?* He walked upstairs to the master bedroom closet. That was where they were going to leave the missing beer bottle from Will Adison's cabin. With traces of methanol undoubtedly still inside, it was the perfect piece of physical evidence to secure Grant's guilt.

He checked his watch. It was time to leave.

As he opened the closet door, something on the floor fell over. James let out a gasp. The bottle had already been placed there. He ran down the stairs and opened the front door. As he fought his way down the drive, bending over to block the wind, he looked down the street. There was no sign of the car. Steven was gone.

When he saw headlights moments later, James breathed a sigh of relief. Then the car slowed and Agent Sam Davis stepped out, drawing his gun.

Friday, February 7—three weeks later

"Ladies and Gentlemen, thank you all for coming this morning. This press conference has been called to announce the discovery of a new drug, able to cure …"

The members of the press, representing national and international media circuits, murmured with awe and excitement. News of the discovery had been leaked in two smaller papers in the Midwest, but this conference, held by representatives of MacPhearson Pharmaceuticals, seemed to support the rumor. As Robert Dawson took his place behind the podium, the crowd grew silent.

"I am pleased to tell you MacPhearson Pharmaceuticals has in fact found the compound to cure and prevent bronchiosclerosis in both children and adults. Three persons in particular worked tirelessly to make available to the world a cure for bronchiosclerosis, a disease that took the lives of thousands of children in our country this past year alone. Please join me in applauding the dedicated efforts of Steven MacPhearson, Doctor Oliver Klein, and Barbara Adison, acting on behalf of her late husband, Doctor William Adison." Steven approached the microphone.

"Thank you. Due to the severity of this devastating disease, we have already submitted an Investigational New Drug application with the Food and Drug Administration. In the meantime, while the cure is in the process of gaining FDA approval, MacPhearson Pharmaceuticals will sponsor a program for those patients diagnosed with advanced bronchiosclerosis."

The press conference lasted for more than an hour, reporters swarming with questions about the compound and the path to discovery. Before the conference, the press had been told that any questions about James MacPhearson's involvement in the murder of Dr. William Adison would not receive comment.

~

Beth hung up the phone and looked at David with weary eyes. She nodded and took a deep breath.

"It's time to go to the hospital. I just can't believe this is happening," she whispered, sliding her purse off the table in the front hall. As he opened the front door for her, she turned and looked back, thinking of the days when she, Grant, and Katie had lived there together. There had been happy times.

Things had changed so much since then.

~

Grant's thoughts were interrupted by the shrill ring of the telephone. It was only the second day he had spent in his own bed, arriving home from the hospital on Wednesday afternoon. If Sergeant Donnelly and Agent Davis had arrived any later, he wouldn't have made it out of the garage alive. So far he'd made a remarkable recovery. Even the headaches had subsided.

He had watched the MacPhearson press conference on television. The fact that other children would not have to endure what Katie had made his heart feel a bit less heavy. He didn't want any other parent to experience what he had been through in the last few weeks.

"Grant, I think you'd better come to the hospital. The doctor says it won't be long now. She really wants to see you."

Twenty minutes later he walked into Woodwinds Hospital. Barbara Adison was already there. She took Grant's hand. They exchanged words for a few moments and then headed down the hall toward her room. He wanted a few minutes alone with her, so Barbara waited outside.

She was resting when he first saw her. All the tubes and monitors made her seem so vulnerable. As he closed the door she stirred and opened her eyes, smiling up at him.

"I'm so glad to see you," she said weakly.

"I told you I would come, didn't I?" he said softly. He sat down on the bed and gave her a strong smile. "How's the baby?"

"They've scheduled me for a C-section this afternoon," Jessica whispered. At the hospital on the night of Grant's attack, she started having contractions. She had been immediately admitted and placed on bed rest to delay the onset of labor. But she couldn't carry the baby any longer. He was showing signs of fetal distress. "We'll be fine. How's *your* baby?"

"Katie's going to be okay," Grant smiled. "Thanks to you, Jessica."

"Oh Grant, when I heard your daughter was in the hospital I called Sergeant Donnelly. But if I had come forward as soon as I heard that telephone conversation, neither you nor Katie would have been in danger."

"Jessica," he said firmly, "if you hadn't gone to the police, both Katie and I would be dead. You did what you felt you had to. James MacPhearson threatened the life of your baby. I, of all people, understand what that's like. You have to do everything you can to protect your child." He couldn't fault her for doing exactly what he himself had done. Tommy Garrett had died so that Katie could live, and he was responsible for that. How could he sit in judgment for what Jessica had done to protect her baby? "Barbara told me you wanted to see me. I'm sorry I wasn't able to make it here earlier. I'm actually meeting Beth and David upstairs later. Katie is being released from the hospital this afternoon."

"I am so glad to hear that. Grant, I just wanted to apologize in person and see for myself that you and Katie are going to be okay. I need to close that chapter of my life before my baby is born."

"I understand, Jessica."

"It means so much to me that you came," she said, her eyes losing focus. Grant patted her arm and left her as she drifted back into sleep.

"How is she?" Barbara asked as he closed the door to Jessica's room.

"Tired," he answered honestly.

"The doctor says the baby will probably have to stay in the hospital for a while because he's a few weeks early, but he should be just fine."

"So it's a boy," Grant said, looking at her, not really knowing what to say.

"Yes. She's going to name him after Will."

Epilogue—Friday, February 21

Pat Donnelly shook his head when he walked through the door of his office. He had just come from a meeting with the county attorney. Even with James MacPhearson's statement, the county attorney had decided to offer a deal to Steven MacPhearson. In exchange for his testimony against James, the charges against him would be reduced to obstruction of justice. The chances of him serving jail time were slim, and Pat Donnelly was beside himself with rage.

After questioning James MacPhearson, he believed the two brothers were involved in Adison's murder together.

"It's this goddamn system," he shouted as he threw the file in his hands across the desk, sending papers flying in every direction.

"What did she say?" Melinda asked, although she already knew the answer.

"She's offering a deal to his attorney this afternoon," Pat said through gritted teeth. "The slime is going to walk out of court a free man in return for testifying against his brother."

"We don't have any reason to believe James MacPhearson is even telling the truth," Sam said under his breath. They had no evidence to corroborate his story.

"She said she couldn't run the risk of them both getting off. I think what she means is she can't risk not winning a big case before the fall election," Pat said bitterly. "Adams didn't know if Steven was involved or not. The fact that he thought he heard James talking to someone at the townhouse during his attack would never hold up in court. A person under the effect of methanol is not a reliable witness. And Jessica Monroe would be no better—she never knew who was on the other end of that phone call she overheard. The county attorney seems to think Steven's testimony will make it an open and shut case against James—maybe won't even have to go to trial. All she'll charge Steven with is obstruction of justice for lying to us about his brother's whereabouts on the night of the murder."

"Then she can also claim responsibility for saving the taxpayers' money," Melinda added sarcastically.

"That's the way Steven planned it. He had the whole thing set up—leaving his brother stranded, holding the evidence," Pat sighed. "I don't know which of the two is worse."

"Jessica Monroe could have overheard James MacPhearson talking with Carruthers," Sam said.

"Carruthers was one of the only people who could tell us the truth," Melinda commented quietly. Doctor Andrew Carruthers had been killed in a single car accident the evening of the attack on Grant Adams. "We may never know."

"Officially, the case is closed. My hands have been tied by the county attorney," Pat told them. There would be no opportunity to follow his instincts.

"I'll see you both out," Pat told them, opening the door to his office.

"Unfortunately not all loose ends can be tied," Melinda said, shaking Pat's hand. "It was an honor to work alongside you, Sergeant."

"You as well. I'll call you as things get underway," he promised.

"We'll talk soon then." Sam shook his hand and the two of them walked out into the brightness of the afternoon.

Pat dragged his feet on the marble floor on his way back to his office. He grabbed his coat, deciding to leave early. The walls of his office felt confining. All he wanted to do was go home.

~

Barbara Adison heard the doorbell ring as she slipped her diamond bracelet over her wrist. She was going to Beth and David's wedding. The couple had decided to forego all of the formal plans and have a small wedding, inviting only family and friends. Barbara was going with Grant.

"You look beautiful," he told her as she opened the door. It was true. She was gorgeous in a pale blue jacket and silk dress. The thought of spending the evening with her was making Grant look forward to the wedding. Being in a relationship, even the very beginnings of one, was enough to help him get past Beth once and for all and accept her happiness with David.

"Before we go, I have something for you," she said, handing him a folder containing two pieces of paper. Confused, he began reading over the documents. He looked from one to the other, the realization washing over him.

"It's all there," she said, nodding. "After you told me what you had done, I looked in Tommy Garrett's file at the clinic. Just out of curiosity. I pulled the test results from his file and then told the lab they were missing. They were more than willing to provide me with another report. When you compare them, the numbers don't match.

The lab report you altered didn't even belong to Tommy Garrett. Grant, you didn't have anything to do with him being denied participation in the study."

"They just wanted me to think I was responsible for his death. They set the whole thing up—Carruthers suggesting if the records were changed Katie would get in; leaving me alone in the office with the file sitting out in the open on his desk. He baited me, and I fell for it."

"You were desperate and they knew it," she stated evenly. "While you were still in the hospital, I explained what had happened to Sergeant Donnelly. Forgive me for not saying anything sooner but, with everything you've been through, I didn't want to get your hopes up until I was absolutely certain. Donnelly called me this afternoon. You have been completely cleared."

"I can't thank you enough. Feeling responsible for the death of that little boy was unbearable. And because of you and Oliver, Katie was able to receive the cure. You saved her, Barbara. And so many other kids just like her," he said, smiling.

After speaking with Oliver at the hospital, Dorothy and Beth had given him their consent to administer the cure to Katie, with neither the knowledge nor consent of Dr. Paul Nguyen. All three felt the fewer people who knew the truth, the better. As far as the hospital staff was concerned, Katie Adams's recovery was nothing short of a medical miracle.

Grant cleared his throat and his expression became more serious. "I wish I could remember more from that night, but I can't. Barbara, do you believe what James told the police? Do you think it's possible Steven was working with him from the beginning?"

"Grant, Steven and I have been friends for a very long time, and I knew him in a way that I never knew James. He made a mistake in trying to protect his brother, but he's no killer. He just doesn't have it in him. James was looking for a scapegoat and it didn't work. He'll pay for all he's done—to both of us."

"I hope you're right," he sighed. He had to move on with his life, and this night was a step in the right direction.

"Come on," she caught his hand and they walked out the door together. "We have a wedding to attend and I have a bouquet to catch."

Sitting in the backseat, Katie watched her dad and Barbara as they walked toward the car. They were laughing as he opened the door for her. Katie smiled. She liked Barbara Adison, and had the feeling her dad felt the same.

~

Steven sipped his martini slowly. He ignored the stares of the other members of the St. Croix Country Club. Let them gossip. The rumors had been circling for weeks. Robert Dawson set down his phone, wearing an expression full of satisfaction.

"That was the county attorney. She's offering you a deal," he said smugly. "Did you wire the money to her account?"

"That little gesture of thanks should be enough to fund her campaign for the senate in a few years, when all of this has blown over. You know, people are wrong. Money really can buy happiness. So, no jail time?"

"You'll be fined, assigned to some sort of community service, and will probably have your sentence suspended."

"And James?"

"Mason is certain she'll get a conviction."

"Well done, Counselor. James always wanted to be in control. Thought it would be better if he handled everything," Steven smiled.

"His arrogance played right into our hands," Dawson concurred. Steven toasted him and the two tapped their glasses together to celebrate. "I've told Barbara you'll sell your shares to her. They're worth significantly more now that the cure will be on the market. Amazing that the whole time it was Klein who had the disk with the curing compound for bronchiosclerosis. And we thought Adams had taken it."

"I hear Barbara's asked Klein to run the company with her. They'll be changing the name at the start of the next quarter." Steven licked the alcohol from his lips. "How long until we can get another company up and running?"

Dawson nodded. "I'd say we could be ready to go within three years' time. You have the rest of Adison's notes?"

252

"What Barbara had was just the tip of the iceberg. I have extensive notes from almost twelve years of Adison's research. We get his theories in the hands of some young, hungry, scientific minds—"

"And just wait for the money to roll in," Robert finished for him. "It's going to be perfect."

"Now, tell me more about this small bio-tech company in central Florida," Steven insisted as he leaned back in his chair, finally able to relax.

the end